New Orleans
Beat

Also by Julie Smith

*Published by Ivy Books

NEW ORLEANS BEAT

A SKIP LANGDON NOVEL

JULIE SMITH

FAWCETT COLUMBINE • NEW YORK

A Fawcett Columbine Book
Published by Ballantine Books

Grateful acknowledgment is made to the following for permission to reprint previously published material:

Henry Holt and Company, Inc.: Excerpt from "The Oven Bird" from The Poetry of Robert Frost, edited by Edward Connery Lathem. Copyright 1944 by Robert Frost. Copyright 1916, © 1969 by Henry Holt and Company, Inc. Reprinted by permission of Henry Holt and Company, Inc.

Llewellyn Publications: Excerpt from The Goddess Sekhmet by Robert Masters. Reprinted by permission of Llewellyn Publications, Box 64383, St. Paul, MN 55164.

Phoenix Publishing, Inc.: Excerpts on pp. 189–191 are from Eight Sabbats for Witches and Rites for Birth, Marriage and Death by Janet and Stewart Farrar. Copyright © 1981 by Janet and Stewart Farrar. Reprinted by permission of Phoenix Publishing, Inc.

Library of Congress Cataloging-in-Publication Data
Smith, Julie, 1944–
   New Orleans beat : a Skip Langdon mystery / Julie Smith.
      p.   cm.
   ISBN 0-449-90743-0
   1. Langdon, Skip (Fictitious character)—Fiction.   2. Policewomen—Louisiana—New Orleans—Fiction.   3. New Orleans (La.)—Fiction.
I. Title.
PS3569.M537553N47   1994
813'.54—dc20   93-46506
                                                                                                    CIP

Manufactured in the United States of America

First Edition: July 1994

10   9   8   7   6   5   4   3   2   1

For Hendrika de Vries,
who taught me where stories come from

Acknowledgments

What would I have done without the WELL? Many thanks to David Gans (tnf), Scott Marley (hudu), and Thaisa Frank (thaisa), for advice and support; to Jon Carroll (jrc), for that and more; and to Jim Petersen, the real (bigeasy), for the loan of his user ID.

Greg Peterson, Richard Sabatte, Betsy Petersen, Steve Holtz, Chris Wiltz, Nancy Moss, Kit Wohl, Becky Light, and Diane Rubin were generous with their expertise. Chris Smither contributed advice on love.

Captain Linda Buczek of the New Orleans Police Department, with her delicate understanding of a writer's needs, nuts-and-bolts knowledge of police procedure, and generosity of spirit, was immensely helpful (not to mention patient and kind), as always.

My deepest thanks to all who assisted.

1

● ●

People hate New Orleans because it's hot—certain people, that is, from the sort of bland, tepid climate that spawns good mental health and consuming boredom. In a hot climate, anything can happen. A quiet dinner can ignite. "Bobby," a wife may say to her husband, "you never fuck me anymore. Bobby, why don't you fuck me anymore?" Her tone will change here. "Because when you do, you're soooo good at it."

Just as the guests are beginning to smell danger, she may say, "He is, isn't he, Emily? Isn't he good at it?"

Emily's husband knows he should do something, but what? Defend his wife? Yet he's torn—maybe he's about to find out something he needs to know.

But Bobby says, "Precious lamb, I never fuck you anymore because ever since you went on Jenny Craig you're such a little bitty thing I can't even find you in the covers."

Thrilled, she answers, "You really think it did some good?" and all is well until the next course, when the neighbor from next door, drunk and deciding suddenly to remodel, may pound a hole in the wall.

"Burton," the host will ask coolly, "what do you want?"

Burton will raise one finger and begin to fall through the new doorway, passing out about fifteen minutes too late to avert disaster. "Ham and cheese on rye," he will answer, crashing loudly onto the floor. But still, he will open one eye: "Hold the mayo." And that is the part of the story that makes it worth repeating.

This sort of thing would never happen in Sweden—or even in California—according to Steve Steinman, the great and good friend of New Orleans detective Skip Langdon, and a resident of California himself. Steve claimed to have been at the gathering where the above events occurred, and as a result had formed a theory that the heat of the place causes chemical changes in the brain that loosen the inhibitions. Skip said it was only the alcohol, but he said that and the heat, taken *together* . . .

Steve had some quaint notions, Skip thought, and furthermore, he had never been to New Orleans in late fall and winter.

The cold can be piercing. In those magnificent rooms for which the city is celebrated, the ones with the fourteen-foot ceilings, occupants sigh and reach for their thermostats, reflecting that, expensive as heat is, it's nothing compared to air-conditioning. In November, it's merely crisp—a welcome cold, a refreshing chill, one that won't last. Those in sweaters today may be in shorts by Thanksgiving—or not, depending.

It was early in the month, the tenth, the first really cool day, and Skip woke up shivering. She was in a new place, one she'd never slept in in winter—it was the slave quarters behind her old apartment building, which had been restored to its original status as a single-family house and was now inhabited by her landlord, Jimmy Dee Scoggin, and the two children he'd acquired when his sister died.

Jimmy Dee had gutted the slave quarters and turned it into as posh a showplace as the Quarter had to offer when he'd lived there himself. But it now had a new name. His adopted children were from Minneapolis and hadn't grown up with the city's brutal history. Determined to protect their innocence, he insisted upon calling the outbuilding a *garçonnière*. "In the old days," he told them, "they had special houses just for the boys," which prompted eleven-year-old Kenny to ask why he couldn't have it instead of Auntie.

"Because," answered Skip, "now that I'm there it's going to take an earthquake to get me out."

She had four times as much room as in the studio she'd rented before, ten times the luxury—and about twenty times the open space, as her three or four sticks of furniture didn't really make a dent. She thought it was a mansion and she was as close to happy as she'd ever been in her life. But what she didn't have, she was discovering, was central heating.

She called Jimmy Dee.

"Make a fire, darling, a fire. So romantic, don't you know."

"Dee-Dee, it's seven-thirty A.M. I'm going to work."

"Well, then, what's the problem? I've oatmeal to make if you don't mind." In the background she heard a chorus of "Ick, oatmeal!" Fatherhood was proving a little more than Jimmy Dee expected.

Skip dug out a black wool skirt and cocoa sweater, dressed, and hoped the day didn't warm up. Somewhere she found a brown blazer that "pulled the outfit together," as her friend Alison put it. She didn't get it herself, but she had to admit it looked better than something she'd have picked herself—probably something red, singularly inappropriate for a homicide detective.

She was at her desk, drinking her second cup of inky coffee, when her sergeant, Sylvia Cappello, handed her a day record from the coroner's office, along with its autopsy report.

"Take a look. I just talked to the coroner about this."

It was an "unclassified," or suspicious, death. A thirty-one-year-old, healthy white male had been found dead after an apparent fall from a ladder.

Cappello said, "Notice it says he fractured his ankle *and* his skull? Pretty unlikely, apparently. You'd either land on your feet or your head, not both."

"I can see that."

"But if you landed on your feet, broke your ankle, and you were too badly hurt to move, somebody could come along and bang your head against the concrete pretty easily."

"Surely someone from Homicide went out on it."

"Lasko and Drumm. But it looked like an accident and they thought that was how it should be classified." She handed Skip the brief report they'd done. "And now they're up to their eyebrows with that triple shooting in the Magnolia Project."

"It happened Thursday." Skip sighed. "And today's Monday. I hate to think about the crime scene."

"Well, what the heck—what else have you got to do?"

A macabre joke that drew a snort from Skip. The city's homicide rate was sky-high and climbing.

"Thirty-one's too young to die."

"But too old to live with your parents."

Yet Geoffrey Kavanagh, the victim, had lived with his, in a rambling old house on Octavia Street. From the outside, it looked like the sort of place the neighborhood kids would call "the haunted house"—the one with its yard overgrown, the one that hadn't been painted in a couple of decades. The occupants must not be particularly friendly people, must not want much contact with the outside world, to live behind such an urban forest. Skip approached with trepidation.

Inside the house, a dog barked. What sort of people were like that? Antisocial people by definition. Crazy people, probably. Neglectful people.

Depressed people.

Alcoholics.

But as she entered the jungle, she saw that there was a certain pattern to its wildness, an artfulness, a cultivation of the inherent drama of the thing. Deadwood had been cleared and so had paths; leaves had been raked—in fact, the jungle was an illusion, only a tangle at the front of the yard. Past that was a neatly mowed lawn and some beautifully tended beds. Three or four sleek cats sunned themselves in what patches of light they could find. Those who lived here weren't neglectful, despite the desperate paint situation.

Just as Skip had decided that, a woman who belied it answered the door. She wore baggy, faded sweats. Her face was drawn, without makeup, her cheeks sunken, the half-moons under her eyes purplish. Her hair was drawn back in a loose ponytail, but it lacked body and shine. She could have been sixty, judging by her ravaged face, but her hair was black; she had some fight left in her.

"Mrs. Kavanagh?"

"Terry. Marguerite Terry."

Skip identified herself. "I wonder if I could ask you some questions about your son?"

Immediately, her eyes filled. "My son? But he's . . . I don't understand."

"About his death."

She seemed relieved. "I'm sorry. I guess I'm still half asleep; I've been sleeping so much. . . ."

Skip nodded slightly but said nothing, hoping Marguerite Terry would remember her manners, but she only looked expectant. At her heels, a white dog with brown ears wagged its tail in a vague sort of way. "I wonder if I could come in?"

"Oh. Of course." She glanced at the dog. "Okay, Toots?" The dog gave another vague wave, apparently acquiescing.

Skip stepped into a room as gloomy as is appropriate in a house where there's been a death. The curtains were drawn, making it cavelike. Newspapers were piled on the floor, as if no one could be bothered to remove them. There was a glass or two on a coffee table and a rumpled blanket on the couch; otherwise the room was dusty and looked seldom used. The rug was threadbare and the floor was bare wood, its finish long since worn away. The upholstery was frayed. The ancient wallpaper had never been replaced.

Yet once someone had cared; there were good quality pieces here, a look of severely reduced circumstances, poverty that might be genteel if anyone could be bothered to vacuum and dust. Skip was back to neglectful.

Obviously embarrassed, Marguerite opened the heavy, dusty drapes. They looked as if they'd been chosen forty years ago and hadn't been disturbed since, had simply hung here, collecting dust, outlasting the fashions of nearly half a century, creating a pall of gloom.

The room was better with a little light.

"We don't spend much time in here," said Marguerite. "Everybody's so busy. . . ."

"Everybody?"

"My husband, Coleman, a self-described and self-taught computer nerd, as he likes to say. He has his office here, but he's off at a meeting today. And Neetsie, our daughter. Well, she moved out a while ago—she has a studio of her own, can you imagine? Eighteen years old. And Geoff"—her voice caught—"I was so used to him. You know how you get used to a person?"

Skip thought it an odd thing to say about a son.

"Like a dog or something, I don't know. Won't you sit down?"

"Actually, I'd like to see where the accident happened if I could, please."

"You want to see—?" She stared, as if trying to understand.

"Where you found him," Skip finished. "I'm sorry. I know this must be hard."

"Oh," said Marguerite, and Skip thought she meant not so much that it was hard as that she understood. "Come through here."

The dog at her heels, she led Skip through a dining room as drab as the living room, as dark and dusty, but clearly used—if only as a catchall. The table was piled high with stacks of mail, more old newspapers, magazines, the sort of everyday debris that accumulates somewhere in every house—but that usually gets cleaned up every few days. This looked like months' worth. They went through a kitchen that seemed more lived in, was quite messy, in fact, in a homey sort of way, and finally through a mudroom. Three steps led down to a flagstone patio. "Up there," said Marguerite. "That's where Mosey was."

"I beg your pardon?"

"You don't know what happened?"

"I just know your son fell from a ladder."

"Well, I woke up about ten o'clock and when I came in the kitchen I heard the most piteous meowing. So I went out and there was Geoff, lying on the patio with the ladder on top of him. Mosey, our little gray cat, had gotten up on the roof and Geoff fell trying to get him down." She paused, remembering, her face drawing tight as she fought to control it. "It was like a story that told itself with one glance."

6

"What was he wearing?"

"A T-shirt and a pair of old sweats, as if he'd gotten out of bed and thrown something on to come outside. No shoes. His feet—"

"What?"

She looked miserable. "His feet must have been cold."

Skip didn't want to think about it either. "What did you do?"

"I don't know. I think I must have screamed or something."

"And then?"

"I pulled the ladder off and put his head in my lap; and stroked him. But his head didn't feel right."

"How did it feel?"

She winced. "Not right. Soft."

"Was anyone else home?"

"No. Cole was in Baton Rouge. I had to call 911 myself. I knew he was dead; I was hysterical."

"How did you know?"

"He felt so cold. And his head."

"How long did you sit there with his head in your lap?"

"Maybe a few seconds. Not long."

"When you got up did you let his head come down hard on the flagstones?"

"He was my son!"

Skip waited.

"I put him down very gently."

Skip looked up at the roof. "Had Mosey gotten up there before?"

"Oh, that cat. He goes everywhere."

"But there?"

"I don't know. Not that I know of."

"I'm just wondering—did you hear the ladder fall? Or Geoff yell or anything?"

"No, I'm on the other side of the house. And besides, I could sleep through a hurricane. I take these pills to sleep and they put me so far out I wouldn't know if a bomb fell."

Skip thought that might explain why she seemed so out of it. "Did you take one today?"

"Last night, but I got up with Cole and then went back to bed.

7

I'm okay to talk. Shall we go back in? Maybe I could make some coffee."

Skip liked it better outside and she didn't want more coffee. But she said, "That would be nice," thinking Marguerite might drink some herself. She seemed so dull and listless, her voice so devoid of expression, it might help, she thought. Back in the kitchen, she said, "Let me do it."

"That's okay. I can manage." Marguerite seemed very thin as she moved about her messy kitchen, pathetic and lonely in her baggy sweats. Skip thought it odd that she was alone so soon after her son's death, that the house had not been touched, as if visitors had not come. When Marguerite opened the refrigerator, Skip saw that it was nearly empty, not filled with food the way it should have been—with casserole dishes and hams, cakes and pies from friends and relatives.

"Do you think you should be alone?" she said. "Could I call someone to stay with you?"

Marguerite said, "We're always alone." She looked off in the distance. "Neetsie's friends used to come over now and then. I don't know—I guess Cole and I aren't very social. We don't . . . belong to a church, or clubs or anything. Neither of us goes out to a job."

She sounded as if she were wondering aloud how she had come to this friendless state.

"Do you have relatives?"

"Cole doesn't. My dad died a long time ago. My mother's in a nursing home."

"All the same . . ." She stared into space again. "We're having a memorial service. People might come over afterward—is that what they do?"

Skip shook her head—working in Homicide didn't make her a funeral consultant.

Marguerite looked panicked. Two cats, a tortoiseshell and a black-and-white one, rubbed against her ankles. "I guess I should clean the house."

That was a job Skip didn't envy her.

"Hello, pretties. Hello—should Mommy feed you? Mommy's

so bad. Such a bad mommy that can't even feed the kitties." She tapped some cat chow into a bowl. At the sound, another cat glided in, a black one. Skip had now seen half a dozen cats, none of whom was Mosey, and one dog.

"Does your dog bark when strangers come around?"

"Sometimes—she barked at you. But sometimes not—she's a lousy watchdog. Why?"

"I just wondered about the day Geoff was killed. Did you hear her then?"

She frowned. "I don't think so. But the pills. She could have barked two feet away and I wouldn't have known it."

Marguerite asked what Skip took in her coffee, handed her a steaming mug, and picked up a mug of her own. "Shall we go in the living room?"

At least, thought Skip, there was some sun in there.

"I don't have much time to clean," said Marguerite. "I have so many projects."

"Do you keep the garden yourself?" She looked out the window, more appreciative than ever now that she'd seen the inside of the house.

"Why, yes. Do you like it?"

"Very much."

"I can do creative projects; I just don't seem to be able to handle the daily maintenance stuff. Neetsie's just like me."

"I know what you mean." Skip noticed that Marguerite smiled when she spoke of Neetsie, almost for the first time. She picked up on it: "What does Neetsie do?"

"She's a very fine actress, actually. She's going to be good. I really think she's going to make it. She goes to UNO at night, just a couple of classes, and supports herself with little jobs she gets." She smiled again, the indulgent mother.

"She must be very talented."

"Oh, she is."

"And Geoff?"

"Geoff?"

Skip smiled, tried to make herself as nonthreatening as possible. "What did he do?"

9

"He was into computers. Like his dad."

"His dad? But he and your husband have different names."

"His stepdad. They were very close. Cole taught him about computers and it brought him right out of himself; he blossomed into a new person."

Skip thought a thirty-one-year-old man who lived with his parents hadn't come that far out of himself. She said: "He had a job in computers?"

A shadow crossed Marguerite's face. "No. Geoff was a very, very bright young man. Exceptional. But we couldn't afford the good schools—we had to teach him ourselves. He didn't adjust to other kids very well. He wasn't socialized."

Skip nodded and smiled, absolutely in the dark as to what she meant.

"He was brilliant, really. But he read comic books as a kid. You know how some kids do that? He never seemed to outgrow it."

"I beg your pardon?"

"That kind of mentality. Kind of withdrawn. He was a very quiet, very inward-looking boy. He had a girlfriend, though. Things were looking better for him. I don't think he'd really had one before."

"How about other friends?"

"Well, he did have a male friend." Her nose wrinkled, as if he stank. "Layne something, I think."

"Maybe we could look in Geoff's address book if he had one. Did you say he had a job?" Skip knew perfectly well she hadn't.

"Well, yes. He—uh—worked at a video store. Mondo Video, down by the Riverbend."

Skip wondered if it was a porno place—judging by Marguerite's embarrassment, that didn't seem out of the question. Impulsively, she said, "Do you have a picture of Geoff?"

"What for?"

"I'm just trying to imagine him."

"Could I ask why?"

"I'm curious, that's all."

"I don't think you said why you're here."

"Something came up that we needed to investigate; just cover-

10

ing bases. You know how it is." Again, she smiled, using her smile as a shield: *No more questions, Mrs. Terry. Okay?*

Marguerite looked uncomfortable. "I don't really know where the old photos are."

"That's okay, it was just a thought. I wonder if I could see Geoff's room."

Marguerite looked at her quizzically. "Of course."

His room was just to the right of the mudroom, his window almost directly beneath the section of roof where Marguerite said the cat had been. "Excuse the mess," Marguerite said. This would have struck Skip as funny, considering the condition of the rest of the house, if it hadn't been so sad, looking at the prized possessions of someone who no longer existed, piecing together the story they told.

The story itself was sad, Skip thought, of a piece with the cracked plaster of the house, its icy dormancy. A gray cat, Mosey perhaps, slept in a hollow of the bed, the saggy spot that indicated Geoff had been overweight, or that no one ever bothered to turn the mattress, or both. She wondered briefly if they had been close, the man and the cat, or if in some feline way, it sensed that he had died coming to its rescue, or even if it was somehow attuned to his spirit.

Skip didn't believe in spirits, or anyway, didn't tend to dwell on them.

This place, she thought. *It's creeping me out.*

Yet other than the ghostly cat and the sagging bed, the room was perfectly ordinary. But it was a boy's room, not a man's, so obviously the room of a boy who still lived with his parents. Makeshift bookshelves lined the walls. A desk had been made from an old door and on it rested some sophisticated computer equipment. There was also a television, VCR, and shelves of videos along with the books. A lot of them were science fiction, and so, she saw, were most of the books. But there was lots of nonfiction, too— computer books, some quasi science and actual science, history, all volumes that dealt in facts except for two or three on self-hypnosis.

That fits, she thought, *everything else in the room induces some sort of trance. Why not skip the middle step and go straight for it?*

They intrigued her, these books. She clung to them. Only they and the cat were outside the all too obvious stereotype presented by the rest of the room's furnishings, the cat because it was a warm, living being, the books because they were nonrational. People like Geoff, like the man she imagined him to be, though they lived in a fantasy world, a world of time travel and other galaxies, had no time for inward journeying. They spent their lives either devouring facts about the rational world or trying to escape it.

She felt she could probably describe Geoff. He must have been overweight, soft around the belly; but he had never accepted the fact, or else had so little sense of himself that he simply wore T-shirts a size too small without giving it a thought, T-shirts that gapped over his white and hairy belly, mostly black ones bearing skulls and Judas goats and the names of death-rock bands—Napalm Death, perhaps, Controlled Bleeding—odd, violent symbols and words that didn't fit with the gentle, unkempt man who wore them. He had a short, roundish beard and limp brown hair that always needed shampooing. He wore glasses. Running shoes. Jeans that rode low, displaying the crack of his butt, which was flat. He had once played Dungeons and Dragons, and maybe still did. He was the very personification of "nerd," a bright young man turned inward, poorly socialized, who felt so little kinship with his own planet that he routinely traveled to the ones invented by his favorite authors, who thought of that secret, dreamy place his computer took him to as cyberspace—somewhere exciting, a place more real than his own life, a land he could conquer, not a drab teenager's room in his parents' house.

Skip knew her imagination was on overdrive, but the picture she got was so vivid it spooked her. "He must have been a very nice young man," she said to Marguerite. "Do you mind if I look through his papers?"

Skip could see by Marguerite's face that she did but couldn't think of a reason to say so. "No," she said finally. "I guess not."

Skip sat at the makeshift desk. What she really wanted was to get at Geoff's electronic files, the ones in his computer, but for now she contented herself with going through the things on his desk;

slowly, ever so slowly. She wanted Marguerite to go away. And eventually, she did.

Quickly, Skip checked under the mattress, fully expecting to find at least some old copies of *Playboy*. But there was nothing. She went through his drawers and saw that she'd been wrong about one thing—no death-metal T-shirts; tie-dye instead. Perhaps he'd been a Deadhead.

She turned on the computer. There were files and files and files; she didn't know where to start. There was a box of backup disks— maybe Marguerite would let her take these with her.

"Mrs. Terry?" Skip went back into the living room, to find her hostess stretched out on the sofa, covered with the rumpled blanket, staring into space, the white dog at her feet. It thumped its tail briefly when Skip entered. She asked if she could take the box of disks and was given permission, rather desultorily; Marguerite seemed to have fallen into a fit of depression.

"Just one other thing and then I'll leave you alone. Can you give me the name of Geoff's girlfriend? And his other friend— Layne?" She had found no address book, no Rolodex.

"Of course. Lenore Marquer. She came over once or twice. Layne did too, but I never caught the rest of his name."

"Do you know where Lenore lives? Her phone number?"

Marguerite shook her head. Skip thanked her and left, drawing in her breath when she stepped outside, grateful for the cool fall air, realizing only now how dead the air had been in the house, how sour and stale. She felt her step lighten, a weight leave her shoulders. Had it been that way for Geoffrey Kavanagh? Had the place felt as much like a tomb to him as it did to Skip?

And Marguerite Terry? She was mistress of it, had made it that way. How was it for her?

Geoff's body had to have crashed hard—but having met his mother, Skip could believe she'd slept through it; she was barely awake when her eyes were open.

But surely someone had heard something.

She knocked on doors.

The neighbor next door hadn't heard the crash but had heard

the cat meowing; had been awakened by it shortly before seven and had looked out the window, but had seen nothing—only a ladder propped against the house. She'd wondered why the cat just didn't get on it and walk down. She didn't hear a crash, but she had been gone for half an hour, between eight and eight-thirty, when she drove her husband to work.

The neighbor on the other side had heard a thump and a clatter—but had thought nothing of it. She later realized the thump must have been Geoff and the clatter his ladder, but it hadn't seemed grisly at the time—just a neighborhood noise. She thought it must have been slightly after eight.

Unfortunately, neither of these neighbors, nor anyone else on the block, had seen anyone outside at all, much less anyone strange.

No one knew Geoff or the Terrys.

Skip headed to Mondo Video.

• •

If she'd expected Mondo Nerd, in keeping with the image she'd formed of Geoff, she was wrong. The manager was a freckled red-head, hair a quarter of an inch long, if that. He was broad-shouldered, button-down-shirted, clear-eyed, and looked as if he wanted desperately to be wearing a navy blazer but knew it wouldn't look right in a video store. He was about five feet nine and made Skip, who at six feet was used to shorter men and could take them or leave them, feel as if she ought to hunch over to talk to him. He had the firm grip of a kid who'd learned it at a good prep school, and the last name of a dynasty. "Knowles Kennedy," he said, applying the grip.

Skip squeezed back, identified herself, and stated her business.

"Geoff," said Knowles. "One of our best men. Really bright and knowledgeable. Not real ambitious, though."

He was about twenty-four, Skip guessed, and already he'd done better in life than Geoff ever had.

"Bet he really knew his science fiction."

"That was his thing. How'd you know?"

"I just had a feeling."

"What a memory! That guy could tell you every scene of *The Day the Earth Stood Still* or—what's the one about the pods?"

"*Invasion of the Body Snatchers.*"

"Yeah. Both versions. But he knew all the obscure stuff as well. And all the new ones. Other stuff too—I mean, besides science fiction. He could sing every theme song from every James Bond movie."

"He must have been popular with the customers."

A shadow passed over Knowles's face. "Well, not really. He was kind of shy, I guess. He could talk to them about the movies, but he never thought about 'How're you doing today?' Not real outgoing, I guess. He lived in his head, you know? It was like whatever was going on in there was the real world and what happened out here just got in the way."

Skip grinned. "Space case?"

"You could put it that way. I mean, he functioned; he did a great job here, but the guy was brilliant—face it, this job was way below his abilities."

"How could you tell he was brilliant?"

"Well, you know—by the way he talked. He retained things; like I said, he remembered everything from every movie he ever saw; and he knew a lot of just plain stuff too. Mostly science. I don't think he even went to college—at least not for very long. He was self-taught; and there wasn't much he didn't know about. If you want to know the truth, he could be kind of a know-it-all."

"Liked to hear himself talk?"

Knowles looked uncomfortable. "Well, I don't think it was that, exactly. He didn't have enough whatever-you-call-it—self-esteem—for that. I think he just didn't notice when he was lecturing. It was his only form of communication. See, he could tell you all this stuff about the War of the Roses or the Holy Roman Empire, but he didn't know he was a big fat bore when he was doing it because he didn't know enough to check your reactions. He didn't even look you in the eye—he'd be staring off into space or something, lecturing away and thinking you were fascinated. But like I said, he

15

couldn't remember about 'hi, how are you?' He was just shy, shy, shy. But nice. He meant well."

"Oh?"

"Oh, yeah. He wanted everybody to enjoy his favorites as much as he did. He couldn't remember their faces or names, but when he saw the movies they'd brought back, he'd ask how they liked them—and then he'd go crazy helping them find something suited to their tastes."

Geoff was sounding more and more the sort of person his room had spelled out. On impulse, Skip said, "What did he look like?" .

"What did he look like? Was his face—uh—?"

"No, no, I'm just curious."

"I think I might have a picture from a party we had." He disappeared and came back. "There. The one in the weird T-shirt."

She had been almost completely wrong and yet somehow right: the man in the picture was the perfect sidekick to the one she'd pictured. He was thin, not fat, average height, and clean-shaven. But a beard would have been a good idea. He had a pointy, elflike chin. Three things she'd guessed perfectly: he did indeed wear glasses; his hair was limp and greasy-looking; and he was the very exemplar of "nerd."

What was it about these guys, she wondered? Why were they such a type—brilliant, withdrawn, dorky, into computers and science fiction? She knew the answer, or thought she did. They were unhappy with the real world, had little self-esteem (as Knowles Kennedy, who had a surfeit of it, had observed), and sought alternate universes.

Okay, fine. That was who they were as a class, but who was Geoff Kavanagh other than the nerd from Central Casting? His nerdiness was all too apparent; what was his *Geoffness*, so to speak? Well, she couldn't say that aloud. "What was unusual about him?" she asked finally.

"Unusual?" Knowles looked puzzled. "Well, he was . . . so smart and all. I don't know—he was kind of your average—"

"Nerd."

"Yeah."

"Did he have any enemies?"

"What? You mean he was murdered?"

Skip shrugged. "I have to ask."

"Did he have any enemies! He didn't even have any friends."

"How do you know?"

Knowles looked ashamed. "Well, I don't. I really don't know. It's just that he never talked about them. He never talked about anything except things; events; stuff you could get out of books. Not life. He hardly ever got any personal calls. He could always work late or take someone else's shift. I think he even lived with his parents."

"Did anyone here know him any better than you?"

"Well, Jody might have. She worked with him a lot. Hey, Jo!"

A plump young woman ambled over, black, wearing clothes a couple of sizes too small and, from her saunter, well-pleased with her appearance. "Jody, this is Officer Langdon. She's looking into Geoff's death."

"He was a good guy. Everybody liked Geoff."

"You did?"

"Sure I did. Talkin' to Geoff was like goin' to college."

"Did he ever talk about his personal life?"

"Claimed he had a girlfriend."

"Did he mention her name?"

"Lenore. Oh, sure he had a girlfriend. Like everybody's named Lenore. He probably picked the name from some book. You know, I'd talk about this place or that place, right around here, and he wouldn't know what I meant. Tell you the truth, I don't think he got out much. Stayed home with that computer of his. On the town every single night; always on the town. It was like that was his world. You know the town?"

Skip gulped. Knowles looked as confused as she felt.

"The town. It's like a computer thing. Wait a minute, now, he told me once . . . let's just see if I can get it." She put her hand to her forehead and closed her eyes. "I got it. The Original Worldwide Network."

"Oh. The TOWN. Is it a bulletin board or something?"

She shrugged. "More like a religion. Or maybe a real town. He'd talk about all these things going on on the TOWN, just like, you know, they were really happenin'." She shook her head. "I thought he needed a girlfriend, I was gon' fix him up, but that was when he said he had one. Had to be lyin', though. You know what? He was one weird dude."

"Well, what was weird about him? What was different?"

"He looked right through you, didn't even see you."

"He was shy," said Knowles.

"Bullshit. He wasn't shy, he was only half alive."

2

• •

Maybe, Skip thought, the girlfriend could shed some light. Marguerite Terry had given her a phone number, which produced the following message: "If it's daytime, I'm at Stringalong. If it's night, don't ask—especially at the full moon." This was followed by one of the more fiendish cackles ever heard outside a production of *Macbeth*. Just as well it was daytime, but what was Stringalong?

According to the phone book, it could be found on Magazine Street. A store, maybe.

Once inside, Skip still wasn't sure. It was a store, but was it a business? It was if selling beads wasn't a front or a money laundry—because beads were all Stringalong had to offer. Tiny beads, large beads, glass beads, crystal beads, amber beads, jet beads, carved beads, beads in every color and beads of pristine clarity, about enough beads to fill up a shoe box if you dumped the entire inventory into one small space. But of course that would be no way to sell beads. They were displayed in hundreds of small plastic cases, and cost ten cents apiece and upwards. But still. How could you make a living selling beads? Who bought beads?

There was only one person in the store, a small woman, thirty, maybe, with darkish hair that more or less just hung, a slash of red lipstick and a short black dress that showed off half a dozen doubtless handmade necklaces. She had a tiny face, heart-shaped; a gamine face with a pointy chin that reminded Skip of Geoff's. If this was Lenore, it was a Mick-and-Bianca kind of match. She was a fawnlike creature, in her slimness, her elusiveness, but she wasn't pretty, and she probably wasn't innocent—she simply looked as if she'd spook easily.

Stepping closer, Skip saw that she had a mole near the corner of her mouth, a tiny flaw that lent personality to her face. She had a feeling talking to her was going to be like trying to catch water in your hand.

"Lenore Marquer?"

The woman's mouth quivered. "Yes. Is Caitlin all right?"

"Caitlin?"

"My daughter. You didn't come about her?"

"No."

She breathed in. "Thank God. She's in day care—I live in fear."

Skip smiled, happy to reassure her. "It's not about that at all. I'm Skip Langdon from the police department—"

"Omigod, it's about Geoff! Shit! I knew it. I knew it. I told them. Shit! He was murdered, right? We all knew it. It was only a matter of time. . . ."

"Hold on a minute. You seem to know more about this than I do."

"It's not about Geoff?"

"No, it is."

"You decided to move on the autopsy report, right? Finally. We thought maybe you wouldn't. God, we were worried sick, but now that it's staring me in the face, the cold reality of it . . ." She put her hands to her mouth, apparently to stop the sobs that were coming out anyway. Tears flowed like a hot rain, in no time turning the tiny face a blotchy crimson, almost puce. She was out of control, and Skip had to remind herself that Geoff had been dead only five days; the wound was still open, still angry and dangerous.

"Lenore, maybe you'd better sit down." Skip looked around for a chair, but didn't see so much as a footstool.

Lenore's body was still heaving. Unable to sit, she came out from behind the counter, pulled the door open, and made a show of gulping in fresh air. She had a tattoo on her ankle, a handsome coiling snake.

Skip was in agony. Obviously Lenore couldn't talk if she couldn't even breathe, but it was killing her not to be able to fire questions.

Two women starting to pass the store were obviously drawn by the face at the door. "Oh, look," said one. "Let's go in there and look."

Lenore stepped aside.

"What's this—a bead store? You sell beads here?"

Lenore managed a smile. "And a few necklaces we make on the premises."

"Are you all right, dear?"

"Fine—uh—allergy attack. Is there anything I can help you with?"

The woman turned to her friend. "Steff, this could be just the thing." To Lenore, she said, "I have this suit that has a peculiar ocher color in it and I just can't find the right thing to wear with it."

"Well, let's see. What color blouse do you wear with it?"

Skip considered smashing all the display cases. Better yet, smashing Steff and friend. But there was nothing to do but wait. Ten minutes later, Lenore shot her a helpless look and said to her customers, "Could you excuse me a moment?"

She came over to Skip. "I'm sorry, but I just work here, I don't own it. I can't afford to lose this job, I really can't."

She had a way of making everything into high tragedy; Skip really hadn't planned to cost her her job. But before she could speak, Lenore said, "Look, I don't know anything, anyway. Why don't you go see Layne? He's Geoff's best friend and he works out of his house. He has time."

"Layne who?"

21

"Bilderback. He lives in the Quarter."

That was convenient: so did Skip. This way she could take a sandwich home and put her feet up for a few minutes between interviews.

I could even meditate.

In the privacy of her car, she laughed. That was her little joke with herself—she would meditate if she could, she just couldn't sit still. She was especially unable to sit when her adrenaline was flowing, as when she was fascinated with a case, the way she was with this one. Even putting her feet up would take a major effort. In fact, the hell with it. She ate her sandwich at her kitchen counter, opening her mail as she did it, wondering how Lenore Marquer had known about the autopsy report before she did.

She ate fast, knowing she'd be sorry in a few minutes, but unable to concentrate on the task at hand, only on getting to Layne Bilderback.

He lived on the border of the Quarter, on the downtown side of Esplanade, just off Dumaine. Not the greatest neighborhood, some would say, but beautiful; breathtakingly beautiful. With its tree-lined center divider ("neutral ground" in New Orleans) and its gracious old houses—houses that seemed almost alive, almost to bow and click their heels, they were so welcoming—it was hard to imagine a flourishing drug trade behind the walls, but the neighborhood had that and everything else; Skip knew because she'd worked VCD—the Vieux Carre District—now prosaically called "the Eighth."

A black man sat on the steps of the house Layne lived in. "How're you?" he said, as friendly as if it were fifty years earlier and the races weren't permanently angry at each other.

Skip stopped to enjoy the moment. "Fine, thanks. But cold." She shivered a little.

"Yeah. My wife won't let me smoke inside—she'd rather I freeze to death."

"At least she lets you come home." It wasn't that funny, but she and the man shared a big laugh, pals for a moment—the sort of moment you didn't get in every city, she thought when she liked New Orleans, which she did right now.

22

I'm actually happy, she thought with surprise, and remembered guiltily she was on a murder case.

"Does Layne Bilderback live here?"

"Upstairs."

She pushed the button. In a moment a young white man appeared on the balcony. "Yes?"

"I'm Skip Langdon—did Lenore Marquer call about me?" She was trying to avoid saying the "p" word out on the street.

"No. Should she have?"

"I'm from the police department. Could I come in, please?"

"Let's see your badge."

The smoker disappeared quickly, either spooked or minding his own business. Skip held up her badge.

"What's this about?"

"I think you know, don't you?"

"About time you got here," he said, and let her in.

He was short by Skip's standards, about Knowles Kennedy's height. Though he wore a sweatshirt and jeans, she could see a well-muscled, slim-waisted torso; clearly he worked out. He was pale, had barely any hair, and wore glasses. Not really a nerd, this one, but probably an intellectual. She deduced that by his surroundings as much as his appearance. It was the usual gorgeous high-ceilinged, French-windowed French Quarter gem, but the paint was a dirty beige, as if he could care less, the furniture functional, to say the least—other people's castoffs, it looked like—and there were more books and magazines on the floor alone than in certain library branches. There were bookshelves too, but they were only partly filled with books—cardboard boxes were stacked on them, board games, apparently, but more than Skip would have thought existed.

"Are you from Homicide?" He gestured toward the trashed-out couch with a fake Navaho blanket thrown over it, probably to hide the rips and stains.

She sat. "Yes. What am I here about?"

"Geoff Kavanagh. Can I get you anything?"

She shook her head impatiently, hoping he'd go on; she wasn't disappointed.

"So you guys finally caught on to that autopsy report. We were wondering if we were going to have to storm headquarters or what." He sat in a broken-down rattan chair.

"Would you mind telling me what's going on here? And who 'we' is?"

"It's the talk of the TOWN, Officer."

"Detective," she snapped. Rank usually mattered not a whit to her, but this guy was making her angry. "You mean the computer bulletin board?"

"Oh. You know about the TOWN."

"Not nearly enough, apparently."

"Come on, I'll show you."

"Let's talk a minute first." She felt a need to regain control. The case was spinning out of orbit. "What was your relationship with Geoffrey Kavanagh?"

He blushed. "We weren't lovers if that's what you mean."

"It isn't."

"Well, I mean—he was my best friend, and I'm about as openly gay as you can get."

It was all she could do not to glance at her watch. *I guess you are,* she thought. *We've known each other—what, two minutes?—and I now know one thing about you. That.*

"How did you two meet?"

"Online."

"I beg your pardon?"

"On the TOWN. We were both in the Southern conference and found out we both lived in New Orleans. So we met; we had a lot of interests in common."

"Like what?"

"Oh, computers. Virtual reality. Virtual communities. Virtual sex."

"Virtual what?"

"I just threw sex in to wake you up. They haven't developed it yet, but everybody's on the edge of their seats. Virtual communities exist, though. The TOWN's one. We all know each other and care about each other even though most of us have never set eyes on each other or heard each other's voices and never will; its headquarters is in California somewhere, and that's where most users are. But I know Darlis and Busy from out on the coast as well as I know anybody in New Orleans."

"Layne, you've got to get out more."

"Well, I can't. I work out of my house and everything I like to do you do indoors."

"Wait a minute; what do you do?"

"You mean for money? I'm a puzzle constructer."

"A puzzle constructer."

"Yeah. Like crosswords and logic puzzles. For puzzle magazines mostly, plus one or two general publications."

"Well, I guess somebody has to do it."

"It doesn't sound like fun?"

"Oh, it does. I'm just reeling from the weirdness of it. I guess I never met a puzzlemaker before."

"But you always wanted to." He gave her a winning smile, displaying such friendly blue eyes that she'd have sworn he was flirting—and he probably was. She'd noticed lots of gay men flirted with her and she loved it—no danger of awkward misunderstandings.

"I guess I must have." She'd almost forgotten her irritation. But it came back when she realized the implication of his job. "So you see Geoff Kavanagh's death as a puzzle to solve."

He shrugged. "When your best friend dies, you do what you know. I've got a friend who works for a newspaper out in California. Every time another gay man dies of AIDS, he makes sure he writes the obit. That's his way of dealing with it."

"Was Geoff gay?" Skip knew she was getting off the track, but this was turning out to be a pretty free-floating conversation.

"Not that I know of. And, as I said, he was my best friend." Beneath the cleverness, Layne had a simplicity of expression she liked, a straightforwardness she wondered if she could trust.

"Okay. How'd you find out Geoff was dead?"

"Lenore called me. She'd called him at work and he hadn't shown up. She tried home and his mother told her. I got all excited and posted about it. And then everybody else started, from all over the country. There's a whole topic about it—we think he was murdered."

"Hold it, you lost me a mile back. I can understand looking at a death like a puzzle because you're a puzzlemaker; I can even understand trying to block out the pain of a friend's death with intellectual activity . . ."

He winced, probably hating the mention of emotion of any sort.

". . . but I don't really see why you'd come to the conclusion your friend was murdered just because he died in an accident."

"Oh. I guess you don't know about the flashbacks."

"Is that some computer term I don't know?"

"You really don't know, do you?"

"Know what, goddammit?" She was starting to realize how much she hated the feeling of being out of control.

"Okay, if I understand correctly, you just came because of the autopsy report. All you know so far is Geoff's death was classified 'suspicious'—right?"

"I'll do the questioning, all right?"

Layne leaned back in his chair. "Go ahead."

"Tell me about the flashbacks."

"Well, I was about to. I just wanted to know what you already knew, so I could save us some time."

She held her peace, though her teeth clenched with the effort of it.

But Layne couldn't leave it alone: "Are we having our first fight?"

She was angry at herself for allowing him to see how irritated she was, and wondered how to get out of it. She tried a smile that she hoped wasn't a rictus. "Flashbacks."

"Okay, we'll work it out later. Well, it was in Confession—"

"I beg your pardon?"

"Confession. That's the name of the conference."

"And what's a conference?"

"It's a place where you can go and talk about a subject—a virtual place, that is. Sometimes you go to Confession and a new topic might be sex, say, and people just post things like 'I haven't done it in two months. What about you?' It's luck of the draw, you know? Sometimes it's like that, and sometimes people really get down."

"There was a flashback topic?"

"Oh, no, it was 'Murder in Nice Neighborhoods' or some such thing. I don't know. Somebody just got the idea to post about that phenomenon of everyone saying 'He was such a nice, quiet young fellow' whenever a serial killer gets arrested. And then to ask if people knew anyone they thought was capable of murder. Needless to say, that got interesting, and then the topic changed slightly to something you might call 'Murder at Home,' only it had a slightly different name."

"You're losing me again."

"Well, don't worry, I'm about to catch you up. Murders in people's own lives that weren't called that, or for which nobody was arrested. Like the guy whose grandma fell out a window with his grandpa in the room. Did he push her or not? The topic went on for about a week and then Geoff posted that he thought he'd actually seen a murder once."

"What?" Skip sat forward, unable to keep still.

"The murder of his father."

She sat back. "Keep talking."

"He said he'd had this weird dream when the topic first came up about yelling in the night, somebody trying to break in; scary stuff. He wrote it down, trying to figure out what it meant, and he thought he could actually remember something like that. The feeling, anyway. Being real scared.

"And what he actually knew was this: when he was four years old, he and his mother came home one night to find his father dead on the bedroom floor. Shot with his own revolver—he was a cop."

"A cop!"

"In your very own department. He thought he could remember coming home—climbing the stairs with his mother, going into the bedroom, and finding the body. But once he'd asked her, and she said it wasn't like that at all. She said Geoff ran right up the stairs and went to the bathroom; meanwhile Marguerite—that's his mother—went into the bedroom and turned on the light. It was all she could do to keep from screaming, but she didn't want little Geoffrey to know what was going on, so she turned out the light, closed the door, and went downstairs to call the cops."

"Pretty damn cool."

"Well, who knows what really happened? That's just what she told Geoff. Anyway, it got him to thinking his own memory was bogus—or might be. And after he had that dream, he kept getting these weird flashbacks, if you want to call them that, like incest survivors are supposed to have—little half-memories. Like being in bed and hearing an argument. Running down the hall. His mother's face. His dad on the floor . . . actually, he had that one all the time, from before his mother told him he'd never seen that. Do you see what I'm getting at?"

"He posted this stuff?"

"Yes."

"Under his own name?"

"You can't hide your identity on the TOWN—you have a user ID, but anyone can check you out in about two seconds. Geoff was Vidkid."

"So if it was true, if he really had witnessed the murder, or had even been in the house when one was committed, he was putting it out there for the world to know. Is that what you're saying?"

"That was our reasoning, yes. When we found out about the 'accident.' "

Skip could see why this was the talk of the TOWN. "Okay, anybody on the TOWN could find out who Geoff was. Was there any way for him to know who was reading the postings?"

Layne shook his head. "Absolutely no way in hell. The TOWN has almost ten thousand subscribers all over the world. Someone in Marrakech could have seen the postings and come to New Orleans for the sole purpose of dispatching Geoff before he got that final damning memory."

Or maybe he'd already gotten it; and confronted the murderer. It needn't be anyone on the TOWN at all—all it had to be was someone who knew he knew.

"What was he thinking of?" she wailed.

"To post like that? Well, it's kind of a TOWN tradition. When you're going through something bad—and he was—you come to your buddies for aid and comfort."

"He didn't even know these people."

"Yes, he did."

"Excuse me. Ten thousand of them?"

Layne looked uncomfortable.

"Good God!" she continued. "This is what shrinks are for."

"The TOWN's a hell of a lot more accessible—and cheaper."

"Not in this case."

Now he looked downright sheepish. "It might have been one of us. We know that."

"What's the deal with the autopsy report?"

"Lenore got it—don't ask me how. She posted it and RX, who lives in Portland, Med from Pensacola, and Sayah of Savannah all gave their medical opinions. A lot of the stuff on today is about whether or not we should notify the cops."

Skip sighed. "You might as well show me what the monster looks like."

Layne grinned like a kid. "I was hoping you'd say that."

His computer room looked a lot like the starship *Enterprise*. Clearly, much more thought had gone into the design of this than the decor of the rest of the apartment. Skip sat down in front of the color monitor.

"Okay, I'm logging on. See? I'm typing my user ID—Teaser. Now it's going to ask for my password." He hit keys, but nothing appeared on the screen. Then the announcement: "You're On The TOWN!"

"Who knows your password?"

"You and the sysop. That's it."

"Come again?"

"The systems operator."

She nodded.

"Shall we go straight to Confession?"

"By all means."

He typed out a few things and pretty soon "Murder at Home" was on the screen, its actual name being: "What Murderers Do You Know?"

"This is going to take a long time to read. There are four hundred and eleven postings on this one. Let's get out of it and I'll show you Geoff's."

The first posting was Layne's: "Geoff Kavanagh (Vidkid) was found dead at his home this morning, apparently the victim of an accident. Who believes it?"

The next entry said: "The flashbacks! Somebody saw his posts."

Geoff's body had been found at ten A.M. Thursday—this post was at twelve-thirty P.M., two and a half hours later and about ninety-three hours before the beginning of the police investigation.

I'm just learning this now, Skip thought, *and this cyberpunk knew it three days ago.*

The attached user ID was Gorilla. "Who the hell is that?" she growled.

"Her name is Nancy, I think, and she lives in Boise or someplace. Want me to look her up?"

"No. Let's stay in the topic."

"Well, it goes on in this vein for a while. Everybody coming to obvious conclusions. Then somebody—Med, I think"—he scrolled down—"got the idea of getting hold of the autopsy report and indeed Lenore was able to do that. She uploaded it and then things really took off—all those doctors saying the report wasn't consistent with that kind of accident, everybody with their theories."

"Has anyone accused anybody?"

"Not publicly." Lane looked troubled.

"But anybody could E-mail somebody. They could know something special they might not want to share, right? And simply contact the person directly."

"Yeah. I've thought of that too. Blackmail's what you're talking about, right?"

"That or simple grandstanding."

He nodded, apparently following completely. "Have you ever been to one of those mystery weekends?"

"No, why?"

"Well, I've put a few of them together." He spread his arms modestly. "I do games as well as puzzles. A weird thing happens to people. They all start thinking they're Sam Spade and they do stuff they'd never do ordinarily. They break into each other's rooms, they steal phone messages, they shadow people—it's very disconcerting the first time you see it."

"Oh, shit. This is no game."

"A strange kind of reality kicks in once you get on the TOWN. It's kind of like being in a car and yelling at people you'd never yell at in any other circumstance. You know that feeling of invincibility?"

Skip felt queasy. "They think because they can't see the person they're talking to they're not really talking to him?"

"Well, it's weird. The actual illusion is that you know people intimately when all you see is a few words on a screen. But because that is an illusion, you get bold. The most obvious example is flirting. People flirt online, or anyway it starts out that way and next thing you know, they're talking dirty to a perfect stranger."

"Oh, God, you're not making me feel any better. They feel safe, is what you're saying."

"Yes." His brow was really quite wrinkled.

"How can I get a printout of this stuff?"

"I'll make you one if you like."

"Now?"

"Sure."

"And I'll need the sysop's number."

"Okay, but you've got to talk to Bigeasy, too."

"Who?"

"Our fearless leader. Bigeasy. He knows more about this stuff than anybody in Louisiana."

31

3

• •

Skip spent the rest of the day going through Layne's printouts and waiting for a callback from the sysop, user ID Wizard. Aside from the terrifying thought that the murderer was monitoring the entire discussion, probably even participating in it, there were other revelations. Plenty of them.

Geoff had posted, in front of ten thousand people, not only that he thought he might have witnessed a murder and was soon hoping to get a flashback of the face, but that he'd always thought it kind of funny his mother got married so soon after his father's death. She'd waited eight months and married his Uncle Mike, his father's brother.

Mike Kavanagh was a name Skip knew. Like his brother Leighton, he was a cop—a working cop even now assigned to Robbery, and a cousin of her nemesis, Frank O'Rourke. This was less than wonderful news. O'Rourke had proved time and again that he'd do anything to sabotage her—why, she didn't know, except that he didn't like women, didn't like cops who came from Uptown, and had the disposition of a copperhead. With his cousin a suspect in the case, no telling what he'd pull, if he was in town. Fortunately, he wasn't.

There was another notable thing about Geoff's postings—they weren't complete. Sometimes there'd be a blank space with only the word *deleted* in it.

Just as she was getting her eighth or ninth cup of coffee, more out of boredom than otherwise, so eager was she to be out in the field, the phone rang.

"Hello, this is Wizard."

"Hi, Wizard. I got a problem down here."

"Yeah, I've been expecting to hear from you."

She felt once again the irritation that had surged up at Layne's: How dare these people know more than the police? "Can you let me know all your Louisiana users?"

"I've got to talk to our lawyers about anything you ask me."

"Okay, that's Question One. Question Two is technical. Is there a way to recover deleted material?"

"Not mail. Anything else, yes."

"Who can delete material, by the way? Can anybody on the TOWN?"

"Anybody can delete his or her own posts. And the conference hosts or I can do it if we need to—for legal reasons, say. But other than that, one user can't delete another's."

"I notice a lot of Geoff's are missing. I'd like to know why."

"My guess is he did it himself. I'll see what I can find out."

"Thanks. Here's what else I need: everything Geoff Kavanagh ever posted; and everything he posted that ended up deleted. Can you get that for me?"

"I'll ask the legal eagles."

Legal eagles. He was probably the kind of guy who said "thingie." They all probably did. They were nerds by definition.

"Hey, listen," she said, "what kind of people subscribe to the TOWN? I mean, just in general—do you have any kind of demographic breakdown?"

"Not really. There are thousands of lurkers who never identify themselves other than to give their names."

"What are lurkers?"

"People who don't post. You could monitor every conference except the private ones and no one would even know you're there if you don't speak up. That's a lurker.

"Anyway, we've had these sort of self-surveys online, but they don't really mean anything because the lurkers so far outnumber the posters. On the TOWN, I think it's about eight to one."

"Well, of the posters—or at least those who respond to the surveys—what are most people like?"

"For openers, they're all ages. Lots and lots of them are in computer-related jobs, of course. But we've got a fair number of writers and actors—we're near L.A., so I guess you'd expect it."

"No dearth of doctors, I noticed."

"I think one of them is even a forensic pathologist. Yeah, we've got just about everything you can name. I'll tell you one thing—we have a reputation for being one of the least nerdy bulletin boards."

"Did you say something about private conferences?"

"Yes, anyone can start one. The most popular ones are the Men's, Women's, Gays, and Recovery, but we have lots that have just two or three people in them."

"Can I find out if Geoff was in any of them?"

"I'll talk to the . . ."

". . . legal eagles. You do that thingie."

Another dead end. Disgusted, she packed up and went home.

There were other things she could have done; she felt a little odd about giving up so easily the first day of a big case, but the truth was, she was feeling overwhelmed by this one. She needed a good night's sleep to get her mind in cyberspace.

• •

She had painted her new apartment melon, like the one she had left, in the Big House. As its former tenant, Jimmy Dee, had had it a deep, masculine aubergine, that hadn't been easy, but it had been worth it. Melon walls, white trim, gauzy curtains, and French doors made a cool, light, airy, happy place, though she could have done without the cool and the air at the moment. She had a beautiful blue-and-white Chinese lamp that stood on an antique table, a shiny, dark wood coffee table, her almost-new gray-and-white-striped sofa, and very little else, except for her cherished Marcia Mandeville painting and a new bed, since she now had a bedroom. In the smaller apartment, she'd just used the fold-out sofa. Next she was going to need a set of fireplace tools, that was obvious. Even with the wide open spaces caused by an unconcealable dearth of furniture, she would have been perfectly happy here if she hadn't had to wear three sweaters.

Of course, she could always go over to the Big House.

She'd been doing that a lot lately, and it had only just turned cold. Jimmy Dee had said he needed her, that's why he'd given her the garçonniere so cheap, and why she'd accepted. That and the fact that it was an offer no one in her right mind would dream of refusing. It was one of the best apartments in the French Quarter.

But now she was developing a strange uneasiness about intruding in the Scoggin-Ritter family. The kids had been without a father quite a while before their mother died; and they'd never really known their Uncle Jimmy Dee very well. They weren't used to men; she didn't know if they knew he was gay, but she was damned sure they weren't used to gay men. So they clung to her. Which made Jimmy Dee look sad, even though he knew she was the bridge between himself and them; that he'd been right in more than one way when he said he needed her. And it made her feel slightly panicky—panicky because, much as they weren't used to men, she wasn't used to kids. She didn't know how to replace their mother, which was apparently what they wanted her to do. And she knew it wouldn't solve anything—Jimmy Dee had to be their main parent, no matter how painful it was for everybody.

So instead of Jimmy Dee, she called Steve Steinman, her California beau: "Something weird's happening."

"What? In the weird capital of the world? Stop boring me."

"No, really. This is one for the books. I got this murder case—I mean, a coroner's case that looked like murder. I went out to ask a few questions and all the victim's friends had already seen the autopsy report, had solicited doctors' opinions, and been out with their deerstalker caps and magnifying glasses for a good two days before the police ever even heard of it. I was last on my block to know and, let me tell you, it wasn't fun."

It was a good thirty seconds before Steve Steinman stopped laughing.

"What's so funny?" She was impatient.

"You. You're such a cop. You people hate it if anybody knows more than you do."

"Something wrong with that?"

"Who's dead?"

"Guy named Geoff Kavanagh."

"Oh, shit. Not Vidkid."

"I'm asleep; I'm dreaming. This isn't really happening to me."

"The autopsy report and all that stuff—the people who did that are all on the TOWN, right?"

"Don't tell me you are too."

"What happened to old Vidkid? I'm sorry to hear about this."

"Obviously, you haven't been logging on, or you'd know."

"Not in about three months, actually. I burn out on it after a while."

"You're going to love this." For once, she was unfettered by the police code of secrecy, since almost everything she knew about the case was public—had been public before the murder. And he *was* going to love it; Steve was a sucker for a good yarn, and also an excitement junkie.

He was beside himself. "I can't believe what I've been missing."

"You can know a person and not really know him."

"What do you mean?"

"I had no idea you were a TOWNsperson."

"Well, you know I'm heavy into computers."

"Oh, yeah. You took some sort of course recently."

"Some sort of course that changed my life, that's all. But the TOWN—I guess I never talk about it because it's so boring."

"Oh, right."

"Well, this is our first homicide. Really low crime rate, usually."

"Do you post or lurk?"

36

"Got the jargon already, I see. I lurk, mostly, but now and then—" He paused for a long time.

"What?"

"I was just trying to figure out what. I can't explain it; something comes over you."

"Like a spell?"

"An evil spell."

"Oh, great. First virtual sex. Now black magic. What's your user ID?"

"I'm afraid it's a little unimaginative."

"Hit me with it."

"Steve."

"Steve?"

"Don't be so merciless. Look, you've got to get on this thing."

"My thought, exactly. But I don't want them to know I'm lurking—and you can't hide it, right?"

"Oh, sure you can. Nobody asks for your driver's license. All you really have to do is join using someone else's credit card. The TOWN bill goes to them, but you can log on from anywhere; so if you're working at home, you'll just get the phone bill yourself. Pretty neat, huh?"

"But not very inventive, criminally speaking."

"Well, here's something even less inventive—but more elegant. Why don't you be me?"

"Can I do that?"

"Sure. All I have to do is tell you my password."

"And you'd do that?"

"I'm not so sure. It's a little embarrassing."

"Why?"

"Oh, hell. Just get a pencil, okay?"

"Got one."

"You can't use real words because there are programs that can go through the dictionary until they get to your password."

"You lost me."

"Hackers do this. They'll break into your personal file and into the whole TOWN if they want to."

"Oh, who could be bothered?"

"Did anyone ever tell you there are a lot of strange people out there?"

She was almost angry at the senselessness of it. "Why don't they just get a life?"

"A lot of them are computer wizards working in computer jobs. They do the whole day's work in an hour or two, maybe three, but they can't leave or the boss would notice. So they screw around."

"I see what you're saying. These are people who literally have nothing better to do."

"Idle hands are the devil's playthings—or however that goes."

"How about the password?"

He said something that sounded like "Skip to my Lou."

"Huh?"

"I said it was embarrassing."

"I think it's sweet."

"Take it down—Skip2mLu. My darlin'."

"Aren't you romantic."

He was silent.

"Hello?"

"I don't know. That's a good question."

"What's a good question? What are you talking about?"

"We'll talk about it later."

"What? We'll talk about what later?"

"I'm just not ready yet. I can't talk about it now."

She hung up with fear at the back of her throat. It wasn't like Steve to put her off, to say ambiguous things.

He's met someone else, she thought.

Why wouldn't he have? There were two thousand miles between them. They couldn't go on like this forever, and they didn't plan to. Steve talked all the time about moving to New Orleans. He loved it, it was becoming his second home. Or so he used to say.

And now she knew she would call Jimmy Dee. Anyway, he had a computer and she didn't. On second thought, why call?

She popped over.

"Auntie!" Eleven-year-old Kenny ran for her. He was still cuddly, still a little boy.

38

"That sounds sooo dumb! Why don't you just call her Skip?" said Sheila, the thirteen-year-old.

Kenny looked crushed.

"Because it's not my name. Auntie is my name."

"Short," said Jimmy Dee, "for Aphrodite. Because your auntie is a goddess among women. Or, if you want to know a secret, simply a goddess. It used to be Affie, but she's so modest she insisted on Auntie so no one would know. Keep the secret, would you, angels?"

"Affie! Affie!" Sheila was convulsed in giggles, giggles of the most contemptuous thirteen-year-old sort. "Affie, Affie, Affie."

"Stay for dinner?" Jimmy Dee was keeping his tone light, but Skip saw the plea in his eyes. She needn't have worried about intruding.

"What are we having?"

"To you, fettuccine quattro fromaggi. To Kenny"—he dropped a hand on the little boy's shoulders, and Kenny smiled up at him—"macaroni and cheese. To Sheila—"

"Pig slop."

"I beg your pardon, my good young lady. I bet you've never seen a pig in your life, much less slop."

"I used to ride horses," she said, and stalked out.

Skip said, "You know that expression 'tossed her head'?"

"I do it often." He pantomimed removing his head and throwing it to Kenny, who laughed as if it were the first time he'd seen it.

"But some people really *do* it."

"Come, let's go toss a salad."

The kitchen was shiny as a new car and up to the nanosecond. Two teams of workmen had worked for six months to tear out the four apartments into which the gorgeous old house had been divided and make it whole again. The kids' mother, ill with cancer, had died in the meantime, and they'd stayed for a while with their grandparents. Skip couldn't believe it had happened so fast, but here it was—hardwood floors, paint as fresh as a breeze, and perfect, storybook rooms for each of the kids. Jimmy Dee had hired not only decorators, but child psychologists; he had consulted mothers, dads, and kids about how to furnish the rooms, what toys to get for Kenny, what half-teen-half-kid things for Sheila. Predictably, neither had said a word on seeing their perfect new rooms.

Later, Kenny had grudgingly admitted he liked his, and Sheila had begun to complain about hers. "At least she's talking," Jimmy Dee said.

Skip looked at him sideways. "You're going to wear out your cheeks trying to keep smiling."

"How do you get a kid to like you?"

"Expensive gifts?"

"Didn't work."

"Time."

"Cut up this tomato, will you?"

"Dee-Dee, really. Her whole world's been turned upside down. And besides that, she's thirteen. If she weren't surly, she wouldn't be normal."

"See this hair?" He picked up a strand of it. "It's turning gray."

"It's been gray for years."

There was a bump from the other side of the house, followed by a loud wail from Kenny and then the sound of running footsteps. Sighing in unison, Dee-Dee and Skip ran to the back, to what Jimmy Dee was pleased to call the library, because he'd put all his books in there, but what, in fact, was more or less a very elegant TV room. It was full of dark wood and flowing draperies that were almost apple green, but deeper than that, with a golden sheen. It was a room so beautiful Skip thought it would make her weep if she ever saw it uncluttered with toys and schoolwork. And yet she liked the way the kids had made it theirs, doing their homework on the low, broad coffee table, pulling pillows off the sturdy cocoa-colored couches to lie on while watching television.

Kenny was just changing the channel. He looked up, his face reproachful. "She kicked me."

"Sheila!"

Sheila's chunky frame appeared in the doorway, feet planted apart, long hair snaky. "What?" She had made one syllable sound a lot like "Want to make something of it?" Her jaw looked as if it would take a team of oral surgeons to get it to move.

Kenny pointed a skinny finger. "She changed the channel and then when I went to change it back she kicked me and pushed me over."

She ran at him. "You kicked *me*, you little shit!" And this time she did kick him. He fell over howling, holding his injured leg, milking it for all it was worth.

"God damn it, Sheila!" said Jimmy Dee, going for her, grabbing her arm.

"You let go of me." She wriggled loose on her own, unfortunately having built up enough momentum so that she stumbled forward, fell over her huddled little brother, and landed in a heap on top of him. He set up a new howl, and Skip saw Sheila's face as she rolled over and came up—not merely flushed and angry and sullen, but absolutely miserable. It was a face that said, "No one loves me; I haven't a friend in the world."

"Oh, honey," said Skip, reaching for her.

"Leave me alone!"

Jimmy Dee was trying to comfort the screaming Kenny, whose dignity was no doubt hurt a great deal worse than his leg. Sheila ran from the room.

Sighing, Skip turned off the TV. "Maybe it's time for homework."

"You're going to punish me for something she did?"

"Punish you how?"

"I was watching a show!"

"Actually, it's time to wash up," said Jimmy Dee. "Dinner in five minutes."

"I'm not hungry."

Dee-Dee, in the manner of parents, had lied about the five minutes, of course. But in fifteen or twenty, they were all four seated at the kitchen table (the kids much preferred this to the dining room), Sheila and Kenny actually looking combed and fresh, as if they hadn't just been mixing it up like a couple of street thugs.

They were an odd contrast, these two, exactly the opposite of everything everyone said about kids. Boys were supposed to be rambunctious and aggressive, yet Kenny was gentle to a fault, the kind of kid a bully could smell a mile away, and wanted nothing more than to please. He had freckles across his nose and neat brown hair that he actually knew how to part and slick down. When he did that, Skip wanted to rumple it and say, "Lighten up, kid." But he was so proud of this adult skill that she held back.

She wished sometimes that he'd come home one day with a mohawk, done in pink and purple stripes, and a nose ring.

Sheila was another story entirely. She was big for her age, tall and carrying baby fat, with a lot of color in the face and wavy blond-brown hair with gorgeous sunlit streaks that she let fall over one eye and that was quite often a little on the greasy side—she wasn't yet at the hairwashing-every-five-minutes stage. She was big and full of beans and she was one tough customer.

While Kenny was content to sit on the floor and color, she flounced about the house seemingly from pillar to post, trying to work off energy, at times kicking or hitting anyone who got in her way, sometimes deliberately attacking her little brother, or so it seemed—physically attacking him, as he'd reported tonight.

If Kenny should lighten up, she should calm down, and Skip had to swallow those words as well. Often, Jimmy Dee didn't. He lost his temper with her, he yelled at her. These were the reasons she resisted him, but on the other hand, Skip knew perfectly well, she taunted him. He wasn't used to children; he didn't have the skills yet to know how to defuse her. He saw her simply as a big kid attacking a little one and his instinct was to defend the underdog.

She had to blame someone for her unhappiness, for her mother's death, her father's desertion, for being uprooted and moved to a strange town. Jimmy Dee was simply handy, Skip thought. Sheila had had two sessions with a therapist and after that had put up so much resistance to going that it had been easier to let it go for a while.

Skip adored her—adored them both, actually, but she identified with Sheila. Sheila was uncomfortable with her body, as Skip had been with hers most of her life, before she realized size could be an advantage and had become a cop.

Sheila was in a place she didn't want to be. Throughout her

childhood, Skip had felt like an alien who'd somehow wandered into a culture she didn't understand—Sheila actually was one.

Sheila had a lot of attributes that were supposed to belong to boys; so did Skip.

"Maybe we should just get Kenny some Barbie dolls and Sheila a football," she had said once.

Dee-Dee had raised an eyebrow: "As if being raised by a gay uncle isn't confusing enough for them." But he'd thought about it a minute. "Uh-uh," he said. "It's more like this. Kenny might like to do needlepoint, I think. Or knit, maybe. And Sheila needs a Samurai sword."

"You really don't like her, do you?"

His face twisted into a grimace. "How can you not like a child? But she's violent. What am I supposed to do with that?"

"Well, let's see. First we'll have her pledge Kappa at Newcomb—"

"Oh, cut it out."

There were two ways to get around both kids—one was to take them on an adventure, any adventure, and promise ice cream as part of it. The other was to have Auntie tell a few grisly cop stories. Skip had to censor, and she felt a little funny about telling stories from the streets, necessarily violent and scary stories, but she knew her tales were nothing compared to what was in the rest of the culture. Anyway, she liked to think she was a good role model.

Tonight, she told them about a suspect who vaulted a fence when she was chasing him, and in the course of it lost his wallet, which contained his identity and address. When she got to his house, his wife claimed he'd been in bed with the flu all day. Skip arrested him anyway, but had a bad moment when she came down with the flu two days later.

Kenny, the one who'd looked forward to "macaroni and cheese," almost forgot to eat. Sheila, who'd called dinner "pig slop," shoveled pasta mechanically.

Kenny stared. "He didn't do it. Somebody stole his wallet."

"No, he did do it. He'd made bail by that time, so I went back over to his house, with a temperature of a hundred and two. What do you know, he was lying in bed, a whole different color from two days earlier, and sweat all over his forehead. We both got the flu from his wife, who got the idea because she was sick."

"Criminals have lousy imaginations," said Sheila. She looked at Dee-Dee, then Skip, and Skip felt a momentary tingle. For a moment all was forgiven; uncles and aunts were okay people.

Kenny said, "She wasn't the criminal; he was."

Sheila hit him. "Oh, shut up!"

Kenny set up a howl.

Jimmy Dee had had a glass of wine by now. Skip thought this nearly always improved his parenting. "Sheila, could you apologize to Kenny, please?"

"I didn't do anything."

Jimmy Dee sent Skip a "help me" look. She said, "Honey, we have this thing in police work. Do you know what excessive force is?"

Kenny answered for her: "It's like when you hit somebody and you didn't really have to."

Sheila raised her hand again, ready to give a second swat. But she caught Skip's eye. "Overkill?"

Skip nodded. "Overkill. As in, that'll be enough." She changed the subject quickly. "One of you wouldn't have a laptop I could borrow, would you?"

"I've got a notebook. That's better."

She went home with a computer she could take to bed. Jimmy Dee had shown her how to attach her phone so the modem would work. All she had to do was ask it to dial the number of the TOWN (programmed in by Jimmy Dee at her request).

Sure. She knew how that went. In about a week the glitches would be ironed out and she'd be connected.

But not true; magically, the TOWN identified itself and asked her for login: Steve. Then her password: Skip2mLu. And zap, she was on the TOWN.

Now what?

It was quite a lot like being in a real town—say, New York or Paris—with eighty million different options. She could walk down to the corner for coffee or she could take in the opera. And why do just one? Why not the movies, then the opera, then coffee and after that, ice cream?

There were categories: Body and Mind, the World, Interactions, the Arts, Sports, Politics, Hill and Dale, Computers—on and on like that; she counted twenty-three. And under each category, there were conferences. In some twelve or fifteen; in one or two, a hundred or so. At random, she picked one: Pets. She ended up at the top of a list of topics. As instructed by Steve, she pressed BR for "browse, reverse." Now she was at the bottom of the list, where the current topics were. The last one, Topic 256, was "TOWNies recommend vets"; most of the entries had to do with West Coast practitioners. Number 255 was "When Calicoes Turn Bad."

She tried another conference: Relationships. Worse still—there were 733 topics. Already she was overstimulated and she'd only been here five minutes. She could see how a person might feel safe on this thing. It was so enormous, surely you were just another graffiti artist. She realized with a shock that was what this felt like— illicit scribblings on someone else's wall.

I'll just see what looks interesting and go there, she told herself.

First, she went to Confession. It was nothing if not lively. The topic devoted to Geoff's death had the rather flip title, she noticed, of "Out on the TOWN." Outraged, Lenore (whose user ID was her name) had started a new topic called "TOWN Without Pity," in which TOWNspeople were invited to assess their own voyeurism, cruelty, and lack of feeling. Someone called Bboy had answered: "Now, hold on, Lenore. I think about ninety-nine percent of the posts in that topic are really very caring. The topic name is a little over the top, but surely you realize that one of the main ways people have of dealing with grief is black humor."

A third user, none other than the legendary Bigeasy, had said simply: "Great book on that subject—*The Grief Cycle* by T. M. Collins."

To which Greenie had riposted: "I think Lenore has a good point. Haven't we been acting a little like vultures?"

"Speak for yourself, Green One. :-)." wrote Arthurx. The little pictograph was something both Steve and Jimmy Dee (a veteran of America Online) had told her about—a little sidewise face called a "smiley," the idea being to defuse anything that might sound sarcastic, to show that the writer was just kidding.

If the idea, thought Skip, was to make you feel like you were in a real conversation, this topic was a terrible advertisement. Because a lot of conversations *were* like this—banal. A lot of forgettable remarks came out of people's mouths, but fortunately they were forgotten two minutes later. These were here forever; legitimate graffiti.

She went back to "Out on the TOWN." Now this had a lot more going for it. She had to admit that scribblings that escalated from a simple newsflash that a TOWNsperson had died to getting the autopsy report and launching what amounted to a coast-to-coast investigation was a use of computer technology she hadn't really thought of before. Lenore, Layne (Teaser) and Bigeasy were large in "Out on the TOWN," Lenore and Layne especially. Both were deep in the drama of it; wanted to keep it going, maybe keep Geoff alive that way. (Or maybe throw suspicion off themselves.) But there was no new information—nothing she hadn't already seen with Layne.

As long as she was just browsing, she found a topic that explained the nuances of smileys and another that was essentially a guide to TOWN abbreviations. F2F, for instance, meant "face-to-face," a type of interaction most TOWNies seemed to want to avoid. Then there was IMHO: "in my humble opinion"; SMTOE: "sets my teeth on edge"; MIML, as in "the MIML says": "man in my life"; and Skip's personal favorite, AFOG, as in "I broke up with my boyfriend; it wasn't true love, only AFOG": "another fucking opportunity for growth."

Just to round things out, she went to "Sex." Topic 543, at the top of the reverse list, was "The Sensuality of Ears." She went down the list, finally settling on "What's Your Favorite Perversion?" It was quite amazing. People whose names could be looked up by pushing a button were perfectly candid on threesomes, dogs "trained to give pleasure," nippling (an invention of the person who described it), and various degrees of bondage.

Dazed, Skip hustled out and over to "Books" as an antidote. If she had expected high literary discourse, she didn't find it in the first topic she tried, "What's so great about *The Secret History?*"

The postings went something like this:

"Loved, loved, loved it. Do yourself a favor and race right out."

"Couldn't stand the characters."

"Well, I've known assholes like that. But what an absurdly implausible plot!"

She was tempted to post something like: "I think what the author was trying to do, Georgie and Rinty, was create an allegory in which neither the plot nor the characters really mattered. Rather, it was her view of the moral bankruptcy of the modern college student—"

Something stupid and meaningless—well, laughable, actually— but at least it would show these creeps who were taking up her time with their unsolicited goddam opinions. *Who cared?*

Certainly not Skip. Not even a little bit. She was bored nearly to distraction by "liked it," "didn't," "did for a different reason," "didn't either," which truly seemed a big part of most conferences that weren't specifically set up for something—like games, or working out computer problems, or trading information on where to buy things. Every time she nearly numbed out from the boredom she simply went to another topic, another conference. She was absolutely astonished when she checked her watch and noticed it was three-thirty A.M.

4

• •

"**M**ama, no!"

"No what, honey?" asked Lenore. Caitlin had been fussy lately.

"Yuck!"

"You don't like the soup?"

"*Hate* the soup."

So she had to dump it and make noodles. Caitlin had eaten noodles for the fifth straight day in a row. They said at day care that she ate other things at lunch, even now and then consumed a vegetable or two, but Lenore wasn't sure she wasn't going to get anemia and vitamin deficiency from steady starch.

"An orange for dessert?"

"No!"

"Yes."

"Uh-uh." And she banged her spoon on the table to make her point.

"You're so cute when you're mad."

The child just stared at her, unable to comprehend. Or else she did comprehend and thought the remark as stupid as Lenore did.

But she had said it out of the sudden rush of love that came over her as Caitlin's alien gold curls caught the light.

Her father had been black—"had been" because Lenore only saw him once. Or at any rate he had been a Creole, someone with more white blood than black, probably, but "black" all the same. He was a beautiful tall tan man (as well as she could remember) with hair lighter than Lenore's, but not nearly so light as Caitlin's, which was curly as poodle fur and shot through with gold. Not blond, but pure gold. Her skin was dark walnut, the most beautiful color Lenore had ever seen on a human being, and she was chubby, with tiny little creases in her arms and legs.

"Okay. Mom's dumb, huh?"

"Yes. Yes!" Now Caitlin was banging happily, delightedly.

"Honey, don't get so worked up so close to bedtime. Let's go take a bath, okay?"

"No!" But she smiled when she said it.

Half an hour later, Caitlin was fresh in a white nightgown with Mickey Mouse faces all over it, and Lenore was suddenly overcome with the burdens of the day, with missing Geoff.

"Bedtime, honey."

"Story!"

"Not tonight. Mama's too tired."

"G'night, Moon."

"That's right. Good night to you too, Moon."

"Book."

She spoke sharply. "I said no, Caitlin."

And suddenly, it was the great flood of Tupelo. Damn! The slightest little thing and a kid tuned up and cried.

"Goddammit, Caitlin, shut up!"

That only made her cry more.

Well, there was nothing to do but rock her, which Lenore did until they were both asleep. Lenore came to with a start, grateful she hadn't dropped the baby in her sleep.

She put Caitlin to bed, but she couldn't go herself yet. There were things to do. Many, many things to do.

She began to get things out—the black altar cloth, the black candles, the cauldron, the ritual black-handled knife. She was so tired. . . .

A bath first. It would wake her up and she needed to do it anyway, to purify herself, to get ready. She put out her black robe.

She put herbs in the water—vervain, marjoram, peppermint, rosemary—a special mixture for the things she needed; healing, especially.

Afterward, she decided against the robe. Better to work sky-clad. But she wore her cord, from which hung charms that were still working, each tied in its own silk or leather bag, and around her neck she slipped a pendant, a silver pentacle hung on a black silk cord.

She found the four candles she needed to call the quarters—yellow for east, red for south, blue for west, and green for north. She got ready some paper and matches—later there was something she would burn in her cauldron. (Some held that the cauldron was really a cup that should never hold anything but water. Lenore did not subscribe to that; she needed fire in hers.) She got the water and salt she needed, her altar pentacle; her chalice. And a bolline, a white-handled knife, for carving words in the candles, the black ones. And then another thing—dragon's blood to anoint the candles.

Was that all? She thought so.

She was exhausted. But she had everything together and she had already written the incantation she would need.

It was just past Samhein and the veil was still thin—she could feel the pull from the other side. She felt it often at this time of year, but more so now; because of Geoff, she thought. She couldn't cope on her own; she thought she would never be rid of him, rid of this horrible weight on her shoulders, this knife in her heart. But what she was about to do would help.

She picked up the black-handled knife.

●   ●

Pearce Randolph poured himself a nice friendly little drink of bourbon before logging onto the TOWN. It was a nightly ritual, one he had come to love. To adore.

Sometimes he would light a cigar, puff on it, rub his softening belly and think smugly to himself, I own this TOWN, I'm somebody here.

Tongue firmly planted in cheek, of course. Pearce Randolph was in no way a stupid man, a fact of which he was well aware and reminded himself when he needed to. But yet, when the silly old thought came, he rather relished it. Especially if he was well into that friendly little ritual bourbon.

He also had more serious thoughts, along the lines of Get out of TOWN by sundown.

And You'll never eat lunch in this TOWN again.

He had the power to make someone disappear. He was loved on the TOWN. You couldn't do it by hate, by being nasty to someone—the TOWN didn't work that way. What you had to do when one of these arrogant assholes came along, these goddam know-it-alls, was simply outpost them. Outperform. Upstage.

They were there partly because they thrived on competition, but mostly because they had to be top of the heap all the time. So Pearce had his work cut out for him. He was mayor of the goddam TOWN, and that wasn't easy to do, considering the vast majority of heavy users were concentrated in California and actually knew each other F2F.

That he did pride himself on; that was the fun of it. Of course it helped that he was a professional writer and what you did on this thing, when you got right down to it, was you wrote.

He could do what he had to do in thirty minutes, but he usually spent a leisurely hour, even an hour and a half, dropping witticisms here, bon mots there. First, the TOWN Hall, everybody's favorite conference. If the TOWN had been the COMPANY, this would have been the virtual watercooler. As it was, in twentieth-century America there wasn't an analogous meeting place in a real town. Which was one of the things, in Pearce's opinion, that made the virtual one superior. You dropped in, you said hello, you got the news, you bantered a bit, and you went on to your other favorite conferences. Pearce liked Writing, Movies, Books, Confession, Games, Weird Stuff, and Sex, but he never posted in the last, just lurked. It was amusing to match up the ingenuous disclosures here with the pomposity affected by the same users elsewhere.

Pearce skipped Sex, Games, and Weird Stuff tonight. He was addicted to Writing for the companionship with other writers, and to Books and Movies because they provided lots of scope for what he did best—writing and thinking.

But tonight he just went through the motions. Confession was the undisputed hot ticket. Poor old Geoff wasn't even cold and the TOWN had turned him into a game. Still, Pearce had to admit, Geoff was its leading citizen right now, which might have pleased him. Geoff hadn't been much of anything in life, except a nerd, much like everyone else on the TOWN.

Pearce typed out g con—"get Confession"—and then went to "Out on the TOWN." But in the end it was disappointing; nothing new, really. The latest topic, "TOWN Without Pity," had some merit if you liked to observe the maunderings of self-righteous assholes. Predictably, all the politically correct, put-you-in-the-wrong types were posting here. Living in New Orleans instead of L.A., Pearce had never met them, but he knew who they were: guys with scrawny shoulders and dirty blue jeans, women with fifty pounds they didn't need and scrunched-up, toady little faces. There were those types, the PC ones, and then there were the Henry Clays, those who'd missed out on dynamic careers as diplomats permanently assigned to the Bureau of Tempests in Teapots. They were always posting the sort of little gem that was meant to defuse but made you want to rip their throats out: "I can really see Lefty's point, Bilious, but I just wonder if it isn't time to put this behind us and quit fighting among ourselves. After all, what's really important here?"

Out-self-righteousing the PCs.

Back to "Out on the TOWN." At least Lenore hadn't posted today. One of the worst things about Geoff's murder, as far as Pearce was concerned, was the ready-made stage it gave Lenore. Privately, he called her "the TOWN crier." If Lenore had a problem, the whole TOWN had to be consulted, and if she didn't she was going to make one up.

So far they'd seen her through unwed motherhood: "Should I

Have an Abortion?" was the topic she'd posted in Confession. The woman had no shame. That was followed by "Lamaze or No?" and a seemingly endless stream of self-involved dramas having to do with whether she should tell the baby's father the kid existed, what she should name it, and of course, how much motherhood meant to her; she'd known, of course, she'd been told, but she really couldn't have imagined . . .

Right. Firm grasp of the obvious. That was Lenore.

Pearce had helped to get "Out on the TOWN" going; that had been fun (though at the time, the way he felt, it seemed more like a necessity—he had to talk to somebody, even if it wasn't really talking). But it was fun because it was an opportunity to use his mastery over his subjects. He always enjoyed that.

However, the thing it had become wasn't his cup of tea. These people were serious. They were sorry Geoff was dead and they were seriously trying to do something about it (in their lame little ways, of course). They actually thought they could solve a murder just by yakking electronically at each other. All of which might be amusing if it wasn't such bad taste to display wit in the face of grief, and wit was Pearce's forte. His baby had turned into an ugly duckling.

Disgustedly, he typed EXIT. He might as well use his computer for what he'd bought it for.

He opened a file called "Regrets," possibly a chapter in something, he wasn't sure yet, but definitely an exercise he needed to do right now. He typed 1967, and the very sight of the four digits excited him, conjured up the scent of patchouli oil and pot smoke; the sounds of throngs shouting "Hell no, we won't go!"; the touch of a thousand skinny girls in peasant blouses, with center-parted waist-length hair. The most beautiful of them all was . . . he couldn't bear to think of her, not yet, not without setting the stage.

He rummaged through his records—he still had all of them, along with his old-fashioned stereo. The CD player would come, as soon as he sold a novel or two. Or his screenplay. That was probably what he should be working on—everyone knew it was easier, quicker, and worth more money. But lately, he'd been working on this other thing, this "Regrets," whatever that was. That was the way writing worked for him; it bubbled up and couldn't be stopped. If it wanted out, he released it.

Bob Dylan was what he wanted, something along those lines. But what he found was better—the Jefferson Airplane, *Surrealistic Pillow*. He found the cut that, of any song in the world (except maybe "Light My Fire") was the most evocative of 1967, of the way he'd felt about her. Its first line was this: "Today I feel like pleasing you."

He poured himself another bourbon and settled down to write:

> She was older than I was, but not by much. Twenty-nine, I thought, maybe even thirty, which excited me in an odd sort of way, because of course that was over the line. It meant you couldn't trust her. But then trust was the last thing on my mind when I saw her there, smoke swirling blue around her head, the glare of the lights cruel as napalm; and yet even whited out as she was—a lesser beauty would have been a caricature of harsh lines and tiny sags—she exuded a tropical lushness; smelt, practically, of ylang-ylang or plumeria.
>
> A rubber band held her hair at the nape, but loosely, so that it fell in wings to her chin, and when she bent her head—so serious, so moody—over her guitar, a shadow fell across her chest. She wore bell-bottoms and a white peasant blouse. A ropy sort of belt that she had woven and then decorated with some flowered thing was tied round her waist, the ends allowed to flow at her right side. The same trim, a strip of pink flowers embroidered on a yellow background, had been sewn to the hems of her jeans.
>
> But the thing you noticed most was the way she clutched that guitar—like a lover; like a baby; like the thing she held dearest in the world. She was singing an Appalachian folk song, a ballad about a faithless husband and the unfortunate way he'd disappeared one day, after seeing something odd in the woods—

Pearce stared at the screen. He could recall every detail of her clothing, her expression, he even knew how long her nails were (clipped short), but he couldn't remember the words of the song. What had the husband seen in the woods? An elf or something? A dead animal? This was why it was so hard to finish things. They had to be right. He knew he couldn't finish this piece until he had the song. He'd have to go to the library and research it. He put an asterisk on the page; it was going to take up the rest of tomorrow. . . .

The mood didn't end. He didn't have the song, but he couldn't shake the rest of the memory. To his amazement, it was coming out against all odds.

When her set was over, I found my mouth dry, my tongue stuck on the roof of my mouth, my feet paralyzed. What if she didn't come back? What if I never saw her again?

She came back! She did "Wildwood Flower" for an encore, and it was oddly appropriate, somehow described her. It evoked a mossy smell, a springlike scent, a mysterious waft from something ephemeral and delicate, like the thing the faithless husband had seen in the woods. Something magical, something that would escape if you blinked.

Like her.

I saw now that this was who she was; despite her lush appearance, her bold tropical beauty, in her soul she was a wraith; she was Rima from Green Mansions, or maybe some tiny winged creature from A Midsummer Night's Dream. It was her voice that gave her away—so high, so clear, and pure as the heart of a nun. I knew that now she would disappear for good, and she did. A being like that does not drink in a bar.

And yet, the next time I saw her, it was in a bar—the Dream Palace, on Frenchmen Street, the kind of place you went in 1967 for an interracial kind of experience, a bohemian thrill in a safe (though often noisy) kind of way. It was a dark, ramshackle old cavern of a place, with tiny tiles on the floor and a celestial mural on the ceiling.

She was with friends, a man and a woman, all three of them wearing jeans, the man looking like the pictures of Jesus in my Bible storybooks. Thinking they must need another man to join them—wishing that, actually, not thinking anything at all—I marched over as if I had all the confidence of a person on drugs (which, at that moment, I wasn't).

"Aren't you Marguerite Kavanagh?" I said, for the first time thinking it odd that so exotic a being should be Irish.

"Yes." And she gave me a smile that said she knew what was going to come next.

"I heard you sing. I just wanted to say . . ." I was losing my nerve ". . . I thought you were . . ."

"Yes?" This time it had a teasing quality.

I am not given to hyperbole, and, if the truth be told, I find it hard to compliment people; I'd rather not. And yet, I'd never in my life so desperately wanted to be liked.

"You were wonderful," I said, hoping my Adam's apple wasn't bobbing like a rube's.

"That's very kind of you."

The man she was with, the Jesus impersonator, waved casually at a vacant chair. "Sit down. Join us, why don't you?" and I glanced for a moment at Marguerite to see if she approved. I thought I saw something in her eyes, something that said she didn't, but it looked more like fear than anger. I didn't care, I was sure I could change her mind. I was going to sit there if the place caught on fire in the next thirty seconds.

But her hesitation, whatever it was, was immediately replaced by a warm light, the beginnings of flirtation. "This is Geordie," she said. "And Joyce. A matched pair."

"Pair o' wot, I couldn't tell you," said Geordie. He had a vaguely British accent.

"And who might you be?" said Marguerite.

"Pearce Randolph," I said, wanting her to hear both names, to remember them.

"Oh, my God! The reporter."

"You know my work?" I puffed out my chest a bit.

She twirled her glass and looked at it, embarrassed. "Well, no, I don't think I do." She looked up again. Defiant. "Just your name."

"Oh?"

"From my husband."

I died a little inside.

"My husband speaks of you."

It came to me who she must be, and I was overcome with regret—that I'd become a reporter, that I'd ever been born, certainly that I'd ever embarked on a certain fruitless investigation of police corruption. And yet, I still couldn't believe the connection, couldn't imagine such a thing. "Leighton Kavanagh?" I said. "You're married to Leighton Kavanagh?"

He was a monster, this man. A great big ugly redhead with shoulders that would hold up an overpass, nasty penny-size freckles on his face and arms, hair so short he must have shaved it. But no belly; the man was in shape. And he was ornery—"the orneriest sumbitch in Louisiana," according to some of his colleagues—some who'd given me a bum steer now that I thought of it, but still, if ever there was a case of Beauty and the Beast . . .

She cupped her chin in her hand, using the other to play with her straw, flirtatious as you please. "Sure am. Beautiful little baby son, too—would you like to see a picture?"

I started to stand up. "Look, I'm sorry I bothered you. I'm sure you——"

"Don't go," she said.

And I stayed.

5

• •

Feeling grumpy from lack of sleep, Skip was thinking with distaste that the case, despite its high-tech aspect, was actually hung with Spanish moss, steeped in the miasma of ancient fears and rages, the stink of memory, of acts better forgotten, never forgiven, of passion just below the surface.

What I've got here is a geriatric unsolved murder, she thought, and poured herself a cup of the pitchy substance they called coffee in Homicide. *The entire department couldn't figure out who killed one of its own and now I'm supposed to do it twenty-seven years later.*

Her heart speeded up at the hopelessness of it, the panic it spawned, and yet she recognized a tiny simultaneous surge—the triumph of hope over common sense, the same thing that made a dog hare off after a cat, probably even the thing that caused Layne Bilderback to piece out crosswords. The challenge. The thrill of the chase. She might not get to the bottom of this, but she'd kill herself trying.

The thing to do was get as much background as she could on the case and the major players. Maybe she could solve the whole thing from the office, like Nero Wolfe or somebody.

Dream on, she thought.

Still, another cup of coffee would go down well while she made a few phone calls. She poured one and dialed her friend Alison Gaillard, who knew everything about everybody.

"*Officer* Langdon. I was just thinking about you. I might write a reference book—*Who's in Who.* What do you think?"

"Why were you thinking about me?"

"I need your opinion, of course."

"It'll never sell—you'd have to update it every twenty minutes."

Alison hooted. "Especially in this town."

Alison and Skip had been sorority sisters at a time when Skip had about as much business belonging to a sorority as to the Ladies' Black Hand Auxiliary. From a distance, she had thought Alison beautiful, shallow, brainless, and malicious until she had become a cop and one day needed information. In fact, she had found her warm and bright—they'd made friends for the first time. And if Alison ever called in her markers, Skip was going to owe her big— she'd provided information on so many cases Skip had lost count.

"You calling for a consultation?"

"Mmmm. Usual giant fee, of course."

"It'll be about Marguerite Kavanagh, I guess."

"Now how on earth did you know that?" Skip had perused the paper quickly, and there was no mention of Geoff's death or the department's interest in it.

"Emmeline Norwood called her to say she was sorry about Geoff and Marguerite told her about you."

"Which Emmeline couldn't wait to report to you."

"Not exactly. She told Reenie Vauxhall, who's my day-care lady. Marguerite's a lot older than we are, of course, but I took music lessons from her mama; half the kids in town did. Christina Julian—remember her?"

"I took ballet—to make me graceful."

"Skippy, cut that out." One of the things that endeared her to Skip was the fact that, though she participated in Southern self-deprecation to a tedious degree, she never let Skip do it. "Old Mrs. Julian was married to Wyndham Julian, known as Windy to friend and foe alike, and generally agreed to be the world's most boring man. He taught history at Newcomb."

"Wait a minute—I think I've heard stories about him. Is that possible? How long ago was he there?"

"Oh, about twenty years before you were, I guess. But Windy was famous. Died one day, right in class. Witnesses at the scene said they didn't even notice. Well, Christina truly had a beautiful voice—I mean, really spectacular. She used to sing in the choir at Trinity—remember?"

"I guess not." Skip felt silly. She'd been made to go to church at Trinity nearly every Sunday of her grade school life, but under torture from Torquemada couldn't have said what had gone on there. Her mind had been elsewhere—on the compelling subject, for instance, of ingenious ways to dispatch a pesky sibling; or on modes of transportation that led far, far away from the city of her birth.

"Everybody thought she could have been an opera singer, but it didn't turn out to be true—she went to New York before she was twenty-five, but nothing worked out. When she came back, she was a broken woman. Of course, everyone suspected a failed romance contributed to her low spirits, especially when she up and married the egregious Windy. She knew enough about the piano to teach, and also she gave voice lessons, but I guess there wasn't nearly as much demand for that. Had this big old house over on Octavia Street—"

"Marguerite still lives there."

"Well, that's part of the story. My mother used to go there for her lessons. But by the time I came along, Mrs. J lived in an apartment. God, it was a drag!"

"What?"

"Just going over there. She was so sad—her whole approach to music was sighs and languor. Or maybe that was her approach to life. She didn't get what she wanted and spent the rest of her life in mourning for it. She was a nice woman, though. Aside from being a terrible snob."

"She was a snob?"

"I can't think why. She was from Mississippi or someplace.

60

Anyway, she was nice to her students, I think—most of the girls liked her a lot, but God knows what she was like with her own daughter. I mean, Marguerite did everything she could think of that her mother would really hate—there must have been a reason for it, don't you think?"

"All this must have happened years before your time."

"Well, it did, of course. Marguerite was always held up to me as an example of how a daughter can disappoint—not to mention how she'll come to a bad end."

"What did she do that was so bad?"

"The worst thing a kid could do in 1967. Grew her hair long and became a folksinger."

"She was a hippie?"

"My mother said she was, but I'm not sure a woman married to a cop really qualifies. That was the other bad thing she did— married a cop. You know how I found out all this stuff? I asked my mother how come Mrs. Julian lived in a tiny little apartment instead of a house. God, can you imagine what a little snob I was?"

"Imagine! I can remember."

"Now, now. We're all products of our environment."

"Marguerite just brought Leighton to the old family mansion?"

"Why Christina let her I'll never know. Probably didn't want to rattle around in that big house by herself. But then she moved out almost right away."

"The whole thing has a Stanley Kowalski feel to it."

"Frankly, I think Leighton was that kind of guy. To hear my mother tell it, Christina just had a broken heart. Couldn't stand to see her daughter with him, so she left. Now I admit it would have made more sense to chuck Marguerite out, but this was so much more martyred. Now that I think of it, that might have been the key to Mrs. J. Nothing ever seemed to go right for her. Anyway, the minute she left, Marguerite started letting the whole place go to hell, about which Mrs. J and my mother could cluck for hours. I guess part of the fun was disapproving."

"And then of course Leighton got killed."

"Uh-huh. Marguerite was visiting her mom the night of the murder."

"With Geoff?"

"I guess so. From what I gather, when Marguerite went out and sang—which she did quite a lot—she'd take Geoff over to stay with his grandmother."

"Ah. Grandma the martyr."

"The saint, according to my mother."

"Alison, I have to hand it to you—you're always in the right place at the right time."

"Usually, yes, I cannot deny it. But this is different, I'm not kidding. Everybody at Newcomb took lessons from Mrs. Julian. Probably McGehee's too." McGehee's was Skip's school.

"Okay, what do you know about Cole Terry?"

There was a silence. "Who?"

"That's who Marguerite's married to now."

"I can't believe this—I never heard of him."

"It just shows you're human after all."

"Come to think of it, Marguerite kind of disappeared from the scene, I guess. After she married Mike. Once my mother and I ran into her—the only time I ever saw her, to tell you the truth. She was working as a hostess at the Rib Room.

"Oh, wait, there's another chapter. After that, she sent a brochure around to all the Uptown ladies, claiming years of experience in what she called 'the hospitality industry.' She was starting a party-giving business, and my mom used her once. This was when I was still taking lessons from Mrs. Julian and it got embarrassing. It seems Marguerite screwed up royally. And then there were all these stories from other hostesses—it was always the same thing." She stopped for breath. "Do you think I get my habit of carrying tales from my mother?"

"Probably."

"Why couldn't I have got curly hair like you did? Anyway, it was this way—she always went over budget, and she always had fights with the caterers. Nothing was ever good enough and she kept making people do things over again, which cost everyone involved a bundle. She was just a perfectionist, I guess."

"It sounds like she was into histrionics as well."

"I guess so. Anyway, the business failed and after that I never heard of her again. Until today, I mean. Maybe she dumped Mike, and Cole came along and rescued her."

"I don't know. If they've got any money, why don't they get the house painted?"

Skip hung up, thinking Alison was one of the most satisfying human beings on the face of the earth—and marveling once again at what a small town New Orleans could be. Sometimes she thought it was only tiny if you stayed within certain class and race boundaries, but she was always being proved wrong. The Julians and the Kavanaghs were certainly not in Alison's social circle—and yet she knew every detail of their family history. (Though she was one of the few people in the world interested enough to remember every detail.)

But Skip had lived in San Francisco and she knew how different it was. Such things were treasured in the South, remembered and repeated by people who weren't even gossip pros like Alison. As a region it had its faults—so many Skip felt strangled at times—but you couldn't say people here didn't care about each other.

She called another Newcomb acquaintance who came in handy sometimes (fortunately, she'd met a few people before flunking out). This one hadn't turned out nearly as multifaceted as Alison, but she was dependable. Eileen Moreland, who worked at the *Times-Picayune*.

"Well, if it isn't that double-crosser, Skippy Langdon."

"Double-cross? *Moi?*"

"I thought you were going to let me interview you."

"Well, I am. That's what I'm calling about."

"Uh-uh. You're calling because you want a favor."

"That's only coincidental. I'm calling because I owe you and I know it. That other time, I just had this little undercover thing going."

"Great. When can we set up the interview?"

"Oh, let's see. Maybe in a couple of weeks?"

"Let's see, Thanksgiving week's coming up."

"The week after, maybe?" By then Skip would think of some excuse to wait even a little longer. "Tell me something. Can you get clips on a twenty-seven-year-old murder case?"

"I can, but it's a major pain in the rear."

"How about December seventh? I could do the interview then."

Eileen sighed. "What murder case?"

Skip told her and arranged to pick up the clips that afternoon. Next, she went through the department file on the case. The investigating officer had been one Rene Lafont. A call to the pension board produced his address—in Westwego, on the west bank.

Despite its proximity, it was a place most New Orleanians would never see. She could probably name people who'd been to Australia and six or eight African countries who were probably going to die without crossing the Mississippi. Was it worth a drive over there? Much as she hated the idea, she thought it had to be done. Lafont might be an old grump who'd have to be coaxed to talk.

An hour later, approaching his small but neat house, she couldn't imagine how she could have thought that—and revised her opinion when he answered the door. He was a very thick man, thick in the neck and the jaw as well as the belly. Either his hair was still dark or he dyed it. It wasn't brown and wasn't black, but a kind of steely color, like the muzzle of a rifle, and it was slicked with something greasy. His features, like his body, were thick, his brown eyes narrow above dark pouches dotted with skin tags. He wore khakis held up with a belt that could have fit around a steamer trunk, and a cheap white shirt. He stepped outside the door and simply stood there, waiting for her to say something.

She showed him her badge. "I wonder if you could help me out with something?"

"A lady cop. I thought I avoided 'em by retirin'." The words weren't the world's friendliest, but he smiled when he said them, and his whole demeanor changed. She realized that she'd gotten his street-cop look, the one the punks saw, and now she was probably seeing the one his grandchildren knew.

She decided to play his game. "Can't avoid 'em. We're everywhere."

"Well, my wife's got to see this." He opened the old-fashioned screen door. "Ruthine! Guess what I got here?"

He ushered Skip through a painfully neat living room—the

kind with plastic covers on the furniture—into a kitchen where a stout white-haired woman was loading the dishwasher. She was probably a great cook, judging from the size of both Lafonts.

"This is Officer Skip Langdon, a bona fide lady cop."

"Well, it's about time we had some of those. How 'bout some coffee?" She reached for a cup even as she spoke.

Twenty minutes later, Skip had seen pictures of their grandchildren and, sitting in their breakfast room, outlined her own checkered past with judicious editing—noting, for instance, that she had transferred to Ole Miss, rather than flunked out of Newcomb.

When they knew enough about each other to start their own FBI files, Rene asked what he could do for her. She told him the whole story.

She had judged her audience correctly. He nodded and grunted loudly at the end of almost every sentence, providing his own punctuation. And when she was done, he whistled so loud Ruthine looked over, startled.

"That's some story, young lady. Nothin' like that ever happens on Prodigy."

"I beg your pardon?"

"Prodigy. That's the bulletin board we're on."

"You're kidding. You're on a bulletin board?"

"He is," Ruthine called from the kitchen, where she'd repaired for some chore or other. "It's kind of his hobby now. Whole days go by I never see him."

"Ah, Ruthine, you know that's not so."

"I know it is."

"I was wondering," Skip said hurriedly, "what you could tell me about Leighton's murder. You were first on the scene, weren't you?"

"Well, no, I think a district car got there first. But I was a close second. Terrible thing." He closed his eyes. "Terrible. I knew Leighton too. I worked with him over to the Fifth District." He said "woiked with him."

"What was he like?"

"Mean bastard. And none too smart. But you hate to see that happen to a young person. Beautiful wife—nice little boy."

"What was Geoff like that night? The boy."

"Real scared. Like any kid would be."

"Did you get the idea he could have seen anything?"

"I didn't question him; he was four years old. And that mama of his—the word 'hysterical' was made up for women like that. I'm lucky I got anything coherent at all. Tell you what I thought was strange, though. Two things. It looked like Leighton came home from work and caught a burglar in the bedroom. They struggled, and somehow the guy got Leighton's gun and shot him. Only thing was, the gun wasn't there. Now why take a gun that could only incriminate you?"

Skip grinned. "The guy was stupid?"

Rene grinned back. "Most likely. Other thing was, the place was wrecked, more or less, and only one thing was taken—a ring that Miz Kavanagh said wasn't even valuable. An heirloom—somethin' she got from her grandma—and she said wasn't that always the way, they took somethin' meant a lot to you and wasn't worth that much to anybody else. But she had some nice pearls there—why didn't he take those?"

"Probably thought they were fake."

He grinned again. "Most likely. But he could have taken a handful of stuff."

"What kind of ring was it?"

"Yellow. A great big stone, but just about worthless. Citrine? Could that be right?"

Skip nodded. "That's a kind of gold color."

"Yeah. That's the word. Funny, I haven't heard it in all these years."

"Maybe he knew the Kavanaghs. Maybe there was some reason he wanted that ring."

"That's what I was thinkin'. Couldn't find anything to hang it on, though."

"How about another murder? To hang it on."

"Yeah. How about that?" He stared out the window. "Mm. Mm. Mm."

Skip couldn't have agreed more.

On her way back to the office, she picked up the clips, unfurling them as she walked out of the building. The first thing she saw was the most interesting item they had to offer. It was the byline, the name of the reporter who'd covered the murders— Pearce Randolph, also known as Bigeasy.

6

• •

There was nothing to do but appeal once more to Eileen. Skip went back and asked her about Randolph. He was long gone, it turned out. So once more they checked the clips, finding only one story of interest—on his marriage to Honey Diefenthal. The write-up made clear she was very much a society lady. Which meant another call to Alison.

"Honey Diefenthal! Of course—the Marguerite connection."

"Wait a minute—you're going too fast for me."

"You'd like Honey. Really, you would. She's got a tongue on her you could slice a roast with. She's a good friend of my mom's—they were on some board or other together. One day they were drinking sherry, or more likely gin and tonic, and talking about the good ol' days. Honey swore she was a hippie and Mother said she never even knew one unless you counted Marguerite Julian, who she didn't really know, and Honey confided she worshiped Marguerite—followed her around like a little sister." Alison paused. "But this is intriguing, don't you think? Who knew she married a man Marguerite met when he came to cover her husband's murder? Do you suppose Marguerite introduced them?"

68

"You're asking me?"

"Even Alison the Magnificent is not omniscient. Now, here is your assignment: find out and tell me."

"I promise. Are they still married?"

"Oh, God no. That's ancient history. I'm not sure whether Honey's married to anyone right now, and I haven't a clue about Pearce, whom I know nothing about, by the way."

"That must mean he's nobody."

"I take deep umbrage at that, Skippy Langdon. You are dealing with a pro here and don't you forget it. I will gossip into the night about people who are nobody, as you so tackily put it, as enthusiastically as if they were Di and Fergie. So will Honey, by the way. If I were you, I'd give her a call."

Next, Skip ran record checks on Pearce, Marguerite, and Honey, and then went in to bring Cappello up-to-date. The sergeant frowned, as if she didn't believe a word Skip was saying. "Now let me get this straight. This Pearce Randolph is Bigeasy, right?"

"Right. What's the big deal?"

"Is he still a journalist?"

"Long since retired. Why?"

"Because I just had a call from him—he says he's doing a story on Geoff Kavanagh's murder."

"Whoops. I think I better talk to him next."

Almost next, she meant. Taking Alison's advice, she called Honey next. But Honey was out, and it was getting on toward noon. So she phoned her pal Cindy Lou Wootten, psychologist extraordinaire, and asked her to lunch.

Cindy Lou was one of Skip's favorite people. Skip liked to look at her, for one thing; the woman was gorgeous. She learned a lot from her, for another; the woman was afraid of nothing and no one. That included Frank O'Rourke, the Homicide sergeant who hated women in general and Skip in particular.

She was such a near-perfect creature Skip could have envied her too deeply for friendship if Cindy Lou hadn't had an all-too-human failing—when it came to men, she was hopeless. Even Skip, who had probably had a quarter as many boyfriends and a tenth as many suitors, could see her friend picking Mr. Bad News time after time. Cindy Lou didn't even seem to care: "I know I'm a psychologist," she'd say, "but I can't help it, I just have terrible taste."

They met at the Dante Street Deli, where you could wear anything at lunch, but Skip was made aware of her clunky blazer and skirt when Cindy Lou appeared in a gold-colored suit nipped in at the waist. As always, she could easily have stepped out of *Vogue*. She was black, and liked to dress in colors that complemented her skin tones. It didn't hurt that she was about a size six, with smooth, shoulder-length hair and a finely sculpted face.

She made Skip feel like a moose, though, oddly, she looked incredibly tall from a distance. When Skip had first seen her, addressing a roomful of cops, she had thought her about five-ten.

Today, despite her sophisticated appearance, Cindy Lou had the canary-feathers look of a teenager up to no good. "Guess who I've got a date with."

"Oh, Jesus. Probably the governor."

"Uh-uh." She named a name Skip didn't recognize.

"You mean you're not a Saints fan?"

"Please, not an athlete. He'll kiss you good-night and crush you to death."

"I like big guys. Don't you?"

"Big for me is a whole different story and you know it."

"You've seen pictures of him, haven't you?"

"I don't know. I'm a sports ignoramus—I wouldn't know Joe Montana's picture."

"Promise you'll find one. I want you to see how cute he is."

Skip sighed. "Cindy Lou, you're acting like a teenager. You're gorgeous and brilliant and you could get anybody."

"It's not an ego thing—I mean, not that kind. It's that you always harass me about my bad taste; I want you to see that at least I have the aesthetics down."

"This one's married, I suppose?"

"Oh, yes. And I'm sure there's nothing she doesn't know about his roving eye."

Skip rolled her eyes. "I just hope you plan to have safe sex."

"Hello," said Cindy Lou to a just-arrived waitress. She and Skip glanced quickly at the menu and settled on salads.

"Well, now, sex," Cindy Lou said when they'd ordered. "I don't plan to have it at all. One date—just for the thrill—and I'm out of there."

"Because he's married? You were never so scrupulous before."

"And I'm not now. Look out the window. See a car that looks like a plain brown wrapper? Little white guy hunkered down in it? Mrs. Saint's having me watched."

Skip held her head, causing her to miss the return of the waitress. "Uh—excuse me?" said the woman.

"I don't know if I'm hungry."

The waitress looked confused.

"Sorry—I'm just carrying on. Cindy Lou, are you crazy?" The waitress left.

"I'm a shrink, girlfriend. How could I be crazy?"

In a way, Skip rather enjoyed her friend's parade of losers—it was like reading Dick Francis books to see how he'd work the horses in. Each new swain was an all-new and ever more fascinating form of unsuitable. Skip worried about her, but she had to admit that of all the women she'd ever met, Cindy Lou got her vote for best able to take care of herself.

Skip poured dressing over her salad. "Could I ask one thing? Why go out with him at all? Bad things could happen and there's no future, so what's the point?"

"You forget I'm from Detroit. Danger's a way of life with me. Besides, he'll be fun to look at across the table, and maybe one day he'll get divorced."

"And he'll remember the lovely lady who refused his suit on moral grounds—you'll put it that way, I'm sure."

"Of course. But enough about me—since you're treating, I assume you need advice on something or other."

Skip ran down the case for her. By the time she was done, so were the salads. Settling in, they ordered coffee.

Cindy Lou had a faraway look. "Man. I wish I could have talked to that kid. Geoff."

"He was no kid—he was in his thirties."

"Yes, but he was a kid, really. That's your impression, isn't it?"

"I guess so. He was a lot like other social misfits. But I can't figure out who he was."

"He was probably an egg that couldn't hatch until he got that memory dealt with. A perennial four-year-old terrified of the world because of what it did to his daddy."

"You think he could have seen something?"

"Oh, sure. That's how memories start to come back—a little at a time. That's what he said, isn't it?"

"It's what he posted."

"He was so isolated he didn't even talk; he just posted."

"We don't really know that. He might have talked to Layne and Lenore—maybe other people."

"So if he remembered a face, he might have told someone."

"Well, he did have vocal cords."

"Oh, stop. A lot of men have hearts but they act heartless, now don't they?"

"You'd be the expert on that. Of course he could have told someone—he could even have tried to blackmail the killer."

"Somehow I doubt it, given the guy you've described. I wonder if he kept a journal."

"What?" Skip's ears pricked up.

"That's a common technique for people who're trying to bring something into consciousness. Especially if they're dreaming—and the first thing he posted was a dream."

"Hold it—about this journal idea. I didn't know about it. Does the average person do that?"

"Sure, if they've ever been in therapy. But I think a lot of people just do it—it helps them organize their thoughts. Someone from the TOWN might have suggested it."

"Could be. They're helpful to a fault. But I didn't see any mention of it in his topic."

"How about E-mail?"

"I'm not sure yet; the sysop's not being all that helpful. You know what a sysop is?"

"Sure. I'm on Internet."

"Come to think of it, he had some books on self-hypnosis."

"He did? Now that's interesting. Maybe he was trying to get at it that way."

"The thing is, if there was a journal . . ."

"What?"

"Well, it's as likely to be on the computer—maybe even in his personal TOWN file—as written down in a book."

"You've got your work cut out for you." Cindy Lou started to collect her belongings.

"Let me know if you want me to introduce you to a nice man." Where Skip would find one she had no idea, but that was no problem—this was part of their standard good-bye.

Cindy Lou wrinkled her nose. "Hate 'em." This was the rest of it. "By the way, how's your man?"

"Okay, I guess. He sounds a little funny, though."

"Sounds funny how?"

"I don't know. He made a remark I didn't get."

"Miss Sensitive. You need to get out more, you know that?"

"Speaking as a shrink?"

"Speaking as a friend—especially a friend who wants to go see the Boucree Brothers. You up for that?"

"When?"

"They're playing Thursday at The Blue Guitar."

"I don't think . . . I mean, this case . . ."

"It's a date."

Skip thought about it. "Boucrees or bust."

It was true she almost never went out anymore. The way she got involved in cases, she just didn't think of it—and now that Sheila and Kenny were there, it seemed more fun to stay home.

But they're not my family.

She told herself that often, felt she had to, to avoid disappointment, keep her perspective.

She decided to drop in on Honey Diefenthal instead of calling her. Honey lived nearby, in a wonderful restored camelback, which had been painted a delicate peach.

I like her already, Skip thought.

Honey—clearly just back from lunch—wore black wool crepe

slacks and a pink starched shirt, elegant but informal, the kind of outfit you didn't have to put any thought into, and you still looked great.

If you were Honey Diefenthal.

She was petite, a quality about which Skip had a deep ambivalence. In some ways her size made her feel powerful—in others, simply awkward, like an ostrich among canaries.

Honey was not only petite, but as blond as her name implied, as peaches and cream, as capital-S Southern. She wore her hair in something resembling a crew cut, which could have looked butch but instead looked delicate and caplike. Skip envied the confidence it took to pull it off.

She identified herself.

"Oh, yes. Pearce said you'd probably get in touch."

"Pearce? But we don't even know each other." Skip felt the flash of annoyance she'd come to associate with the TOWN and its denizens.

"Well, he knows you. He said to give you some tea and crumpets. Won't you come in?"

Skip entered a room full of chintz and light, not especially an original look, but it went with the house, and it worked.

"Sit down. Would you like that tea?"

"No, thanks. I've just come from lunch. Why on earth did Pearce think I'd call on you?"

"To check up on him, I guess. He's a little on the self-important side."

"Well, he's sort of right. But I mostly came because Alison Gaillard said I shouldn't miss you."

"Alison! How on earth do you know her?"

"She and I were sorority sisters at Newcomb."

"Oh, you're the Kappa cop. You're famous." She paused, letting pennies drop. "Now I get it. You must be Elizabeth Langdon's kid."

Skip grinned.

"I know her from . . . let's see, the Opera Association, I think, and maybe the NOCCA board. I don't even remember what-all. We're sort of in the same business."

"Professional volunteers."

She laughed. "We say 'community activists.' "

It was the sort of thing Skip had gotten used to. She got ready for twenty minutes of "who-do-you-know," and when that was over, she asked about Pearce. "He must be a nice man, if you still keep up a friendship."

"He's a perfectly terrible man. We don't have a friendship at all—he just calls me to borrow money and read his manuscripts. The former calls are a *great* deal more frequent than the latter."

Skip laughed.

"And thank God. I could tell you about his writing, but you mentioned you just had lunch."

"Gory?"

Her face grew serious. "Just depressing. He has talent, he just can't seem to get on with anything."

"Must be pretty slow stuff."

"In a sense. Do you know how long the average screenplay is?"

"A couple of hundred pages, I guess."

"About a hundred and twenty. Think about it. If you wrote one page a day, you could do a whole one in about four months."

"Providing you'd already plotted it, I guess."

"Well, say you took six months doing that. And then you took a month or two for research. You could do it in a year. Then maybe you'd want to rewrite—give it another six months, say a year to be generous. That's two years, which is a tremendous flyer to take if you're not getting paid for it. Just to take off two years—wouldn't you say?"

Skip nodded, not sure where this was going.

"Well, Pearce has been working for seventeen years. That's almost twenty years on a hundred and twenty pages—on a project nobody wants and nobody'll ever want. And if they did, they couldn't get it because it wouldn't be finished. And if it were finished, it would be a different story from the one they bought. Because he keeps changing it." She sighed. "Every week he's got a different great idea."

"No wonder he has to borrow money."

"Oh, the man is pathetic. A bitter, bitter old man."

"Old? But I thought he was about your age." Around fifty, she thought.

"Old, old, old before his time. He's a person who never fulfilled his own potential—he *could* have been a writer. Or a lawyer, for God's sake, or a bailbondsman. Something. But he isn't anything. He's accomplished nothing. But he wants to be recognized anyway—that's what the problem is. He tells everyone he's a writer, and he *does* write, so as far as he's concerned he is, and he just can't understand why he doesn't get fame and adulation. Which is what he wants. I don't even think he cares that he doesn't have any money—he just wants his talent recognized."

She paused for breath. "So every now and then he does some piddling story like the one he's working on now, about this young man's murder. And he posts on the TOWN, of course. I guess that's a form of writing. For all I know, people love him there." She grinned evilly. "That would be so much easier if you'd never met him. You could imagine he was a dashing, witty sophisticate instead of a broken-down old boozehound."

"He's an alcoholic then."

"Oh, didn't I mention that? It's the main thing, I guess."

"I could see that."

"It's why I dumped him." She wrinkled her nose again. "Well, that and the fact that I couldn't stand the man after I found out who he really was. You know how people can pretend to be something they're not?"

Skip nodded.

"Men, I mean—when they're trying to get your attention."

"What did he pretend to be?"

"Oh, someone nice. Caring, as they say nowadays. Sweet and generous. Considerate. Who wouldn't fall for that?"

"Sounds good to me."

It sounds like Steve, except he's real.

I hope.

Honey shrugged. "He married me for my money, of course. He always paid a lot more attention to Marguerite—that should have been a clue."

"Marguerite? Geoff's mother?"

"I just thought he was one of those guys who always flirts with the wife's friends—you know what I mean? New Orleans is full of them. But, honestly, looking back on it, I really think he was about half in love with Marguerite."

Why is she telling me this?

"I've been thinking about her lately, wondering what's become of her."

"She married a man named Coleman Terry."

"Have you seen her?" Something hovered in her eyes.

"Yes."

Honey was quiet for a moment, coming to a decision. Dignity didn't win out. "Well?" she said. "How does she look?"

"Like someone whose son has just died, I guess." Skip tried to keep judgment out of the words.

"God! I'm so tacky I can't believe it. Well, I can't help it, I've always wondered about it. Marguerite and Pearce, I mean. Because after Leighton died, I don't know what happened—my friendship with Marguerite just deteriorated, and so did my marriage."

"I had the idea your husband met Marguerite when he went to cover the murder."

"Oh, no. The three of us used to hang out together all the time. Leighton wasn't exactly the type to go boogie at Las Casas. God, Pearce was fun then!

"But then I guess I was too—that was before I became a do-gooder. I had a great pair of old-lady shoes that I sprayed gold."

"Hair down to your waist, I guess."

"All that stuff. A drink in one hand, a joint in the other."

"I wish I'd been around in the sixties."

"Oh, my dear, forget it. If you had been, you wouldn't be young now."

"How did you meet Marguerite?"

"Well, let me think." In a moment, she said, "We went to hear her sing—at the Dream Palace, I think. Pearce knew her and took me—that was it. He was impressing me."

"And you two hit it off."

"Oh, God, yes. Marguerite was wild. I envied her desperately."

"Why?"

"Why? Because every man's head turned when she walked into a room."

"Oh, come on, you're not so bad yourself."

"And because she'd do anything."

"Like what?"

"Well, I don't know that I actually saw her do anything off the wall—maybe she just talked a good game. Or maybe it was because she had this weird cop of a husband—no offense. Do you know about Leighton? What a straight arrow. Hair shorter than mine is now. Anyway, she had Leighton and a little kid and she still hung out every night. And she sang! Everybody loves an artist."

"What happened after Leighton died?"

"She just—I don't know—never wanted to get together anymore. I thought she was depressed. But maybe there was something I didn't know about."

7

• •

And maybe there's a lot she didn't tell me, Skip thought as she pulled up in front of Bigeasy's building. It was above a laundry, one fine old room with fourteen-foot ceilings, where Pearce worked, and a tiny bedroom, both jammed with ancient books and manuscripts, some on shelves, some merely piled. There were two tall windows that opened from the floor, but for some reason Pearce had them covered so that the place was dark. That would have been depressing enough, but the stink of the mildew that permeated the books and papers mingled with that of alcohol—somewhere, Pearce had left the dregs of a drink.

He wasn't a bad-looking man, she thought, about average height and average build, with hair that had turned white and looked good on him. He was slightly doughy around the middle, and his face was a little florid, with a few broken blood vessels, but it wasn't a bad face, not bad at all. He wore khakis and a faded-out polo shirt. His shoulders were slightly stooped.

Your typical aging Deke, she thought—a very specific New Orleans type. But he wasn't that, probably wasn't even from New Orleans.

An aging reporter was probably much the same. As she thought it, she realized that Honey was right—the man looked sixty, not fifty; she'd never have thought to use the word *aging* with Honey herself.

He said, "I was wondering when you'd drop by."

"I'm surprised you didn't have people looking out their windows, monitoring my progress."

"You overestimate us. There are probably only about eight TOWNspeople in the whole city."

"You're kidding."

"It just seems like a lot because they're all such busybodies." He held out a hand, inviting her to sit in a beat-up rocking chair whose caned seat was rapidly coming unwoven. She perched gingerly.

"They?"

He smiled, accepting the jibe graciously. "All of us, I guess."

"It's your first murder, I hear."

"But not our first death. Somebody committed suicide once, after making a lot of depressed postings and finally erasing everything he'd ever written."

Skip said nothing, trying to figure out what Pearce was getting at.

"Thereby committing virtual suicide first."

"Oh, come on."

He shrugged. "That's what people thought."

"Doesn't anybody on the TOWN have a life?"

"A lot of them don't, though they'd say they do. It's just that it consists of parking their butts in the same chair and staring at the same square foot every day all day. The TOWN selects for heavy mental artillery and poor social adjustment. Great verbal skills, not much else. We even joke about it. Did you ever see that *New Yorker* cartoon of the pooch at the computer terminal? The caption says, 'On the Internet, nobody knows you're a dog.' "

"I was wondering about that. But so far most of the people I've met seem fairly normal."

"You should have met Geoff."

"Oh?"

"Sweet kid. Really sweet. But painfully shy; no idea how to talk to girls—or anybody for that matter. Just not social."

"He had a girlfriend."

"Yes. Lenore. I wonder if they met online. No, I think they knew each other before. Most of the local TOWNspeople did—that is, they talked each other into getting online. By the way, that suicide wasn't our only drama. We had a threatened one once. Somebody broke up with a boyfriend—you know, I do believe it was Lenore; maybe she and Geoff did meet on the TOWN, because she had another guy at some point. He unexpectedly dumped her and she turned the TOWN into the Ashland Shakespeare Festival.

"People from all over the country were sending her virtual chicken soup and giving her strokes and offering to fly out to keep her company—and I don't mean just guys, either. All kinds of people—" He turned his palms up. "Out of kindness, it would seem."

"But you don't think so."

"Oh, I do. I just think it's a little odd—don't you? I doubt any of them had ever seen her or talked to her."

"Yes." Skip sat back in her chair.

"Yes what?"

"Yes, I think it's extremely odd." That didn't begin to describe what she really thought of it. "Who was the boyfriend?" she said.

"Lenore's? I don't know if she ever said."

"It could have been Geoff, then."

He considered. "I suppose. But I really didn't get that impression."

"Or it could have been someone else on the TOWN."

He grinned at her. "You've got a real talent for small-town gossip. You'd fit right in."

"Actually, it's my job." Annoyed at the concept she kept running into—that of TOWN as entire world—she made her voice crisply professional, slightly icy. "Did you know Geoff well?"

"I guess. The local folk get together now and then."

"You're sort of their guru, I hear."

He grinned. "Modesty forbids comment."

"I was wondering if Geoff talked to you—about any of his problems, for instance."

"He did now and then. Why?"

"Did he talk about this memory he was trying to retrieve? The murder?"

"No. Never."

"Where were you the morning he was killed?"

"What is this? I thought you came to ask me about the TOWN."

"Oh, I did. And somebody on the TOWN murdered Geoff Kavanagh, didn't they?"

"Young lady, I don't think I like your tone."

"I wonder if you'd answer the question." She owed him no apology, but she didn't like her own tone. She had no idea why she was being so rude—it was something about the man's arrogance, a coldness she sensed, a failure to connect with Geoff and maybe others that was getting to her.

"I can't say where I was."

"Why not?" *Don't you remember?* she wanted to add.

"It could compromise someone."

Skip frowned, but forebore to say anything. *Let him stew.*

"I'm really surprised you're taking this line of questioning."

"I have to ask everyone the same thing. But you know more than most people. For instance, you knew Geoff as a little boy. What was he like?"

"You're mistaken. I didn't know him then."

"Wasn't he there when you covered Leighton's murder? He couldn't have had a memory of it if he wasn't."

"I see. You know about that, do you?" His brows knit together and his own voice grew cold. "Of course he was there. But he was just a baby, clinging to his mother's skirts. I didn't have any impression of him."

"You were Marguerite's friend. Weren't you an odd choice to cover that story?"

"Not at all. I'd covered Leighton Kavanagh before—that is, I tried. I worked on a story about police corruption that didn't pan out."

"Marguerite didn't know about it?"

"Oh, she knew. She certainly knew. But she didn't seem to care a lot. I don't know much about that, to tell you the truth. She never talked about it."

"What did she talk about?"

"Music. Politics. The war and Lyndon Johnson. In those days"—he looked at her like she was a pet dog—"we had a lot of angst."

"So she was angst-ridden."

"Marguerite?" He seemed surprised. "Maybe she was. I just thought we all were, but thinking back on it, she had a certain—I don't know—preoccupation about her. Almost a melancholy, like she was perennially worried." He paused, apparently unsure whether to say what was on his mind.

Skip waited.

"Maybe that's what made her so attractive."

"Why would that make a woman attractive?" It wasn't on the point, but she had to know.

"You think you could make her happy."

"Leighton wasn't doing that?"

"Well, they seemed to have precious little in common. I didn't know Marguerite well, you understand—we saw each other in clubs, and now and then for lunch. Well, for lunch once or twice when we first met." He smiled ruefully. "But that didn't go anywhere. When I met Honey—the woman I married—I took her along to hear Marguerite sing, and they got to be friends; then they had lunch together. But we never had Marguerite over to dinner or anything."

"Why not?"

"Because we'd have had to have Leighton, of course."

"It sounds as if you had a crush on Marguerite."

"Oh, God, a bad one. She was the most beautiful, quicksilver, compelling woman I ever saw in my life." He moved his shoulders heavily, shrugging off his regret. "But she was married, and besides that, she wasn't interested."

"Meaning she was interested in someone."

"Marguerite was . . . well, she was a flirt."

"Was she having an affair?"

"With Mike Kavanagh, you mean?" His voice had a sudden nasty edge. "Not that I know of. I barely knew the man existed until she married him."

"Even though you investigated Leighton."

"Mike was clean. At least his name never came up in the kickback stories."

"Do you see Marguerite now?"

"Oh, God, no! The last time I saw her was probably the night Leighton died. She leaned on me that night—cried on me like I was her daddy. And after that she never returned any of Honey's calls, or mine. I think I can take a hint."

"Why do you think that was?"

"Who knows? Honey said she was depressed." He looked depressed himself.

"When Geoff showed up on the TOWN, it must have been quite a shock."

"It's pretty hard to shock somebody as old as I am."

"When he started posting about his memories, why didn't you mention you'd been there that night?"

"Because it's nobody's business but Geoff's. I E-mailed him, of course."

"Oh, you did? So you had a private correspondence with him."

"I had that long before the Confession topic ever came up. You've got to remember, we're all pretty close on the TOWN."

Now it's "we" thought Skip. When it suits him, it seems to be "they."

"Would you mind showing me?"

"Your own letters aren't in your file—they just get sent as if they were on paper. And I never save my mail, so I don't have the stuff he sent me."

"I see. You said he didn't talk to you about his father's murder; but obviously he wrote you about it."

"Not really. Not much, anyway."

"Look. Did he confide *anything* to you—anything that might help me?"

Pearce, whose eyes had strayed to his neglected computer

screen, snapped back to her, suddenly alert. "Wait a minute. I think he did. Do you know about the stolen items?"

"Yes. Leighton's revolver and a ring. Citrine, I think."

"Marguerite has the ring."

"Wait a minute—you mean she lied when she reported it stolen?"

"Now that I couldn't tell you. But it would seem not from what Geoff said—which is that it simply arrived in the mail one day a few years ago."

"How many years ago?"

"He just said when he was a kid."

"But how could he possibly know it was that ring?"

"All I know is that he was there when she opened it, and that she turned pale and started crying. I guess he figured out later what it must have been."

Skip raised an eyebrow. "I guess I'd better not take up any more of your time." She stood up. "You've been very helpful."

"That was fast. I guess I know where you're going next."

"I appreciate your help," she said, more or less trying to make peace—she was so grateful for the tidbit she was suddenly feeling downright benevolent toward him.

"Coming to the funeral?"

"When is it? Tomorrow?"

He nodded. "You really should come. You can get a gander at our little community."

"Maybe I will."

"Wait a minute! I've got a better idea—a much better idea. I mean, you can come to the funeral too, but we're all having dinner tomorrow night—'Geoff would have wanted it that way' kind of thing. Why don't you join us?"

"Who is 'we'?"

"The local TOWNspeople. It's a perfect opportunity to meet everybody at once. We'd love to have you."

I'll just bet. I'd be the main course. "I don't know—"

"Look, the murder's bound to be Topic A. Basically, what you've got is all the suspects gathered together. Someone might confess."

"Right. If this were an Agatha Christie novel."

"Seven-thirty at R&O's. We'll save you a place."

A blast of cold wind hit her as she went outside. She turned her collar up, swearing. She'd learned she got the best results when she steeped herself in her cases. It was grotesque, but she knew she had to go to the damn dinner. It was an easy way to talk to them without making them suspicious. They'd get to know her a little, be a little more at ease when she questioned them later.

8

• •

"How about something like this?" Marguerite held up a simple black dress, nipped in at the waist, plain straight skirt.

"I don't think so, Mom."

"What on earth is wrong with it? It's about as simple as you can get."

Her daughter, Neetsie, barely kept the sneer out of her voice. "It's the wrong length."

"It's knee-length. What's the problem?"

"Short's good; long's good. Just not knee-length. Why don't you get it?"

"Me? It's not my style."

Why was she even worried about a thing like that? Marguerite wondered. It was for her son's funeral; Neetsie's brother's funeral. Why did she care?

I don't care.

But they had already been to three stores and rejected everything. How hard could it be to pick out a couple of dresses for a funeral? She sensed Neetsie getting impatient. Her daughter didn't want a dress anyway. She kept insisting she'd wear her black wool skirt, which was ankle-length, with a black sweater. And she'd look lovely in it, Marguerite thought. (Except, of course, for the holes.) Dramatic, yet comfortable with herself.

That was okay, that was fine, to wear the old outfit; but Marguerite wanted to give her something. Neetsie was the only child she had left, and she wanted her to have something special, something Marguerite had given her.

"Let's look at the Anne Kleins."

"Oh, Mom, they're too expensive."

"You need something nice. Come on. I'd like to buy you something nice."

"Mom, we need to get something for *you*."

Her voice was getting shrill.

"Oh, I don't need anything. I should be home working on my opera."

"Right, Mom. That's what you always say. Why should today be any different just because your only son's dead?"

Marguerite felt quick tears spring to her eyes. "Well, you look like *you're* dead—wearing black all the time, red lipstick, ten holes in each ear and as if that weren't enough—"

"Mom!"

"—another in your nose."

"Mom, we've been over and over that."

"You're such a pretty girl. You have lovely features and beautiful hair—gorgeous blue eyes. But nobody notices because all they see are the holes."

"You're exactly like your mother, you know that?" People in Saks were starting to stare.

"You don't even know my mother. You weren't old enough to know her before she lost it."

"Pearce Randolph told me about her."

"Pearce? How do you know Pearce?"

"From the TOWN. Geoff took me to a couple of their dinners. I said you were always complaining about my piercings, and he told me a story you told him. About a guy you dated—before you married Leighton, I guess. She told him he had lovely features and lovely eyes, but nobody could see them because his hair was long."

"At least he didn't have a nose ring."

"Mom, will you back off?" Neetsie spoke sharply, in a voice different from the habitual ones they used for bickering, a voice that meant business. Marguerite felt the tears sting again.

"Oh, honey, I just love you so much, that's all. You know how proud I am of you. Last year, when you did *The Ballad of the Sad Cafe*, I thought you should be on Broadway, you were so hot. You were great, you know that. I just want—"

"You just want me to be perfect."

"Is there something wrong with that? Is that too much to hope for my one and only child? You're the only child I have left, do you realize that? Cole just never seems to get it together, year after year after year. . . ."

"Oh, come on, how about you? You've been working on your 'opera' for twelve years. Or so you say—nobody's actually seen you doing it."

"Why is this necessary? Why are you trying so hard to wound me?"

"Look, Mom, let's go back to Maison Blanche. I'll just get that first dress. It'll be okay. You could get a suit, maybe. You'd look wonderful in a really sharp black suit. With a deep blue silk blouse, maybe. Subtle; almost black itself. A midnight blue, sort of."

"I can't afford anything like that. You know I can't, Neetsie. I haven't had any money for so long, and all my clothes are full of moth holes—and fifteen years old, too. You just don't know how hard it is."

Neetsie looked alarmed. "Mom, let's go to the ladies' room."

She turned on her heel, apparently perfectly confident that Marguerite would follow. Which she did, tears streaming, hardly able to see in front of her.

She had blown it again. She had meant to say how proud she was of Neetsie, to convey somehow how much she loved her, and that if she'd just respect herself a little more, she could live up to what Marguerite knew to be her true potential. She was beautiful, she was talented, she was nearly perfect. Why not go for the whole ball of wax? Marguerite just couldn't understand it.

When they were there, in the ladies' room, Neetsie said, "Mom, are you okay? You seem really out of it."

"Geoffrey—"

Neetsie shook her head. "You sure? You sure that's all?"

Marguerite leaned on the vanity top. She felt sobs welling up in her diaphragm.

"That's it, Mom. That's it. That's just what you need. Go ahead and cry all you want to." Neetsie left for a minute and came back with a huge wad of toilet paper, which she handed to her mother.

Marguerite dabbed at her eyes, embarrassed, hoping no one would come in and catch her bawling in the bathroom.

There was something else, all right. She hadn't felt this stressed out since the day Geoffrey had died.

She was terrified. The thought of seeing Mike Kavanagh filled her with dread.

And he was sure to be at the funeral, had insisted on keeping up a relationship with Geoff long after the marriage was over (never mind the fact that the boy hadn't cared two figs for him).

When the sobs started to subside and the toilet paper was saturated, Marguerite looked into the round blue eyes of her daughter (Cole's eyes; Neetsie had been so lucky to get them) and she saw how sad they were.

"Neetsie. Neetsie, could I just ask you a question? You know I don't ask you for much."

Neetsie pulled together a smile. "Sure, Mom."

"Could you take out the nose ring for the funeral? Would that be possible at all?"

• •

Cole picked up the phone and dialed the nursing home. "This is Coleman Terry, Marguerite Terry's husband. I don't know if you know that there's been a death in our family—we'd like Mrs. Julian to go to the funeral with us."

He waited as the secretary got his mother-in-law's chart, as she conferred with doctors, nurses, probably administrators. Eventually, he was told he could come get Mrs. Julian the next morning, but that, as usual, he shouldn't expect her to know anybody.

Next he got out the vacuum. These sorts of chores usually fell to him. Marguerite took care of her animals and her garden; sometimes she cooked a little; she may have worked on her opera, he wasn't sure. She was a creative person, not one for the constant repetition of household chores; a fair flower of the South who needed to be taken care of, not the sort to get her hands dirty, and it was Cole's privilege to assume her care. He only wished he could do it better. His pending deal had to work out . . . it just had to.

The house was falling apart and if he were any kind of husband, he'd take care of it, he'd have the place full of maids and gardeners and contractors. Sometimes Marguerite got so frustrated she flew into rages, and he didn't blame her. He felt like raging himself, but he couldn't, he had to keep working, he had to keep the family together. She was especially fragile right now, with this tragedy, Geoff's terrible death.

But there was a bright side: *At least it wasn't Neetsie. She loves that kid like she never did love Geoff. I probably feel worse about him than she does.*

God, if it had been Neetsie, I'd probably have to check Marguerite into the hospital with her mother.

He changed the attachment and began to vacuum the furniture, shocked at how dusty it was, how deep was the cat hair. He didn't know if there'd be visitors after the funeral, but if there was even one, it was worth cleaning. Otherwise they might get reported to the health department.

In fact, if anyone from the TOWN came, everybody else on the whole damn network would know the condition of the Terry household, down to the last flea on Toots.

I wish I'd never gotten Geoff on that damn thing! Hell, I wish I'd never joined it myself—waste of time, and not only that, it's not safe. All that speculating, that monitoring of people by strangers—

He smiled grimly even as he had the thought, remembering that it had been very unsafe indeed for his stepson. But he was disturbed by what had come after as well. It was sudden and creepy and unexpected—the energy behind it, the taking on of a murder as if it were a hobby.

Don't those assholes have anything better to do? he thought.

The whole phenomenon made him mad, especially that Pearce

Randolph, whipping up these young kids, these marginal personalities—getting them all worked up, like he was some goddam electronic guru. Geoff had loved him, all the kids loved him, but he rubbed Cole the wrong way.

Shit! I'll be done with him and all his kind if only the deal works. Goddam, if it hadn't been for that idiot partner of mine, we could be in Costa Rica by now, Marguerite and me. Everything he's ever done he's screwed up. Why does God make idiots like that? Can you tell me that? Huh, Mosey? Huh, Calabash? Huh, Toots? Could you tell me, please?

He spoke the last few words aloud, prompting Toots to wave her tail unenthusiastically, as if fulfilling an obligation, and then to start barking. The barking started softly and got louder.

"Hey, what'd I say? I thought you'd agree with me."

Toots had trotted to the door, and now stood there barking at it. Cole turned off the vacuum in time to hear the last chime of the doorbell. "Oh, well, at least I got most of the cat hair."

A large woman greeted him, six feet tall probably, and built to make an impression. She had buttoned her brown tweed blazer, something you didn't often see women do. There was aggression in the way she stood. He had an immediate reaction against her—he couldn't have said why, there was just something about her that was in your face.

"I'm Skip Langdon," she said, and held up her badge. "You must be Coleman Terry."

I should have known, he thought, as she explained she was there about Geoff. "Your wife showed me his room," she said, "but I wonder if I could take another look."

"Do you have a search warrant?"

"No, I just thought you might not mind. Of course, if you do—"

"Oh, no, it isn't that. That's just what they always say on television."

She smiled. "We like to do things informally when we can. Is Mrs. Terry home?"

"I'm afraid not. Did you want to see her?"

"It's okay. I can come back later. But why don't we check Geoff's room now?"

He stayed with her while she looked, though she conducted her search so slowly he wanted to tear the place apart for her. "Are you looking for anything special?"

He saw her hesitate, probably wondering if it was safe to ask him. She seemed to realize that at this point it made no difference, she wasn't going to find it—whatever it was—by herself. "Do you know if he kept a journal?"

"I don't think so. I guess I'd be surprised if he did. Geoff wasn't a particularly introspective boy."

"Wasn't he? I thought he kept to himself."

"Well, maybe he *was* introspective. He just never seemed all that aware of other people. Shy. Painfully shy. He was a good kid, though. A really, really good kid."

"Were you close to him?"

"Probably closer than anybody. The way to his heart was through the computer, and I was able to introduce him to it. He liked me almost as much as the machine." Cole gave her a big smile.

"And what did you think of him?"

"Like I said, we were close."

"I see."

Did she close down a little? Cole thought he saw a shadow cross her face.

"Listen, would you mind if I took his computer down to head-quarters?"

"What for?"

"Evidence."

".What sort of evidence?"

"That's all I can really say about it. Of course, if you don't want me to—"

"Did you want to get into his files? Is that it? See if he's got a journal in there?"

She smiled again, but he saw the tension at the corners of her mouth. "You never know what you'll find."

"Seizing computers is a pretty hot-button issue. The EFF would drum me out of the country if I didn't say something."

"EFF?"

"Electronic Frontiers Foundation. You could just download the disks, you know. The idea is, it's bad enough to lose your software, but if your hardware's missing, so's your livelihood."

"I think in this case . . ."

"Yes, of course." He shrugged. "I thought I should at least register a protest."

She began to unplug the computer and gather it up, as if he'd given her permission. "Mr. Terry, as long as I'm here, I thought I might clear up a couple of loose ends. I'm wondering where you were when the body was found."

"Didn't anyone tell you? I was in Baton Rouge. That's why it was such a horrible shock for Marguerite; she had to go through the whole thing herself. Of course I got here in a couple of hours, but it was terrible for her—all alone like that."

"May I ask why you went to Baton Rouge?"

"Of course. It was business. I'm a partner in a software company and we're in negotiations with a company that wants to market our product."

"I see. And where'd you stay?"

"Oh, just a Holiday Inn."

"Which one?"

He gave her the address. "Can I help you carry that to the car?"

"Sure."

"By the way, did you get the floppies? He could have put anything and everything on floppies." He rummaged through Geoff's files. "Here they are."

"Thanks."

As they walked to her car, he carrying the hard disk, she the floppies, she said, "Tell me about your business."

"Well, it's kind of interesting, really. I had another business, an electronics store—this was, oh, years and years ago when nobody had PCs. I was one of the first on my block and I was trying to find a program to keep the books, but none of them were any good. So I designed my own, and from that moment I was hooked.

"I went out and read every book I could find about computer programming; I took my first course in it long after I'd already founded a software company."

"You're self-taught?"

"Except for that one course, which I just took to see if I'd missed anything."

"And had you?"

"Not a lot."

She opened the trunk and they packed it with Geoff's equipment.

"That's pretty impressive."

"You'd really think so if you knew the rest of my history."

"Why is that?"

"Well, I fall out of love easily." He smiled at her. "Except with Marguerite, I mean. But I've had quite a few jobs—I sailed a boat around the world for a captain of industry; I went to law school and passed the bar; I founded a bluegrass band that was pretty hot up in Baton Rouge a few years back; I even taught at a state college for a while—history, one of my favorite subjects."

"You seem like a pretty well rounded guy."

"Not anymore, I'm afraid. For the last few years, it's been nothing but get up in the morning and work all day, and then work half the night, then get up and do the whole thing all over again. If things had gone right, and I hadn't fallen in with a pack of idiots, Marguerite and I'd be millionaires. But now things are taking a turn for the better. We've got a deal going that's finally going to do it."

"That's terrific."

"We've waited a long damn time for it."

He was ready to say good-bye—he still had to mow the lawn—but she leaned lazily against the car. "Are you from Baton Rouge?"

"No. Why?"

"Because that's where the band was."

"Oh. Just passing through. I was born and raised in Metairie. Lived a lot of other places, though."

"How long have you been married?"

He had to pause and figure it out—Neetsie was eighteen. "Nineteen years," he said. "I can't believe it."

"That's a long time."

"It's been good, though. It's been great."

"Happy marriages don't come along every day."

"Neither do women like Marguerite."

She smiled at him more warmly, he thought, than she had before: *All the world loves a lover.*

It was hard to convey the way he felt about Marguerite. "Did you ever meet someone that you knew in that instant was right for you—was your life's partner?"

"I don't think many people do. How did you two meet?"

"Well, it wasn't even that we met—I saw her across a crowded room and wouldn't rest until I found out who she was. It took me an hour to work up the courage, though. Lucky for me, she was just out of a marriage to a very abusive man. What can I say? We fell desperately in love."

"Leighton or Mike?" she said.

"I beg your pardon?"

"Who was the abuser?"

"I guess they both were, now that I think about it, but I met her after Mike. Otherwise I'd have snapped her up a few years earlier. Neetsie was born about a year after we got married, and meanwhile Geoff and I formed a real father-son bond. Mike had been abusive to him as well as to Marguerite; but maybe you knew that."

She nodded, not giving anything away.

"He was withdrawn at first, but I found the cyberpunk lurking under the quiet exterior."

Her smile looked painted on as she said good-bye, he didn't know why. Maybe he'd run on too much. It was a habit, Marguerite said.

9

• •

Skip hated to leave without talking to Marguerite, but she had a feeling it might be for the best—better to catch her without the doting hubby hanging around.

Cole had surprised her.

He was vaguely handsome in that clean-cut, fraternity-boy way so many New Orleans men were blessed with. But he had something else—a kind of wild energy, a charisma. He was a fast talker, and a little short on modesty, but she felt herself drawn to him, drawn to the whirling center of all that electricity. How did a man like that sit at his computer all day? He seemed as if he should be out playing tennis. Not only that, how did he hook up with a dud like Marguerite?

But she must be missing something about Marguerite. The woman appeared to have had very nearly the male population of New Orleans in love with her at one time, and it didn't seem to have abated much. What did she have that men saw and women didn't?

Skip pulled into her parking place, thinking that the biggest mysteries she encountered weren't always who did what to whom.

Remembering that Ted Bundy had been famous for his charm, she wasted no time checking Cole's alibi—but his business associates confirmed the meeting he'd attended, and the Holiday Inn said he'd checked out at midmorning the day of the murder.

She turned her attention to a note she'd found on her desk when she walked in: "Call Mike Kavanagh ASAP."

Gladly, she thought. *About time we met.*

Kavanagh had a classic New Orleans accent, not exactly yat, but pretty close. He said he'd be right 'dere.

He was overweight and red-faced, veins popping on his nose. He clearly ate too much and drank too much. His hair had been red, but it was mostly gray now. When he shook hands with her, he stood close enough so that she could smell the alcohol on his breath. She hoped he wasn't too attached to his liver.

She hated cops who gave cops a bad name, and Mike Kavanagh, she could see at a glance, was capable of that. She had taken what Cole said about his being abusive with a grain of salt, but now she wondered.

"What can I do for you?" she said.

"I came to ask you that. May I sit down?"

"Of course." They both sat.

"I knew you'd find me eventually. Terrible thing about Geoff." He looked at his lap and shook his head. "Terrible thing. Wasn't it?"

She nodded, thinking he looked shaken indeed.

"I thought you'd like my ideas on the case." He attempted a smile.

"You have some?"

"Nah, not really. But you do—you think I'm a pretty good suspect, don't you?"

"Are you?"

"Well, Suby told me about all this memory stuff. She says half that goddam thing—the TOWN—thinks I did it."

"Suby?"

"My daughter. Geoff got her on the goddam thing."

"I don't understand. How did they know each other?"

He brought his fist down on her desk. "See? See? You don't

even know. Geoff and I were close, goddam it! Marguerite didn't tell you that, did she? I went to see that kid every week after we got divorced, and then welcomed him into my home after I got married again; he came to see Suby in the hospital the day she was born. They were like cousins, those two. Practically brought up together."

"I guess I didn't know that."

"That bitch Marguerite's not gon' tell you. I don't know why I ever married her—I must have been crazy."

"Maybe you were crazy in love."

"With skinny ol' Marguerite?" He sat back in his chair, regret on his face. "I tried. I really did try. But the only good thing I got out of it was Geoff."

"She was very beautiful, I hear."

He made a face. "Shee-it. I don't know, maybe she was. She was my brother's wife and that was the end of it. I never really paid her any attention. But Leighton, he worshiped her. Thought the sun rose and set on her. Then when he died, she just seemed so . . . I don't know, so sad and small somehow. Real fragile, and real burdened. I just felt real, real sorry for her. She had that little boy—bad little kid. Really bad. But then after we were married, he just kind of settled down. He needed a father was all."

"Are you saying you married Marguerite because you felt sorry for her?"

"Well, that was why I started seein' her. I'd take her and Geoff to the movies, the Audubon Zoo—I thought it was my duty as an uncle. Leighton and I were like that." He held up two mashed-together fingers. "It was what I had to do for his son and his widow."

His eyes clouded as he went back in memory. "Sometimes she'd cook me dinner. Or we'd go out to the lake and get crabs. It just seemed we were together a lot." He shrugged, apparently trying to piece it together for himself as well as Skip. "It seemed like the thing to do to get married. It sounds kind of funny now, but I did it out of duty, sort of. Can you understand something like that?"

"Not really."

He slammed his fist down again. "That's how it was, goddam it! You can believe it or not."

"I didn't say I didn't believe it. You asked me if I could understand it."

"Are you a Catholic?"

She shook her head.

"Well, that explains it."

When she said nothing, he poked at his chest with the fingers of both hands. His face got redder and redder. "I didn't get who she was, see. I believed Leighton—did that ever happen to you? Somebody you're close to likes somebody so much you talk yourself into that person?

"I remember the first time I met her, I thought, this woman is trouble. She's up to something I don't understand. She's gonna hurt my brother. But then she didn't and he married her and he kept on thinking she was a saint even though she looked like a goddam hippie. She had to do that for her job, he said. Because folksingers had to look that way. And I was so dumb I just believed him. You know what? You should always trust your first impressions. I had a lot of clues and I was too dumb to notice. Like what a bad little kid Geoff was."

"Bad how?"

"He was always in your face, always asking for things, demanding things, and throwing tantrums when he didn't get them. Nothing was ever enough for that kid. I thought it was just natural—his father dies, it upsets a kid. Ha! There's this other thing—his mother pays no attention to him the first four years of his life, it leaves a real big hole. That's what the kid was like—some kind of bottomless pit. Of course, Leighton and Marguerite probably fought a lot too. That probably didn't help."

"I thought he thought she was a saint."

He looked uncomfortable. "Well, Leighton was different from me. I like a peaceful kind of woman."

Right. Subservient, you could even say.

"I think he was into kissin' and makin' up."

"Why do you say that?"

100

He looked down at his flat, blunt fingers, thoroughly embarrassed. "Because Marguerite was."

He seemed inclined to stop there, but Skip was having none of
it. When he hadn't spoken for thirty seconds, she said gently,
"Oh?"

He looked her full in the eye, apparently determined to come
clean. "She got me with this helpless act. Then we get married and
she wants to go out every night all by herself and drink and hang
with a bunch of hippies and do every kind of drug you can name.
Now think about it—what's the next thing women do when they
do drugs?"

"I guess that depends on the woman."

"You know what it is. They're hangin' out in a bar with a
bunch of lowlifes—you know what they're doin'. She wouldn't
come home until two or three—she'd leave the kid over at her
mother's—but finally she'd get back and I'd be good and mad.

"Well, she knew I was going to be good and mad. How could
she not know? Same thing happened every time. She'd fight with
me a while, then she'd get real seductive. I fell for it the first few
thousand times."

"Ah. You got off on it too."

"Well, now, that's the thing." He was talking to her as if she
were a man, not embarrassed anymore, simply analyzing what happened. "I didn't get off on it. The first few times, I was so surprised
I just reacted like a piece of meat. Then after a while, I started realizing it was kind of makin' me mad. I was feeling kind of used,
to tell you the truth. And eventually, I didn't want nothin' to do
with her after we'd been fightin'." He paused and took a breath,
even smiled.

"Well, that made her mad. I mean, really mad, and I caught on
that the other kind of fightin' was an act and when she didn't get
what she wanted, that was when she got bitchy. See, the way I
piece it together, Leighton always gave her what she wanted—got
jealous, got into a fight with her, got seduced and had a rare old
time. You gotta remember, he wasn't married to her as long as I
was."

"How long were you married to her?"

"Six years. Seemed like sixteen. Anyway, after I caught on to what was happening, I just left her alone. And then that started a whole new deal about why didn't I care anymore and I must have another woman and all that kind of crap. But I'd had it by then. I just wasn't falling for all that stompin' and screamin' and carrying on anymore.

"Anyway, by that time I could see I wasn't going to get what I wanted out of the marriage."

"And what was that?"

"Well, I was crazy about that l'il ol' Geoff. What I wanted was a kid." For the first time he looked sad rather than unpleasantly angry. "But Marguerite just wasn't interested." He was quiet for a moment. "You know, sometimes I think I'm kiddin' myself, that I didn't marry her out of duty or because she was kind of pretty or anything. I just fell in love with that kid." There was real pain in his voice.

"That must have been the hardest part about getting divorced."

"Always is, they tell me. The kid. That's why I stuck with her so long in the first place. In the end, she was the one wanted to get divorced. I guess I kept hopin' she'd change." He shrugged. "But both of us met someone within six months or so, got married again, and had a daughter. That always pissed me off, you know? That more than anything. That she had a kid with him when she wouldn't have one with me. But I tried not to let it bother me; I had to be civil to her to keep up with Geoff. I miss that boy, you know that?" He had tears in his eyes.

"You still married?"

"No way. Got me another bitch, second time around. Totally different from Marguerite; I thought if I got an ugly one she'd stay home and take care of me like she was s'posed to. Helen was short, fat, and dumb—and just as mean as Marguerite. That's it for me, lady. No more of this marriage shit."

Skip didn't reply, more or less struck speechless.

"But it was worth it. Got me a beautiful daughter that time. You know what? I got a picture right here." He pulled a worn wallet out of his back pocket and extracted a photo of a teenage girl who'd obviously gotten both parents' fat genes. But he was right, she was lovely just the same, mostly because of her skin, which was almost translucent, delicately pink.

"Light of my life. I'm crazy about that kid." His moony face looked like the sun for a moment. He rested a hand lightly on each knee, a man at ease for a second in the torment he seemed to find life on Earth. He smiled a distant smile, looked fondly at the wall for a bit, and came back, patting his knees to signal his return.

"Well, I guess that's it. I just wanted to tell you my brother was the only thing I ever loved except for his son Geoff and my daughter Suby. I wouldn't hurt Leighton, Ms. Langdon. And I wouldn't hurt Geoff. I'd rather cut off my arm."

I could believe the first part, anyway, the way this guy hates women.

She thought briefly about letting him get away with the way he'd addressed her, just to avoid a confrontation.

But why should I put up with that crap? He probably makes a career out of pushing women around.

"Officer Langdon, Officer Kavanagh. Thanks for coming by."

"Well, sorry to offend you, *Officer*."

"Thanks for getting in touch." She didn't smile as she said it.

"A lot of good this did me," he said, and walked out of the room.

"You, sir, are a grump," Skip said to the air.

•   •

Marguerite needed talking to, but Skip decided to leave her until after the funeral—Lenore needed talking to just as badly. If Geoff had told her things in confidence, she might be ready to come out with them. And how *had* she gotten that coroner's report?

Skip gave her time to get off work, get home, and put her kid to bed. She turned up about eight-thirty, and was dismayed to see that the house looked dark. The curtains were drawn, but one of them moved slightly, and she thought she saw a flash of something, maybe a TV screen. Or a candle. The notion made her sigh—if she was about to interrupt a romantic evening, so be it.

She walked to the front door and raised a hand to ring the doorbell. But even as she started to press it, something stopped her.

103

Chanting.

Was it "Om"? Or just "Ooooooooooooooooo"? She'd never heard anything like it. It made her spine tingle and her scalp prickle, made her want to get in the car, step on the gas, turn on her red light and drive to Mexico.

Come on, she told herself. *It's just voices. What's the big deal?*

The chant changed: "Maaaaaaaaaaaaaaaaaa."

The voices were women's, she thought, and they were playing with the sound, drawing it out, some singing in different keys, at different pitches from the others. The effect was eerier than bag-pipes.

Shivering, trying to shake off what she knew was irrational fear, Skip moved to the side of the house. As she'd hoped, there were windows here whose curtains hadn't been drawn. The trick would be to look in without being seen.

She needn't have worried. The people inside were standing in a circle, arms around each other's waists, swaying, eyes closed, so deeply involved in the chant she could probably take her time.

Candles burned at odd places about the room, some on what appeared to be an altar—or a coffee table that had been turned into one. In the light they cast, the ones on the altar were easy to see. There were two tall ones, one black and one green; and there were several votive candles, all black.

Also on the altar was a candle snuffer, a knife or dagger with a fancy handle, and some kind of small round plate with a star engraved on it—*Pentacle,* she thought, not quite knowing where the word came from. A large ceramic chalice was filled with some kind of dark liquid—*red,* she thought. *Or am I crazy?* And oddly, a curiously mundane item nestled in the midst of the macabre—a china plate of cookies. Next to the cookies was a skull.

Not a cow's skull, or a cat's skull.

A human skull.

The people chanting wore hooded black robes. Candlelight glinted on something shiny on one of the faces—something strangely metallic. Skip stared until, revolted, she realized it must be a nose ring. But she couldn't tell anything about the face itself—

that one or the others. Not even if the robed figures were men or women, black or white.

Voodoo, she thought.

But it didn't seem right. She had been to the voodoo museum on a case, had read a little about it. This looked a little too stark for voodoo. There should be figures on the altar, perhaps. Offerings of rum and cigars. And she didn't think the robes were right. Shouldn't they be white?

But the cookies must be an offering of some sort.

Why cookies?

They were creeping her out, those cookies, so plain and wholesome sitting there next to the skull. Had she come face-to-face with the infamous banality of evil? The phrase had always puzzled her.

The chant was winding down.

I'd better get out of here, or they'll sacrifice me and drink my blood.

She ran back to the car. It probably would have been safer to walk, but she couldn't help it, she ran.

Once inside, windows up, keys in ignition, radio at hand, she felt her heart beating as if she'd run five miles. It was cold outside, but she tasted sweat.

Jesus Christ, what in the hell was that?

She tried deep breathing. *Can I meditate?* She wondered. Usually, she couldn't—she hated to sit still—but she had to get her center back. She sat and breathed until her heart slowed down. Only then did it occur to her to wonder what had gotten to her. Why was the thing so scary when there probably wasn't any danger at all? The only weapon she'd seen was the dagger on the altar and she had a .38. What was the big deal?

She honestly didn't know.

Much as she would have given anything to go home and pull the covers over her head, she settled down to wait for the strange ritual to end. It was no night to beard Lenore, but she had to try to find out who'd been in there.

She wrote down the license numbers of the nearby cars and hunched down.

She had plenty of time to meditate; she could have written a sonnet or a symphony, too, if she'd been the creative kind. It was an hour and a half before the door opened and women's voices chimed merrily.

" 'Bye!"

"See you soon."

"Give Caitlin a kiss for me."

Skip shivered.

They hugged their hostess good-bye and tripped daintily to their cars, as if they'd just been to a tea party. They looked pretty normal except for the one with the nose ring—and she would have without it.

Several of them went to the cars Skip was watching.

Excitedly, she ran the plates. Two were noteworthy: one was registered to a Michael Kavanagh, one to a Nita Susan Terry.

Yes, now that she thought of it. The heavy girl who'd gotten in Kavanagh's car was probably the one in the picture he'd shown her. The other one, the one with the nose ring, was about the age to be Neetsie Terry.

When she got home she ran all the names she had—six in all—through the TOWN's data bank. Three were TOWNspeople—Neetsie (SaraB), Suby (Michelle), and someone named Kathryne Brazil (Kit), a tall slim woman who seemed a good deal older than the others.

10

• •

Skip found, as always, that once logged on it was difficult to get off. It wasn't that she was fascinated—in fact, she was more or less bored—but there were so many choices, so many possibilities. . . .

Who could resist checking a few of them out?

First, of course, she went to Geoff's topics. Nothing new, which was wonderful news. Maybe she was up to speed with regard to the TOWN; that should improve her self-esteem.

What next? This was supposed to be a place where you could get information. Was there anything that could help her? How about religion? Yes, there was a Religion conference; she went there. There were 305 topics, mostly, it seemed, dealing with various forms of Buddhism and with channeling.

Ah, there it was—"Is It True What They Say About Satanism?"

Eagerly, she dropped in.

Reading quickly, licking her lips, she went through 150 entries in about half an hour. The gist of the discussion seemed to be whether Satanism was somehow an urban myth, a product of false memory syndrome, rather than a real phenomenon. Some of the people who posted, for instance, found it hard to believe that women were systematically gotten pregnant and forced to give birth to babies who were then sacrificed and eaten.

The whole Satanic scare, it seemed, had started with a book called *Michelle Remembers* that blew the whistle on the baby sacrifices and such described by people who claimed to have grown up in a Satanic cult. The name Michelle, Suby's user ID, gave Skip a tiny bit of hope, but it was the only thing that did. Neither Lenore, Suby, nor Neetsie had posted in the conference.

Kathryne Brazil (Kit) had, however. She noted that nearly all the victims of the Inquisition had confessed to witchcraft and had described it in the same terms as all the other confessors—something about having sex with the devil, who had a memorable member. Though none of the women complained of frostbite in a usually warm area, Kit couldn't see why, unless they were lying. Well, not lying exactly—simply asked certain leading questions under torture. She had said she didn't know whether that was quite like a shrink questioning a kid about his adventures with Mom and Dad's naked pals, but it was funny the subject was the same.

That tells me exactly nothing, Skip thought. *Oh, well, what next?*

I know. What's with tattoos and nose rings?

In her mind, the two went together. Lenore had a tattoo and Neetsie had a nose ring. She associated both with heavy metal, which seemed rich in Satanic imagery.

Sure enough, there was a whole topic on body piercing, with a tattoo thread running through it. By the time she had read it, she knew quite a number of interesting things, but not whether the two went together (though some posters said one was a subset of the other) and not why people did them.

One thing she knew was that people sometimes got piercings in a sort of ritual with drums and hand-holdings, perhaps not unlike the one she'd just witnessed.

Another thing she knew was that, if you got your nipples pierced, you probably didn't have to worry that it would interfere with breast-feeding unless you got badly infected; as a side issue (known on the TOWN as "topic drift"), she knew that a nipple has about 120 milk ducts.

She also knew two positions for labia piercings, each grosser than the other, and she knew that, if she should ever desire such a thing, it would be okay to bring friends to hold her down, and okay to videotape the procedure. She wondered if even Miss Manners was aware of these nuances.

Finally, she knew six different ways the penis could be pierced, including the ever popular Prince Albert ("parallel" the poster had gravely explained, "through the urethra").

She had to admit that nose rings were pretty tame when there were questions like these to be explored.

She had found the piercing topic in the Sex conference and what the hell, she thought, why not stay there?

An entirely unembarrassed crowd of men and women who couldn't see each other's faces frolicked happily on their virtual bed, merrily tackling such questions as "The Best Phone Sex I Ever Had," "What I'd Never Do Again," "Flirting Online," and "Who I'd Most Like to Do It With."

None of the people she'd met posted here except Layne, who seemed more earnest about seeing that the gay side was presented than carefree about dirty talk in cyberspace.

She had to admit to a fascination with "Flirting Online." Here people described (presumably in front of the people they were talking about) what happened when you knew only what a person wanted you to know about him or her. They liked each other's postings, they bantered publicly, they engaged in E-mail, they wrote in a chatty, friendly way, and somewhere they crossed the line into flirting. Next thing you knew they were turning out porn and slavering for each other. So they did what civilized people do at the fin de siècle—they made a coffee date.

And went "Yuck" on sight.

Or else they didn't—maybe they liked each other fine, maybe they even fell in love for a while.

Or maybe they never met at all. Looking through, Skip could see what appeared to be a lot of stories about "relationships" that were never consummated by a meeting F2F.

It seemed a metaphor for the whole phenomenon of virtual communities somehow—a lot of people pretending they knew each other. And liking it a lot better that way.

In a way, she thought with horror, *this is my life. I don't really know Steve Steinman at all. In a way, all we've got is a phone relationship. Oh, sure, we see each other every few months, but I wonder if we really know each other—if you really can in a few days here, a few days there?*

And then the inevitable thought: *What's wrong with me? I've got to be crazy, trying to have a long-distance relationship.*

But wait, he's supposed to be moving here.

Unless he isn't.

I don't know him at all. Maybe he never meant to. Maybe he likes long-distance things because it's so much easier to get along with somebody you don't have to be with. To pretend she's who you want and never see who she is.

She logged off and went to bed.

● ●

After Pearce's urging, she'd decided definitely to go to Geoff's memorial service. Feeling insecure after last night's doubts, she called Steve before she left, time difference be damned.

She'd awakened him, but, happily, he wasn't mad; seemed delighted, in fact. "Skip. I was going to call you today. Listen, we really have to talk. Something great's happening to me. I haven't told you because I wasn't sure it was going to work. Then when you asked the other night . . . I don't know. I wasn't ready."

"What?" Her heart raced. He'd said it was great, but it wasn't, it was bad news; she felt it.

"What's wrong? You don't sound right."

"Nothing. I just don't have much time, that's all."

"This might take some time."

She felt as if she knew what the medieval witches meant about the devil's icy member. She was feeling nailed to the wall by something cold and hard, something male and deceitful.

Worst fears confirmed, she thought. *He's not moving here.*

She said, "Damn! Cappello's calling me. Call you back, okay?"

"You're at work already?"

She wasn't.

She was sitting at her kitchen table. She didn't move for a while, waiting for the numbness to wear off. She cursed herself:

Didn't I call it? Didn't I know? And I got right in it anyway. I believed him. Shit. I acted like I believe in virtual reality or something.

Because a guy in L.A. is not the real world. Definitely not.

Fuck! How could I have been so dumb?

Feeling spacey, not trusting herself to drive, she had another quick cup of coffee. She felt a little hopped up and a lot better when she arrived at the church.

She saw Cole Terry with a stunning woman in a sleek black suit and blue blouse. Surely it couldn't be Marguerite.

But it was. Skip saw how she could have caught men's roving and wandering eyes so many years ago, and probably still did. She was obviously a genius with makeup, someone who could upstage a bride at her own wedding if she wanted to. Her formerly lank, greasy hair now looked shiny and handsome, pinned up in a becoming tight bun.

The Terrys were with a young woman who was obviously their daughter. She was as beautiful as Marguerite, or she was going to be, Skip thought. She was a little thin, slightly stoop-shouldered and gangly, but otherwise gorgeous. It was the first time Skip had seen her in the light, but she recognized her, even without her favorite accessory. Neetsie'd left her nose ring at home.

Be proud of your height, Skip wanted to say. I'm four inches taller than you—don't embarrass me.

She was six feet tall and wearing heels.

Neetsie was about five-eight, with shiny dark hair like her mother's, and a sprinkling of freckles. She wore a sort of jumper that fell to her ankles, and Doc Martens, indisputedly the hippest footgear at the funeral. Her parents had probably made a deal with her—she could wear them if she dumped the nose ring. They were as ugly as any shoes Skip had ever seen, which indicated they were probably the hippest thing going.

The girl was the picture of filial perfection—petal-soft face, intelligent but innocent, not a mark on it yet, no tiny wrinkle or frown left by one of life's little lessons.

But anybody could be a Satanist. You didn't have to wear black lipstick.

A very old woman was sitting with the Terrys, Marguerite's mother, perhaps. That was good. Skip was dying to talk to her.

Lenore was here too, looking forlorn. She had with her one of the prettiest children in Orleans Parish.

The kid won't last through the service. She'll have to take her out.

Kathryne Brazil was also with her, the handsome woman from the cult.

I wonder if I should get some garlic or a cross, maybe.

There was a man with them too, someone about Brazil's age. Her husband, perhaps?

The service started.

Speeches were made; sermons delivered; hymns sung. And suddenly, Mike Kavanagh was going for the pulpit.

Skip had been drifting, hadn't heard what had been said the moment before, but it seemed as if people had been asked to give spontaneous eulogies. Mike wore a brown suit buttoned over a body that had changed size twice since its purchase. His hair was slicked back with water. His face was the rosy pink of impatiens in the springtime. His voice was full of tears.

"I've known Geoff Kavanagh longer'n anybody in this room except his mama and she's only known him about thirty minutes longer. His daddy was my brother and losin' that person in a person's life is probably more than a person can take. 'Specially if the person's four years old.

"Now I didn't know Geoff as well the first four years of his life as I did the next four or five, but when we got together he was one crazy mixed-up kid. He was the baddest little kid you ever saw in your whole life. Why, he used to pee on the living room rug just to watch his mama burst into tears."

Skip glanced at Marguerite, and a more perfect expression of hatred she couldn't conceive.

Mike waited for the Southern politeness that constituted a laugh track in such situations. "I'm tellin' you that boy and I went through just about everything you can imagine and I don't mind telling you, I used the back of my hand once or twice."

This time it occurred to Skip to look at Cole. His jaw was clenched and so, she thought, was his whole body. She couldn't see his hands or Marguerite's, but Skip imagined them entwined and white-knuckled.

Mike went on for nearly half an hour, telling the story of a little hellion turned into a worthwhile human being by the story's hero, Mike Kavanagh. And then he spent five minutes praising Geoff—Dr. Frankenstein admiring his creation; Pygmalion adoring his statue. When he stepped down, he stumbled.

God, I hope somebody has something else to say. What a miserable little send-off.

Fortunately, people did: Knowles Kennedy from the video store, and Layne, and Pearce Randolph, who gave a graceful little talk about Vidkid on the TOWN that sounded almost like an adventure yarn. Marguerite smiled through it.

Then one more hymn and it was over. People cried and hugged each other and went to talk to the family. Skip wished fervently that she could divide up into thirty invisible eavesdroppers, capable of covering every conversation at once.

"Pearce was good, wasn't he?" said someone behind her. She turned to see Honey Diefenthal. "And Marguerite looks like a million."

"You look good too." She looked as if her little black suit had been made for her—by Karl Lagerfeld, probably. How did these tiny Southern women do it? Skip felt like a mountain in a dress with no waistline, Empire-style, and short sleeves shaped like stiffly starched bells. Why couldn't she ever find the little-nothing dresses?

Because you don't have a little-nothing figure.

Oh, well, this wasn't a fashion show. "Do you know a woman named Kathryne Brazil?"

"No, why?"

"She's with Geoff's girlfriend." Skip pointed out Lenore. "The man might be her husband."

"Why, that's Butsy." The first syllable rhymed with "put."

"And who might Butsy be?"

"Oh, just some old wheeler-dealer. He's been around for years, with no visible means of income. That must be his little girl. She was Geoff's true love?"

"Marguerite seems to think so. Cute baby, huh?"

Honey shook her head, though even W. C. Fields would have thought so. "That girl just doesn't look like a mother."

"Could the other woman be *her* mother?"

"Oh, God no. Butsy was divorced half a century ago." She frowned, staring at Kathryne Brazil. "I don't think I've ever seen her." As she finished the sentence, she let out her breath in a "Whoof," having been grabbed around the waist by an exuberant ex-husband.

Skip broke away to lurk near the family, but couldn't get near Marguerite and Cole. The old woman sat alone in her pew. Lenore, looking anxious, her baby on her hip, fought her way toward her. "Mrs. Julian?" The old woman's expression did not change. "Mrs. Julian?" Lenore's face was as bright and happy as a schoolgirl's. "Mrs. Julian, it's Lenore. This is Caitlin, my little girl." She got no response, but she kept beaming. "I'm so happy to see you."

"Are you my nurse? Can I eat now?" Mrs. Julian spoke very softly, her voice giving away how little energy she had left, how little life.

Lenore, who throughout the service had not cried for Geoff, began to sob. "Oh, Mrs. Julian. Mrs. Julian; oh, no!" She tried to put her arms around the old woman's matchstick shoulders, but Mrs. Julian sat stiff and rigid as a guard at Buckingham Palace.

Embarrassed, Skip turned around.

"Kathryne! What on earth are you doing here?"

The words had been more or less snarled.

Kathryne Brazil's voice was warm. "Cole. I'm so sorry for your loss."

"You didn't know Geoff!" He sounded outraged.

"Not very well. But I've heard a lot about him from Lenore. I came for her. And for Neetsie and Suby, of course."

"Neetsie? My daughter? You know my *daughter*?" He wasn't pleased about it.

11

• •

Instead of going back to the office, Skip went home for lunch, stopping off for a sandwich to go. She arrived burdened with a paper-wrapped po'boy and a Coke in a giant red cup. She quickly wolfed the sandwich, then allowed herself twenty minutes of languishing about, and ten of closed-eyed napping.

Better than a restaurant any day, she thought, arriving fresh at Homicide. Her phone was ringing.

"Langdon."

It was the 911 operator. "I've got a call about a burglary. I've got a car on the way, but the lady wants to talk to you."

Before Skip could answer, she switched the call.

"Oh, God! I was afraid you wouldn't be there." It was a female voice, close to hysterical.

"Who is this?"

"Lenore Marquer. You remember me?"

"Are you all right? What's going on?"

"They hit my house."

"*What?*"

"I'm so worried. I'm so afraid for my little girl."

"Lenore, what's happened?"

"Somebody ransacked my house."

"Okay, try to be calm just a few minutes more. Could the burglar still be there?"

"Oh, shit!"

"Could he?"

She started to cry. "I don't know."

"Take your little girl and go outside, far from the house—go across the street or down to the corner, and wait for me."

Lenore lived Uptown near the river, in the quiet, old-fashioned area near Audubon Park. It's a funny old neighborhood, run-down in one part of a block, spiffy in another. Some of the streets don't have sidewalks.

Lenore's house was one of the beat-up ones, a shotgun covered with asbestos shingles, the tiny yard overgrown with weeds and planted only with a huge palm.

Mother and child were across the street, as ordered, both crying, both looking in need of a mom. The marked car pulled up at the same time Skip did.

She and the other officer entered the house, guns drawn, threw open the closets, went through the whole place quickly. It was empty.

And one of the most prodigious messes Skip had ever seen.

When she came back out, Lenore practically hung on her skirts. "I'm so glad I got you. Jesus, I'm scared. Caitlin, this is Officer Langdon. Say hello to Officer Langdon."

The little girl hid her face.

"She's tired. I don't know if I can face this. Do you need to look at anything?"

"The other officer does. And then you do. To see if anything's missing."

"Oh, God."

"You have to do it sometime. It's probably better while I'm here."

"You'll wait?"

"I've been wanting to talk to you anyway."

"We could go around back. Would that be okay?"

"I'll meet you there in a minute."

The district officer was a young woman, barely in her twenties. She was average height and slight, but otherwise reminded Skip of herself a couple of years ago—not long ago at all. She was very new and very eager.

"What's your name?"

"Susie Rountree."

"Skip Langdon, Homicide. Listen, I'm going to need a very thorough investigation here, and I'll need prints. Call the crime lab and get them out here." Seeing Rountree's puzzled expression, she said, "This could be just a burglary—or it could be related to a homicide."

Rountree perked up.

"Do as thorough a report as you can, okay?"

Rountree looked as if she'd died and gone to heaven.

It was all Skip could do not to wince. *Was I ever that green?*

Rejoining Lenore, Skip was surprised to find her seated near a small oval swimming pool.

Skip said, "I didn't expect that."

"It was the original reason I rented the house—otherwise it's pretty run-down. But then Caitlin came along and it got to be a big safety hazard. Now I have to keep it filled up even in the winter—" It did have water in it, and lots of grunge. "I mean, if she falls in water, at least she's got a chance, right? She's already had swimming lessons, and in the summer we do have fun." Her eyes moved to the little girl and she slipped into baby talk. "Isn't that right? Isn't that right, Petunia?" She picked the baby up. "Caitlin's really tired. I'll hold her and maybe she'll go to sleep."

There were a few plastic chairs on an old patio near the pool, some nice palm trees, and a banana or two. Someone had once cared about the yard.

"Good thing there's sun today." Lenore pulled Caitlin onto her lap, and Skip noticed for the first time that it was a very lovely day indeed. A day that might have been manufactured in September and saved for a couple of months, till it had reached full golden mellowness.

She sat in one of the chairs. "Tell me about you and Geoff. How did you meet?"

"Oh, we've known each other forever—since we were kids. But we met again on the TOWN. It's wild—just about everybody who's on it here got on it through somebody else—I mean they all knew each other and that's how they got on. But I started taking computer classes at UNO and got interested that way. When I saw Geoff was on it, I started flirting with him."

"You started it?"

"Well, I don't really remember, but anyway—"

"What?"

"I'd almost forgotten it started that way. I think people thought I was his girlfriend—his family and everything."

"You weren't?"

"Not really. I was kind of lonely at first, so—well, maybe a little then. But neither of us was really interested. What we wanted was a best friend."

"I thought Layne was Geoff's best friend."

"Is that what he says?"

"It's not true?"

She looked vaguely around the garden. "I don't know. I guess they were kind of close."

While her eyes wandered and her baby cuddled, Skip hit her with the thing she really wanted to know. "How'd you get the autopsy report on him?"

If she'd expected a big reaction, she had to be satisfied with a shrug. "I know someone in the coroner's office."

"Who?"

"Tom Renault."

"And how do you know him?"

"Through a group I belong to."

"A group." Skip let it sit there. Skulls, black hoods, coroner's deputies—did these things go together?

"Parents Without Partners," said Lenore.

"Come on, Lenore. Tom Renault's gay."

"Well, he hasn't always been. His ex-wife's a hopeless alcoholic; and his lover died, poor man." Skip didn't ask for details. She could check it easily enough.

"Tell me something else—did Geoff tell you any secrets?"

"What kind of secrets?"

"Anything to do with what he remembered. Anything at all you think might be important."

Lenore shut her eyes, thinking. But she came back shaking her head. "I can't remember anything." Her eyes wandered again and when they returned to Skip, they were watery. "When we were kids, we just played together—it wasn't a big deal. But his grandmother was my music teacher. I only took from her a year, but I'll never forget it."

"Why not?"

"Because she was just about the only adult who ever was nice to me. It was so awful to see her today. She's lost it, did you see?"

Skip thought Lenore knew very well that she had seen—that Lenore had seen her watching, and noted it for reasons of her own. She said, "You must know Neetsie and Suby too."

"A little, sure. But not through Geoff especially, through the TOWN. Neetsie's dad got her on it, the same as he got Geoff on. And then Geoff got Suby on."

Time to ask her about Kathryne Brazil? Something told Skip to wait.

She certainly wasn't ready to ask about the skull and robes.

Lenore said: "God, I miss Geoff! But I'm doing a little better. I'm handling it, I think." She blew her nose.

When the crime lab and Rountree had gone, Skip asked Lenore to go through the house.

"Would you mind going with me?"

"Okay."

And without asking, she handed the baby to Skip.

If I were a male cop, I wonder if she'd have done that.

But the little girl cuddled sweetly, so she could hardly be mad.

It was a funny thing. Skip had read somewhere that most police officers, queried as to why they'd chosen their jobs, said they "wanted to help." *How often,* she thought, *do you really get that opportu-*

nity? It wasn't glamorous, it wasn't busting scumbags, but there was something satisfying about following Lenore from room to room, holding little Caitlin.

Lenore went through her jewelry box; her underwear drawer, where she'd stashed a wad of cash; her medicine cabinet, where she had what she called "prescription drugs"; and her living room, where her TV and VCR reposed.

Skip noticed that some of the candles from the other night were still in place. "You must like candles."

"Ummf."

The altar had been dismantled, but some of its accoutrements were scattered about the room, including the pentacle plate. "How unusual!" Skip said, picking it up as if to admire it. "What's it for, exactly?"

"It's my lucky star." Lenore gave her a warm smile. "A friend gave it to me."

So much for innocently teasing out cult information. Yet Lenore didn't seem particularly rattled. She gave Skip a puzzled look, absently holding her arms for Caitlin. "It looks as if everything's here."

"Did Geoff give you anything to keep? A book, perhaps?"

"No, why?"

"You must think this has something to do with his death—you asked to speak to me."

Lenore took a moment to answer. "I don't know. Maybe I do. It's funny, I didn't think about it. I just saw you at Geoff's funeral and I thought of you." She paused, serving to turn the idea over in her head. "You're the only cop I know."

That was New Orleans—you talked to whom you knew, and you just about always knew someone.

Skip said, "Are you going to the TOWN dinner tonight? Pearce invited me."

"You're kidding. That'll be great." She really seemed to brighten.

Lenore genuinely seemed to like her. And she *had* asked for Skip—like a good little citizen—when she discovered her burglary. Could it all be an act?

120

Easily.

Skip spent the rest of the day at Geoff's computer, calling up his directory and reading his files, end to end, one after another, until her eyes hurt and her body twitched from boredom. Most of what he had used his computer for was computer-related; at any rate, it didn't seem to be English.

Neither, on the other hand, did it seem to be a secret code. Disappointed, she had to conclude that if Geoff had kept a journal, he had done it the old-fashioned way. There were a few letters and some notes on movies and books, but other than that, almost nothing personal.

● ●

R&O's, the restaurant set for the TOWN dinner, was sometimes confused with the elegant Arnaud's, but offered a very different dining experience. It was a barn of a place out by the lake, serving all the basic seafoods and sandwiches—nothing fancy, just good. A little noisy for a meeting like this, but otherwise you couldn't fault it.

Lenore was the first person Skip saw when she arrived, sitting once more with Kathryne Brazil. Bigeasy was there too, already at the bottom of a beer.

She held out a hand to Brazil and introduced herself.

"I'm Kit," said the other woman. "Are you new on the TOWN?"

"I'm not on it at all. Pearce invited me—I'm a police officer investigating Geoff Kavanagh's death."

Something that wasn't delight crossed Kit's face.

"Oh, dear, is that a problem? Maybe I shouldn't stay."

But Layne arrived and broke into an ear-to-ear grin. "Skip. Nice to see you."

Kit had the grace to turn pink. "I'm sorry. I didn't mean to be rude. Lenore, are you okay with this?"

Lenore nodded, somehow quieter around Kit. Submissive almost.

"Stay, please," said her protector.

Layne said, "Who else is coming?"

"Neetsie and Suby." Pearce signaled a waitress. "Another beer, please. Anybody else?"

When orders were taken, Skip turned to Kit. "Do you work with computers?"

"Me? No, I'm a nurse. I just got on the TOWN because of a private conference I knew about. And because everybody I knew was on it."

"Oh?"

"Well, that was in Kansas City, if you can fathom that. There's a really great medical conference, and the people I worked with lived and died for it. They were the ones who told me about the other one—the private conference." Starting to relax, she smiled. "So of course when I moved here, I got in touch with all the TOWNsfolk. Great people. Suby, hi. Neetsie—I'm glad you came. I didn't think you would."

The two young women had come in together, and now hugged everyone but Skip. Neetsie's nose ring (out for the funeral, in again now) made her want to avert her eyes. She thought of herself as a rebel, and hated being such a fuddy-duddy.

But it isn't judgment, it's aesthetics. Can I help it if the thing turns my stomach?

She wondered why Neetsie had it. In L.A., it would be one thing; in New Orleans, it was quite another. Here, everybody would notice. Almost no one would like it. Yet Neetsie seemed in most ways perfectly conformist. Maybe she liked stirring people up.

But that's hostile.

And why shouldn't she be hostile? Two murders in one family is more than the national norm.

Skip reflected, as she did when she saw family violence, that you couldn't know what goes on in a household.

Once, when she'd been sent to the scene of a nasty beating, the atmosphere in the house had seemed so charged, so electric with brutality and hate, that a line had come to her, a paraphrase: "In these mean rooms a woman must live."

She'd thought about it later—couldn't get it out of her mind— and it had become her phrase for unhappy households, enclosed spaces where families clawed at one another, ripped each other's psyches open, dined on each other's Achilles tendons: *Mean rooms— where you always hurt the one you love.*

She'd walked down her share of mean streets, but not nearly so often as she walked and talked and sat in mean rooms. She saw them every day, in every case, and usually they looked and felt like any other rooms. She was quite sure those on the mean streets came out of them.

Kit said, "I'm not as much in love with the TOWN as all these folks."

"Oh, Kit, you spend two hours a day on it."

"Two hours a week's more like it. And that's just because I don't have time to have real relationships. That's what I think's wrong with it. It's a pacifier. You think you're in a relationship, but you're not."

Neetsie rolled her eyes. "Can we ever forget the cybercad?"

Skip was interested. "Cybercad?"

"Well, you know how people have romances online? I mean they start E-mailing people and then one thing and another?"

"I told her all about it." Pearce was trying to sound bored, but Skip sensed he was slightly uncomfortable.

She nodded. "But not about the cybercad."

"What happened was, someone in the women's conference was crying publicly about her lost love. She mentioned a few sweet nothings he'd whispered before he disappeared and someone else said, 'Hold it. This has a familiar ring.' So they compared notes and what do you know, they'd been through the same thing with the same guy.

"It seems he had a little system—he'd flatter and carry on, and tell a few of his deepest secrets just to let them know how intimate it all was, and encourage them to tell secrets. They would and then he'd know all their vulnerable spots. Funny thing—when it was all over, it turned out there were six of them and every single one of them overweight. A lot of it was specific flattery about their particular body types. Who knows? Maybe he just liked big women, but they didn't think so. They thought he'd sought them out because of their lack of self-esteem.

"Anyway, he'd call them first thing in the morning (which he could do because they lived all over the country), and have phone sex with them."

"Phone sex?"

"Uh-huh. They said it was some of the best they ever had, meaning, I guess, that he wasn't the first guy they'd done it with. Then he'd say he'd love to see them F2F, but he just couldn't afford a plane ticket and would they help him out? By this time, they'd be deeply obsessive, and they'd split the cost of the plane ticket. Then he'd come and treat them to great sex—they all agreed about this part, though certain other women later said he was lousy—then dump them. And along the way he'd declare his love and insist on exclusivity. But all the while he'd have a bunch of them on the string."

"Don't forget," said Lenore, "he swore them all to secrecy too."

"What a creep."

Layne nodded. "So we had an old-fashioned village stoning."

By now they were all eating some fries they'd ordered to amuse themselves till dinner arrived. Pearce picked one up and waved it like a wand. "Some people called it a lynch mob."

Kit said, "Bullshit!"

"Of course none of them were women."

"But how did it work?" asked Skip.

"They started a topic about it in the women's conference and we decided it warranted a public warning. So we issued it. And all hell broke loose." Kit rolled her eyes.

Pearce nodded. "I can't think why I forgot to tell you about it. A true exercise in virtual community. Okay, here's how it went: A public warning is issued. Then TOWNspeople come to the women's aid, to give support and say what heroes they are for coming forth; next thing you know someone says, 'Wait a minute, we've only heard one side of the story.'

"But the perp's away for the weekend, so his side doesn't get heard for a while. Meanwhile, he gets called names. 'Perp' for one. And 'sociopath' was bandied around quite a bit. About now, people are starting to pat themselves on the back. They're saying things like 'We're important pioneers out here in cyberspace and the fabric of our virtual community was nearly rent. However, we handled it! And a good thing, because things like this are a threat to trail-blazers and virtual towns the world over.'

"Meanwhile another faction is saying, 'Hold it, this is a virtual lynch mob and I want no part of it.' "

"While participating loudly and acrimoniously," said Neetsie.

"The funny thing was," Pearce continued, "it ended up being just like life. People who'd had their own problems on the TOWN and didn't like the fallout took the guy's side, most women took the women's side, and so did most of the hard-core VC types."

"What's VC?"

" 'Virtual community.' See, this isn't just a way of wasting time, it's a whole philosophy. A lot of people are really large on the concept as some kind of futurist ideal."

Kit said, "Excuse me while I barf."

"Could you do that later?" said Layne. The food was arriving.

"Look, the TOWN has done a lot of good things for me. When I first went on it I had a medical problem I needed help with—I'm a nurse and couldn't get it from my own community; strangers helped me. And since then I've met some great people—right, guys?"

The three women glowed at her, but Pearce seemed to be try-ing to force a smile. Only Layne, if Skip read him right, was indif-ferent.

"And I enjoy it. It's like playing solitaire and eating bonbons—you know you could be improving your mind, but screwing around's more fun. But look—" She threw both hands out in front of her, a lot of energy behind the gesture. "Geoff's dead because of it. Okay?"

"Kit, I really don't think the TOWN killed him." Pearce's voice was cold and dry.

And condescending, Skip thought. *The guy's got a mean streak.*

"Well, somebody on the TOWN did. And it could be argued that in a way the system did. He thought he was among friends, he posted things he shouldn't have made public, and somebody he couldn't see was out there."

"How exactly is that the fault of the system?"

"I don't mean the TOWN, or even the idea of bulletin boards.

If people want other people to know something, let them post it. What I mean is the whole virtual community idea—the idea that this thing is anything different from what you'd get if you wrote a letter. Do you really think Geoff would have written letters to ten thousand strangers about his father being killed? Nobody would. They'd have better sense. When they really thought about it, they'd realize it was nobody's business, and had no real point anyway. I mean, think about it—think about ninety percent of the stuff on the TOWN. Why does anyone need to know? What do I care what someone in Idaho thought of a movie, for instance?"

Layne cleared his throat. "Well, I think the TOWN does a service—"

"Service! A lot of services. But I'm just not sure this promiscuous posting of opinions is one of them. And frankly, Compu-Serve and America Online probably offer a lot more in terms of things you can really learn or access."

She sat back in her chair, apparently a bit flustered about becoming so heated.

Suby grinned. "Good use of 'promiscuous.' "

Layne looked thoughtful. "In a way, you have a point. Kit, I mean, not Suby. In fact, Suby's point made me think of mine—which is that you don't see all that many carefully composed epistles on the TOWN, not all that many good uses of words."

Pearce snorted. "That's because nobody under thirty knows any."

Whereupon Neetsie, seated next to him, slugged him, not altogether playfully, and Suby threw a hunk of bread at him.

There was quiet for a moment and Neetsie said, "I wanted to thank everyone for coming to the service."

"I'm so sorry about your brother," said Skip.

"Thank you," said Neetsie, and her eyes filled. "I just wanted to say that."

"Sorry about my dad," said Suby, and looked down, red spots popping out on her cheeks.

I shouldn't have come, Skip thought. *I forgot there'd be relatives here.*

"You know, I think I really should go," she said.

126

Neetsie stopped her. "No, stay. Pearce would have uninvited you if we hadn't wanted you."

I should have known. He E-mailed them right after I left.

That meant even Kit had agreed.

"Why?" she asked.

"We thought the more stuff you knew about the TOWN, the better your chances." Her eyes got wet again. "Do you know what it means to lose a brother?"

In my case, it might be a pleasure.

Sensitivity prevented her from speaking aloud. Instead, she said, "Can you talk about him?"

Neetsie nodded.

"Are you sure? This might be hard."

"Go ahead."

"What did you really love about him?" Skip asked the question not to torture his sister, but once again seeking the man behind the nerd.

The girl's face turned into a sunflower. "When I was seven years old, he woke me up in the middle of the night to watch Toots have her puppies. I didn't even know she was pregnant—I never even heard the word or anything. Can you imagine what that was like when you're seven, watching little bitty dogs come out of a big one? 'Isn't it wonderful?' he said. 'You could do that some day, but I can't.' Then he said, 'It's life. That's really life,' and he just kept staring at her, birthin' those babies, and finally, when it was all over, he said, 'Go back to bed before Mom catches us. I told her I wouldn't wake you up.'

"But he did, anyway. He really wanted me to see that."

12

• •

I had imagined him dead so many hundreds of times, and yet I could not have conceived of the horror of it. I must have seen two hundred dead bodies by that time, but when it is someone you know, no matter how much you may have hated him—and for good reason—no matter how much he may have hurt someone you love deeply, you love life more. It is a fact of biology, of our DNA, and is perhaps as simple and basic, as ignoble in the end, as the urge to rut.

Whatever my mind told me, my good, rational, U. Va., white male mind, I was ill at the sight of him, would have given anything to pluck out the bullet and repair the torn flesh.

I believe Marguerite felt the same. She cried torrents, as if he had not made every moment of her waking life a living hell. She was beautiful in her grief, her despair not for Leighton, but for the same thing for which I grieved—for the rawness of life itself. And perhaps for her child; I cannot say that I will ever really know what went on in Marguerite's mind, only that she is a force of nature.

She was magnificent today. I believe if I had seen her for the first time in that church, in her severely chic widow's weeds, instead of so many years ago in the Dream Palace, she would have had the same effect. Cole Terry, on the other hand, is rather a horse's ass.

• •

Pearce had written a little bit of "Regrets," the thing he cared about, as a sort of warm-up to working on the story about the murder. He really did need to get started on that.

Because this was the story that was going to resurrect his entire career. And his life.

He knew how to do it now.

He could scrap the damn stupid screenplay he was working on—about the eighteenth story in as many years—and turn this one into a movie. And it would sell too, because it would make national news and maybe *People* magazine, which everyone knew was the bible of every producer in Hollywood.

The plan was simple. He could hardly believe he'd been so brilliant as to think of it—it really did kill quite a few birds with one stone.

("If you'll excuse the expression," he said to himself, stroking his mustache devilishly.)

Who first? he thought.

But there was really no competition.

Without even calling first, he drove to Lenore's. She had decided late last night, at the TOWN dinner, to call in sick again today.

"Pearce!" she squealed. "I was okay last night, wasn't I?" She seemed surprised to see him. "I mean, I know I was weepy, but under the circumstances—"

He took her hand. "I was worried about you, that's all."

"You're such a sweetheart. Honestly, I think Kit's wrong about the TOWN. All my best friends are on it—I don't know what I'd do without you."

He had to get her talking, get her loose. "I thought you might want to take a walk."

"Oh. Well, I kept Caitlin home today. She's asleep."

"Let's have a beer then. I want you to relax."

She came back with two beers, smiling for a change. That wasn't especially like Lenore. He wondered if she'd dropped something. Maybe Prozac. The whole world was on Prozac these days. "You're such a good friend to me," she said.

She sat beside him on the sofa, rather than in one of the chairs. Did that mean what he thought it did? He put out a hand and let it rest on her neck for a millisecond. Gently, he began to massage her. "I was thinking last night how stressed out you must be."

"Neetsie too. She lost a brother."

"You lost your best friend. Maybe that's worse."

She settled into his working hand, adjusted her body to accommodate it. "I've been thinking about Geoff a lot."

"We all have."

"I was so mean about stuff."

"Oh?"

"Sex, I mean. I never wanted to have sex with him."

"Why don't you put your head in my lap? I can't get to your other shoulder."

She complied.

"I mean, what would it have hurt? I can't help it. I feel so guilty about it."

"You and Geoff didn't have sex?"

"Not very much." She giggled. "Not if I could help it."

"But you did something even more important."

"What?" She lifted her head she was so surprised; the young were absurdly single-minded.

"You confided in each other."

She lowered her head. "Oh. Well, yeah, we did."

• •

Lenore hadn't realized he was such a big teddy bear—he was just Bigeasy, TOWN guru. But not really the uncle type.

It was sweet of him to check up on her; she hadn't really thought he was that good a friend. But she shouldn't have doubted. The TOWN was the village and he was the village elder; it was natural he should call her on. It made her feel warm and fuzzy, almost as if she'd had to lose Geoff to find out she had other friends. Usually she was so busy with Caitlin she didn't have much time left over.

I must take time, she thought. *I have to start a new life.*

130

Geoff had filled up a lot of holes for her. He had always been there when she wanted some oysters, wanted to go to a movie.

For now, the beer was really very relaxing. And it was nice of Pearce to rub her neck, something Geoff never did. He was really a very thoughtful man and there were so few thoughtful men in her life. In fact, no men at all unless she counted her father.

Lying on her stomach, she felt Pearce pat her upper back, almost like burping a baby. "You'll get over it, Lenore. We've all lost somebody valuable but we'll all get over it."

She realized she was crying.

Astonished, she sat up. "I wasn't crying for Geoff. I was crying for me."

"Well, it's only natural."

"No, you don't understand. I was feeling sorry for myself because I realized that without Geoff, days could go by and I'd never see another adult except the people at the store."

"Young lady, you're going to have to get out more."

"What'll I do? What do people do who've just lost someone close?"

"Let's have another beer, shall we?"

She went to get a pair of them.

When Pearce had taken a healthy sip—in fact, slugged down about a third of the bottle—he said, "I'll tell you what you can do. You can keep an old man company every now and then."

"You're not old." She knew he was just being nice, that he didn't need company and had no intention of hanging out with her.

"I'm old and I'm lonesome."

Lonesome. Now that was something else. Did he find her attractive?

He must, she thought with sudden interest. *Of course he does. Why wouldn't he?*

But put in that context, he *was* old. She couldn't . . . no, she just couldn't possibly . . . he was nice and everything, but he was her dad's age.

"It's sweet that you and Geoff could confide in each other. I envy you that."

"You don't . . . uh . . . have anybody . . . ?"

"Come on. Who'd want to tell me their secrets?"

"Well, you're a nice-looking man."

"But do I have an honest face?"

"Sure."

"Well, tell me something. Did you and Geoff talk much about the flashbacks he was having?"

"We talked about things a lot. Thoughts. Stuff on the TOWN."

"Did he ever say anything to you about a citrine ring?"

"What's citrine? I never even heard the word."

"Let me rub your feet, shall I?"

•   •

Neetsie had called at midmorning. "Dad, I need to talk. I just don't . . . I can't . . ."

"What is it, honey?"

"I don't know. I got through yesterday fine; I even went to dinner with friends and they talked about Geoff and I was absolutely okay. But today I woke up crying and I . . ."

"It's hard on all of us, sweetheart."

"But I couldn't even go to work. I mean, that isn't even the point. It's not just that I feel sad, it's that I'm afraid."

"Afraid of what?"

"I don't know. I'm just . . ."

"Well, look. I'll come get you."

"No!"

"What?"

"I don't want to see Mom."

So Cole had gone to Neetsie's, to comfort a daughter coming face-to-face with her own mortality. She had always come to him when she was afraid, and it seemed to him that she was afraid a lot, of one thing and another.

He didn't know how to comfort her, how to tell her that the worst might be over, that if she had even the slightest success in the world, she'd never again have to live in the kind of poverty in which she'd been brought up.

Not that her apartment was a step up—the opposite, in fact. It was a roach-infested studio in the Faubourg—a big one, but in disrepair, although furnished cleverly. Neetsie was nothing if not clever. She could have been a designer. Instead, she had some piddling job at a computer store, and wouldn't get another because she didn't want anything that took too much of her energy; she needed to have an arid work life so that her real work, her acting, could blossom.

This was her theory.

His was that as long as she had to work all day, she might as well do something that paid well.

He found her wearing jeans and a long black sweater, Kleenex in hand.

"Oh, Dad!" She stared at him, a hard, beseeching, "give-my-brother-back" kind of stare, but she didn't throw her arms around him. He sensed that she didn't want to be held.

"What is it, honey?"

She flung herself on her duded-up bed; he sat in her one director's chair.

"Life is just so fragile." She sobbed out the last couple of words, apparently in the grip of a depression she couldn't shake.

"Let's go for a walk."

"Why?"

"Because you'll feel the wind in your face, and it'll make you feel alive. And you'll move your butt; endorphins will kick in."

She made a face. "That's the last thing I want to do. I don't feel like budging. I can barely get to the bathroom when I have to pee."

"You said you felt afraid." How many conversations had he had with her that started like this? How many with Marguerite?

"I don't know. I might have a lump in my breast."

He might have panicked, but he had been here before. "You're pretty young for that."

"Well, it might just be a rib. But I feel hot all over, and then cold, and it seems like my heart beats really fast. Do you know what palpitations are, Daddy?"

"You get them when you fall in love."

"I'm not kidding, I think I'm sick."

"Two people in the same family can't die within a week. What do you think the odds of that would be?"

"It happens all the time. Somebody gets stressed out and drops dead at the funeral."

"The funeral's over. Anyway, those people are a lot older than you." He wanted to go over and take her hands, but he knew better. When she was this way, she was in a shell that she didn't want violated. "Listen to me. You're fine. You're just upset and you are stressed out. But at your age, stress can't do all that much to you."

"It can give you ulcers."

"How's your tummy?"

"Fine." She actually smiled. "It's my chest that feels funny."

"Dr. John says you've got a broken heart."

She laughed. "Do Dr. John."

Dr. John was a part he'd always played for her when she was sick; it was based partly on the voodoo priest of the slave days, and partly on the contemporary musician, whose records Cole would play, and whose hoarse voice he'd use, when "curing" her.

He raised his hands and made them into claws. "By lizard and snake and skull and scorpion, I lift the hurt and ease the pain." His voice was like gravel. He got up and began to dance in a circle around Neetsie, the choreography inspired by movies whose makers had failed to research Native American culture.

"Dr. John put a spell on you! Put the gris-gris on that hurt!" He pronounced it "hoit" like the musician, which made Neetsie laugh.

He stretched out his arms, made V's of his fingers and chanted, "Anita Bonita Juanita be cured! Mojo work and gris-gris take root. Out of this girl, broken heart be lured!"

"Daddy. It's the only heart I've got."

"Oh. Okay." He did the whole thing again, with the V's and the gravelly voice. "Out of this girl, the sadness be lured!" He made the last word a big deal. And then he started to dance around some more, singing the mojo song, like he always did when he played Dr. John: "I got my mojo working, got my mojo workin', and it sure do work on you."

He dropped into a squat at her feet. "Feel better?"

She nodded, smiling, almost her normal self. "I love Dr. John. Maybe it's why I want to be an actress."

"Sweetheart, I hope you can do better than that." He picked himself up and sat in his chair again.

"You know what that cop asked me? She came to the TOWN dinner last night."

"That's strange."

"Pearce asked her. You know how he is."

Cole nodded. "What did she ask you?"

"She asked me what I liked best about Geoff. I told her about the time he woke me up for the puppies. What did you like best?"

"When I first met him, he was just a little boy about eleven or twelve, and he came over to me and said, 'Do you know how to play baseball and basketball?'

"I said, 'Sure. Why?' But he didn't answer, he just said, 'How about chess?' I said, 'Uh-huh.' And he said, 'Poker?' I don't even remember all the things he asked, but you see what he was doing? He was checking out my daddy qualifications. Just when I thought it was all done, he said, 'Well, what kind of cookies can you bake?' I said, 'Chocolate chip,' and he said, 'Uh-uh. Oatmeal,' and went away. So I knew I was in, as long as I brought some oatmeal cookies every time I came over."

"And that was it? That was the best thing he ever did?"

"Well, no. See, he used the cookies too—like, at first they'd be an excuse to stay around while he ate them. Then he'd offer me some; and then he'd say he'd play catch for a while if I'd bring him some more. You know how kids don't want to say they like you?"

"Boys."

"Okay, boys. Well, that was his way of doing it—pretending he was just in it for the cookies."

"Now you're going to cry."

"I might." Sure enough, his throat had gone tight, but he blinked before anything came out of his eyes.

• •

Marguerite felt hot, was almost sure she was running a fever. She lay down with a comforter. *Sweat it out*, she thought, and wondered if she should make herself a hot toddy.

But Cole should make it for her. Where was he?

Oh, yes, with Neetsie, who for some reason wouldn't come over. Well, at least he had made her take her pill before he went. It was almost working. She almost didn't feel the fever, the sweat at her hairline, on the bottoms of her feet, the cold panic in her stomach.

Cole had said to her, "Two people can't die in the same family in a week," but she thought they could. One death made the rest more vulnerable.

She had to get the opera finished, the work to be dedicated to her mother. If she never did another thing in her life, she had to do that. Because if she didn't do it soon, it probably wouldn't happen, because she had cancer. She knew she did. She didn't examine her breasts because she was sure there were lumps there, didn't look at her back in the mirror (that was where the melanoma probably grew), would rather die than look in the toilet for blood—it would fill up the bowl. It was just a matter of waiting until it wore her down, till she could no longer take care of her animals. But if she really put her mind to it, maybe she could finish the opera first. As soon as this fever broke. Tomorrow.

She closed her eyes.

She must have slept a while. She felt foggy when the dogs barked her awake. The doorbell rang, for the second time, she thought. It was probably someone bringing food; people had come yesterday, after the service. They had been the first guests since Neetsie's slumber-party days. Perhaps it was another one.

She had lain down in her sweats, so she was decent. She merely looked dreadful. But no matter; her son Geoff had just been buried and this might be a mourner. She owed it to him to get up.

It was the cop again.

Oh hell, she thought. *Instant replay.* And opened the door.

Here was a girl who could use a fashion consultant. Even a little advice from a friend would help. Or did you have to wear unflattering knee-length skirts when you were a cop? Gray ones, topped by houndstooth blazers? Surely if you weren't in uniform, you had a choice.

Also, the girl could stand to lose a few pounds. And a hair stylist wouldn't be amiss either. Marguerite had never admired the wild curly look.

"Sorry to bother you again."

"Come in," said Marguerite. This was something one had to do. At least the living room was decent; Neetsie and Cole had picked it up yesterday, after everyone left.

"Sit down, won't you?" She was damned if she was going to offer lemonade.

"How are you feeling?"

"Better, I think."

"I saw you at the funeral yesterday. I wonder if that was your mother with you?"

"Yes, it was. She doesn't get out much, but she and Geoff were very close."

"I'd like to get in touch with her."

"Really! What on earth for?" She maintained a cool exterior, but inside she was boiling. Her mother! How dare this bitch?

"It's all just part of the investigation."

"But, Officer, my mother is in a nursing home, and not only that, she's over eighty. Do you really think she managed to break out, hitchhike over here, and heave to the ground the ladder on which the apple of her eye was standing?"

"Let me assure you she's not a suspect. I just have a couple of questions to ask her."

"What kind of questions?"

"That's not really something I can talk about."

The bitch!

Not really something I can talk about. How does she have the nerve to try this crap?

"She's not well at all, to tell you the truth. I'm afraid she really can't be disturbed."

"I'm sorry, but I'm afraid I have to insist."

"She isn't lucid. It's a shame, but . . ." She let the sentence stop in the middle.

"All right then. I'm sure you know I can find her, Mrs. Terry. One other thing. Remember the citrine ring that was stolen when your husband died? I wonder if you know where it is now."

"The ring? What's all this about?"

"I'm just wondering if you've ever seen it since."

"Young lady, my son was buried yesterday! Don't you have anything better to do than come around to a bereaved family asking questions about something that happened twenty-seven years ago?"

The girl had the gall to smile at her. Her grooming wasn't perfect, but she did have perfect teeth. "So you haven't seen it?"

"Of course not! And if you come back here, I'm going to report you."

She smiled again, damn her. "Sorry for the inconvenience."

● ●

Something was up with Marguerite, but Skip wasn't sure what. It was just possible she was so out of it that she really hadn't read Pearce's TOWN stuff in the paper.

But it wasn't likely.

Still, it hadn't been a wasted trip. Skip had gotten the lay of the land, anyway; Marguerite, for whatever reason, was playing dumb. But she'd been entirely too testy. When she broke, she was going to break wide open. The time would be right soon.

That afternoon Skip drove home singing with the radio, knowing she was going to get a break from the case—tonight was the night she and Cindy Lou were going to see the Boucree Brothers.

She had done quite a bit of paperwork after seeing Marguerite, and she'd left work early to do some research on the computer—since she hadn't heard from Wizard, the sysop, she'd gotten impatient; she wanted to work on Geoff's posts on her own.

It was barely after three when she arrived home, but the day was cloudy and it was already getting dark. There was a nasty chill in the air.

But Sheila was on the patio, working on something, maybe homework.

"Hey, babe. Aren't you cold?"

"I'm fine." The girl didn't look up.

Uh-oh, forget about work for a while.

"Come in, why don't you? Let's have some cocoa."

"I don't think so."

Oh, hell, what was it going to take?

"Coffee and beignets?"

Sheila looked up. "Really? I could really have coffee?"

"Well, beignets, anyway."

"I knew it. I knew you didn't mean it."

"Well, I almost meant it. Going once, going twice . . . yes or no to the beignets?"

"Oh, okay."

Skip was almost disappointed, had half wished Sheila would continue to sulk and let her go about her business. "Just a second, okay? I've got to do a little piece of business."

"Can I go with you?"

"Sure."

Sheila followed her inside. "Your place is really nice."

"But freezing. Aren't you cold?" She didn't take off her coat while she phoned the TOWN and left a message for Wizard. "What were you doing outside?"

"Oh, nothing."

"I mean, why weren't you inside?"

"I get tired of it in there."

Skip backed off. The girl wanted to see her, that's why she was outside. "Come on. Let's go get those beignets."

What was going on? she wondered. Was this a bonding attempt, or did she have something on her mind? Maybe she was getting her period or something; she was about the right age.

By way of feeling her out, Skip said, "You know, Jimmy Dee was thinking of getting an au pair to stay with you and Kenny when he's not home. But I talked him out of it. I thought you'd be involved with after-school activities, and then if you were home, there's always Geneese." The maid, she meant—the extremely motherly maid (Skip had seen to that) who doubled as a baby-sitter.

"What the fuck's an au pair?"

"Well, you certainly are a trash-mouth."

"Fuck you, too."

Something was on her mind.

Skip sat down. "What is it, honey? Something's bothering you, isn't it?"

"I hate this place, that's all! And Uncle Jimmy and—" She was yelling, loud, but apparently she couldn't get herself to finish.

"Me."

Instead of answering, she turned and ran.

"Sheila!" Skip followed.

"Leave me alone!" The girl ran through the gate and back to the street, where she fumbled with her key.

"Okay, honey. I will for now. But come talk to me when you want. I'm sorry I called you a trash-mouth—I don't care how you talk. You can say anything you want. Really."

Sheila gave her a glance, just once, before she disappeared, and Skip thought she'd never seen anyone look so pathetic.

13

• •

She booted up her computer and started going through Confession again. But Geoff could have been posting in a hundred other conferences in the same time period. She needed to know his favorites. She called Lenore and Layne, got neither of them.

What did she need to do next?

Warm up.

She made herself a cup of tea and opened the phone book. Where did you order firewood?

If I had a beautiful, warm room, it would be more inviting for the children.

She called around, got some wood on the way, and made a vow to get some furniture. But then she had a better idea.

Art.

I can't afford it.

Well, maybe a little something. A tiny little watercolor? Something by Carol Leake. One of her garage sale things.

Or maybe a few of them.

And plants. I'll have art and plants and a beautiful rug—no, for now, just a warm one, a nice warm gray one, to match the sofa. The kids can lie on it and play Scrabble or something.

She felt a big lump in her chest when she thought of Sheila, but she didn't know what to do about it; the girl had Do Not Disturb signs hanging all over her.

I could call Jimmy Dee.

Later. You'll never get your work done.

But she got it done in an hour—or more accurately, seeing the hopelessness of it, abandoned the project and called Dee-Dee.

"Come to dinner?" he asked hopefully.

"Can't. I'm going out with Cindy Lou."

"Oh."

"Maybe you should rethink the au pair."

"Yeah, maybe I should." He couldn't keep the discouragement out of his voice.

And maybe, she thought when she had hung up, I should rethink the case.

The same theme kept replaying itself: *I want to know more about Kit.* She popped in the shower, to get her mind off it. Cindy Lou was right—you couldn't eat, sleep, and breathe a case.

Even if you need to keep your mind off your boyfriend. Who seems to be in the process of dumping you.

Well, not dumping me. Just not . . .

Committing?

What a stupid word! What a dumb, late-twentieth-century female cliché.

She was surprised to find herself wishing for a joint, a sign that she was depressed and hadn't yet admitted it.

She sighed.

In the old days, Jimmy Dee would come charging through the door and hand her one, right about now. But of course there was no smoking at Chez Scoggin any more—Jimmy Dee didn't know all that much about being a parent, but he had caught on that you didn't do drugs around the kids.

She was meeting Cindy Lou for dinner in a few minutes. She put on black leggings and a long green sweater that she felt matched her eyes. She thought Jimmy Dee might approve if he was still in the mode of barging in to dress her when she went out.

She felt as if she looked pretty good, pretty damned acceptable, till she saw Cindy Lou, who had on jeans, a white shirt, and a black leather jacket. People at the restaurant were whispering to each other, trying to remember what show they'd seen her on. Skip knew because it happened all the time. Sometimes they waited till Cindy Lou went to the ladies' room and then they buttonholed Skip: "*Who* is that woman you're with? I've seen her in commercials, but she's got her own show now, doesn't she?"

When they were seated (which didn't take long; the maître d' seemed as friendly as anyone with a star on the premises), Skip said, "Mind if I run a few things by you?"

"If it's about the case, yes. This is girls' night out, remember?"

"Teeny question. Itty-bitty."

"Oh, okay."

"I saw Geoff's grandmother at the funeral and she seems to have lost it. Am I wasting my time to try to talk to her?"

Cindy Lou shrugged. "You could give it a shot. You know what they say about the short-term memory. She might not know her own daughter and still have a perfect recollection of that fateful night long long ago. In a galaxy far away."

"You seem a little distracted."

"Trying to distract *you*. Night off, okay?" She took a sip of wine. "Have you heard from Steve?"

"I've heard a little too much from him."

"How's that?"

"I don't think he's going to be moving to New Orleans. He's sort of hinting around that things are really great in L.A. right now." She didn't meet her friend's eye, but sneaked a peek to see if she looked alarmed.

She didn't. "Well, good. When he gets here, he'll have some money."

"Hey. Whose side are you on?"

"He'll be here. The guy's crazy about you."

Skip didn't answer. If a guy was crazy about you, he didn't get your hopes up and then disappoint you. Did he? But she didn't feel like arguing. "You're the shrink."

"I mean it, you know. This guy is a gem. Things happen with people. Maybe he can't move here now, and that's just bad

timing—nothing to do with his level of commitment. You're thinking about that, aren't you? I know you."

Skip nodded.

"Give it some time, girl. You're disappointed and therefore
you're pissed and I don't blame you—I would be too. But do me
a favor, okay? Count to ten. Give things time to shake down."

Skip was pissed and not only at Steve. *Little Miss Shrinky-Poo,* she
thought. *How dare she? The way she runs her life.*

Cindy Lou caught her look. "Oh, chill out—the music'll do you
good."

It was true. She knew it, and when they walked into The Blue
Guitar, one of the hot new spots that were popping up like weeds
in the warehouse district, she was like a teenager again—a person
who hadn't yet settled on murder as a career.

*Jeez. Think about it. Murder as a career. Cindy Lou's right, it takes more out
of me than I think.*

In her younger days (which weren't all that far away) she'd
spent a lot of time in joints like this, swigging illegal Dixie and listening to the blues, which, she believed, had been invented just for
her. Nothing else so perfectly described her miserable little life; and
nothing could make her feel so alive.

I wish Sheila were old enough for this.

She will be soon enough.

Too soon.

Cindy Lou said, "Let's get a couple of Abitas and grab those
spots over there."

It was the kind of place where you stood, preferably as close to
the stage as possible.

"Make mine a Dixie."

"Hey, good-lookin'."

Skip felt herself grabbed from behind. A strange black man had
his arm around her.

She was tensing up, about to give him the shove he deserved
when something rang a bell. "Tyrone?"

"Ms. Skip? Officer Skip?"

"I didn't think you'd remember me."

"How'm I going to forget you? There we are playing the

JazzFest, biggest crowd we ever had, we're trying to figure out what we did right, and you come on stage tryin' to arrest us all."

She laughed. That hadn't been what happened at all, but she was pleased to be remembered.

"Are you talking to the famous Tyrone Boucree?" Cindy Lou had gotten the beers and now handed one to Skip. She turned her full wattage on him.

"Cindy Lou Wootten, Tyrone Boucree."

"Buy you a beer?" said Cindy Lou.

"Well, no, I think Skip owes me one after nearly scaring me to death at the JazzFest. In fact, I think she ought to buy the whole band a round."

"I would, but half of them are underage."

"I'll have a Dixie," he said.

Skip turned to get his beer, knowing perfectly well he just wanted some time to stare at Cindy Lou.

When she came back, he said, "Did y'all come to see us?"

"Uh-uh. We thought the Nevilles were here."

"When our lead singer grows up a little, we're going to give them a run for their money. Right now, it's kind of hard, playing in places where they serve alcohol." Someone tapped him on the shoulder. "Uh-oh, I gotta go do it. Y'all stick around. I'll buy you a beer." He went off toward stardom.

"Cindy Lou, he's married, and not only that, he's Joel Boucree's father and Joel's Melody's best friend."

Melody was a kid from another case, a kid toward whom Skip felt extremely protective.

"You don't get it about me. When I say I have bad taste in men, I mean abysmal. Tyrone Boucree is preceded by his reputation; the nicest guy in town, right? I think *New Orleans Magazine* singled him out." She wrinkled up her nose.

"Was that the problem with the Saint?"

"God, no." She shrugged. "Maybe shrinking other people's taking its toll. I'm just kind of tired of the game, that's all."

"Have you got a radio or anything? I've got to get a weather report."

"What are you talking about?"

"I think hell just froze over."

Cindy Lou turned slightly away, to hide her smile, Skip saw, and the band started up. The two women edged closer to the stage. For the next hour and a half, Skip was in a trance, moving with the music, part of the human motion machine that now filled the club, forever swelling, bouncing and bobbing, jukin' and jivin', in a collective world of its own.

Cindy Lou was right. She did feel better.

"That was *fabulous.*"

"Let's go outside."

The Blue Guitar boasted a courtyard, a place where you could sit and talk and cool off. Even in November, it felt good.

"Omigod, look over there." Skip pointed at the bar.

"What?"

"Melody. Buying a beer."

"She's only seventeen, huh?"

"Not even that—unless she didn't invite me to her birthday party."

"So what are you going to do? Bust her?"

"I've got to do something." She started walking. "Melody!" The girl tried to hide her beer. "Haven't you heard? There's cops in here."

Melody gave her a wan smile. "Hey, Skip."

"Come on. Let's have a hug."

She got one, a warm one, except for the cold bottle that pressed against her back.

"Haven't seen you since . . ."

"July."

Skip had taken her a small gift. She wanted to stay in touch, but wasn't sure how to do it. "Hey, do you baby-sit?"

"Not much. Why?"

"I've got kids now." She told her about Jimmy Dee and his two wards.

"Wow, weird. Can I meet them?"

"Sure. I'll call you. I've got to tell you something, though. You're breaking the law."

Melody flushed.

"Who're you here with?"

"Some friends from school."

"You're all breaking the law."

"We have to leave, huh?"

"It's a school night, anyway."

"Can't I stay a minute? Just to introduce my friends to the guys?" The Boucrees.

"Honey, I'm a police officer. What if you said, 'Can't I just rob that old guy over there?' "

"It's not the same thing." She started to pout.

Skip was miserable. Here was a kid she was crazy about, about to impress her friends by knowing the Boucrees, and instead she was getting them thrown out of the club. Skip truly felt for her. But before she could say a word, a genie appeared out of nowhere—a coffee-colored one, tall and reedy, about thirty or thirty-two, with close-cropped hair and a pair of eyes that didn't miss a thing. But still, they were soft, kind eyes; eyes that could take a joke and give one back. She'd noticed him onstage and been impressed.

"Hey, Melody. I'm s'posed to be lookin' for this big good-lookin' tall woman. Wouldn't be this one, would it?"

Skip liked his looks, his wiry energy, but she hated lines; obvious, unimaginative lines, at any rate. "Not unless you're giving away money," she snapped.

"Is your name Skip? You're supposed to be with a bourbon and Diet Coke."

"I beg your pardon?"

"A skinny little black bitch. 'Scuse my French; I used to be a bartender." As if that cleared it up.

He was looking at Skip now, and his expression had changed. "I mean, I didn't mean your friend's a bitch. It's just a . . . you know . . . bartender humor."

"Oh." She couldn't decide whether to continue being outraged or let it go.

"Listen, Tyrone sent me. He wants to get out of here, go somewhere quiet. Y'all up for it?"

"Where's Tyrone?" asked Melody. "Couldn't I just say hi to him?" Ostensibly, she spoke to the genie, but she looked at Skip beseechingly. The look said, "I'm going to die right now if you embarrass me in front of this cool dude."

Skip nodded. What was another minute going to hurt? But she also said, "Don't forget to give Cindy Lou her beer."

Despite all her efforts to be cool, the genie said, "That somebody else's beer? I was just gonna read you the riot act, child. Tyrone's packing up in the back. Say your name, they'll let you in."

She went off to find her friends.

"I used to do that," said Skip.

"What?"

"All that teenager stuff. Drink; stay out too late; lie to my parents."

"Whoa. Didn't we all."

"You must be a Boucree."

"Oh, didn't I say? I'm Darryl. You didn't see me on rhythm guitar?"

"Mmmm. Guess I did."

"You didn't really notice. That's because I'm ugly, have no sex appeal, and women hate me. Agggg. Thanks so much."

"Sorry. It's just that there are so many of you."

"And we keep switching around. I bet there are fifteen different Boucrees play different gigs, different times." He flashed Skip a smile that could have lit the path if they'd been lost in the woods.

She found herself smiling back. Smiling and not being able to think of a thing to say, which meant her mind had been more on form than content. His form.

A bad sign, a very bad sign. Cindy Lou, where are you?

"Maybe I should find my friend."

"Oh, yeah. The bourbon and Diet Coke. There she is. That her?"

Skip scanned the crowd. "Where?"

"Over there. The one that looks *real* nice. Nothing like a bitch at all." He gave her another of his dental extravaganzas.

"Ah. The one that's waving." Skip beckoned her over. "Cindy Lou Wootten, Darryl Boucree."

They said they were glad to meet each other, and Skip outlined the plan—to join the band someplace quiet.

Cindy Lou waved a manicured hand. "Sure, sure. I'm up for anything. Let's go wait out front."

"I'll meet you in a minute." The cop in her had to make sure Melody went home.

They ended up at the bar at Snug Harbor—not the world's quietest spot, but it beat The Blue Guitar. And, face it, Skip thought, there probably weren't that many places where a crowd of five or six black guys and two women, one of them white, would be all that comfortable.

She had a lot to catch up on with Tyrone—mostly Melody's career. Tyrone, as the father of her pal Joel, and also just a good strong, earthy guy, was Melody's idea of the ideal dad. She idolized him, and also fought with him, more or less as if he were her own dad, because she knew him about that well—he was her boss. Melody was the underage lead singer Tyrone had mentioned.

There were problems, with Melody being white and everyone else black, but both sides wanted to work them out.

"Best singer I ever saw," Tyrone said. "Ever. Well, except maybe Etta James. You like Etta?"

"Mm-hmm."

"But you know what about Melody? She's got to quit coming to see us in bars. One of these days she's gonna get in trouble."

"I almost gave her some trouble tonight."

"Yeah, me too."

"But neither of us did, did we?"

"I didn't want to embarrass her in front of her friends."

"Me neither. Kids are hard, you know that?" She wanted to tell him about Sheila, but the story was so complicated—and at the moment so depressing—she didn't feel like going into it.

Darryl came up behind Tyrone and leaned on his shoulder. "Don't Bogart that lady, Tyrone. When do I get to talk to her?"

"Here, you want my stool? I got to go work out something with Louis. Why don't you just talk to Ms. Skip a while? You might have met your match, Mr. Darryl. Go to it, now." He walked off chuckling to himself.

Darryl looked disconcerted. "What'd he mean by that? You don't look a *whole* lot like the Bride of Frankenstein."

"Did anyone mention I'm a cop?"

"Holy shit, you're kidding! A cop?"

"Homicide." She tried to make her smile as dazzling as his.

"Whoa, boy."

"What's wrong? You a murderer?"

"No, man, I *love* cops. That's what I always wanted to be . . . just one thing and another, it didn't work out."

"Oh, come on."

"Well, the family frowned on it—after they sent me to Yale and all."

"Yale! I thought Joel was the first Boucree—" She stopped, realizing she was blundering.

"What? Headed for a profession? Now one thing he is: he's the first to go to one of your fancy white folks' private high schools. Went to Fortier myself. And, unlike Joel, I actually *wanted* to be a musician. Also, I'm better at it than he is. But, see, I was good at other stuff too. So they gave me this scholarship and there was no stopping the Boucrees. They wanted their little black boy to go up to New Haven, Connecticut, and freeze his scrawny butt for four years.

"So I did it. I was a good boy. What I didn't do, I didn't do the rest of it."

"You certainly don't talk like a Yalie."

"Jeez, don't you hate the way they talk? It's enough to make you lose your chitlins and greens. Excuse me; chitterlings and verdant vegetable matter. Anyway, I didn't go on to better things—like law school or something."

"So what's your day job?"

"I'm back at Fortier—teaching English and creative writing, which turned out to be what I really liked. 'Course, you should hear me in the classroom—I still don't talk like a Yalie, but I try not to drop my g's. Those kids don't know shit—you know that? Gotta set an example, however tiny. Anyway, when I was in high school I went to the cop lecture on career day."

"When did the bartending come in?"

"Oh, well, I lied about that."

"You weren't a bartender?"

"No, I said I used to be one. Still am. You should try getting along on a schoolteacher's salary. Besides, I like the variety."

"Two jobs is murder, though. You have kids?" That, she thought, might be a reason for doing it. Surely that was it, she thought. But his answer was a clear challenge:

"Not married. You?"

She looked into her drink and shook her head, desperately trying to think of a way to change the subject. There was something high-octane about this guy, a kind of magnetic masculine energy she couldn't help responding to. But for one thing, she was already involved; for another, she felt slightly squeamish about the uncharted territory of dating a black man.

Oh, for heaven's sake, she told herself. *He hasn't asked you for a date. He's just flirting.*

Well, I could use a little male attention.

"So what does a cop do for fun?"

"Not that much. This is the first time I've been out in a couple of weeks. I read a lot, I guess."

"Who's your favorite author?"

"I don't know. Flannery O'Connor, maybe."

"Whoa. Good taste. How about contemporary authors?"

"Who do you like?"

"Oh, Elmore Leonard sometimes. Jane Smiley; Amy Tan. Depends on the mood I'm in."

"No black authors?"

"Oh, sure. But I feed 'em to the kids. That's the job, you know? I like a break once in a while."

"I know men who say they don't read women authors."

"Well, they didn't go to Yale. Princeton, probably." He took a long swig of beer. "Did you go to college?"

Skip was surprised at the question. "You think cops don't?"

"Do they?"

"To tell you the truth, I flunked out of Newcomb. Made it through Ole Miss, though."

"Why'd you flunk out? No, let me guess. Drinkin', drugs, and hellin' around. You're one of those outlaw cops."

"Former outlaw. Current cop."

151

"You pretty sure about that? You never break the law anymore?"

"What are you getting at?"

"I'm just gettin' a feel for who you are, that's all. I bet you hate kids."

"Oh, don't be such a know-it-all. I live with kids."

"What do you mean, you live with kids? I thought you said you didn't have any."

"I don't, but my landlord does. And he's my best friend."

"Ah." He turned back toward the bar and sipped his beer, as if chastened. "Your boyfriend."

"No. My best friend. Don't you think men and women can be friends?"

"My best friend's a woman."

"Oh, yeah? Tell me about her."

"Lady I work with at the bar. Waitress."

"Well, that tells me a lot."

"She's a writer, I'm a musician—we've got something in common, you know what I mean? Only I've got something she hasn't got—'cause I'm a teacher too. Writing is her whole life—I mean, it's gonna make her or break her. It's her *passion*. Whoa. I feel for her, man. Some of the Boucrees are like that." He gestured with his chin. "Tyrone is, really. Music's the whole world to him. *Man*, it's made him unhappy."

"What's her name?"

"Why you askin'?"

" 'Cause maybe she's not real. Maybe you made her up."

He looked as amazed as if she'd just told him he was under arrest. "Now, why on Earth would I do that? You are one strange chick, you know that?"

"Sorry. I guess I am." *Can it be he really doesn't know how appealing that little story makes him?* She smiled, hoping it made her look normal. "What's her name?"

"Tricia." When he smiled back, she let out her breath. She hadn't known she was holding it.

"Tricia who?"

"You're weird, you know that? Tricia Lattimore."

152

The name was as familiar as her own, but by now she was expecting it. "She was my best friend at McGehee's." Her high school.

"You're makin' that up."

Once he said the first name, she had known it was going to be Tricia Lattimore, though Tricia had been in New York when last heard of. Something about Darryl Boucree was starting to look the tiniest bit inevitable.

Watch out! Early warning signal. If he's like a magnet, he's got to be bad news, right? AFOG, as they say on the TOWN.

But on the other hand, how do people ever get together at all if they aren't attracted first?

She tried to remember if she'd been attracted to Steve at first. She couldn't, but one thing she recalled perfectly well: *He was attracted to me. Does that mean I'm AFOG for him?*

She didn't want to think about Steve. She wanted to flirt.

Which she proceeded to do until Cindy Lou strolled up: "Come on, girlfriend. It's a school night."

"I," said Darryl, "am taking this lady home."

"I think I better go with Cindy Lou."

"Uh-uh. You live in the Quarter and it'll be the perfect walk."

Skip slipped off her bar stool. "I don't think so."

But Cindy Lou was already edging out the door. "Oh, you young people." She had an evil grin on. This was a lot more her style than Skip's.

Darryl said, "Just a beautiful walk, I promise. Hands to myself. I'll even put 'em in my pockets." Instead, he hunched his shoulders, folded his hands under his arms, and thrust his head forward. He looked so endearingly goofy Skip burst out laughing.

Well, why not? I'm a cop. I can take care of myself.

She felt free as all outdoors.

14

· ·

It was a brisk walk in more than one way. The wind had a bite to
it, but in a way it felt festive, as if harvest balls were in the offing.
On the other hand, a little body contact might have cut the chill—
the hands-off policy had its down side.

"Well, this certainly has been an interesting evening," Darryl said
as they neared her house. "You are just . . . *interesting*, you know that?"

"I thought you thought I was weird."

"Uh-huh. That too."

She held out her hand. "I had a great time."

And that would have been it, if Jimmy Dee hadn't called her
name about then, so loudly they probably heard him back at The
Blue Guitar. He was on his balcony.

"Dee-Dee, what is it?"

"Sheila's gone."

"Omigod, I'll be right up. Darryl, I'm sorry. Gotta go."

"What is it?"

"His niece. She's thirteen." She was trying to keep the panic out
of her voice.

"I'll help you look for her."

154

"No, that's okay." She turned away and started fiddling with her key.

"No, really. I'm good with kids."

"Dee-Dee and I can handle it."

They could have argued another five minutes if Dee-Dee hadn't said, "Bring him up, for God's sake. Just get here."

Can't hurt, she figured, and followed orders. "What happened, Dee-Dee?"

"I don't know. She had dinner with us—actually, she stalked off in the middle, so I just left her alone. I didn't check on her till I went to bed, which was about eleven, and she wasn't there."

"What did you do then?"

"Threw up." He shot her an accusing stare. "And then called you."

"And I wasn't there. I'm really sorry, Dee-Dee." She rubbed his arm absently.

"That's all right. You were obviously doing yourself some good." Seeming to remember his manners, he turned to Darryl. "Sorry to speak of you in the third person."

"But it means he likes you." Skip knew the whole thing had been calculated; he had quite deliberately been rude to Darryl, knowing he could get away with it if he camped it up. Sure enough, the corners of Darryl's eyes were crinkling; in some mysterious way that had never happened with Steve, Darryl and Jimmy Dee had taken instantly to each other. But she didn't have time to marvel about it. "Did you call the police?"

"Yes, and they said they'd keep an eye out. Someone came over and talked to me; that was about that. And of course I couldn't leave because of Kenny."

"Where would she go?" Skip knew the runaway scene pretty well, thanks to the same little Melody she'd seen tonight. There was a whole circuit, complete with bars that catered to the underage crowd.

But not that many thirteen-year-olds. Sheila was too young even to be noticed by most kids on the streets.

The thought of her out there made Skip shiver. Kids wouldn't notice her, but adults would. The wrong kind of adults.

Dee-Dee said, "She doesn't really have any friends, but I called everyone I could think of."

"Did you check my house? And the courtyard?"

"I took the liberty. You don't mind, do you?"

"Good God, Dee-Dee." Each had a key to the other's place and they went in and out like family members.

Skip caught Darryl's eye and saw that his whole demeanor had changed. With the merriment gone from his face, he looked incalculably sad; melancholy in a way that made Skip want to tell jokes and chatter and make soup all at once to cheer him up. "We got to get out there," he said.

"Oh, Darryl, it isn't your problem. Why don't you go home and I'll go look for her?"

"I'm not sleepy. I'll go with you."

Jimmy Dee said, "Somebody has to stay with Kenny." She could see he was itching to get out there, but they couldn't leave Darryl to baby-sit—he might be a Boucree, but he was still a stranger—and Jimmy Dee wasn't the right person to find Sheila, of that Skip was pretty sure.

"I think it's got to be you, Dad. I hate to say it, but right now I think Sheila might be happier to see Auntie than Uncle Jimmy. What did you fight about, by the way?"

"The proper way to eat spaghetti. She favored the two-finger method."

Darryl said, "One dinner I'm glad I missed."

"I'm going to take a quick spin around her room."

The bed was unmade, but that meant nothing—she might not have made it that day, or she might have gone to bed for a little while. Skip looked around for coats—a fleece-lined jean jacket was all that was missing. And Sheila had been wearing jeans that afternoon.

"Okay, Dee-Dee, we're out of here. Darryl, do you really want to come?"

He nodded. " 'Course I'm coming."

Truth to tell, she would have been disappointed if he'd given any other answer. After seeing that look of utter sadness, she knew there was only one way it was going to fade. A man who could look that way about a missing child wasn't going to get any sleep if he went home.

They could see their breath when they stepped out on St. Philip. "Okay, let's think. I couldn't stand to talk about it in front of Dee-Dee."

"Do I have to call him that?"

She couldn't help smiling. "Quit making me laugh. They say over at Covenant House that runaways don't run to anything, they just run away."

"Would she go to Covenant House?"

"I doubt she's ever heard of it. But if she did, they can keep her for a while without letting anyone know. I think we better try the streets."

"Would she try to go anywhere?"

"Like back to Minneapolis? She hasn't got anything back there, and she hasn't got money. I guess that's what she'd need first."

"If she had a plan. My guess is she didn't. She just split. Saying to herself, 'Everyone hates me and they'll all be sorry.' "

They turned right on Bourbon Street. "She'd walk towards Canal Street, towards the people. Did you ever run away?"

"Uh-uh," said Darryl. "I was happy. You?"

"Oh, yes. Several times, for about half an hour. I thought you might have, since you mentioned not having a plan. I always went home because I couldn't think what to do next."

"It was probably quiet and dark on the street where you grew up; here, it isn't quite so scary. But even if you weren't scared out of your wits, you'd have to find some place to hide."

"Either that or depend on the kindness of strangers."

Despite his promise, he took her hand. "Try not to think about that."

They walked silently for a while, looking in doorways, scanning the crowds, which were thin now, it being almost two on a Friday morning. If people turned off Bourbon (and Sheila would follow the people), they would probably walk toward the river, maybe to the Napoleon House, the Cafe du Monde. . . . "I know!"

Skip shouted. "The Cafe du Monde. It's open all night, a minor can go there, and it's warm. Anyway, pretty warm." The tables were outside, but there was heat.

"Or Kaldi's maybe," said Darryl. A coffeehouse on Decatur.

"Maybe. But the Cafe du Monde's in the thick of things. It might seem glamorous to be there alone in the middle of the night."

"Let's go."

It was bustling, as usual, but there was no sign of Sheila. They questioned the waiters. Sure enough, she'd been there. Not only that, she'd been there twice. Once about ten o'clock and later, around midnight. She'd had hot chocolate and beignets both times.

"I wonder where she went in between?"

"Kaldi's?" said Darryl.

"Let's go check."

But it had been closed for hours.

"She must have found some warm place close around here."

They walked up and down Decatur, the street where the runaways hung, talking to strollers and loiterers, asking if they'd seen a thirteen-year-old in jeans and denim jacket. One guy said he had, but he couldn't remember where or when.

"Know what I think I'd do?" said Darryl. "I might go over to the cathedral. They used to say in Sunday school that churches are refuges."

It was a good idea.

They found her there, in one of the cavernous doorways, her head on her knees, maybe even asleep. A grown street person, a woman, Skip thought, was curled up not ten feet away.

Skip bent over Sheila and said her name, not wanting to get too close for fear of scaring her. "Honey, let's go home."

Sheila sat up and peered out of her eyes so innocent they weren't even frightened. When she had oriented herself, the fawn look turned to answer. "No way I'm going back there."

Skip knelt. "This is my friend Darryl."

"Hi, Sheila." He held out a hand to shake. She stared at him for what seemed like a long time, and finally shook.

Skip said, "Well, at least let's go get something to eat."

"I'm not hungry."

"Well, I am," said Darryl. "I'm having a major Big Mac attack. You don't want some fries or anything?"

Sheila's eyes got round. "We could go to McDonald's?"

"Sure. Or maybe we could get pizza. You want some pizza?"

She shook her head. "McDonald's."

Skip gave Darryl an utterly amazed look. Not daring to say anything, she stuck out a hand for Sheila to grab. "Up you go."

"Do Uncle Jimmy and Kenny have to go with us?"

"Honey. You're shaking." Thinking she was probably cold clear through, Skip put an arm around her.

"I'm okay!" The girl shrugged away.

Darryl said, "No, Uncle Jimmy and Kenny don't have to go. Kenny's sound asleep and Uncle Jimmy'd probably be glad to be."

"I have to call and say I found you, though. He's worried sick."

She let that pass and said to Darryl, "Who are you, anyway?"

"Well, I'm a pretty good guitarist and a damn good English teacher."

"No way."

"No way what?"

"You're not a teacher. Teachers don't say damn."

"Well, this one does at this time of night. Excuse me. Morning."

"Are you Skip's boyfriend?"

Skip spoke up quickly. "He's a friend of the family, honey."

"You mean Uncle Jimmy? Eewww."

"What you got against Uncle Jimmy?"

But she fell silent.

When they had reached the house, she took Sheila and Darryl into the garçonnière and gave Jimmy Dee a call. "She's fine; we've got her. She can stay with me tonight, okay? And no school tomorrow, I think."

She hung up, feeling beat. "Does everybody really want to go out? What about some sandwiches here?"

Sheila teared up. "You mean we can't go?"

Darryl said, "I want to go."

159

"I'm outnumbered." Trying hard to smile, she picked up her car keys. "Wait. What if they're not open?"

She made a couple of phone calls—and got no answers. But the look in Sheila's eyes said she better come up with something.

"I know," said Darryl. "The Clover Grill's open all night."

"Have they got fries?"

He nodded soberly. "And shakes."

Sheila meant business. She got a burger, chocolate shake, and fries. Not to be outdone, Darryl did too. Skip made do with a Diet Coke and bites of theirs.

As soon as Sheila's mouth was full, which assured Skip the floor, she said, "I'm getting the idea you aren't happy with Jimmy Dee and me."

"I'm afraid of Uncle Jimmy."

"Whatever for?"

"My mom said he's queer." She squinted at Darryl. "Are you queer too?"

"Do you know what that means?"

Sheila nodded vigorously. "Gay."

"Well, why would that make you afraid of him?"

"Andrew told me gay people do bad things to kids."

"Andrew's full of it," Darryl said.

Sheila flared. "Well, sure, you'd say that. You're gay too."

Darryl grabbed Skip and planted one on her. "I am not."

"Hey!"

Sheila giggled.

Skip said, "Who's Andrew anyway?"

"My boyfriend."

"You've got a boyfriend?" She didn't even have breasts.

"I'm afraid to ask him over 'cause he might find out about Uncle Jimmy."

"That's why you ran away?"

"No! I ran away because Kenny gets everything and I don't get anything."

Darryl said, "Did Kenny get to go to the Clover Grill at two-thirty A.M. on a school night?"

She gave him a half smile, the slightly flirtatious look of a child who's exasperated with a grown-up but too polite to say so. "Uncle Jimmy didn't take me."

"Well, he probably would if you asked him."

"Uh-uh. He won't let us eat burgers and fries."

"I bet he will now." Skip had a feeling Jimmy Dee's ideas about nutrition were about to be eroded.

Darryl said, "Are you really afraid of Uncle Jimmy?"

Gravely, Sheila nodded.

"Do you remember your dad very well?"

She shook her head.

"You've never really lived with a man, have you?"

Again, she shook her head, pouting.

"We're not so bad."

She gave him another closed-mouth smile. "Maybe you're not."

"Well, what's so bad about Uncle Jimmy?"

She lowered her eyes, looked at her plate. "Nothing." She thought better of it. "He doesn't cook like my mom."

"You miss your mom, don't you?"

She nodded.

He put an arm around Skip. "Well, you got a nice auntie here. Maybe you should spend more time with her."

Sheila looked at him hopefully. "And you too? Could we do things sometimes? Without Kenny?"

Skip's heart went out to her. "Sure, honey."

Later, lying in bed, Sheila tucked cozily into her fold-out couch, she thought, *What's with this man? He charmed Jimmy Dee, who hates any man I'm with, and Sheila, who's afraid of men in general. Damn. And me.*

● ●

Friday was a big day for Cole, only the biggest of his life. Marguerite had wanted him to cancel his meeting, but not even for her would he do it. It was the culmination of all his work. Twenty years of struggle: little deals, almost deals, deals that weren't worth making, deals that never panned out; and finally, he had a chance at the one that counted.

161

His software was a group scheduler, basically a calendar—a way to keep schedules for entire companies, to know where everyone was at once, and what he was supposed to be doing. He'd gotten raves from the companies who'd used it; the problem was, they were little companies.

Trying to sell it individually to everyone in the world was a sucker's game. What he needed was somebody like Microsoft either to buy it outright or distribute it and pay him a royalty. Bill Gates hadn't called, but this morning Cole was meeting with a software publisher that was about to be nearly as big.

They had been negotiating for six months, Cole and his partner, mostly with a man named Burke Hamerton. A figure of $1.5 million had been named.

At ten A.M. sharp, Cole walked into the meeting room at the Windsor Court that the company had reserved. He had gotten up early and ironed a shirt. He had packed his briefcase and re-packed it.

This morning, because the talk was all about whether the up-date of the project was going to work, it was just Hamerton and Cole, not Cole's partner, and no one else from the company. Cole much preferred it this way. He only half understood the financial nuances, and they bored him. If, instead of having a partner, in-stead of participating at all, he could have hired someone to work it out and let him know the bottom line, he would have.

But he'd learned the hard way, in the first five years of his ca-reer, that business didn't work that way. There was only one person in the world he could rely on: Cole Terry.

The room was sunny, well appointed. Cole couldn't have felt more cheerful and confident. "Good news, Mr. Hamerton, I think I've got it. I should be able to make the modifications in the pro-gram in six months, maximum. And I mean maximum—it could take as little as four."

"Sit down, Mr. Terry." There was something about his tone that Cole didn't like. "Have you seen this letter?"

It was from the IRS, attaching the bank account of a company called Psypid. Cole's company. It was addressed to Cole's partner.

"What is this?"

"You tell me."

"I've never seen it." It was dated a week earlier, meaning it must have just arrived. The gist of it was that Cole and his partner—who employed about twelve people—had underpaid their payroll taxes and were being given no second chances. He sat down. "I don't know what it means."

"It seems pretty straightforward to me."

"We haven't paid our taxes?" He couldn't seem to take it in. How could it be? And how could Hamerton know before he did? "Where did you get this letter?"

"It was in a pile of papers Cutting delivered yesterday."

Cutting. My own partner! My shit-eating, motherfucking lamebrain fool of a partner.

"My company has a fiduciary duty to its shareholders, Mr. Terry. We were about to put a million dollars in advertising into your product. And this letter very plainly indicates our supplier's days are numbered. You understand, of course, that we can't possibly do business with a company that's on its way out."

"On its . . . what?"

"Look at that letter. Do you have enough money to pay those taxes? If you don't, say good-bye to Psypid."

It was too much. Not only was Cutting a crook, he was an idiot who couldn't be bothered hiding the evidence, who actually *delivered* it to a potential buyer—accidentally, Cole was sure; he knew Cutting.

He brought his fist down on the table. "Fuck!"

"Mr. Terry. Please."

Even Cole had been surprised at his bellow.

"Goddam motherfucker!" As Hamerton cringed, Cole picked up the telephone and threw it. "*Goddam!* Where is he?"

"I don't know. I haven't talked to him."

"I'm going to kill him."

He drove to his partner's house, walked to the front porch, beat on the door, and called his partner's name so loudly that neighbors looked out their windows.

When there was no answer, he kicked the door in and without even bothering to close it, began methodically destroying the contents of the house.

•   •

Lenore wished she'd gone back to work. She had told her father she'd be home, and here he was, having nothing better to do than go visiting.

"I was just going to take Caitlin out."

"It won't take a second, darlin'. Let your old dad in, will you?"

Caitlin came toddling into the room. He bent down. "There you are, you precious thing. How's Grandpa's little angel, huh?"

It infuriated Lenore to hear him talking to her daughter.

"What can I do for you?"

"Well, I've got a little problem. I had a real good opportunity to make a lot of money fast, so I borrowed a little from the company to make the investment. You know how these things are—there's no way of predictin', really. Things didn't pan out and . . ."

"And you didn't pay it back? Is that what you're telling me? You *embezzled* from your own company and now you need me to bail you out? Is that what you're saying?"

"I prayed about it, baby. You know I did. I asked for guidance from the Lord and . . . I don't know; I did what I thought I was s'posed to."

"Your precious Lord told you to steal?"

"Now you know better'n that, Miss Lenore. You know the Lord wouldn't say a thing like that. He told me I was gonna be able to pay back the money real fast, with plenty of interest. It was a good investment for the company, you see what I mean? Just something went wrong is all."

"What is this? Now you're caught? Are you going to jail?"

"Well, I probably am. The IRS says I didn't pay' em."

"I see." She'd remembered to take some deep breaths, and she was calming down a little. "You used the money you were supposed to pay the company's taxes with."

"I'm in a bind, baby girl. It was good your mama left her money to you, I mean straight to you instead of going through me first. You need that money and I'm real glad for you to have it, in your situation. . . ." He looked down at Caitlin, who was amusing herself with a green plastic dinosaur. "But she really didn't provide for anything happening to me. I know Jesus must have meant for her to do it that way, but I need you to show a little Christian charity to your old man."

Lenore's hard-won calm shattered as if dashed on a hard pavement.

"Christian charity! You have the nerve to speak to me about Christian charity after the things you said to me. You disowned me, Cutting Marquer. Have you forgotten that?"

"Well, now . . ."

"Well, now, nothing. Let me just remind you of a few things you said. For openers you said I was a whore and a slut. You said I was a blight on the family's precious goddam reputation—as if anyone ever heard of the Marquers—and a disgrace to God-fearing people everywhere. Is any of this ringing a bell?"

"The good Lord says to forgive, and I've made my peace with all that, Lenore."

"You forgive *me*? Is that what you're saying?"

"Well, I do, and you know it. We talked about that six months ago."

Indeed they had. He'd asked for money that time, too, and she'd given him some. Tearfully.

"Let me mention a few other things I should have brought up on that other occasion six months ago. You said you were sorry, but you were going to have to shut off familial relations—that's what you said, 'familial relations'—because my sluttish reputation was not only against God's law but would probably queer your precious business deal. Remember that at all?"

"Perhaps I spoke in haste."

"You spoke before you knew the contents of Mama's will."

He looked at her with tears in his eyes. "For the love of God, Lenore. I haven't got anywhere else to turn."

She sat down, sorry for him in spite of herself. "How much do you need?"

"I need quite a bit, to tell you the truth, but fifty thousand might keep me out of jail."

"*Fifty thousand dollars?* Did I hear you right?"

"Seventy-five, if you can spare it."

15

• •

Morning came about a week too early.

Skip lay in bed, waiting for her coffee to brew and trying to decide what she had to do next no matter what. Unfortunately, the answer involved getting somewhere earlier than she'd have to be at the office.

She had to see Kit. And she had no idea where Kit worked, which meant she had to pop by her house.

Nothing to do but leap.

In twenty minutes, she'd dressed, left a note for Sheila, and another for Geneese, the maid, which she delivered to the Big House on her way out.

Dee-Dee had eye bags you could pack and take to Europe. "What's going on?"

"She's okay, no kidding. I mean, really she is. And she's going to get through this fine, I promise. Geneese can take care of her today. I'll phone you from the office, but I've got to get somewhere fast."

"Just one more thing—who *was* that masked hunk?"

"The Pied Piper, I think."

Kenny came in rubbing his eyes. "The Pied Piper was here? I thought that was a fairy tale."

Jimmy Dee said, "That's appropriate," and Skip blew Kenny a kiss.

"Uncle Jimmy, can I have some shredded wheat?"

Skip left shaking her head: *Shredded wheat. Any other kid in the world would want Lucky Charms or something. It must be really hard on Sheila having a perfect little brother.*

On the way to Kit's, she tried to think of ways to make Sheila feel more at home, but the only thing she seemed to want was to see Darryl again.

Who can blame her? The thought popped up before she could trample on it.

Kit lived in Lake Forest, a fairly new, suburban-looking area of one-family houses. Because it was extremely well integrated, it wasn't fashionable, but Skip found the racial mix more attractive than otherwise. She sighed, knowing that was a minority view among white people.

Both kinds of kids were walking to school—she liked that. They might pull knives on each other in the halls, but for the moment, all was peaceful.

Kit's house was modest, but comfortable-looking. However, Skip didn't see the inside—Kit emerged as she was locking her car, wearing a nurse's uniform and smoking a cigarette—an odd combination, Skip thought.

"Hey, there. You want me?"

"Too late, huh? I need to ask you a question or two."

"I could take a break about ten-thirty—want to meet me at work?"

She's awfully cooperative. I wonder why?

Nevertheless, Skip agreed to turn up at the South Louisiana Medical Center, a private hospital across Magazine, in the Irish Channel.

She went back to the office and called Jimmy Dee, now at his office. "I think what it is, Dee-Dee, is Shelia's never been around men that much. She doesn't know what to make of having an uncle who's a daddy and so, brace yourself, she says she's afraid of you."

"What? Mild-mannered Uncle Jimmy Dee?"

"Well, she says it's because you're gay, which apparently her mother told her, but frankly I think that was just a way of getting into it. It does develop, though, that she has a homophobic boyfriend."

"A *what*? She's only a baby."

"I think at her age talking to someone in class qualifies him as your boyfriend. We do need to do a little education around being gay, though. I could do that if you like."

"No, I think I should. Otherwise, it's like it's still in the closet or something."

"The hell of it is, I know this is hard to take, but so far as I can tell, basically she wants her mama."

"She's got you," he said hopefully.

"Poor unlucky child, if that's the best she can do. But unfortunately it is and that's part of the problem. I think it's the whole thing—strange city, strange adults, and a whole lot of grief for everything she's lost. She's going to get through it, though. I even see running away as a good sign. By doing that, she told us how bad things are for her."

"Well, what are we going to do about it?" He sounded hopeless.

"Take her to McDonald's, for one thing."

"Do *what*? And get the social services on our backs for child abuse? Why don't we just beat her while we're at it?"

"A tiny trick I learned from Darryl. He's got quite a little way with kids."

"I like that dude. I think he's okay."

"High praise, indeed."

"And what does her tininess think about him?"

"He's got quite a little way with everybody."

There was certainly no accounting. Why on earth did Jimmy Dee find Darryl less threatening than Steve? When Steve was around, the two of them squared off like bull elephant seals in mating season.

It's something male, she thought. *Something they can smell. They know something we don't, but they don't know what they know. Maybe he likes Dar-*

ryl because he's not threatening. He doesn't really want me and Dee-Dee knows it.

It was a good theory. She checked her watch and headed for her meeting with Kit.

The hospital was old, dark, almost spooky. Decorative plaster cornices bespoke better days. The ceilings, especially in the corridors, seemed thirty feet high. It smelled of Pine-Sol. Skip found it thoroughly depressing.

But to her surprise, she were ushered into a small corner office, light, cheerful, and furnished with plants and photos. "I'm a supervisor here," Kit explained. "So I get one perk and this is it."

For the first time, Skip really looked at her. She was a handsome woman, the sort who might have been called "rawboned" in another era. She was tall and strong, slender without, somehow, that being an issue. Her bones were big and her body narrow. She had brown hair, which she wore carelessly pinned up, Katharine Hepburn style, and hazel eyes that looked as if they could laugh. Her hands were certainly a nurse's hands, capable hands, with the nails cut blunt and short. She wore only one silver ring, twisted into an ankh. She had a fast metabolism, Skip thought, and probably ran on nervous energy. She was over forty, though how much over it Skip couldn't have said. She could have been from New England or the Midwest, perhaps; definitely not New Orleans—her bones were not delicate enough; she was too earthy. If she had tattoos or piercings, they didn't show, and wouldn't have looked right.

She looked at her watch, setting a certain tone. "You're wondering how well I knew Geoff?"

"Sure, among other things."

"He came to our TOWN dinners, but he didn't talk much. I knew about him mostly, through Lenore, who's become almost . . ." She hesitated, then shrugged. "I may as well say it—almost like a daughter to me."

"Ah. Then tell me about Lenore. How did you get to know her?"

"Online, originally. Then we were in a group together and sort of discovered mutual interests."

"May I ask what sort of interests?"

170

If Kit were the type who could blush, she might have. As it was, she merely looked caught out. "Caitlin, I guess. I feel so terribly sorry for her, having to raise that child alone. I worry, I really do. And Caitlin's such a sweet little girl; so sunny."

"What kind of group were you and Lenore in?"

"Oh, just a sort of women's thing."

"Social?"

"You could say that." She looked acutely uncomfortable.

"You said 'were' as if the group isn't still meeting."

"Did I? Well."

"But you are."

"Well, Lenore and I've become terribly good friends."

"Who else is in it?"

"Oh, dear, I really can't remember." She looked at her watch again. "Does this really have to do with Geoff?"

"I was wondering—why do you worry about Lenore? Does that have to do with Geoff?"

Kit busied herself with papers on her desk. "I suppose you could say that, yes. Or it did. I used to worry that she'd marry him, just to be with somebody." She looked up, straight at Skip. "You know, Geoff just wasn't the sort you'd marry. He lived with his parents, after all."

"You couldn't see him taking care of a baby?"

"He was a baby himself." It came out with a lot of vehemence.

"I saw you with Lenore at the funeral."

"That poor girl, all the things she's been through . . . her mother's dead and her dad disowned her, did you know that? For being a single mother. He's a Christian, I guess, and an unbelievably nasty piece of work. I just feel so sorry for her."

She looked off in the distance and when her eyes met Skip's again, it was as if Kit read her mind. She made a rueful little snorting noise. "I should mind my own business, I guess. . . ."

"Oh, Miss Brazil. May I see you for a second?" A young black woman, her hair in dozens of tiny braids, poked her head in.

Kit rose with a graceful sweep, not even putting her hands on the desk for balance. "I'll just be a minute," she said as she left, not bothering to turn her head toward Skip.

Skip stood and strolled to the window. Casually, so that it would look as if she were simply bored, she turned to face Kit's desk and scanned it quickly. An ordinary desk calendar lay open-faced, inviting riffling. But there was no need—something intriguing was written on that day, Friday. "Full moon," said the entry. "Outside, p.u. Suby 7 P.M."

That was so good Skip turned back a few days, to Tuesday. That day, too, Kit had had a date at 7 P.M. On that page, she had drawn a star with a circle around it—the pentagram Skip had seen on the altar at Lenore's. Just doodling, probably, but it gave Skip the willies. She turned the calendar back to Friday.

She sat down, trying to make sense of it. In Satanic cults, children were sacrificed, weren't they? Little Caitlin seemed perfectly healthy, but what about Geoff? Usually cults had men in them—if this one didn't, maybe that meant something. Kit had been pretty harsh on the subject of Lenore's father, and not all that lenient on Geoff.

But that was ridiculous. A ritual murder accomplished by the pushing over of a ladder was too lame to contemplate.

On the other hand, who knew what these people were about? Perhaps there was some strange initiation.

Maybe Lenore was required to seduce a man and then kill him, black-widow style. . . .

Maybe Geoff knew something he wasn't supposed to. . . .

Maybe he threatened Kit's job, or Lenore's.

Skip shrugged off a shiver. A little paranoia goes with the territory, but let's not get carried away.

Kit came back pushing up her sleeves, efficiency personified. "Look, I sound weird, like I'm fixated on Lenore, and I guess I am. I guess, basically, I'm a mother in search of a child to take care of, and she's satisfying that need right now—she and Caitlin together."

She pushed back a lock of hair that had come loose. "I never had children because my husband didn't want to. I didn't go to medical school—which I also wanted to do—because I put him through school, then helped him get his business started. We had a deal—I'd support him for a while, then he'd support me. Only I

172

never got to collect—we broke up over the child issue. I got married again, but by then . . . I don't know, maybe it was too late. Anyway, I'm divorced again." She shrugged. "So I need something to nurture and Lenore's it for right now. I guess if she'd married Geoff, I'd have had three children instead of two. I don't know, maybe I'm as crazy as anyone in a certain ward of this fine institution."

Maybe, Skip thought. But one thing was painfully obvious—this was a terribly unhappy woman; a woman who didn't know where to turn to get out of the doldrums.

I wonder if she has a boyfriend.

It doesn't matter—whoever he is, he isn't enough.

"I have to get back to work."

"Could I ask you one more question? Neetsie told me where she works, but I forgot. Do you happen to know?"

"Sure. All Systems Go." At Skip's blank look, she said, "Are you sure she told you?"

"I guess not. Maybe it was Suby."

"Well, it's not classified information. It's a computer store."

On the way back (driving being Skip's favorite time to philosophize), she thought about the irony of Geoff, the computer wiz, working in a video store, while his sister, the actress, spent her days flogging computers.

● ●

Right before lunch, Steve called. "How's everything?"

"Just awful. Sheila ran away last night."

"Sheila?" He couldn't seem to place her.

"Dee-Dee's kid."

"Oh, sure. What's the matter with me?"

"I mean, she really ran away. We didn't find her until two o'clock."

"In the morning? You were up till two in the morning?"

"Three-thirty, actually. We had to bribe her to come home by taking her for a burger."

"Yikes, I hope you didn't have to go to McDonald's. Better to leave her to freeze."

"Steve!"

"Hey, I'm kidding. Joke, okay? I didn't mean anything."

"Sorry. I'm sleep-impaired."

"We'll talk tonight."

But she couldn't, of course. She had to spy on a bunch of cultists.

Anyway, she didn't want to. Bad news could wait.

She hung up feeling snappish. He had seemed blithely unconcerned about Sheila; in fact, seemed to have forgotten her entire existence.

She was angry at Steve anyway, and this didn't help. She couldn't help thinking, *A real man would show some concern for children.*

To which the corollary was all too obvious: *Like Darryl.*

She called Wizard, the TOWN sysop. "Oh, yeah, I've been meaning to phone you."

"Did you talk to your lawyers?"

"Yeah," he said. "I'll send you the stuff. You knew I'd have to, didn't you?"

"I knew you would if I subpoenaed it. I was hoping it wouldn't come to that."

"Yeah, well, if I'd had my way, it would have."

Is this something I need to know? Why is this man so irritating? "Could you send it today, please? Federal Express?"

"Are you going to pay for it?"

Arrrgggghhh. "If you like."

Skip rang off. *Self-important bastard.*

Then: *I'm evil today.*

It was a phrase she'd picked up from Cindy Lou, whose grandmother used to say she "got evil" when she reached menopause. "So far as I could tell," Cindy Lou had said, "it's like galloping negativity. You don't like anything or anybody and you snap at whoever you run into."

Apparently, more things than menopause could cause it. Lack of sleep, for one.

The phone rang again. "Goddamn it."

"Hi, it's Layne."

"Oh. Hi."

"You don't sound that glad to hear from me."

"Sorry. What can I do for you?"

"It's what I can do for you. I've got a present for you."

"Information, I hope."

"It's this great piece of software I designed. You can track who posted where and when and how many times and all kinds of neat stuff. Sort of a detective bureau on a disk. So you can manipulate your computer data just like other stuff—like putting it on three-by-five cards."

"Wait a minute. You mean I could figure out what somebody did in a given session on the TOWN? If they posted in a lot of different conferences?"

"Sure."

"Would it tell me when? Like what order it all happened in?"

"Elementary, my dear."

She was warming toward him. She could track Geoff and Lenore and anyone else she wanted to.

"So shall I come over tonight and install it?"

"I don't think that's the way to do it."

"Hey, I'm gay. Did I mention that?"

She laughed. "It's not that. It's just that until the case is over we need to maintain a professional relationship."

"Huh?"

She kept quiet while the penny dropped.

"Hold it. Hey, hold it, I think I just got it. I'm a suspect, is that what you're saying?"

"Like the man said, I suspect everyone."

"I can't get over it, I'm a suspect." He laughed for about a minute and a half, making her feel evil again.

"Listen, thanks for the offer, but maybe I should come to your house."

"I've got a better idea. You live in the Quarter, don't you?"

How the hell does he know where I live? "It's okay, I'll come to your house."

"No, let's meet for coffee. That place on Royal Street with the funny name and the little art gallery. You know, it's . . ."

"Right by the Eighth."

"Huh?"

"The police station."

"Yeah. Coffee and Concierge, something weird like that."

"Is five-fifteen okay?"

"Well, *you're* certainly all business."

"Wait a minute. I don't know a damn thing about installing software—do you think you can explain it in a way I can understand?"

He was quiet a moment. "You know, I'm not really sure."

"What if I bring along a nerd friend?"

"I have to admit I'd feel better."

She phoned Jimmy Dee, explained the situation, and asked if he'd mind acting as translator.

"Charmed, I'm sure. In fact, perfect. My car's having surgery. You can pick me up."

She had one more thing to do before she could leave—report to Cappello and make arrangements for that night.

The sergeant frowned. "So. You really think these babes are Satanists?"

"That thing at Lenore's spooked me. Bad." She shrugged. "I've researched it a little. If they are, killing Geoff could be one crime in a long list of them."

"Who do you want for backup? Hodges okay?"

Skip broke into a grin. "Perfect."

Jim Hodges was an older black man, solid as a concrete wall—a tough pro who'd seen it all and carried pictures of his grandchildren.

"You got him." Cappello shook her head, not liking the turn the investigation was taking.

• •

Finally, wearily, Skip left for lunch, which in this case meant a nap at home. She could get a sandwich later.

At one-fifteen sharp, she woke up and put on coffee. There were things she could do from home—why not do them instead of going back in right now?

Sheila's bedclothes were still on the couch. She whipped up a BLT, and cuddled up in them, reaching for the telephone.

"All Systems Go."

"Neetsie Terry, please." Skip wondered suddenly if Neetsie wore her nose ring to work.

"Who?"

"Um . . . Anita."

"Oh. Nita. Just a second."

Neetsie came on and Skip identified herself. "I called your parents' house," she said. "But I couldn't get any answer."

"Mom's probably asleep. She's been sleeping a lot lately. It's how she copes, I guess."

"I hope I didn't disturb her. She has a lot to cope with. I called because I need to know how I can get in touch with your grandmother."

"Don't we all."

"Yes, I gather she's a little past it."

"What do you need her for?"

"I'm afraid I can't really talk about that."

"Well, I don't see how it can do any harm—she loves visitors. You'll brighten her day. The place is called The Camellias. Gruesome name, isn't it?"

"What's gruesome about it?"

"Camellias. I hate them, don't you? So stiff and proper."

"Actually, I do." But she did like Neetsie. She showed promising signs of being a free spirit.

Well, there'd been one thing she could do from home anyway. Next, she had to get to The Camellias before Marguerite forbade them to let her see the patient.

It was near Bayou St. John, an unprepossessing one-story building that was altogether too run-down for its rather grand name. Skip did notice, though, that there were five or six healthy camellia plants in its otherwise scruffy yard.

A nurse met her at the door, a young woman in her early thirties. She was a little dumpy, maybe thirty pounds overweight. A pair of round glasses sat on a round, happy face surrounded by a wreath of curls. Her skin was as white and soft as one of the blossoms the place was named for, her full, generous lips painted a bold red. She was the sort about whom people clucked, "Such a pretty face; what a shame about her weight."

Oh, well. Guess I am too.

Skip identified herself. "I'm here to see Mrs. Julian."

"I'm Mary Christianson. You must be here about her grandson. Awful thing, wasn't it? And so weird—all those computer people."

"It's an odd one, all right."

"Well, I don't think . . . Mrs. Julian can't really understand much."

Skip nodded. "Does she have lucid periods?"

"I don't know if I'd exactly say *that*." She looked anxiously at Skip, eager to please. "Sometimes she's better than others, though."

"Shall we give it a try?"

"Sure. Let's go find her."

Mrs. Juilian was in a common room with some other old people in bathrobes and pajamas. Most of them had their eyes pinned on a television, but almost none of them looked interested. Two of the old men were shouting at each other, though Skip thought there was no animosity in it; deafness, probably.

"Mrs. Julian, I've got somebody nice to see you."

"To see me?"

"This is Ms. Langdon."

"Marguerite? Are you Marguerite?"

Mary cleared some magazines off a couch.

"It's really nice to see you today." Skip sat down, automatically patting the old woman's wrist. "I wanted to talk about Geoff."

"Oh, yes. Uh-huh."

"Your grandson."

"Shall we start with scales today?"

"Your grandson who died, Mrs. Julian," said Mary helpfully.

Skip was at first dismayed, since she had no plan to bring in the present, but she perked up when Mrs. Julian said, "Leighton. Leighton was the one, but he wasn't my grandson. Was he?"

Mary rolled her eyes, and Skip quickly put a finger to her lips. She said, "Do you remember what happened to Leighton?"

178

"Well, yes, I do." She nodded several times for emphasis.

"Can you tell me about it?"

"Oh, yes. Of course I can."

"The night Leighton died. That was quite a night."

"Well, yes it was."

Mary looked at Skip and shook her head. "She does this a lot. If you ask her a direct question, she'll say yes, no matter what it is. Go ahead. Try it."

"The night Leighton was killed. That was V-J Day, wasn't it?"

"Yes, it certainly was."

Skip sighed. "Is she ever any better?"

"Oh, yes. Sometimes she gets on a roll and talks like it's goin' out of style."

"What about?"

"Usually, things that happened to her a long time ago."

"Ah. Has she ever mentioned Leighton?"

"I think she has. Yes. I really think so."

"What did she say?"

Mary frowned. "I guess I can't really remember."

In her eagerness to please, she reminded Skip of Mrs. Julian. Skip wasn't sure you could get a straight answer out of either of them.

16

• •

Jimmy Dee kept Skip waiting ten minutes in front of his office, her motor running, her temper rising.

"Dammit, Dee-Dee, this is a business appointment."

"Well. Aren't we Miss Congeniality."

He could make her smile even when she was angry. "I'm sorry. I didn't mean to snap."

"You probably think you're suffering from lack of sleep."

"Uh-oh. This is leading up to something."

"Precious angel, you've been bitten by the lovebug."

"You mean Darryl Boucree? He's black, Dee-Dee."

"And beautiful—or didn't you notice?"

"Remember in Jungle Fever how shocked the guy's friend is when he says he's seeing a white woman? Darryl Boucree wouldn't go out with me."

He stuck out his hand. "Oh, yeah? Fifty bucks says otherwise."

"Anyway, there's Steve."

"Isn't there?"

She looked at her watch. "Damn! It'll probably take ten minutes to park."

"Let me. You go handcuff the guy or something."

"Okay." She turned the car over to him.

Layne was just draining a cup of espresso. "I thought you'd forgotten."

"My friend was late. Would you like something else?"

He shook his head. "No, thanks. Aren't you pleased I'm doing what you said?"

"What?"

"You said I should get out more."

"Congratulations. I think your color's coming back."

"Here's the thing." He handed over a package of software, which she opened immediately.

"Oh, no. Those big floppies. I have the little ones."

"Oh. Nerds always have both kinds because we get stuff from lots of different sources. But it's not a big deal. You can still upload it, you just need the hardware to make the transfer."

"Jimmy Dee probably has it."

"Who, me?" He came in jangling her keys.

"Dee-Dee, you're in the nick. This is Layne Bilderback. Jimmy Dee Scoggin."

She bought Jimmy Dee a latte, and for the next ten minutes, the two men spoke a language she didn't.

"No problem. Piece of cake," Dee-Dee said finally.

"Great." She looked at her watch. "Should we get going? You still have to cook."

"God, yes. Anyway, I'm worried about Sheila. She could be halfway to Chicago by now." He stood and spoke to Layne. "You have kids?"

Layne grinned. "Uh-uh. Times like this I'm glad I'm gay."

"Don't get too cocky, son. It's not over till it's over."

"Darling," said Dee-Dee when they were back in Skip's car, "I simply can't keep track of all your men."

"Well, that one's a murder suspect."

"Pretty friendly for a desperado."

"Probably just trying to butter me up." She thought about Layne. "He is nice, though. It's hard being a cop sometimes."

"I'm crying. Has he gainful employment?"

"Employment, anyway. He's a puzzlemaker. Or puzzle constructer, as he prefers to be called."

"He's pretty open about his preferences, wouldn't you say?"

"Oh, come on, Dee-Dee, tell me you didn't know."

"Well, I was hoping."

"What? You *liked* him? You never like anyone."

"Pish-tush. I would trek to the North Pole to get Darryl Boucree a piece of ice for his Coke."

"I mean . . . this seems different."

"Young Mr. Bilderback has taken my fancy."

"You've *got* to be kidding. I don't believe this."

"You think he's single?"

"Dee-Dee, he's a murder suspect. Remember Sheila and Kenny."

"We're not getting married, for God's sake. Not for months yet."

She honestly couldn't tell if he was just carrying on (as was his wont) or if he was genuinely interested.

As was her wont, she entered her apartment throwing off clothes. As soon as she had stripped down to panties and bra, her doorbell sounded.

"Who is it?" she hollered.

"Darryl Boucree."

She pulled on a robe and stepped out on her balony. "Darryl! What are you doing here?"

"Got a present for Sheila."

"Well, aren't you nice. Hang on a second."

She wriggled into a pair of jeans and looked around for her red sweater. It wasn't anywhere.

She picked up another, but it was drab brown. No good. She hunted some more, down under the bed, in the closet, before it occurred to her what she was doing.

What do you care about Darryl Boucree? she asked herself.

She slipped on the brown sweater, but took time to fluff up her hair.

I guess I care.

When she had walked downstairs, and actually stood in his presence, the breadth of his chest, the way it moved inside his sweater, the pull of him, almost a smell, she thought, made her oddly happy.

Watch out! Testosterone is the world's most dangerous drug. Get one molecule on you and you're helpless.

It was too late. She was covered with it.

Drenched.

She didn't need this; didn't want it, didn't welcome it. So why did she feel so happy?

The rapture of the deep, I guess.

When she spoke, her voice sounded thin. "Hi." He held her gaze as long as she was willing to let him. She broke away first.

"How you doin'?"

"Remember Cindy Lou? My friend from last night? She talks about being evil. That's how I'm doing."

"Need your eight hours, huh?"

"How about you?"

He shrugged. "Half a teacher's better than none. In fact, the kids think it's better than one."

She laughed. "Let's go over to the Big House."

"Okay."

"Sheila. Sheila! Look who I've got."

Sheila poked her head out. "Darryl." She came flying down the hall and flung her arms around him, something she never did with Skip or Jimmy Dee. "How you doin', dude?"

"Gimme five."

For an eternity or so, they slapped each other's palms in the complex hand jive that kids and black males were so crazy about.

"Who's out there?" Jimmy Dee emerged, now in jeans, polo shirt, and determined-dad look. His face split in a grin when he saw who'd arrived. "Auntie Skip and Uncle Darryl. You're staying for dinner, of course."

Darryl grinned back. "Best offer I've had today."

Sheila said, "You haven't had his cooking yet."

Skip and Jimmy Dee caught each other's eyes. Sheila had actually cracked a joke. Skip looked back at her to make sure she was kidding.

No question: there was a mischievous glint in her eye.

"Suppose you cook tonight, young lady," said Jimmy Dee. "How's your coq au vin?"

"Cocoa what?"

Skip looked at her watch. "I have to be out of here in forty-five minutes. Tell me you're not making coq au vin."

"Okay. I'm not. Geneese made some gumbo. All we have to do is heat it up."

Skip said, "I'll start the rice."

Kenny had come in, and was standing shyly against a wall. "Hey, sport," said Darryl. "What's your name?"

"Kenny." He smiled his sweet little smile, the one that made all adults love him and Sheila want to kill him.

"Darryl. Gimme five."

They played pat-a-cake for nearly as long as it took to cook the rice and by the time they were finished, Darryl had another disciple.

Skip busied herself peeling cucumbers and washing lettuce while Jimmy Dee set the table. *It's like a family*, she thought. *We're finally having fun.*

Dee-Dee was beside himself, but also nervous as a bride. He knew, as Skip did, that Darryl was the glue holding it together, and who knew who Darryl was? He was still a stranger she'd met in a bar; or maybe a guardian angel who'd come down and tapped her on the shoulder.

Well, what the hell, depending on the kindness of strangers made this city famous.

Sheila tugged at Darryl. "Hey, where's my present?"

"In my backpack. What'd I do with it?"

Sheila ran to get it.

Kenny was leaning against a wall, looking melancholy.

"Bet you'd like a present too, sport."

He looked around, as if sure Darryl were talking to some other kid. "Me?"

"Yeah, you. You want a present?"

Kenny smiled his smile. "Sure."

"Well, I got somethin' for you."

Sheila handed Darryl his pack. He fumbled around for what

184

seemed an inordinate amount of time, and when he pulled his hand out, a different rubber monster head sat on each finger, now waving fiercely in Kenny's face.

The boy laughed out loud. So did Skip and Jimmy Dee and even Sheila.

"You want these?" He caught Kenny's nose with two of them. "Want 'em? Huh?"

Kenny was so enchanted he could only nod.

"And now for Ms. Sheila. Well, I got you something really special. But I better tell you, it's something you're probably not expecting."

She nodded, radiant in her anticipation.

"It may even be something you think you don't want."

"Oh, I'll want it. I know I'll want it."

"Even if it's a—"

"A what?"

"I can't tell you. You're going to be mad."

"I won't be mad, I promise. I promise I won't be mad."

"Okay, it's a book."

"A *what?*" She couldn't conceal her disappointment.

"See, I knew you'd be mad."

"I'm not mad. I could . . . read a book." She wanted desperately to please him.

A truly wonderful sign. She never wants to please either of us.

"Even if it's about a boy?"

"A boy?" Her voice said, *What on Earth are you thinking of?*

"You gotta trust me, Sheila. Even though it's a book and even though it's about a boy, it's going to change your life. You're going to read this and think, 'There's somebody out there who understands.' "

"*Catcher in the Rye,*" the other adults said together, and instantly realized it was a tactical error. They were the enemy; if they liked it, it couldn't be good.

But Darryl turned to them: "Now how did you two know that?"

"Saved my ass," said Jimmy Dee.

"Mine too."

Kenny said, "I didn't think grown-ups were supposed to talk like that."

"Anybody who reads this book," said Darryl solemnly, "can talk any way they want from now on."

"Hold it a minute," said Jimmy Dee. "You don't have to live with these two."

"Yeah, but you know it doesn't matter what I say now. Because you can't stop anybody after they've read it, can you? They come out a whole different person, don't they?"

"Okay, okay, I'll read the damn book."

"Sheila!" said Kenny. "You're not supposed to cuss."

"Darryl said I could cuss."

"Only if you read the book."

Skip sighed: *Back to normal.*

But still. It was the most peaceful—in fact, the most downright enjoyable—dinner she and Jimmy Dee had ever had with the kids.

Too bad Darryl's already got two jobs, she thought. *He'd be the nanny of the century.*

"Margaret, where are you off to tonight?"

"Oh, a little something on the case."

"Policeman's work is never done."

"This lady's no policeman," said Darryl. "She might be the heat, but I got eyes."

Eyes like lasers. Get 'em off of me before I rip your clothes off in front of the kids.

"Gotta go," she said. "Darryl, nice to see you. Thanks for coming by."

"My pleasure, Ms. Skip. Pleasure's all mine." He stared unabashedly as he said it, and she felt her sweater go over her head, her zipper go down in his mental movie.

Beads of sweat are going to pop out of my forehead, she thought, saw Jimmy Dee's amused look, and was pretty sure they already had.

She'd agreed to meet Hodges at headquarters. He was going to drive, since none of the women had seen him; Skip could scrunch down in her seat if she had to.

Driving over, she thought, *What's with this Darryl? What does he want? Surely not me.*

And yet she hoped against hope that he did.

What about Steve?

Damn Steve!

She picked up Hodges and gave him directions to Kit's house. They followed her as she picked up Suby (who came out carrying a large tote bag), crossed the Causeway, drove to Covington, and then turned onto a small country road. That was bad—there were very few cars, which meant they had a good chance of being seen.

They stayed as far behind as they dared, and when they no longer heard Kit's motor, they parked, hoping the other car had stopped rather than surged ahead.

Skip started to open her door, but heard another car behind her. Both she and Hodges ducked, and as it passed, she saw Lenore riding shotgun.

Wonder what she does with Caitlin? Skip was reminded suddenly of Marguerite, out every night when Geoff was a small boy.

She and Hodges waited another fifteen minutes, too keyed up even to talk. A few more cars passed, then all was quiet.

They got out and split up. Skip followed the road a little farther, staying close to the side, where the trees were. It was a warmish night without much wind. The moon was rising and, because it was full, she could see very well—but so could she be seen if anyone happened along. She had an odd sense of anticipation, of excitement, a kind of tingling.

A reaction to danger? she wondered. But it wasn't her usual sort, which involved a lot of heart pounding and sweat. This was pleasurable, almost a sexual sensation—a marked contrast to her fear the other night. For the life of her, she couldn't have said why.

She had walked about ten minutes, until she heard the sound of voices. The women were in a cleared space, perhaps a meadow. In the center of it they had placed a table of some sort—the altar, Skip surmised, and noted with relief that it was neither the size nor shape for human sacrifice. And this time there was no skull. But the moon glinted on the dagger, and she could see the pentacle plate.

Small scarves or bits of colored cloth were scattered at equal intervals around the altar—four of them, with a candle in a jar on each one, and a few other things, Skip couldn't tell what, but they looked like rocks and shells.

The women were still fussing, organizing, arranging, making things pretty. Behaving much like women giving a tea party. Skip thought again of the banality of evil, but tonight she couldn't make it stick; the beauty of the evening, the woods bedecked in silver light, the purity of the air, the softness of the women's voices— somehow, it just didn't add up to degradation and horror.

I'll feel differently when they put on those spooky black robes and get the blood- curdling chant going.

But to her amazement, they put on white robes instead—all but Kit, who had disappeared.

Oh my God, they're playing dress-up. A cult with outfits; just what I need.

•   •

Pearce had seen her arrive after the others, and realized it must be her car he had passed, parked on the side of the road. He had fol- lowed Lenore. She must have followed one of the others, probably Kit.

He had seen her colleague too, the old guy.

He had arrived at the opposite strategy from theirs, had driven past the glen where the women were having their little picnic, had parked, and doubled back. He'd already been in position when the cop arrived. It amused him that he was the better stalker.

They were all in white now, in belted robes with little bags like drawstring purses hanging from their belts; little bags and knives—a very medieval look. But Kit was missing.

Ah—now she was coming, just emerging from her car.

Unlike the rest of them, she wore yellow, a gorgeous yellow robe, belted with some sort of cord threaded through the loop of another, shorter cord. From the shorter cord hung a large metal ankh. The effect was of a rosary, or whatever priests dangled from their cassocks. On her head she wore some kind of headband with a sort of disk on it, affixed so that it stood upright, on its edge. It was gold-colored metal, probably brass, and the moonlight glinted eerily on it.

Her hair had been teased out in all directions, forming an unruly mane around her face, a variation on the Bride of Frankenstein look. And she had painted her face. Even with the brightness of the moon, he couldn't see terribly well, but from his vantage point, it looked as if she'd put horizontal stripes on her cheeks, like cat whiskers.

The women stood in a circle. They took turns lighting the four candles they'd placed around the middle table, each one mouthing some sort of mumbo jumbo about east and west and earth and fire, and who knew what kind of crap. It embarrassed him.

But each one, as she did it, slid a knife from its sheath and drew something in the air with it—what, he couldn't tell.

When it was nearly over, the pattern of the thing began to ring a bell—something about the four directions and the elements. Wasn't this a common part of religious rituals? Was it Masonic? He thought it was, perhaps, but he thought he'd read something about its origins; he had the impression it was vaguely Cabalistic.

Something told him he was in for more than he bargained for—this wasn't a bunch of women doing some little improvised Halloween skit. He didn't know what it was, but it was starting to spook him.

He rifled his pockets for his tape recorder; he was close enough that it might pick up. And, to make sure, he took notes as well, on his ever-present four-times-folded sheaf of paper, the only proper notepad for reporters, the old-timers had told him, because it fit in the palm of your hand and didn't make anyone nervous.

Neetsie came forward and with a fanfare drew the dagger on the altar from its sheath, held it out the full length of her arm. Kit also came forward and pointed likewise with her ankh.

Neetsie began speaking a language Pearce couldn't understand. He couldn't get it at first, couldn't make any sense at all of it, but she kept repeating it, chanting it, and finally he just started writing down what it sounded like:

> Eko, Eko, Azarak,
> Eko, Eko, Zomelak,
> Eko, Eko, Shining One,
> Eko, Eko, Terrible One!

As she chanted, she walked around the circle, Kit following, the two still pointing with their weapons.

> Darksome night, and shining moon,
> East, then South, then West, then North;
> Hearken to the witches' [room? tune? he wasn't sure]
> Here we come to call ye forth! Earth and Water, Air and Fire
> Wand and pentacle and sword,
> Work ye unto our desire,
> Hearken ye unto our word!
> Cords and censer, cup and knife,
> Powers of the witch's blade,
> Waken all ye into life,
> come ye as the charm is made!

> Queen of heaven, Queen of hell,
> Horned hunter of the night—
> Lend your power unto the spell,
> And work our will by magic rite!
> By all the power of land and sea,
> By all the might of moon and sun—
> As we do will, so mote it be;
> Chant the spell and be it done!
> Eko, Eko, Azarak,
> Eko, Eko, Zomelak,
> Eko, Eko, Shining One,
> Eko, Eko, Terrible One!

They walked the circle three times in the course of the chant, and when it was over, Neetsie said, "The circle is cast; we are between the worlds."

The other women answered in chorus: "So mote it be!"

A woman Pearce didn't know came out of the circle, picked up a bowl of water from the altar, drew her knife, put it in the bowl, and said, "I exorcise thee, o creature of water, that thou cast out from thee all the impurities and uncleanliness of the world of phantasm; in the names of the Lady and the Lord of light and darkness."

She held up the bowl for all to see.

Another woman, also a stranger, came forward, picked up another bowl, put her knife in it, and said, "Blessings be upon this creature of salt; let all malignity and hindrance be cast forth here from, and let all good enter herein; wherefore do I bless thee, that thou mayest aid me, in the names of the Lady and the Lord of light and darkness."

She then poured the salt into the water; both women put their bowls back and rejoined the circle.

Neetsie again took center stage and admonished the group: "Listen to the words of the Great Mother; she who of old was also called Artemis, Astarte, Athena, Dione, Melusine, Aphrodite, Cerridwen, Dana, Arianrhod, Isis, Bride, and by many other names. At her altars the youth of Lacedaemon in Sparta made due sacrifice."

He had thought she would continue, but Kit directed her ankh toward the heavens (toward the moon, he realized later), and all the women spoke in unison:

"Whenever you have need of any thing, once in the month and better it be when the moon is full, then shall ye assemble in some secret place and adore the spirit of me, who am queen of all the witches. There shall ye assemble, ye who are fain to learn all sorcery, yet have not won its deepest secrets; to these will I teach things that are yet unknown, And ye shall be free from slavery—"

Here Pearce's tape recorder jammed, and he fiddled with it during the rest of his speech. There was something about the "secret door," though, "which opens upon the Land of Youth, and mine is the cup of the wine of life and the Cauldron of Cerridwen, which is the holy grail of immortality."

Sign me up, he thought. *So what if we have to sacrifice a few virgins?*

"Nor do I demand sacrifice," they said.

Ha! What about the youth of Lacedaemon?

There was another phrase he liked: "All acts of love and pleasure are my rituals."

Again he thought, *Sign me up,* but given the spooky tone of the ritual, he couldn't help wondering what on Earth the phrase was supposed to mean. Were these women some sort of modern maenads, as likely to tear strong men apart as light a candle or two in the moonlight? Kit looked the part.

A little scenario came to him: What if Geoff's death wasn't quite as cut-and-dry as it looked? What if he'd been killed somewhere else and taken to his patio, the ladder placed just so . . .

Or maybe the ritual had been there in the first place.

Exactly how it might escalate to death he'd worry about later, but a less pleasant thought hit him now—maybe these women really were dangerous when full of religious fervor or whatever you called this.

If you were in the wrong place at the wrong time . . .

A sobering thought, but no way in hell was he budging. In all his years as a reporter, he'd never seen anything like this damn thing.

They finished the speech: "For behold, I have been with thee from the beginning; and I am that which is attained at the end of desire."

But who the hell are you? He wondered, as people had, he realized, since "the beginning" the speech mentioned.

The end of desire. Sure. If only it were that easy.

Neetsie seemed to have another announcement to make. This Neetsie certainly wasn't the one he knew. She was much more poised, surer, more confident.

More adult.

He found himself a little in awe of her, a circumstance he couldn't have imagined before tonight.

She spoke to the moon. "You who are with us always even when you are not; Moonmother! Shining One; dark one; large one; small one; pregnant one; barren one; crescent and circle. You who are as we are—maiden, mother, crone—though now at your height. Diana, Luna, Cybele, Aradia; Ishtar, Astarte; Inanna. Come to us tonight. Come to us!

"Be here now!"

Obviously following some sort of script, the others shouted: "Be here now!"

Neetsie lit a black candle and picked up a green one. She spoke to it: "And you, Lord Cernunnos. Horned one; leaper; lover;

brother and son. Virile one, keeper of the animals, join us as well."
She lit the candle.

"Be here now!"

"Be here now!" the women chanted, and it was all Pearce could do not to shout the words with them. Though what it was they were calling, he wasn't sure he wanted to know.

If it has horns, it probably has little cloven hooves as well.

Neetsie spoke again, this time to the group, having apparently finished her colloquy with heavenly bodies and demons. "Women of the Cauldron of Cerridwen! Tonight we will speak with one as old as the pyramids. Wiser than all the pharaohs and all the gods; more terrible than an earthquake. Sekhmet, the Lady of the Fifth Way! Those who work with Sekhmet mention indescribable delights and unspeakable horrors. So is it with our lady."

Mixing things up, aren't they? Cerridwen was Celtic, I think, and the pyramids are Egyptian. And how the hell does Our Lady fit in?

He was trying to think sophisticated thoughts, striving to muster up his usual cynical attitude, but he couldn't stop a crop of goose bumps.

"Priestess Brianna, come forward."

That proved to be Kit, who had rejoined the group and now came to the center again. "Priestess Brianna, are you ready to receive the Lady of the Bloodbath?"

"I am."

"Are you ready to receive the Giver of Ecstasies?"

"I am."

"So mote it be."

The answer came: "So mote it be."

Once again, Neetsie spoke to the moon: "Lady Diana [she pronounced it "Deeonna"], it is your night; it is your moment. And so we beg your indulgence to call into our priestess your counterpart of the daytime hours, another Shining One, a lady of the sun."

Pearce half expected the moon to bellow out, "So mote it be!"

"Cover us," commanded Neetsie.

Suby stepped forward, picked up a silvery scarf from the altar, and draped it over both women's heads. It looked as if, inside, Neetsie held Kit by the shoulders.

"Mother of the gods!" she shouted. "Come into our priestess. One Who Was Before the Gods Were! Flaming One! Lady of the Scarlet-Colored Garment! Awakener! Lady of Enchantments! Sekhmet of the Knives! Satisfier of Desires! Sublime One! Mother of the Dead! Enlightener! Destroyer by Plagues! Lady of the Waters of Life! Great One in Heaven! Devouring One! Bountiful One! Warrior Goddess! Beloved Teacher! Beloved Sekhmet! Come into Brianna!"

Under the scarf, he saw Kit straighten suddenly. Neetsie lifted the scarf and stepped away. Kit's bearing was different, Pearce thought; and one of her hands had drawn itself into a clawlike shape. With the other, she raised her ankh, slowly, agonizingly slowly, and pointed it straight ahead: "I am the Lady of the Place of the Beginning of Time. I am Sekhmet, Great One of Magic. Come forward, you who would know."

One of the women stepped forward and spoke quietly to Kit, who answered her too softly for Pearce to hear. The supplicant then lit a candle she had brought with her, a white candle in a jar apparently meant to serve as a wind shield.

She stepped back and another came forward, then another, till everyone had had a turn.

Meanwhile, the ones who weren't eating from the tree of knowledge, or whatever they were doing, chanted some godawful spooky thing: it could have been "Om" or just "O," Pearce couldn't say, but it sounded like the baying of all the hounds of hell.

For a while, though, he forgot to be unnerved or even cynical and was caught by the beauty of the scene—women in flowing garments, candles, chanting.

Oh, God, watch it, Pearce; this is how people slip into things. This is how smart people get converted to cults. They hypnotize you. They know techniques that work on your reason.

Well, forget me. This is a nut that's not gonna crack. Who the fuck does Kit think she is, the Pythian Sibyl?

Those poor little girls. They actually believe that crap she's handing out. Whatever it is.

He amused himself composing words of wisdom she might be passing to the others:

Give me all your money and jewels.

Do whatever I say for the rest of your life.

Go out and make your bones—sacrifice a human being to prove your allegiance. Preferably a child under ten.

Wait a minute! Sacrifice a human being? That was even better than the other idea—the one where things got out of hand and Geoff died by accident. Could he sell this one to the cops (and of course to his esteemed readers)?

17

• •

Skip came away oddly unnerved. Not terrified, the way she'd been before—instead, somewhat reassured, since no one had been sacrificed and no blood had been drunk. In fact, now she knew what the cookies were for at the last meeting—they were to eat. At the end, Kit had taken off her headgear and her fierce look, and the whole bunch of them had sat down and had a tea party. It was certainly a study in different styles.

She was unnerved at her own reaction.

She'd loved the thing.

"Uh, Jim," she said, "what the hell do you think that was?"

Hodges grinned. He had worn dark clothes and he was dark. His teeth glinted in the closed car. "Don't know, but it shore was pretty."

That helped. Skip had thought so too, but it made her feel weirdly guilty—as if she were breaking some kind of basic rule of society.

She still wasn't sure it was benign—maybe they only did sacrifices once a year, or every two months or something. And there was all that talk of bloodbaths. And of course the skull last time, the pentacle, the reference to "the horned one." And what on Earth was a Sekhmet? In short, there were a lot of very suspicious things still to be dealt with.

Which was why it was particularly worrisome that she felt as if she'd fallen under a spell. After she dropped Hodges, she even had trouble driving home, kept drifting off. Well, they'd called themselves witches. Maybe they'd done some sort of magic on her. Maybe one of those young women who walked up to Kit had said, "I just saw Skip Langdon hiding in the bushes. Why don't we neutralize her?"

What was a witch anyhow? She pondered the word. The black robes fit, but the white ones didn't. And where were the broomsticks, the orgies? What there had been, of a witchy nature, was a cauldron, and apparently some sort of attempted contact with the spirit world.

But she remembered that post of Kit's on the TOWN—weren't witches supposed to have intercourse with Satan? Only if Torquemada insisted they had, the post seemed to say, but there was still that bothersome word: *Satan*.

She fell into bed and dreamed of water—of a tidal wave engulfing her, and awakened, sweating. She got up and sipped water, knowing she had to pursue this first thing in the morning.

I know. I'll talk to Suby.

Suby was probably the most vulnerable. The one most likely to crack under bullying. It was a dirty job, but the fastest means to an end.

However, she now had enough information to ask the department experts first—someone in Child Abuse or Intelligence might know what she and Hodges had seen.

She put in calls and waited—it was a Saturday, so it was a while before the phone rang. "Ramon, Intelligence. Returning your call."

She described the two rituals she'd seen, and he fixed on one word. "Witches? Did you say they're witches?"

"That's what they called themselves."

He laughed. "Look, I've got a whole lot of material on it—I could give it to you if you want."

197

"Could you meet me at headquarters in a few minutes? I want to interview somebody and I don't really want to go in cold."

"Yeah, sure."

What he told her, what she read, was fascinating, but it left most of her questions unanswered.

She hoped Suby didn't live with her dad—she didn't have the heart to accuse her of witchcraft with Mike Kavanagh in the house. She thought not, though.

The house where Kit had picked her up was big, but probably a duplex. A slender girl answered the door, not Suby, but maybe one of the witches. Moonlight changed faces, she realized—all the women had looked beautiful, even Kit with her odd hair and makeup. "Is Suby home?"

"I don't know if she's up yet."

Skip produced her badge. Wide-eyed, the girl went to find Suby, leaving Skip in a living room furnished with what were obviously parental castoffs. She sat down on a brocade couch with the stuffing coming out of one of the arms. A black cat, no doubt the couch-killer, came and rubbed against her.

Somewhere in the back of the apartment, a radio went on; an old jazz tune broke the stillness of the Saturday. WWOZ, she thought.

Finally, Suby appeared, in jeans and sweater, hair freshly brushed but wearing no makeup. At the TOWN dinner, Skip had paid her little attention, had noticed only that her features were like her father's, Irish and rather coarse. A flat, slightly piggish nose spread out on her face, but her skin was lovely and her hair was thick. When she said hello, Skip realized something she hadn't before—that her best feature was her voice, and it was fascinating—unexpectedly deep and throaty, yet at the same time very soft, very feminine. She spoke slowly, which made her sound as gentle and reassuring as your favorite aunt. A nurturing person, Skip thought, and found herself drawn to her.

"Would you like some coffee?"

"I'd love some. Shall I help you?" Despite Suby's protests, Skip followed her to the kitchen. Favorite aunt or no, she wasn't taking a chance on getting eye of newt for breakfast.

"You must be here about Geoff."

"Suby, I need you to tell me something—what's the Cauldron of Cerridwen?"

Suby whirled, her cheeks flaming. "How do you know about that?"

"It's my job to know."

"Why are you asking?" She turned back around and began very carefully measuring out coffee.

"How old are you, Suby?"

"I drive. I'm sure that's on record somewhere."

Skip couldn't believe she'd picked this one believing she'd be an easy target. She took a breath; here was where the bullying started. "It is. You're nineteen; that's still a minor. As you know, I work with your dad. Now, we've had reports about Satanist activity in the area and I wanted to give you a chance—"

She whirled again, this time knocking over a dirty glass on the counter. "Satanist! That makes me so mad!"

"I'm giving you a chance to explain."

"Goddammit! My dad dragged me off to mass a couple of weeks ago and the priest was talking about 'pagans' like we were those heavy-metal types with the spiked hair and the inverted pentagrams. It makes me so goddam mad. There's no religious toleration in this country unless you're goddam *Catholic*. My dad could probably get Kit arrested for contributing to my delinquency or something and she hasn't done a goddam thing except teach me . . ."

"What?"

"Things I need to know."

"I guess I know what your favorite word is, anyway."

"Oh. You mean *goddam*. Sorry. It's just that it makes me so mad. . . ."

"I get the hang of it. Look, I'm not here to hurt you. I just need some information, that's all. What's an inverted pentagram, for openers?"

Suby drew a star and turned it upside down, so that two of its arms pointed upward. "There. It's supposed to be a Satanic symbol—I've never seen one except on, like, album covers. Death-rock kind of stuff." She turned it back around. "Not to be confused with this one, which means the four elements and spirit. Or . . . lots of things, I guess. That's just how I think of it."

The coffee had dripped through its filter. She turned back and poured Skip a cup.

"So tell me about the Cauldron of Cerridwen."

"I guess I have to, huh?" She seemed to have calmed down.

"It's probably a good idea."

"The only thing is, I don't know where to start. Let's see. Well, we're a group that has a name that I'm not going to tell you yet, because it's kind of inflammatory. What do you know about neo-paganism?"

Skip shrugged. "I've never even heard the word before." (Before talking to Ramon, anyway.)

"Well, it's a kind of made-up religion based on—um . . . what? All the religions that ever were, practically. Unlike Satanism, by the way, which is an offshoot of Christianity. We don't even recognize Satan, who is a Christian concept and nothing to do with us."

"Wait a minute—this thing is based on all religions *except* Christianity?"

She flushed. "Well, there are pagans who are also Christians. I just don't happen to be one of them."

"And Kit?"

"I have no idea. The great thing about it is there aren't any rules or dogma. You can believe anything you want and nobody'll care."

"Except about Satan."

She flushed again.

"I take it back. There's a code of ethics. Black magic is precluded."

"Whoa! I'm in way over my head."

"Most of the ancient religions did go in for magic. Think about Native American shamanism, or voodoo. We think they were on to something. But we don't use what we do for evil. As I understand it, Satan's evil by definition."

"You call yourselves witches then."

"That's right. How'd you know that?"

"Tell me more."

"Okay, the word I was avoiding is 'coven.' It's a group of witches who work together. Ours is all women, but we aren't Dianic."

"What?"

"Sorry. That's a technical term for witches who only call the goddess, and that's not us. See, we reject the idea of a male god. That is, only one god who happens to be male. Most ancient cultures had a goddess before they had a god—the god is her consort, but also her son and her lover, depending on what time of year it is." Seeing Skip's confused look, she said, "Most of the beliefs come from agricultural cultures. The goddess represented the Earth itself and the god represented the grain. He dies, so he has to be born again. That's why he's her son."

"Let me get this straight. She mates with him, he dies, and then she gives birth to him again."

Suby shrugged. "They don't call these things mysteries for nothing."

Skip was thinking that this pat little lecture explained a few things, but Suby was making it sound a lot more cheerful than she had found it.

"Come on, Suby. Why would you need human bones for the sort of thing you're talking about?"

"Human bones? What on Earth are you talking about?"

"A skull on your altar."

Her cheeks flamed again. "You've been spying on us."

Skip shrugged.

"Oh, God, we were doing that crone ritual. Oh, Jesus, this is starting to make sense. We even made jokes about it—if someone saw this, wouldn't they freak out, ha, ha, ha. And it would be a cop."

"Why don't we go back in the living room? I've got a feeling we're going to be here a while."

"You want some toast? I'm starving." Now that she knew what Skip knew, Suby was friendly as her own little black cat—which Skip now thought of as her familiar.

Carrying their coffee and Suby's toast, they went back in and settled on the shabby sofa. Suby put a hand to her head. "God.

How can I explain this?" Finally, she pointed outside, at the gray sky. "This is the crone's time of year. Winter. The maiden is spring, and the mother is summer."

"That works metaphorically."

"Ah. That's a word I should have used myself. You've got to think of this stuff as metaphor. We're a very dramatic coven—we've got the right clothes for everything, and these real formal, real dramatic rituals with a lot of memorization and fancy words—mostly at Neetsie's insistence.

"Once we did this ritual to banish all our bad habits and Neetsie insisted we all go do it at the hospital where Kit works, in this spooky old room where she goes to smoke. Can you imagine what that was like? Getting all our robes and gear past the hospital staff? That Neetsie's something else. By the way, it didn't even work that well—Kit still smokes, I still eat chocolate, and Lenore . . . oh, well, that's her business."

"What about the skull?"

"Sorry. I just wanted to emphasize that there's nothing like having an actor around to get a little drama in your life. So naturally, we've got white robes for the maiden, which we also wear at the full moon, and red for the mother, and black for the crone. Also, we use black candles for the crone.

"I know it sounds gross, but basically we're talking death here—that's what winter's all about, right? Halloween is All Hallows' Eve, when the veil between the worlds is thinnest—"

"What worlds?"

She shrugged. "Us and the other side. Death's what Halloween's all about—communing with your dead ancestors, all that sort of thing, and that ritual was barely afterward. Remember? Theoretically, the veil stays thin for a few weeks. And Geoff had just died."

"Oh. You were trying to get in touch with him?" She felt awfully silly talking this way.

"No, although we might have if he'd died before Samhein—that's what we call Halloween. Oh, God, I'm bogged down again. Look, the idea is that the goddess is everything—not just sweetness and light, but everything. Unlike the Christians, who see their god as simply good, and Satan, I guess, as evil, we try to recognize the dark side of life. Are you freaked out yet?"

Oddly, she wasn't. "No, I can kind of see it. If you see it and call it what it is, it can't sneak up on you."

Suby beamed. "Exactly. So we had this ritual to kind of say good-bye to Geoff—to acknowledge that he was really dead and to try to assimilate what that means. Somebody's parents had gotten that skull at some doctor's estate sale—why, I have no idea—but she appropriated it for the occasion." She laughed. "I can truthfully say we've never before had a skull on our altar. Creepy, wasn't it?"

"The whole scene was kind of creepy."

She laughed again. "Yeah, I guess it was. You should have seen the one we did last night. There's this thing where you call a deity into a person. . . ."

"Is that symbolic or . . . uh . . . real?"

"I'm not going anywhere near that one. For our purposes, let's just say it's symbolic. Kit wanted to call this real fierce Egyptian goddess that's supposed to have a lion's head. And one of the things that's survived is a list of her epithets—the things her devotees called her. So we got them out of a book, and called her with her names. Man, you should hear them—stuff like Lady of the Blood-bath. Yikes. But then there's also sweet stuff like Giver of Ecstasies. We tried to intersperse them—I sure hope nobody caught that little gem." She looked at Skip suspiciously.

"It sounds colorful."

"Oh, we're nothing if not colorful. Kit says you really don't have to do all the elaborate stuff we do, but we like it. Especially Neetsie. She kind of orchestrates us."

"I get the feeling Kit's the leader of the band."

"Yeah, she was into it wherever she lived before—Kansas, I think—and she started a topic on the TOWN."

"Do you ever . . . uh . . . sacrifice any animals?"

Suby's young features contorted. She looked around frantically for the cat. "Midnight, you didn't even hear that." She picked up the animal and stroked it. "The Santeros do; and maybe some of the voodoo people do, but if so, they're sure quiet about it. *We* wouldn't hurt a fly." She spoke to Midnight again, "Now, a flea—that's a different matter."

Skip wondered if she'd been conned. It was a pretty story, and not that different from what Ramon had told her, but was this all there was to it?

Quite apart from that, there was a personal question: How could she not have known about a thing like this?

But then she remembered how frightened Suby had been at the thought of Skip's telling her father.

I guess you don't nose it around if you're a witch.

Skip went through her friends and relatives, trying to figure out how they'd respond if she said she was one.

Oh, God. Forget censure. Steve's wisecracks alone would keep me quiet.

Okay, the thing seemed benign enough, but so did Christianity until it got into the hands of lunatics. How did Kit play as the David Koresh of the witch world?

Skip honestly wasn't sure. It did seem a little odd that she was hanging out with a group of women so much her junior. Neetsie had a nose ring and a mother who apparently thought she was Blanche DuBois. Lenore was the sort who'd always be into something. Drugs, A.A., witchcraft—whatever happened along. Suby seemed pretty self-possessed, but her dad was a bully, and she'd responded quickly to Skip's bullying. These women might be vulnerable.

What in the name of Sekhmet was Kit up to?

She headed for the den of the lion.

Kit was in jeans, gray cotton sweater, and an apron. Seeing Skip, she turned pale. "Has something happened to Lenore?"

"No. Why would you think that?"

"I don't know. It's Saturday. I thought it might be an emergency."

"I just wanted to talk to you."

"Well, would you mind coming in the kitchen? I'm in the middle of a sweet potato pecan pie. For—uh—well, Lenore."

"You two seem very close."

"We talked about that, didn't we? We're each other's only family right now. Besides . . ."

She let the sentence trail off, leading Skip through a surprisingly ordinary living room, no occult symbols in view, only a lot of books and some sewing projects. The sofa and a comfortable-looking chair were covered with an earth-toned floral fabric.

She had the light on in her kitchen, which was cheery and at the moment flecked with flour.

Skip would have preferred a more formal interview—in the living room, say—but it was Saturday and she had barged in. She settled for standing when Kit asked her to sit.

"You were going to say something?"

Kit was measuring brown sugar. "I was?"

"You're Lenore's only family. Besides . . ."

"Oh. Well, I really shouldn't talk about Lenore's problems. But believe me she has them. We're in—how to say this without being indiscreet?—we're in a private conference on the TOWN that's a place where people can go for a particular kind of help. I'm kind of her big sister there; it's how we met, actually."

"I see. A Twelve-Step conference—something like that?"

"That's close enough."

"You seem to be an inspiration to a lot of young women."

"Why do you say that?"

"I'm thinking about Cerridwen's Cauldron."

"So that's it. Suby phoned a few minutes before you got here. I should have realized you'd want to know more."

"I gather you're quite the charismatic leader."

She turned toward Skip and brushed away a lock of hair that had fallen in her face. "That sounds a little accusing."

Skip said nothing, simply waited her out.

"I'm not even slightly charismatic. Look, it's this way. After my second marriage broke up, I had a bad bout of depression, and I started working with depressives. I'm a psychiatric nurse, but besides that I do a lot of volunteer work, some of it on the TOWN."

She gave Skip a hard stare to make sure she understood her point—she wasn't exactly giving away anybody's secrets, but she was making it easy to connect the dots.

"You know when you're depressed how people tell you to get something spiritual in your life? I found when I was in therapy, I had a lot of dreams that . . ." She opened her refrigerator and took out eggs. "It's hard to talk about this stuff. They were dreams that pointed in a certain direction. And to make a long story short, I got into this stuff. I already knew Lenore from the TOWN, and when I moved here, I got her involved in it because I thought it might help her the same way it did me. She took to it like she was born for it, and she got Neetsie interested. Lenore knew Suby through Geoff, and of course Neetsie and Suby always wanted to meet each other—they were sort of like cousins who weren't really related. So . . . we have other people, but that's the core of our happy little group. Sometimes, though, I have to admit I wish there were more . . . well, what I'd call adults. You wouldn't want to come sometime, would you?"

"Me?" Skip almost laughed, getting a mental image of herself wearing a weird outfit and frolicking with a bunch of murder suspects.

She said, "Thanks. I'll think about it. Could I ask you something else?"

"Sure."

"How do you know Cole Terry?"

"I used to be married to him. Didn't I mention that?"

Skip felt flames of rage leap up her spine. "Why, no. And I really think you should have."

"Oh, God, I thought you knew. I'm sorry."

"I certainly didn't know." Skip was trying to get her anger under control. "You're telling me you just happened to become best friends—through a computer bulletin board—with a woman who was the girlfriend of your ex-husband's son?"

To Skip's surprise, Kit laughed. "That sounds ridiculous. And you're absolutely right—it didn't happen exactly that way. Technically, Lenore and I didn't meet on the TOWN—it's where we remet as adults. We knew each other when she was a kid. I was married to Cole then, and we knew Butsy, though they weren't yet business partners—"

"What? Cole and Lenore's dad are business partners?"

"Oh, yes. You didn't know that, either?"

"No."

"Well, I believe they still are. They've known each other forever. Anyway, many years after Cole and I had parted company, when I was living in Kansas City, I got on the TOWN because of this conference I mentioned, which is called Down-and-Dirty—it's famous in the depressive community. And once I got there, there were the kids of all these people I knew. It was sort of weird and wonderful."

Skip was trying to take in what this meant—that Kit had been in New Orleans when Leighton was murdered. "You mean Geoff?" she said cautiously. "Were you friends with Marguerite and Leighton?"

"No, no, I just meant Lenore and Neetsie. I never met Leighton and I don't know Marguerite at all—the only time I ever saw her was at the funeral."

"But you knew Geoff eventually, through Lenore. I think you mentioned it."

"Not all that well." Skip thought Kit's eyes were darting nervously.

"No?"

"Uh . . . no, not really." Her phone rang. "Could you excuse me a minute?"

She picked it up and Skip heard her say, "Oh, no! Have you called the police? Good. Listen, Skip Langdon's here. I think you'd better talk to her."

She handed the phone to Skip. "It's Neetsie—she's been burglarized."

Skip said, "Neetsie! Are you still in your apartment?"

"No, I'm calling from a neighbor's."

"Good. Is the district officer there yet?"

"No."

"Okay, what's your address? I'm coming right over. If he gets there first, tell him to contact me by radio—immediately."

"Okay."

This is getting to be a habit, she thought as she drove to the Faubourg Marigny.

18

• •

Neetsie's apartment reminded Skip all too vividly of the place she'd just moved out of, the cozy place she'd lived for two years when the Big House was divided into apartments.

She couldn't believe how little room there was to turn around in, what a feeling of transience it gave her. It was fine for a student or an actress, but not for a fully employed police officer.

I should have moved a long time ago.

But to do that would have meant leaving Jimmy Dee—a thoroughly unacceptable proposition.

Tiny as it was, Neetsie had decorated the place with the flair one would expect of an actress-in-training. The walls were dead-white. She had a mattress on some kind of platform, and above it she had affixed a triangle of poles to the wall so that she could hang a tent of rich fabric that looked like an Oriental rug. The same fabric covered the bed, giving her a houri's divan on a shoestring. Low, white-painted bookshelves served as bedside tables, and one small, worked metal table was piled with books, but could probably be used for tea or coffee in case Neetsie had a guest. A director's chair—only one—would seat him. A thirties dresser with three mirrors had been painted a deep, shiny burgundy, the dominant color of the divan.

Filmy curtains hung at the windows and a smiling sun face of beaten copper, something almost certainly meant for the garden and picked up at the flea market, was the only art.

Plants had been placed strategically, and despite the sparseness of the furniture, money had been spent here. Neetsie had a television, VCR, and CD player, all set on casters. A minuscule notebook computer lay on a cheap and cheerful kitchen table, no doubt something from Pier 1.

It was probably a lovely room, Skip thought, under normal circumstances. At the moment, it was littered with the contents of the dresser drawers, closets, and kitchen cabinets.

CDs and books from the two bookcases had also been flung on the floor, as if to show contempt. "Did they think I kept my money between the pages of *Streetcar?*" Neetsie wailed.

Her laundry was piled on the bed. She'd been at the Laundromat during the break-in.

The district officer, whose name was DuBois, had arrived about five minutes before Skip had. She gave him the same instructions she'd given Rountree at Lenore's burglary and was about to talk to Neetsie when he said, "Wait. Come in the bathroom. There's something you ought to see."

A message had been written in lipstick on the mirror: LOOK OUT, BITCH.

She thanked DuBois, who left to call the crime lab.

Skip said, "Neetsie, could you come in here a minute?"

"Omigod." Her hand covered her mouth. And then she screamed.

Skip swiveled to look at her; eyes darting wildly, she screamed again.

"It's okay, it's just something he wrote. You're going to be okay." Skip was making meaningless comforting sounds, more or less cooing, not even believing her own words.

"It's not that." She pointed, her eyes saying she saw a monster. "He shat!"

"What?"

"Oh, God! He didn't flush."

Skip saw that someone hadn't.

She had seen that kind of trick before—and worse. Sometimes the perp defecated, sometimes he masturbated, and frequently not in the toilet. In a way, Neetsie was lucky.

The bad news was, it was a sexual statement or one of contempt, a violation that could escalate.

"What's that?" Neetsie bent to pick up something.

Skip caught her arm. "Wait. Got a hair clip or something?"

It was a cardboard rectangle. She flipped it over with the clip Neetsie handed her. It was Mike Kavanagh's business card.

Neetsie drew in her breath. "The bastard. It fell out of his pocket when he pulled his pants down."

"Let's go out on the balcony." DuBois was at work in the other room; Skip didn't want to get in his way.

"Suby's dad. I can't believe it."

This looked like the work of a sexual screwball, someone—someone named Mike Kavanagh—who knew both Neetsie and Lenore, who'd upped the ante since the first burglary and would probably do it again.

But even psychopaths sometimes took something. Little souvenirs they thought wouldn't be missed. She needed Neetsie to go through her things.

The door, equipped with only a simple chain lock, had been a piece of cake. The downstairs door—the one for the building—might have been more of a challenge, except that it was moving day for Neetsie's next-door neighbor, who had propped it open while he jammed all his earthly goods into his car. He was now on the way to California and couldn't be questioned.

"How'd you get along with this guy?" Skip asked.

"Petey? He's the closest thing to an angel I ever met. We commiserated about our love lives."

"Could he have been interested in you?"

"Are you kidding? Is there a straight man in this part of town?"

"Okay. Did you call the police right away, or did you check to see if anything's missing?"

"Hey." She looked through the French doors into her apartment. "The stereo's here. And the VCR. I thought they always took that stuff."

"Well, I guess that answers the question. When the crime lab's done, I'd like you to look."

While they waited, Skip thought about the suspect she'd told Kenny and Sheila about—the one who had dropped his wallet going over a fence. It wasn't the only arrest she'd made on the basis of something falling out of someone's pockets. But she didn't know about this card business.

A woman's jeans were tight. Something like a business card might not get jammed to the bottom, might easily fall out while taking them off. A man's pants, on the other hand, had looser pockets; a card would easily slide to the bottom. And why would you keep your own business card in your pants pocket, not in a jacket, perhaps in a cardholder?

But suppose you were a little nuts and unconsciously wanted to be caught. Maybe you'd manage somehow to leave an incriminating clue.

When the crime lab and DuBois had gone, Neetsie looked distastefully at the mess on the floor. She stooped and started pawing among some small boxes, the sort jewelry comes in. Most were cardboard, but one was covered with black velvet. She opened it. "Omigod, here are the pearls I got for graduation. They're the only good jewelry I have." She found a cheap jewelry box that had been upended and rooted around, scooping up beads and baubles. "God, what a bunch of crap. I'm not kidding, I don't have anything good."

Skip pointed. "That's a nice silver pentagram."

Too late, Neetsie's hand closed over it. She stared at Skip, obviously wondering whether she'd just declared herself a member of the sisterhood. Deciding not to take a chance, she said simply, "Thanks," and went back to her task.

"Hey, you know what I can't find?"

"What?"

"There's this ring my mother gave me. This great big yellow stone in some sort of ornate setting. Really cool-looking, but I know it's not worth much. Why didn't he take my pearls?"

"A yellow stone?"

"Something called citrine."

Skip went back to the office and phoned Cappello at home. Saturday or not, she wasn't about to go near Mike Kavanagh without conferring with her sergeant.

She knew Cappello would hate this, could almost see her biting her lip: "He's a policeman with a good record. He's probably got lots of friends."

"Uh-huh. And one relative."

"Who?"

"Frank O'Rourke." Skip's nemesis.

"Oh, shit."

"Fortunately, he's on vacation."

Skip's other line rang. "I've got to go. You'll think about it?"

"Couldn't I just slit my throat instead?"

Skip's caller was the front desk. "The 911 operator just transferred a call to you. A Mary Christianson called to say one of her patients died. You want to talk to her?"

Mary from The Camellias. "Oh, God yes. Give her to me."

There was a click. "Mary? Are you there."

"Mrs. Julian died." She blubbered into something, probably a Kleenex.

"Oh, I'm sorry. But I didn't realize you were close to her."

"I always cry when they die. But—I don't know—something's funny this time. She did have a bad heart condition and it looks like she just slipped away in her sleep. But her room isn't right—some things are out of place."

"Have you notified the family yet?"

"No. I thought . . . somehow, I thought I'd better tell you first. I mean, of course I have to notify the police on all deaths. But I thought you should know too."

"Well, you're right. Homicide has to be notified anyway. Seal off the room and don't let anyone in till I get there. Except the district officer."

By the time she arrived, Mary was more composed, though her delicate skin was blotchy from crying. The district officer was making the necessary calls. Skip said, "Can you show me the room?"

To Skip, it looked perfectly kept, just an ordinary room with an old woman asleep in bed. "What's out of place?"

"The things on her table. Her water glass, and her glasses. I mean the other kind. Spectacles. She kept those real close to her. They're all the way on the other side."

"Anything else?"

"That pillow on the rocking chair." It was covered in flowered chintz.

"It looks fine to me."

"Well, it wouldn't to Mrs. Julian. See how the roses are upside down?"

"Not really."

"Look here." Mary went over and traced the design with her fingers. "See, here's the stem near the back of the chair; the blossom is on the edge, as if it's growing upside down. At least that's what Mrs. Julian always said. She always kept it turned the right way. Meaning the other way. *Always.*"

"But maybe someone else—"

"No way. All the help knew about it. See, people with Alzheimer's, you have to humor them?"

"Okay. Let's keep the room sealed till the lab and the coroner get here. When did you find her?"

"Right before I called you—about forty-five minutes ago. She was still warm, I can tell you that."

"Has she had visitors today?"

"Not that I know of."

"Let's ask around, shall we?"

None of the nurses had opened the door to a visitor, but one thought she'd seen a stranger on the premises—a red-haired woman in a camel coat.

One of the residents had seen a tall gray-haired man, and another an average brown-haired man. One woman burst into tears because the visitor she'd seen reminded her of her daughter, who died in a fire.

"What's security like?" asked Skip.

Mary answered, "What security?"

In the daytime, both doors, front and back, were usually unlocked, and when the heat was on, windows were sometimes opened as well. And closing didn't always mean locking them.

Skip went to find Paul Gottschalk from the crime lab. "Anything?"

"Bagsful. Fibers, hairs, prints, you name it. Housekeeping staff ought to get the chair."

"You're in a great mood."

"It's Saturday. Haven't you noticed?"

"I'm especially interested in the things on her tables—the water glass and spectacles. Could you make sure to dust them?"

"Already done."

She sighed. She still didn't know what to do about Mike Kavanagh.

She called Cappello again. "It looks like someone killed Mrs. Julian. Smothered her, probably—with the pillow from her rocker."

"Shit!" Cappello was quiet a moment and when she spoke, her voice was firm. "Okay, I've been thinking. The last thing we want to do is alert Kavanagh at this point. Spend the weekend building your case and we'll deal with it first thing Monday."

●　●

Now I'm an orphan, thought Marguerite. *They say a parent's death is one of the most traumatic things in the world. But what is it after losing a son?*

Instead of the heaviness, the misery she'd felt when Geoff died—that blindsided feeling—she felt a little lighter, a little better, as if her mother had been released. She wanted comfort food, though.

I actually feel like making it, she thought, and sat up. She put on a pair of running shoes and checked out the kitchen. There was leftover chicken and ham—if she had sausage, she could make jambalaya. Was she up to getting some?

I guess so. I don't feel like sleeping anymore. I'm so, so sick of being exhausted.

She was back with the sausage in minutes. She was looking forward to this, she thought, as she grabbed an onion and started mincing.

I suppose I'm relieved. She suffered so much the last few years. And she didn't have the least idea who anyone was. I guess to me she's been dead for a long time.

Either that or it hasn't hit me.

She finished the onion and reached for a green pepper, but she noticed she was working slowly, not feeling nearly so energetic as she had a few minute ago.

At least all Mother's friends were dead. Geoff hadn't met his yet. He was thirty-one and his life hadn't really even begun.

I wonder why?

Why didn't he go out and live life? Why did he spend all his time behind a machine?

He could have had a wife, children, a brilliant career. . . .

Why didn't he?

It had never occurred to her to wonder before.

She put in salt, two kinds of pepper, a little chili powder, thyme, basil—or had she already put basil in? She couldn't remember.

I'm almost as dead as my mother, I really am.

I can't remember shit.

I have no energy.

I don't know why I bother.

Cole was calling her. "Marguerite!"

"In here."

He came in smiling, as handsome as the day she met him, and she thought, *This is why. I still have Cole.*

"Honey, what are you doing in here? You shouldn't be tiring yourself out."

"I want to. I needed comfort food."

"Well, I can sure see that, baby. If anybody needs some, it's you. My poor, poor beautiful Marguerite." He came up behind her, gripped her upper arms, and kissed her shoulder through her sweatshirt. The warmth of him, his scent, his breadth, felt so wonderfully comforting, so familiar and cozy. She wanted him, she realized.

She turned around, encircled his neck with her arms. She knew her breath was hot, her eyes burning. She could feel the old sensations circulating in her body, electric currents in a house, everything regular and familiar, as it should be.

Yet exciting.

Exciting as always.
Cole stepped away, surprised.
She realized they hadn't made love in months.

19

• •

Pearce's line was busy, probably, Skip thought, because he was logged onto the TOWN as usual. No telling how long he'd be on it, either.

She drove over.

"Well, Ms. Langdon. I never thought I'd see you on a Saturday."

"Policemen's work is never done. And it's Detective Langdon, please."

"You don't look like any policeman I ever saw."

She could almost have said it with him, it was so predictable.

"A couple of quick questions. May I come in?"

"Sure."

She re-entered the black, smelly hole Pearce called home, and thought that this time she wouldn't sit, she would get out as quickly as possible.

"Think back carefully. Tell me what you really think—not for testimony, not for any official purpose, just tell me what your sense is. Was Marguerite involved with Mike Kavanagh at the time Leighton was killed?"

"You already asked me that."

"And you said no. But there was something funny about the way you said it."

"Yeah, maybe there was. Okay, she could have been."

"Why do you say that?"

"Once or twice she stood us up—Honey and me. She'd call at the last minute and say her mother was sick, she couldn't get anyone to take care of Geoff. One of those times we thought we'd drop over and surprise her. Which we did, but no one was home."

"That's it?"

"Well, another time she was late and she was disheveled. And I mean the kind of disheveled women get—you know? Like she'd been necking in a car and the guy didn't want to let her go."

"It could have been Leighton."

He shook his head. "He didn't bring her out to the Dream Palace. He hated it when she hung out."

"All the more reason he wouldn't want to let her go."

His head kept sawing. "Uh-uh. She acted kind of embarrassed. Why do you ask, by the way?"

"I'm a cop and you're a reporter. You know I'm not going to say."

"I think I can guess. So it's *Hamlet*, is it? Oldest story in the book."

She left to find Honey, hoping her parting smile was enigmatic.

Honey was raking leaves, dressed in a red bandanna and striped overalls. Like so many New Orleans women, she had the knack of looking perfectly groomed for every occasion, as if her life were one commercial after another. This one could be for garden tools.

"Hey, Honey. Nice nippy day, isn't it?"

"Hey, Skip. Don't you love it when it's like this?"

It was a rhetorical question. Skip said, "Listen, I was just wondering about something. Do you think Marguerite and Mike Kavanagh might have been involved before Leighton was killed?"

Honey cocked her head. "Well, I never got that impression. Honestly, I'd be a lot more inclined to suspect Pearce."

"Seriously? I mean, you're not just carrying on?"

"Oh, maybe I am—I don't know."

"Were you ever with Pearce when Marguerite broke dates, or arrived late or anything?"

She thought again. "Not that I can recall." She shrugged. "She came, she had fun, she flirted. The only thing is, Pearce had a great big letch for her."

"Which she returned?"

"Well, I think I've mentioned it three times now. I sure think she might have."

"Did you have any reason to think that?"

"Once I found a strange phone number in one of his pockets. I sort of couldn't resist calling. It was some bar where she liked to hang out. Then, too, I didn't always know what he was doing. He worked late a lot. And sometimes when the three of us would be together, Marguerite would go to the ladies' room and Pearce would go for cigarettes. And they'd both be gone a long time. I mean, a real long time."

"Suspicious."

"Uh-huh. Like I said."

"Thanks, Honey." Skip wondered why Honey was trying so hard to incriminate the ex she said she was on good terms with.

It was starting to get dark and Skip realized she hadn't eaten lunch. It was Saturday night and she had no plans.

But no problem—Jimmy Dee would feed her. She tried not to feel guilty about intruding, knowing he truly wanted her there.

Tomorrow she could make phone calls from home, but there was still something she had to do today. She returned to the office and called a friend in Burglary.

"Hey, Dennis. Can you do me a favor?"

"Why, sure."

"I can't tell you why, but I need to know what Mike Kavanagh's schedule was last week, and what it is next week."

"Call you right back."

Mike would be in late Monday, it turned out. That was good—she could go get him at home.

He hadn't been working the night of the murder. That was good too. He could have driven over to Geoff's in the early morning and . . . and what? Waited for Geoff to climb up a ladder?

Suddenly she realized something she hadn't before—the murderer must have put the cat on the roof. Somehow, that made the whole thing nastier.

"Hey, Dennis, who was Kavanagh married to?"

"Helen. That's all I know. Why?"

"I was just wondering who'd put up with him."

"Well, they pay me to do it. And Helen had enough, I guess. They been divorced a long time—longer'n they were married, I think. Least if she's got any sense they have."

There was a Helen Kavanagh in the phone book—if it was the right one, at least she'd kept Mike's name. Maybe she liked him better than Dennis did.

Skip stopped by her desk to tidy it and found a message that warmed her heart: "Darryl called. He said how's Sheila and would you like to have coffee sometimes." It was unsigned.

She picked it up, about to stick it in her purse, when the phone rang. She grabbed it. "Langdon."

"You sound cheerful. It's Layne."

Oh. Not Darryl.

"Listen, I've been checking something out. I read over some old stuff I downloaded—some correspondence with Geoff."

"Yes?"

"And I found something funny in it."

"Uh-huh." *Spit it out, please.*

"It's a quote from *Hamlet.*"

Hamlet. It was a word she'd heard not an hour before.

" '. . . the funeral baked meats did coldly furnish forth the marriage tables.' Remember how that worked? Hamlet's mother married his uncle too soon after his father's murder—eerie, huh? I know because I looked it up today, but I guess when Geoff sent me the quote I didn't bother. I don't know why it's any big surprise—that he suspected his uncle, I mean. But I could kick myself for not trying to figure it out at the time."

Bells went off in Skip's head.

What is this? I'm on the verge of arresting Mike and Pearce mentions Hamlet, then Layne does. Things are getting awfully coincidental.

And cops don't believe in coincidence.

220

Was a setup possible? Was someone trying to point the finger at Mike?

She said, "How'd you happen to think of it now?"

"I didn't. I just came across it. I mean, I was looking over some stuff for you—to see if there was anything you could use."

She looked at her watch. Nearly six P.M. on a Saturday. Well, who knew? Half these computer people didn't have lives—that was already established.

Layne said, "Gotta flee. Hope it helps."

"Thanks a lot, Layne. I appreciate it."

"Say, how's your friend—uh—?"

"Jimmy Dee."

"Yeah. Jimmy Dee—uh—?"

"Scoggin. He's fine. I'll tell him you asked about him."

"Nice guy. Well, 'bye now. Hope it helped."

Maybe that was why he'd called—why he'd spent the afternoon trying to find an excuse to do it. Anyway, he'd given her a song to sing for her supper. Forty-five minutes later, she was singing it, standing in Jimmy Dee's kitchen, a glass of red wine in hand.

"Guess what, Dee-Dee? Layne returns the compliment."

"Layne who?" He opened the oven to peer at his eggplant parmigiana.

"You know what Layne. The one you think is cute."

"How do you know he returns the compliment?" He straightened up and spoke casually, but Skip noticed he brushed the hair out of his eyes, something she'd never seen him do before.

It's probably a habit he had in high school. "Because he called up and asked your last name."

"He did? Just like that? Did he say why he wanted to know?"

"He pretended he was inquiring about your health."

"Ah, the how's-old-what's-his-name maneuver." He pulled the casserole out.

"Ah, indeed. You want to make a bet on whether or not the kids are going to eat that?"

He turned around, right hand already stuck out. "Fifty dollars."

"I get it. You've already taken a poll."

"It's their favorite dish. Can you beat that? Listen, want to work on that software of Layne's tonight? I did try, but there was one little problem—I couldn't get on the TOWN."

"I'm using Steve's user ID and password."

"Oh. Steve."

• •

After dinner, Jimmy Dee uploaded the software and began futzing with it. Skip read magazines. And after a while she went home, leaving him cursing Layne, telling her he was quite sure Layne was the murderer, at any rate he was a sadist. Generally having the time of his life.

Back in her cold apartment, she gathered blankets and tucked herself in to read, but her mind wandered. Should she call Darryl? Not tonight, of course, but tomorrow, maybe? Did she really want to see him again?

She did. She did, badly, but it was dangerous. She liked him entirely too much for a woman supposedly involved with another man.

But maybe Steve is dumping me.

Well, he hasn't yet.

As if on cue, the phone rang. "Hi."

"Steve?"

"Of course Steve. You were expecting, maybe, Tom Cruise?"

Though no one could see, she flushed.

"Listen, we really have to talk. I've got some semibad news, but in the end it's going to turn out really great. I'm not kidding, this is really exciting."

"You're not moving here."

"Now, why would you think that?"

"Every conversation's pointed to it."

"Well, wrong. I *am* moving there. Just not right away."

Oh, sure.

"Hey, are you still there?"

"Go ahead. Talk." She knew she sounded distant, withdrawn; but she couldn't pretend.

"I know this interferes with our plans, but it's only for a couple of years, and things'll be so much better when I finally get there.

I mean, this is really the most important thing that could happen to me at this stage of my career—the most important. For once I'm on the cutting edge—and I really have to stay a while and cash in."

"I guess you'd better tell me about it."

"Remember that computer seminar I took?"

"Vaguely."

"Well, you know I've always been a computer buff. So I took this AVID seminar. Just for fun, really. It was in nonlinear digital editing—have you ever heard of that?"

"Should I have?"

"It's changing the film industry—and incidentally, it's making your boyfriend rich. It's like . . . total freedom. It's so fucking fast it's unbelievable. Anything you want to do, you can do it. It's just split-second stuff."

"So what does all that mean?"

"The old way of editing is wildly expensive and time-consuming. This costs pennies—for the equipment, I mean—and you can literally get a rough cut of a film in one night. It's state-of-the-art, baby, and I'm in on the ground floor."

"But what does that mean to you?"

"It means I'm in big demand," he said modestly. "I'm working on feature films—under big-name editors—which I haven't done before. And here's the best part—I'm making about five thousand a week."

She was oddly intimidated. "That's a lot of money."

"You bet it's a lot of money. It's a hell of a lot of money. Do you see why I have to stay a while?"

"In a Hollywood kind of way I do. But what about your own work?"

"At five thousand a week, I can make a half million dollars in two years. Think how many little baby films I can turn that into."

" 'Little baby films'? You're putting down your own work."

"No, I'm not. I'm just calling it what it is. Besides, I love doing this stuff. I'm crazy about it."

"You're never coming here, are you?" *You're going to buy a house in Mailbu and marry Sharon Stone.*

"Of course I am. Don't you understand that? I'm going to do

this exactly two years and then cash out. By then, everybody in town'll probably know how to do it anyway."

You never had any intention of moving here.

But he said, "So when I'm there, there's a much greater likelihood I'll stay. I mean, that I'll be *able* to stay."

"I guess I should say congratulations."

"I was kind of hoping for that."

"I'm finding this a little hard to adjust to."

"Why? It's only for a couple of years. I'm coming. Don't worry, that place is home to me now. A lot more than L.A. More than L.A. ever was."

"But you're there and not here." She realized how whiny her voice had become.

"Have you got your period or something?"

"What?" He'd never spoken to her like that. Never.

"You don't sound like yourself at all. Look, let's change the subject. How's life with the no-neck rug rats?"

"Shit!"

"What?"

"Steve, I've got to go."

She hung up on him, something else she'd never done—to him or anyone.

He'd try to call back, of course. The thing to do was leave the phone off the hook. Or better yet . . .

Before she realized what she'd done, she dialed Darryl's number.

A moment later, she was holding a dead receiver, glad he hadn't answered, knowing she should call Steve back, but not wanting to talk to him.

What's wrong with me?

Suddenly Steve couldn't do anything right in her eyes. Even without Cindy Lou to tell her, she knew she was acting dumb. This was about her, not him.

But what part of her? The part that was disappointed in Steve? The part that, deep down, still didn't trust him?

Or the part that was wildly, irrationally attracted to Darryl?

And which came first?

If she didn't know, she didn't know how she could tell Steve. She unplugged the phone, knowing she was acting like a baby. Absolutely unable to do otherwise.

• •

Lenore thought she was going to scream soon. Caitlin had turned into a wild energy machine sometime this afternoon. She had been throwing things for the last two hours—some, simply household items, some her eating utensils, and some her food, pea by pea. Lenore had let her do it at first, thinking she'd work off the energy soon, and then had tried to make her stop, but that had involved crying and flailing that she couldn't cope with right now, and so she had gone back to letting her do it.

Had the kid managed to eat enough food to survive until morning? Or should she keep trying to get her to eat?

I don't care. I don't care about anything! I just want to lie down and cry.

She was having an extreme reaction to her old music teacher's death—at least it seemed extreme to her. She hadn't realized she had cared so much about Mrs. Julian, certainly couldn't have predicted that the death of someone she hadn't seen in years, except at Geoff's funeral, could have such an effect on her.

It must be because it came on top of Geoff's death. Or maybe because I did see her. It was so awful, realizing she'd lost it.

She thought it might symbolize something to her—something like the dark night of the soul. The void, the abyss, chaos—something she couldn't quite comprehend but that scared her to death.

I need to do magic. A spell for solace and serenity. I need to get myself together.

But how can you get yourself together when you're tattered? You can't heal yourself when you don't have the energy even to run a fever.

Caitlin tossed a cup, which shattered on the floor.

"Caitlin, goddam you! Can't you give me a moment's peace?" She was shocked at the sound of her voice. The neighbors had probably heard her.

Caitlin, obviously shocked as well, simply stared for a second. Her little lips made a perfect O. And then her lovely face turned into a writhing mask of ugliness. Sound spilled out of her that could be heard, not only next door, but down the block.

Lenore lowered her voice and sugared it. "Caitlin, I'm sorry, honey. I didn't mean to shout." She grabbed for the screaming child, full of remorse, but Caitlin flailed at her.

"Stop it. Stop it, goddammit! I'm sorry." Without thinking about it, she flailed back, striking Caitlin's cheek with a sound like something cracking.

"Oh, Caitlin. Omigod, I'm so sorry. What happened to me?" She had to hold Caitlin's arms to get close enough to pick her up, which only made the baby scream louder.

Once she had her, what to do?

She needed a drink desperately. She had already taken some Valium, but to no avail.

Holding the screaming baby, she went through her cabinets. There was wine, but she didn't need something she had to sip to get a buzz—she needed something she could toss down.

Coke! There was some coke some guy had left. Now where the hell was it?

She put Caitlin down and let her scream while she found it, made herself two neat little lines, thought about leaving one till later, and changed her mind.

She went back to find the baby, noticing the screaming was tolerable now. She could feel love. Behind all her frustration and sadness, her love for her daughter had been lurking all along, and now she could feel it.

She sensed the change in herself, heard her voice smooth out, become lower, and saw with gratitude that Caitlin responded. Now the baby came toward her, arms outstretched. Gladly, Lenore enfolded her, happy that children were so forgiving.

"You want me to read you a story?"

Caitlin nodded.

Lenore got out one of her pop-up books, and they were soon in sync, laughing and having fun as if nothing had happened. When it was over, Caitlin said, "Read me another, Mommy."

"It's time for your bath, honey."

"Please, Mommy?" She looked so sweet, so absolutely adorable and innocent, yet somehow so alert, that Lenore couldn't resist.

"Okay, but after this, we'll do your bath and then bed."

"Okay, Mommy."

"You're *too* adorable, you know that?"

"Umm-hmm."

Lenore found another book and began to read, something about a baby duck that got separated from all its little sisters and brothers, a more complicated book, and Caitlin kept interrupting.

She pointed to a picture at the bottom of the page. "What's that, Mommy?"

"That's a dog, honey."

"Why is he . . . why he is . . ." She was stuttering in that way kids have. "Why is he . . ."

"Caitlin, spit it *out*."

Her daughter stared at her again. Before she had a chance to cry, Lenore said, "I'm sorry, honey, I didn't mean to snap. Would you wait one second for Mommy?"

Another little toot is called for. Just one more and she's in bed and I'm okay.

She had two more, but when she came back, Caitlin seemed to have lost interest in the book. "Mommy, could we read another one?"

"Honey, you said we'd go to bed when you finished that one."

"But we didn't finish . . . we didn't finish . . . we didn't finish . . . it."

Can I make it through one more?

Oh, sure, I've got a second wind.

So to speak.

"How about the one about Rhiannon?" She had actually found a children's book about a good witch, no small feat.

"Okay." Caitlin put her thumb in her mouth, a sure sign she was getting sleepy.

They were nearly through the book when she started interrupting again. "Why is she . . . why is she . . . why is she . . . a witch?"

"Because that's her job, honey."

"Why is it . . . why is it . . . why is it . . . her job?"

"You know how I'm a bead lady? And Auntie Kit's a nurse? Everybody has a job to do."

"What's a job?"

Lenore closed the book with a thud. "Oh, Caitlin, for heaven's sake, you're not interested in the book."

"Yes, I am."

"Come on, we're going to go take your bath."

"No!" She stamped her foot.

Lenore got up and started the bathwater. She went back for Caitlin.

"Come on, baby."

"No!"

Lenore felt a surge of rage travel up her spine. "You come here, young lady."

Caitlin stared at her, unmoving.

"You get in that bathroom." She was screaming again.

Caitlin set up a howl.

"Come to me!"

Caitlin lay down on the floor and howled louder.

"You're going if I have to drag you."

Lenore grabbed her by the arm and began dragging. Caitlin caught a table leg and held on.

"Let go, Caitlin, dammit, let go." A tiny fat figure came crashing down—a little Venus of Willendorf.

"Goddamit, Caitlin!" Furious, Lenore pried the child's fingers loose, dragged her into the bathroom, and commanded, "Stand up!"

Caitlin didn't.

"All right, you're going in that tub with all your clothes on." Lenore tossed her in and held her head under the still-running faucet. The water scalded her hand.

Caitlin screamed louder than ever.

"Oh, my baby, oh my poor baby!" Lenore jerked her out of the tub, grateful she hadn't undressed her, hoping against hope she wasn't going to blister.

She remembered she had some aloe vera and stripped the child.

She had gotten Caitlin out fast enough—either that or her heavy overalls had saved her. And Lenore's own hand had protected the baby's head.

But why did I hold her head under the faucet? What was I thinking of?

Not caring if she lived till morning, Lenore did the rest of the coke when Caitlin was in bed.

20

• •

Skip woke to a loud knock the next day, and tumbled grumpily out of bed, feeling as if she had a hangover. She'd awakened a few times in the night, cold and fretful, and she was still both.

Dragging a blanket, she stumbled onto the balcony.

"Beignets! Time for beignets!" Kenny hollered, happier than a whole kindergarten class.

"Uncle Jimmy said to get you," Sheila said quietly, obviously trying to maintain dignity in the face of Kenny's exuberance. Yet she too didn't seem averse to the plan, which, where Sheila was concerned, meant a lot. Skip wondered if the whole house of cards would collapse if she didn't go.

Probably, she decided.

"Five minutes."

Fifteen minutes later, the four of them were sitting in the Cafe du Monde, the two adults trying fitfully to read the Times-Picayune, the two kids trying to kill each other.

And yet, the attempted murders were much more lighthearted than usual, more like a brother and sister fighting, less like Desert Storm revisited.

Either that or I'm getting used to it.

"Hey, when can I see Darryl again?" asked Sheila.

"He called last night to see how you are."

"He did? Do you think he likes me?"

"Yes. I do think he likes you. But he's too old to be your boy-friend, if that's what you mean."

She looked disappointed. "But, if he really likes me—"

"'Anyway, he's black," said Kenny.

Sheila said, "What's wrong with that?"

"Black people and white people don't date. Do they, Uncle Jimmy?"

"Well . . ." He hesitated. "Sometimes they do. But it doesn't happen every day. I guess you could say that."

Sheila was indignant. "Why not?"

"It's just not easy, I guess."

"But if people really, really like each other, they can do any-thing they want."

Skip saw him choosing his words carefully. "The world we live in just isn't set up for certain things."

"Uncle Jimmy, you're a racist!" Sheila's face was red.

"I'm a . . . ? Auntie, help me out."

"Uncle Jimmy isn't a racist. He's trying to tell you the world is screwed up."

"No, he's not. He's a racist!"

"If it's not one thing," murmured Jimmy Dee, "it's another."

They were silent on the walk back, Sheila fuming, Kenny racing on ahead, and Skip coming to a conclusion: she was going to call Darryl as soon as she got home.

Why, she wasn't sure, any more than she was sure why she some-times overate. Maybe it was Kenny's blithe contention—the prevailing one—that white people couldn't date black people. Maybe it was the man himself. He was a spectacular person (almost, she realized, too good to be true). And maybe it was like eating ice cream when your boyfriend disappointed you, which hers most assuredly had.

Some things you did to make yourself feel better, some things you did because something inside you, something you couldn't name, was calling the shots.

231

She didn't take off her jacket to dial. "Hi. Did I wake you up?"

"Uh, no, I . . . Skip? Is that you?"

"Yeah. You're asleep."

"Well, that's good. Means you didn't wake me up. I hate it when someone wakes me up. You want to have breakfast?"

"I've already had it. How about lunch?"

"Thinking ahead. Good. Least you know where your next meal's coming from."

"I'm going to be at work. Where do you live?"

"Uptown. Hey, I know what. Let's go to the zoo—they have good food and we could go for a walk afterwards. See some bears or something."

"I like 'gators."

"You like 'gators? I love 'gators. 'Cept those white ones—aren't there enough white things in the world?"

"I guess your students don't read *Moby Dick*."

"Sure they do. The whale gets it."

I should have listened to Kenny.

But he said, "Hey, I didn't mean anything. Just light banter, you know? Hate dark banter—enough dark things in the world. That better?"

"You're a case, you know that?"

"And that's without coffee. Notice half my sentences don't have subjects? Caffeine deprivation. Taking shortcuts."

Well, anyway it worked. A lot better than a hot fudge sundae. I think I'll float to work now.

She changed clothes, trying to think how to build a case against Mike. They had enough probable cause to get a search warrant. But she needed to move carefully; Mike was a policeman, not some three-time offender.

She needed to go over to Neetsie's and canvass her neighbors—probably with a picture. She decided to do that first—if someone wasn't home, she could try back later in the day.

She surveyed herself—now in brown corduroys, cream silk blouse, and tweed jacket—and thought she looked fine for a Sunday. She had to go back to the station for the picture and back again to the Faubourg. She was beginning to wish she'd agreed to meet Darryl downtown.

Neetsie let Skip in the building. There were only three other tenants, two of whom were home, and neither of whom had seen or heard anyone at Neetsie's Saturday. The third one, a lady in her seventies, was probably at church, Neetsie said.

Skip tried the next-door and across-the-street neighbors, hoping for stoop-sitters and curtain-peekers. Again, she drew a blank.

Time to pay a visit on Helen Kavanagh.

She lived in a neat house in Metairie, which was probably—if she was the right Mrs. Kavanagh—something she'd bought with Mike.

She fits the description, Skip thought when the door opened. Unlike Marguerite Terry, this woman wasn't pretty. She had a lot of extra weight on her, that was easy enough to see, though she was wearing a muumuulike garment that hid her pretty well. Her hair, which had been allowed to go gray, was pinned up some kind of way, but it was coming down in tufts. Her face was a bit too red, as if she, like Mike, drank too much.

"Helen Kavanagh?"

"Yes." She looked puzzled.

"I'm looking for a woman who used to be married to a man named Mike Kavanagh."

"That's me."

"I'm Skip Langdon, N.O.P.D. I wonder if we could talk a few minutes?"

She waved Skip into a house that reeked of cigarette smoke. "Oh, Gawd, is Mike in trouble?" Without waiting for an answer, she said, "Make yourself at home. I went to early mass; I was just taking a nap."

She disappeared.

"Uh—Mrs. Kavanagh?"

She retraced her steps. "Yes?"

"Were you going somewhere?"

"To put on some clothes."

"No need to do that. This should only take a minute."

"Sorry, I don't receive visitors like this."

She disappeared again, creating a situation that always made Skip uncomfortable—but which she had to live with this time. She could think of no excuse to follow a stranger into her bedroom.

She didn't really know what Helen's relationship with Mike was—maybe she'd call him and say Skip was there, ask him what to tell her. If she did, there wasn't a thing Skip could do about it.

When Helen returned, she had changed into navy polyester pants and a print blouse, a too-tight outfit that gave her an egglike look—she was one of those rare women who gain weight in their middles rather than hips.

But she looked a good deal more presentable. She had tucked up her hair, and her face was losing its rosiness, which Skip realized was probably the result of being pressed against a pillow.

She yawned. "How about some coffee?"

"Not for me, thanks, but I'll come in the kitchen while you make some."

"Oh, no, you just sit right here."

But Skip was already up.

The living room was furnished with cheap, mass-produced color-matched furniture—wood that had been finished to look like plastic, fabrics of petroleum products, a table lamp that was a cone of clear glass around the lamp's standard, creating the effect of innards on display.

It was fairly depressing, but the kitchen, despite the cheapness of its furnishings, was cheerful, a working room in which Helen probably spent a lot of time.

"I was wondering what it was like to live with your husband, whether he was . . ."

Helen took down a mug. "It was hell. Why do you ask?"

"It's part of an investigation."

"What investigation?"

"Now, Mrs. Kavanagh, you were married to a policeman. You know I can't tell you that."

"I know you'd better or I'm not talking to you."

She was reheating coffee she'd already made. As she waited, she lit a cigarette, narrowing her eyes as she puffed. Skip suddenly saw her less as the neighborhood baker and a lot more as a tough old bird. She was definitely no Marguerite.

Skip held her gaze. This was a woman who didn't like her ex-husband. She'd want to talk about him.

Finally, she shrugged. "Oh well. I guess it's not all that important."

"It's about Geoff, isn't it? You want to know if he could have killed him."

Skip shrugged again.

"I've been talking to Suby. Don't think I don't know what's going on. I know all about the TOWN."

"There's no way to keep a thing like that a secret."

Helen finally poured her coffee. "So what you want to know is whether Mike was ever violent."

"Was he?"

"He's an asshole."

"A violent asshole?"

"Verbally, he was about as brutal as you can get. But he never hit either one of us—Suby or me. I'll give him that." She was in her element, coffee in hand, clouds of smoke circling her head.

"You know all about Geoff's flashbacks."

"Anybody who reads the paper does."

"Well, I was wondering—you were married to him, he must have confided things."

"Not so's you'd notice." For the first time, she smiled.

"Do you know if he and Marguerite were already involved when Leighton died?"

"No. No, I don't. What I do know is he claims he had no interest in her, didn't even like her much, till after he lost his brother. When that happened, he felt like he had to take care of her, and then he kind of fell in love with Geoff more than her."

It was the same story Mike had told Skip.

"But then if he killed his own brother, he would make up a story, wouldn't he?" She held up a hand. "I know, I know. He doesn't seem real bright, but he's got some low cunning, Mike does."

Skip smiled, thinking, *Win some, lose some.*

"Know what I think, though? I think he didn't do it."

"Why?"

"While we were married, he cheated on me. And always with big fat women, just like me. Mike doesn't even like scrawny squirts. That's what he calls 'em—scrawny squirts."

"Could I ask you something really personal? I mean, really, really personal?"

"I don't know whether I'll answer it."

"Did he have any sexual perversions? Anything to do with defecation?"

Her whole face changed, went from its in-control complacency, its almost lighthearted enjoyment, to betrayal and hurt. *"What?"*

"Or young girls?"

If the expression on Helen's face wasn't genuine bafflement, Skip had never seen it. "Honey, you got a different Mike Kavanagh. This one can barely stand the missionary position."

"Was he into—uh—scatology or anything?"

"Why in the name of hell are you asking me these questions?" She was angry now, clearly a person who hated being out of control. She and Mike must have been hell on wheels when they were together.

"Trying to check something out, that's all. Thanks so much for your help, Mrs. Kavanagh."

"Wait a minute! You're much mistaken if you think you're leaving without telling me what this is all about."

"You know I can't do that. I'm afraid I really have to go now."

"Just a goddam minute here!"

Skip was glad she was nearer the door than Helen—because Helen, she was pretty certain, was capable of fisticuffs to get her way.

Skip slipped out without answering. Helen stood in the doorway. "You come back here!" Her face had turned red again.

Poor Suby. Raised by a mean drunk and a dragon with attitude.

She was ready for Darryl, ready for his self-described "light banter," his sunny disposition, the way he made her feel good. Was that a trick of his or was it something in her? Was it that melted caramel kind of feeling she always got when she was starting to fall in love?

Not so fast, there. It's only lunch.

Lunch and a walk, actually. A stroll through the 'gators—pretty romantic.

Darryl was waiting for her. "How 'bout some jambalaya? They do a good one."

"Okay. That and a root beer. My treat."

"You crazy? I'm the man."

I noticed.

But she didn't say it, didn't dare. She settled for, "I asked you."

"Uh-uh. I asked you—left you a message, remember?"

"Okay, I won't argue."

"Good thing. Or you'd be 'gator bait."

They picked up their jambalaya and sat down on a roofed deck overlooking a simulated bayou. "How's Sheila?"

"In love with you, I think."

He laughed. "That's me. All the kids love me—they're under fifteen, they want to take me home to Mama."

"How about the big girls?"

"You mean about six feet? Well, I don't know; I was kind of wondering that."

Oh, God, don't blush. Whatever you do, don't blush. "You mean moi?"

"I mean toi."

"You get right to the point, don't you?"

He nodded. "I hate wasting time—I mean, not that time with your lovely self is wasted. I just hope we're going somewhere, that's all."

"Somewhere like to bed? This afternoon?"

"Why, Miss Scarlett, how you do run on. I just wondered if there was anything you needed to tell me."

"You mean, like, whether I have a boyfriend?"

"Bingo, baby."

"I'm not sure."

"Oh, no. Don't tell me it's going to be one of those."

"Well, I did have a boyfriend, out in California. But I hung up on him last night and—"

"And called me this morning. Damn! Had my heart set on a happy ending." He made his face so droll she had to laugh.

"You mean you don't have anybody? Or do you just need your harem rounded out?"

He was so electric the first seemed almost impossible. But on the other hand, she'd caught him on Sunday morning in bed alone—either that or with a masochist, to put up with that conversation.

For the first time since Sheila turned up missing, he looked troubled. "Just broke up with somebody."

"I guess I did too. How long ago did you do it?"

"Mmmmm. 'Bout three days. No, four. Four and a half."

"Pretty recent."

"Well, how about you?"

"Oh, we haven't actually *talked* about it yet. . . ."

"Hmm. One of those future-type kind of things. Like space travel and stuff."

"Hey, what happened to light banter?"

"Am I gettin' too dark for you? You should see me with a tan. Or better yet, yo' mama should. You thought about that?"

"I don't know if I'm ready for this."

"Not sure you are. Let's go see some bears."

"How 'bout the 'gators?"

"Bears are more autumnal. All that fur and stuff. Makes you think you're warm."

As they finished lunch and dumped their garbage, a blast of wind came through the swamp exhibit. "I wish something would."

"Oh, yeah? We can arrange that." He put an arm around her waist and drew her to him. "You ready for this?"

She smiled up at him—she liked a man she could look up to; there weren't that many. "Ready and waiting," she said.

As they walked to the bears' enclosure, his arm very warm around her, she tried to get her balance back. One of the things she loved about Darryl was that openness of his—the way he was right out there, the way most men weren't.

In her experience, they mostly liked to let things ride until a situation was so intolerable you couldn't avoid talking about it for one more second.

Here's a guy who's got some balls; only I don't, it turns out.

After the bears, she tried Neetsie's third neighbor again.

Miss Bertie La Grange was truly a beautiful old lady, an old lady who, white hair, stooped shoulders and all, was as girlish as a debutante. She had somehow—maybe with rouge, Skip couldn't tell— retained a pair of sweet pink cheeks, and she wore her hair in a knot at the neck. Bertie was a name that suited her well, but Petunia would have been better. It was November and she had on a white dress. It took a Petunia to pull that off.

She said, "Do come in, dear. I've been expecting you."

"Oh?" Her apartment was a monument to knickknacks, especially little china dogs, which was odd because she had a live cat. But cluttered as it was, it was immaculate. Each dog was probably groomed once a week, with a bath in soapy water.

"Neetsie said you came while I was at church. I'm so sorry I missed you. Now sit right down and we'll visit."

"Well, I don't think I can do that right now. I just wanted to ask—"

"Now, of course you can. You sit right down."

Skip sat, sighing. "Are you retired, Miss La Grange?"

"Why, I surely am. I taught sixth grade at Lusher for nearly forty years."

"I had an idea you used to be a schoolteacher."

"Did you, darlin'? Can I get you some lemonade?"

"Oh, no, thanks, I just have a minute. I was wondering if you saw anything yesterday—when Neetsie was burglarized."

"Why, no. I don't b'lieve I did. Well, I did open my door—you know, to put out my trash?—and there was a gentleman downstairs. So I didn't go down."

"Could it have been one of the other tenants?"

"Well, it could have been, I just couldn't tell."

Skip pulled out Mike Kavanagh's picture. "Do you know this man?"

"Why, yes, I b'lieve I do."

"How do you happen to know him?"

239

"Now, let me think. I b'lieve he runs the store on the corner. No, no, I don't think it's that. I b'lieve I've just seen him around the neighborhood."

"Where around the neighborhood?"

"I went out for a walk yesterday, and I b'lieve I saw him getting out of a car. 'Course I said 'Good afternoon,' but he didn't answer back."

"Where was the car?"

"Why, right out front. Well . . . down a door or two, maybe, but right close."

"What kind of car did he have?"

"Just a . . . car." Her vague blue eyes went slightly cloudy. "I don't know anything at all about cars."

"Why do you think he didn't speak to you?"

"Well, maybe he didn't see me. He sort of turned away, like he had to get somethin' out of the trunk."

Something like a crowbar.

"About what time was that?"

"Oh, just after lunch, I 'magine. Sometime around one. That's when I always take my stroll."

The time was right. Skip wasn't sure about the witness.

"Now, Miss La Grange, I want you to be very sure about this. Are you absolutely certain this is the man you saw?"

"Well, I think it was."

"I notice you wear glasses. Do you have your eyes checked regularly, that sort of thing?"

For the first time, gentleness failed the old Petunia. "There's nothing wrong with my eyes. Nothing atall."

The orbs in question flashed indignation.

• •

Later, summing up her weekend for Cappello, she said, "The only straws we have to cling to are Pearce and Petunia. Pearce thinks Mike might have had an affair with Marguerite, and Petunia, who probably can't see two feet in front of her face, might have seen him at the time of the burglary."

"Straws is right. Even if they were sure, it wouldn't help us."

"It would make me feel a lot better."

Skip could hear Cappello drawing in her breath, making a decision. "That bathroom stuff bothers me—it's ugly; and Mike's an ugly guy."

Skip was surprised—Cappello was a by-the-book cop; instinct wasn't her thing. She shrugged. "It's not my call, Sylvia."

"It could be a setup, it really could. But something tells me it could be Mike, too." Cappello stroked her lip with her index finger, something she seldom did. Skip thought she was probably deeply ambivalent. Finally she said, "Let's talk to Joe."

It was no more Joe Tarantino's call than Skip's or Cappello's. But he was the lieutenant in charge of Homicide, the first stop on the chain of command that had to go all the way to the superintendent when a policeman was suspected of a crime. The chief of the Detective Bureau and Internal Affairs had to be involved as well.

Joe was a big, pear-shaped, dandruffy kind of guy, as much teddy bear as tough cop. When Skip was a rookie on a beat, green and suffering from terror that she wouldn't make it as a cop, couldn't do the only job she'd ever wanted to, Joe had recognized her ability and gotten her into Homicide. She'd worked with him once when he was a sergeant and had solved the case herself, but that hadn't made her believe in herself. Nothing had but Joe's believing in her; that and doing a good job in response to it.

She adored him.

This morning he gave her what she thought of as his avuncular smile. "Cappello says you've got quite a little story to tell."

She ran the whole thing down for him: Geoff's death, possibly based on a twenty-seven-year-old case; his grandmother's death; the two burglaries; and Mike.

She thought a grim expression came over his face when she mentioned Mike, and not just because she was talking about a policeman. She wondered if their paths had crossed, if Mike had rubbed Joe as much the wrong way as he had her, as he had her friend in Burglary, as he had the entire congregation at Geoff's funeral.

When she had finished, he gave no opinion at all. He said only, "Give me a while on this."

She and Cappello left, not knowing whether that meant he wanted to think about it or he was taking it up the chain of command. Cappello said, "You know, if we get the warrant, I'd kind of like to go out on that search with you."

Skip liked to work alone. She'd been offered partners, but she didn't like someone looking over her shoulder. However, there was clearly only one answer. "Sure," she said, wondering if something personal was going on. Maybe Cappello had had some kind of run-in with Kavanagh.

On Skip's desk lay a message to call the desk officer immediately. "Langdon, you've got a visitor."

"Who, me?"

"You. In the lobby of the Detective Bureau. She's pretty out of it."

Lenore was standing, looking jangled. She was holding a can of Diet Coke and shaking.

"Lenore, what is it?"

The other woman turned a pinched, bruised-looking face on Skip. She had huge purple circles under her eyes, though not from being hit—the eyes were sunken, not swollen.

"You're strung out, aren't you?" *Why in the name of hell had anyone let her in?*

"Not strung out. Up all night." Her speech was slurred.

"What can I do for you?"

That was the signal to let go, big-time. Lenore's face came tumbling down; tears poured in puddles. "Everybody I know's getting killed."

"Who's been killed?"

"Everybody."

"Has someone other than Geoff been killed?"

"Everybody I know. Geoff, Mrs. Julian . . ."

"Mrs. Julian? What do you know about Mrs. Julian?"

"She's dead. Everybody I know's dead."

"Lenore, did you kill her?"

"Did I kill her? Did I kill Mrs. Julian?" She was shouting. "No, I didn't kill Mrs. Julian. But somebody did and you'd better do something about it."

"Easy there. Easy. I thought Mrs. Julian died of natural causes."

"You know better than that."

She didn't have a clue whether Lenore knew something or not. "Lenore, why are you here?"

" 'Cause everybody I know's getting killed and nobody's doing a damn thing about it. Came to make you get on the stick."

"Do you know something about Mrs. Julian's death?"

Lenore looked down at her lap. "Know it was no accident."

"What makes you say that?"

"Conspiracy against me."

"You know, I think we should continue this conversation when you've had a few hours' sleep." She paused. "And you're not on drugs."

Lenore stood up, hands outstretched as if she intended to attack. "You bitch. You bitch! I'm gonna kill you." She looked too pathetic and scrawny to kill a spider.

"No, you're not, Lenore. Go home now."

Skip was on her way out when she thought of something that made her stomach lurch. She stopped and turned around. "Lenore? Where's Caitlin?"

"Caitlin. Oh my God . . . Caitlin!" The baby's name pealed through the corridors.

"Take it easy now. Take it easy."

Skip walked toward her and took her wrists gently, just holding her up.

She was rocking back and forth, body racked with sobs, tears coming at such a rate she was going to get dehydrated. "My baby. I forgot my own baby!"

"She's at home alone?"

Lenore nodded. "Shit. Oh, shit!"

Skip was already reaching for the phone. "Who's your next-door neighbor?"

"He's never home." She shook her head violently. "I've got to go."

She was halfway out the door when Skip caught her by the arm. "You can't drive in your condition." She could barely think, her head was so full of visions of Caitlin sticking her fingers in sockets, pulling cabinets over on herself, opening the door and walking to Nebraska.

"I have to."

Skip said, "Come with me."

"Where are we going?"

"To get someone who can help you."

When Lenore found out the someone was an officer in Child Abuse, she threw another druggy little fit, but by then she was no longer Skip's problem.

Skip was pushing papers around on her desk, stomach nervous, waiting to hear from Joe, when she became aware of something large and menacing behind her. She swiveled, found herself staring into the protruding belt buckle of Sergeant Frank O'Rourke.

"What the fuck are you doing going after Mike Kavanagh?"

"My job, Frank."

"We're not talking some lowlife dirtbag. This is my cousin, Langdon."

She forced a smile. "I guess it runs in the family, Frank."

The color and texture of his face—suffused, but lumpy and dull—reminded Skip of a New Orleans name for tomato sauce, "red gravy."

He squinted and whispered: "You cunt."

"Could you speak a little louder, Frank? When I file harassment charges, I want to make sure everyone heard it." When he didn't answer, she said, "What's that you called me, Frank? It started with a c, didn't it?"

"I'm gonna have your badge, little missy. Who the hell do you think you are, some little rookie from Uptown, going after a guy who's been a rock in this department for thirty years?"

She realized he was so close to her she couldn't stand up. "Would you stand back, Frank? I have to go throw up."

Apparently thinking she was serious, he took a step back, giving Skip the opportunity to stand. She was two inches taller than O'Rourke. "Don't ever call me 'little' again, if you want to live, Short Stuff."

Several detectives who'd been pretending to mind their business could no longer contain themselves. Someone shouted, "Go, Skip!" and someone else said, "Watch out, Short Stuff!"

Skip realized she was shaking. O'Rourke often had that effect on her—he could discombobulate her so badly she lost her composure, but she realized with amazement that for once she'd stood up to him.

Ha. Literally.

Not only had she stood up to him, but the guys were taking her side—and she *was* a relative rookie from Uptown.

She was trying to digest that and figure out how to press her advantage when Cappello sailed in. "What's going on here?"

"Langdon just threatened to whip O'Rourke's ass."

Laughter. Loud laughter.

"We're gettin' up a pool, but nobody's bet on Frank yet."

O'Rourke's face was red gravy again.

"Come on. Let's settle this somewhere else."

Cappello walked back out to the hall, Skip following and O'Rourke treading behind her like an elephant.

"Frank, are you harassing her about Kavanagh?"

"She's got no right—"

"She's got a duty, Frank. She was following my orders—who the hell are you to mess with another sergeant's people?"

"All right, Sylvia, I'm tellin' you. Mike Kavanagh's got a lot of respect in this department. She's gonna get that big ass of hers in a sling."

He slammed back into the Detective Bureau.

"Pachyderm," said Skip.

" 'Pachyderm'? What's wrong with 'Asshole'? The guy's treating you like scum and all you can say is 'Pachyderm'?"

Suddenly she and Cappello were in each other's arms, collapsed in a giggle fit. It would have set women in the department back ten years if O'Rourke had come back.

It was the first time Skip had ever seen Cappello lose it. In fact, there were a lot of firsts here—she'd never heard her swear, never seen her take on another sergeant, and never seen her really mad. And, come to think of it, never seen her so interested in one of Skip's cases.

She knew this was going to happen. That's why she wants to go on the search with me. That's why she's pretended she's personally invested in this case. She knew O'Rourke was going to come gunning for me.

She protected me.

Tears sprang to Skip's eyes. Joe had in many ways made Skip's career, but he'd thrown her to O'Rourke more than once. It wasn't that he wanted Skip to get chewed up, it was that he and O'Rourke had been friends for so many years Joe couldn't stand up to him.

In all her time as a police officer, Skip had never truly felt the protection of a superior officer, truly felt part of the team as she did today.

Jeez, I hope I don't make an ass of myself.

But even if Kavanagh somehow slipped away, Cappello was right there with her.

This is the way it should be, she thought, and wondered why it hadn't been before. *It might be because I'm a woman, but maybe it just takes time. Maybe they're used to me now.*

An amazing thought popped into her head: *Maybe it changed because I stood up to O'Rourke.*

Why had she ever thought she had to take his crap?

21

• •

Cappello said, "The superintendent said go get him."

"You're kidding."

"Uh-uh. He's taken a lot of heat in the press for dirty cops—haven't you noticed? He's taking no chances on this one."

It was nearly noon by the time the search warrant came through. Skip hoped against hope Mike would still be home.

Cappello banged on the door. Almost instantly, Mike answered it. He was wearing jeans and no shirt. His belly made Skip want to avert her eyes. "What's going on?"

Cappello handed him the search warrant, smirking a little, Skip thought.

"What's going on?" he said again, this time more softly, his bravado gone.

"We're searching your house, Mike."

"How the fuck did you get that thing?"

"Oh, went through channels. Asked a judge. All the usual stuff."

"You haven't got shit on me."

"Interesting choice of words," said Cappello, elbowing past him. "Jeez, this place is a pigsty."

As bachelor digs went, it was even worse than Pearce's place. Instead of books and papers, he had tools and empty paint cans, full ones as well, boxes of nails, stuff most people stored in garages.

How in hell are we supposed to find anything?

The bedroom looked a little easier. It stank—stank badly of dirty laundry, which littered the floor. But at least there weren't so many little pockets to hide things. "Want to flip for it?"

"It's yours," said Cappello. "I can't take the stink."

She went back out to the living room and started emptying boxes. At intervals, objects hit the floor with satisfying thuds.

Sighing, Skip opened a window and breathed fresh air.

On top of Mike's bureau were a lot of grime-encrusted, though once-elegant bottles—scents Suby and Helen had given him, probably. And there was a filthy tray he kept them in, and a saucer full of pennies. But nothing in which to hide anything.

Skip opened the first drawer—socks and shorts, his underwear drawer. A favorite for hiding things. And sure enough, there was some money in there—as a cop, Mike should know better.

But there was no citrine ring.

Systematically, she took the bedroom apart, pulled the mattress off the bed, and turned to the unlovely task of attacking Mike's closet. The odor in there was even worse than in the rest of the room. Unhappily, Skip went through all his pockets, to no avail.

She found a stack of dirty magazines on a shelf—not copies of *Penthouse*, but crotch shots and bestiality; and kiddy porn and ass 'zines and tit 'zines and 'zines full of naked fat ladies. Either Mike had truly catholic tastes or, more likely, a collection of stuff found under circumstances a lot like Skip's current one.

She went into the kitchen. It was also filthy and littered, and stank of garbage and two-day-old dishwater. Angry at the grunginess of the chore, she opened a cupboard and started pulling things out. Like Cappello, she was tempted to drop anything she'd looked at onto the floor. But the thought of broken food jars—peanut butter, say, and pickle relish—was too gross to contemplate on top of everything else.

She had to dig around in the peanut butter, though, and in other jars of goo. She pulled out a five-pound bag of flour that sent up a white cloud.

Damn. I didn't think it was open. I must have torn it.

But examining the bag, she saw that it was torn near the top and around the back, so that if it faced out, no one would see the tear. She didn't see how she could have made it.

Gingerly, she poked a finger in. Flour.

She pulled the top off the bag and there it was—one very white ring, halfway buried, obviously pushed into the tear. "Cappello. I've got something."

Mike was outside smoking a cigarette. She hoped he wouldn't come tearing in to see what they had.

Cappello stuck a sweaty head in. "What is it?"

"Come look."

The sergeant peeked in the bag and nodded. With a gloved hand, she fished it out, wiping a little of the flour off. A chink of yellow twinkled. "Ah, yes. Come to Mama."

She dropped it in an evidence bag. "Okay, let's finish up and get out of here." She jerked her chin outside. "Taking his nibs along for the ride."

Mike put up less of a fight than they expected—more or less crumpled when they read him his rights. He'd insisted on calling a lawyer first, but instead had called Helen, apparently to find him one.

While they waited for his lawyer, Cappello said, "I can hardly wait for this. I'm going to enjoy every minute."

"Do you have history with this guy or something?"

Cappello looked shocked. "No, why?"

"You're having such a great time."

The sergeant shrugged. "I never get out in the field anymore."

She was going to want to help Skip with the questioning, which, once again, Skip would rather do alone.

Oh, well. Easy come, easy go.

Cappello said, "Did you get squared away with the druggie?"

"That was Lenore. Geoff's girlfriend."

"Great little gal."

She left for a while and came back. "Mike's lawyer's here. I gave them a few minutes, but we can probably go in now."

"Who is he?"

"Eddie O'Brien. Funny you didn't say 'Who's she?' "

Skip snorted. "For some reason, it just didn't occur. Eddie's okay, though. At least you know what you're dealing with." Eddie was a spark plug of a guy, with a linebacker's build on a five-five frame. He had a military bearing, a stubborn, jutting jaw, rusty brush-cut hair, moles on his face, and a yat accent he'd probably never even considered trying to dump. Like many New Orleanians of a working-class stripe, he still said "earl" for "oil" and "zinc" for "sink." He had the high-pitched, excited voice so many short men seem to get stuck with. He was noisy, bombastic, and, so far as Skip knew, absolutely honest.

She and Cappello arrived in the interview room. Cappello slapped down a file folder she was carrying. Skip said, "Hey, Eddie," and stuck out her hand with genuine warmth.

"Skip. It's been a while. You've got the wrong man this time, baby."

"That's what you always say, Eddie."

Cappello said, "Hey, Mike. Did they give you lunch?"

"You bein' the good cop? Langdon here's going to be the heavy?"

"You've got us psyched, Mike."

Eddie spoke to him sharply. "What'd I tell you, Mike? Let that be the last peep I hear out of you."

Cappello said, "So it's going to be like that, is it? You looked at the warrant receipt, right? We found a real important piece of evidence in your client's house."

"They didn't find shit in my house. Know how I know that? There wasn't shit to find. I didn't do this shit and these babes know it."

"Mike, will you shut your goddam mouth?"

Skip said, "You didn't do what shit, Mike?"

"Not a word, dammit!" Eddie was shouting.

"Eddie, they can't do this to me. Look at 'em—couple of dykes who hate men—probably playing with each other under the table."

"Mike, I'm leavin'. I swear to God I'm leavin' here right now."

"Okay, okay."

Cappello turned to Mike and said sweetly, "Do you always keep ladies' jewelry in your flour?"

"There wasn't nothin' in my flour. I don't know what the fuck you're talkin' about."

Skip said, "We're talking about the lovely ring we found in there."

"Yeah, I know that's your story—I saw the fuckin' receipt. There wasn't any fuckin' ring or anything else in my flour. I didn't even know I *had* any fuckin' flour."

Cappello pursed her lips. "Ooooh. Language, Sergeant."

Skip said, "You don't know anything about the ring?"

"No."

"Well, who else could have put it there?"

"You. That's who did it, right?"

"How about your daughter? Does she have a key to your house?"

He stood up, doubled his fist, and leaned over the table. "You say one word about my daughter and I punch your lights out."

Eddie put his stocky little body between his client and Skip. "Mike. Hey, Mikey, everything's okay. Mikey, Mikey. Take it easy."

Glaring, Mike sat down.

"Mike, now repeat after me: 'I refuse to answer on advice of my attorney.' "

"Yeah, yeah, I know the drill." He hesitated a moment, in the end couldn't bring himself to do it. "Eddie, I gotta tell 'em the truth. I want it on the record that I don't know anything about any fuckin' ring."

Cappello looked pleasantly at him. "May we continue?"

He nodded, but glared as if he'd like to kill her. Cappello was making it known she was having a fine old time.

"Are you acquainted with a Miss Neetsie Terry?"

"Geoff's sister?"

Skip nodded.

Mike looked at Eddie, who nodded as well. "Well, sure, she and Suby are friends. She was at the funeral."

"Weird kid, huh? She wears a nose ring."

Mike said nothing.

"Something about nose rings turn you on, Mike?"

"What the fuck are you getting at?"

"Just wondering how well you know her."

"I don't know her at all. She was Geoff's sister, that's all I know. Why are you asking me this shit?"

"Why do you think, Mike?"

He looked helplessly at Eddie, who said, "Look, Mike, I'm charging you the same amount whether you clam up or not. It's all the same to me what you do with your life."

Mike finally said it, the sentence Eddie was waiting for: "I refuse to answer on advice of my attorney."

And for right now, that was okay with Skip.

It was important at this point not to lean too heavily on the burglary. If Mike were anybody but a policeman, he would probably have been convicted on the evidence they had on him. Skip had plenty to use for leaning on him, getting him to plead to a lesser charge. She'd even considered showing him pictures taken of Neetsie's ransacked apartment and violated toilet. But it would take something worse than the Sharon Tate crime scene to rattle a hard case like Mike—and anyway, who cared about the burglary?

Go ahead, she thought, *clam up. That's just dandy with me. You can look smug today, but I'm going to get you tomorrow for murder.*

Tomorrow you're mine, asshole.

I'm not letting go till I've got you and it's not because you banged Geoff's head till he died; it's not even because you smothered an old lady.

It's because you put that cat on the roof.

What makes me the maddest is the way you tricked Geoff into doing a good deed—you used his own good nature to set him up. Now that's low.

Gang members might gun each other down, but it takes a special breed of invertebrate to put a cat on a roof and wait around to ambush its rescuer. You think you're getting away with it, you're severely misguided.

"Whatever you like, Mike," she said. "But we've got enough to have you for breakfast."

They booked him and had the momentary pleasure of seeing him behind bars, but he was out in an hour, courtesy of O'Rourke.

Joe Tarantino called Skip into his office. He held up his hands in front of his chest, as if she had a gun on him. "Listen, I want you to know I didn't have a damn thing to do with this. Yeah, I'm O'Rourke's friend, but he's got plenty of other friends in this department, most of them a lot higher up than me. Personally, I think the guy did it. I think you're doing a great job, okay?"

"Thanks, Joe." She loved the guy, she really did.

The phone was ringing when she got back to her desk.

"Langdon, you've got a visitor."

"Who?"

"A Mr. Pearce Randolph."

"On my way."

She brought Pearce back to Homicide.

"I heard you arrested Mike Kavanagh."

"Now where'd you hear a thing like that?"

He gave her a look.

"Oh, never mind." She didn't give him the satisfaction of saying his information was out-of-date. "What can I do for you?"

"I didn't get it off the TOWN, if that's what you think. But I do happen to know it. And I also know he didn't do it."

"Didn't do what?"

"The burglary. Isn't that what you arrested him for?"

"Now what makes you think that?"

He was starting to glare. This was a man who liked to be in control. "Look, I'm trying to help here."

"So help."

"I know he didn't do it because I know where he was when the burglary was committed."

"Ah, you know when the burglary was committed. Well, that's more than we know—would you mind clueing us in?"

He got up. "I'm out of here."

And he was striding out when Skip got hold of herself. She was mad at O'Rourke, not him. "Pearce, wait up. I'll buy you some coffee."

As soon as they were in the hall, he said, "What's wrong with you anyway?"

"That's a good question. Listen, I'm sorry. I want to hear what you have to say."

She brought him back in and got him some coffee. It was a good move. He was a little less cocky now, a little more inclined to be helpful rather than merely superior.

"Look, of course I'm in touch with Neetsie. All of us are in touch all the time. You know that."

"I guess I should by now."

"So I know the burglary took place while she was out at the laundry, which was between one o'clock and two-thirty. Something like that. Right?"

"Right."

"Well, Mike was home alone then."

"If he was alone, you weren't with him, right? So how could you possibly know?"

"Because I saw him go out to Schwegmann's at twelve-thirty P.M. and followed him back at one-fifteen. Then I sat in front of his house until three P.M., when he came out and went to a liquor store and drove home again. When he didn't come out by five, I figured he was drunk and went home."

"Hold it. Let me get this straight. You've had Mike Kavanagh under surveillance?"

"That's right."

"Whatever for?"

"Because I figured he was the best candidate for murderer. Suby's on the TOWN; she probably told him all about Geoff's flashbacks. Or maybe Geoff told him himself—who knows?"

"You're leaving something out. Everybody in New Orleans probably thinks he's the best candidate for murderer, but even I, the detective assigned to the case, have not had him under surveillance. Why, pray tell, have you?"

"Well, maybe you should have." Seeing Skip's look, he said, "Just kidding. I know you can't do everything. I'm working on a story about the case. You know that."

She nodded.

"Well, I thought if I—you know—solved the case . . ." He looked so embarrassed she almost believed him.

"You mean you've been playing detective on this?"

"I'm an investigator. I know what I'm doing."

"So you know for a fact he didn't leave his house between one-fifteen and three P.M."

"Yeah." He reached up, as if to straighten his tie. He probably hadn't worn one in years, but had kept the habit. It was probably what he did when he lied.

"How about the back door?"

"He brought his garbage out about an hour after he got home."

"You must keep careful notes."

"As a matter of fact, I do." Pearce pulled out a folded piece of paper. "See: 'Saturday. 2:18; brought garbage out.' Oh, look, I forgot about this. Some neighbor knocked on his door about half an hour later. He came out and talked to her a minute. See: '2:46. Conversation with neighbor.' "

"That's a lot of activity for an hour."

Pearce shrugged. "It couldn't have been him, Skip."

"Damn. I thought I really had something."

"What'd you find in the search?"

"That's police business."

"Come on. I gave you something. You give me something back."

"If you have information about a crime, it's your duty to come forward with it."

"You aren't going to tell me?"

She smiled. "I can't. You know that."

"Well, what are you going to do about Mike?"

She spread her hands, the picture of largesse. "Guess I'll have to let him go."

"Sorry it turned out this way." He stood to give her a good-bye handshake. "But I'm glad you believe me."

Sure I believe you, Pearce. And the Mississippi just changed course.

22

• •

As she was about to leave for the day, Federal Express delivered a bulging package, which she ripped open instantly. It was full of disks from Wizard and some printouts as well.

Everything Geoff had ever posted and everything he'd deleted.

She was thinking eagerly of diving in the next day, with some of the same tingly excitement usually reserved for Linda Barnes novels, when Kit called. "Lenore asked me to phone and thank you for your help. She says she knows she acted like an ass, but she's too embarrassed to tell you herself."

"Is she all right?"

"She'll be better when she wakes up. I guess she was pretty loaded when she saw you."

"I'd say so. What about Caitlin?"

"Caitlin's fine. Lenore didn't forget her at all. She took her to day care, went back home, called in sick, dropped some pills, got some paranoid fantasy in her head and took off to find you."

"She had a close call."

"Yes. I just hope that pill thing didn't mean she's . . ." She seemed reluctant to complete the sentence.

Skip said, "Suicidal?"

Kit made a sound that could have been a sob.

It had been a hard day and Skip had a hard night ahead of her. Her calendar showed that, some time ago in a weak moment, she'd agreed to baby-sit while Jimmy Dee took a client to dinner.

So when Cindy Lou called ("Hey, girl, you want to grab a bite?"), she talked her into dinner *en famille*. Now the problem was figuring out what to make. There was always hamburgers—that went down well with kids—but did Cindy Lou eat meat? Yes, she'd had veal the other night.

Okay, hamburgers. Sheila herself had said Jimmy Dee never made them—he probably had the kids on a perfectly balanced low-protein, low-cholesterol, high-vitamin regimen that Deepak Chopra himself couldn't manage.

It occurred to Skip that Jimmy Dee might be working too hard at fatherhood. No wonder he was so tired all the time and felt so beaten down.

She shopped at the Quarter A&P, arriving with two giant bags she hoped Dee-Dee wouldn't peruse before he left. But of course nothing would stop him.

"Auntie! Naughty, naughty. Potato chips! You've got to be kidding."

"Lighten up, Dee-Dee, they're kids."

"Yeah!" chimed in Kenny. "Auntie Skip, could I have a potato chip?"

He never called her "Auntie" unless he wanted something.

"You can have lots of them for dinner. For now—how about a carrot stick?"

"Gimme a break!" But he trundled off good-naturedly.

"I got cookies for dessert too. I think he's right, Dee-Dee— maybe you ought to lighten up."

"God, I'm doing the best I can! This shit isn't that easy for a fifty-year-old faggot."

"Well, I was thinking—maybe you're making it harder than it has to be."

But he didn't seem to want to talk about it. He said, "Sheila spoke to me today."

"Aha. You must be doing something right."

"I think that genie, Darryl, had something to do with it. We should have him over—tonight, for instance. How would that be?"

"You mean I should have him over. You're trying to promote something, aren't you?"

"I've found my true love. Why shouldn't you?"

She let that hang there a while.

"You think I should call Layne?" asked Dee-Dee.

"Sure—if it turns out he didn't kill his best friend."

"Yeah. Maybe not quite yet. I haven't had a date in four years—just my luck to bring home a murderer. But there's something I don't get. Since he *was* Geoff's best friend, why would he kill him?"

"It might not have anything to do with the flashbacks. Maybe that's a blind alley."

"Oh, sure."

"I don't know—maybe it was Pearce and he's protecting him. Maybe he's Pearce's lover."

"Was, you mean. Was. He likes me now, remember?"

She turned away smiling, intent on washing lettuce for the burgers. Dee-Dee was definitely interested. He'd had so many friends who died, he'd been too depressed even to think about romance for a long, long time. Maybe he had sex with someone or other—Skip didn't know—but he sure didn't have relationships.

The doorbell rang.

"That'll be Cindy Lou. I asked her for dinner."

"How come you never ask anybody good when I'm home?"

God, we're like an old married couple! she thought as she went to answer the door. She wondered if she was about to be as jealous of Layne as Dee-Dee was of Steve.

Sheila moved out into the hall and, catching a glimpse of dark skin, came tearing to the front of the house. "Oh. I thought you were Darryl."

"I'm only Cindy Lou." She would have shaken hands, but Dee-Dee interjected himself between her and Sheila, kissed her on the cheek, and said, "Haven't got time to say good-bye. Hello."

Kenny, who'd popped out as well, was the only one polite enough to chuckle. "Hey, Cindy Lou," he said, and stuck out his hand as if he were grown up and a graduate of all the good schools put together. Cindy Lou lit up.

What a pleaser, Skip thought, and felt a twinge for Sheila, who'd never learned the technique. Life seemed so much harder for her.

But Cindy Lou turned to her. "So you've met Darryl, have you?"

"Are you related to him?"

"Well, I don't know; maybe. We're about the same color, aren't we? But I'm from Detroit."

"Really? We're from Minneapolis."

"Aren't you glad you're out of all that cold and mess?"

"I don't know. Well, sometimes." It was the first time she'd ever said anything even slightly indicating she was happy to be there.

Skip said, "I think it's pretty cold here," which set off twenty minutes of raving—on everybody's part but hers—about what really awful weather was like.

The kids liked Cindy Lou. What was more important, Sheila did. That was two people she'd liked in less than a week. Progress was happening.

Kenny went back to his homework or model-building or collecting for the poor or whatever exemplary behavior he performed when discreetly disappearing like the convenient child he was.

But Sheila stuck around. "Hey, Cindy Lou, are you married?"

"No, are you?"

"Not yet, but—"

"Are you engaged or anything?"

"Well, I do kind of have this boyfriend, but I don't know. Now I like somebody else, but I think he likes somebody *else,* and it's somebody I'm sort of close to."

Good grief, can she mean Darryl? Is it this bad?

"Well, what's his name?"

"The new guy? Michael."

Skip breathed a sigh of relief. She'd probably forgotten all about her crush on Darryl.

"And your friend? The one he likes?"

"Annalise."

"Well, honey, Annalise won't be your friend if you take her boyfriend away. And you know what's important—your girlfriends. Boyfriends come and go—"

"In some people's lives," said Skip.

"I mean at your age," Cindy Lou said to Sheila.

"Oh. Well, then. Maybe if I got an older one, he might be more stable."

"How much older?"

Sheila blushed.

Skip said, teasing, "Someone like Darryl, maybe?"

Without warning, the girl's face clouded over. "Fuck you!" she said, and turned on her heel.

Skip shrugged. "See what I mean? A trash-mouth."

"I think she's adorable."

"What do you think about the way she changed like that—one minute okay, the next a little street thug?"

"I think she felt attacked. I guess she's pretty insecure."

"Wonder why. No dad. No mom—"

"Go apologize."

"Huh?"

"Yeah, go do it. It'll make her feel better."

Skip found Sheila in the TV room, stretched out and pouting. "I'm sorry, honey. I didn't know you minded being teased."

Sheila didn't answer. Skip slunk back to the kitchen, feeling slapped.

"Well?" said Cindy Lou.

"Her Majesty's not speaking."

"Don't worry, it did some good. She'll smooth out. She just needs a little time."

"I'm starting to see another problem, though. She's only thirteen. Isn't she awfully precocious—sexually, I mean?"

Cindy Lou shrugged. "Welcome to the nineties."

Skip was peeling an onion, and it was making her cry. She turned it over to Cindy Lou. "Here. Don't you have contacts?"

"No, but I could use a good cry, just on general principles."

"Something wrong?"

"Just crying for you, babe. About this pickle you've gotten yourself into."

"Being an auntie, you mean?"

"Lordy, as my old mama used to say. Better you than me. And the same goes for that Darryl character, by the way."

"What's that supposed to mean? You're the one with the bad taste."

"Yeah, I'd never mess with him—he's not that bad. But I'm almost attracted to him—and that means he's trouble."

Skip heaved a great sigh. "Are they all trouble? Tell me that."

"That Steve's a pretty good one."

Skip turned from the counter, where she was making patties. She was surprised at the anger in her voice. "Well, he's the one—" She had to stop, to keep herself from bawling. She blinked, but it was too late. Cindy Lou saw the tears.

"You're really upset."

"He's not coming, Cindy Lou. For two years, he says. He says he's developed some great new skill and everybody wants to hire him. But he'll be here in two years, just like clockwork, he says. Right. Sure."

"You don't believe him, huh?"

Skip grabbed a paper napkin, the closest thing she saw to a tissue, and sat down at the kitchen table. Cindy Lou was crying too, from the onions. "I didn't know I was this upset."

"That's because you've been flirting with Darryl to distract yourself. That's baby stuff, girlfriend. You're mad at Steve and upset with Steve and sad about Steve—might as well go on and deal with it."

"Oh, quit sounding like a shrink."

"Sorry." She shrugged. "I guess I just like the guy."

"Always a bad sign."

"Au contraire, regarding other people's men. In this area, I have quite good taste. Steve's a classic teddy bear; that Darryl's a butterfly man."

"What on earth are you talking about?"

"Just a little psychological term I made up. A butterfly man's beautiful—dazzles you with his gorgeous colors. And what a tongue! You know what a butterfly's tongue's like? Kind of this long thing that rolls out? A butterfly man's got a tongue that won't quit—he'll tell you everything you want to hear and when he's done with that he'll make up some nice new stuff, all of it just as pretty as all that plumage. Only two things wrong—"

"He flies away."

"Oh, yeah. He flies. He flits from flower to flower—has to, to stay alive. The other thing's kind of mixed—he's got a real light touch. You know, like a butterfly kiss? In a way that's nice and sweet but, I don't know, in the end you just can't take him seriously."

"Darryl's a teacher. He went out with me at two A.M. to find Sheila and took us out to eat at three. It's Steve who doesn't give a damn about the kids."

"I knew one once who was a nuclear physicist. They can have good jobs, and they can be loving—I guess that's what you're saying about Darryl—and they can be great with kids because they're so childlike themselves. But don't expect them to tell you their innermost thoughts. And if they do, don't be surprised if they tell you something different tomorrow."

Skip was starting to be amused. "Well, who needs innermost thoughts if they're taking care of things? Like the kids, I mean."

"Let me put it another way. 'Butterfly man' is just the highly technical professional term for these guys. On the street, they've got another word for it."

"What's that?"

"Con artist."

"Oh, come on, Cindy Lou. You mean if I called up Fortier, they'd tell me Darryl didn't work there?"

"Oh, probably not. He probably works there. I'm just saying when something looks too good to be true, it usually is."

"He doesn't look too good to be true. He looks just about good enough. Is it too much to ask that a man know how to take care of kids? That's the part I'm impressed with."

"Oh, yeah? This guy doesn't make you feel singled out? He doesn't have some way of focusing on you—maybe on you and your whole family, Dee-Dee and Sheila as well—that makes you feel really special? Like he really has deep feelings for you even though he just met you? Tell me something—is there a person in the whole house who isn't utterly charmed by him?"

"Well, that part's true. And he does have this way of focusing. How'd you know that?"

" 'Cause that's a butterfly man. Are you getting it now?"

"So you're saying he's just conning us? He doesn't really have any feelings for us?"

"Oh, he's got feelings. It's just that they're very, very changeable."

Kenny came in. "Burgers ready yet?"

Skip got up and went back to her patties. "Ten minutes."

"Okay." He smiled ear to ear and left.

"A doll," said Cindy Lou.

"Yeah. Wouldn't you just hate to be his sister?"

"Ooooh. Wouldn't you?" She got up to set the table. "How's the case going?"

"Don't ask. We hit an impasse." Because Cindy Lou often worked as a consultant for the police department, Skip could talk about the case with her. She told her about arresting Mike, only to have him alibied by Pearce. When she got to the end, she said, "Do you think Mike's nuts?"

"Could be. Or maybe he was just drunk. But in that case wouldn't you have found fingerprints? Could he have forgotten to flush the toilet, not noticed he'd dropped his card, and yet remembered to wear gloves for the burglary?"

"I don't know. Maybe not."

Skip turned over the burgers. She dished them up and opened a bag of potato chips. "Tell me what you think about this threesome." She told her about Lenore, Caitlin, and their self-appointed mother, Kit.

"Oh, man. Kit's got her hands full."

"Did I tell you what those women are into? You're not going to believe this."

"You want me to call the kids?" Without waiting, Cindy Lou hollered, "Sheila! Kenny!"

It was definitely time—the burgers were ready, the chips were in the bowl, the table was set, the condiments were on it. But Skip felt oddly disappointed, knowing she and Cindy Lou were going to have to postpone adult talk till after dinner.

She wouldn't have missed that dinner for anything, though. The kids didn't fight, no one stalked away, and they came close to settling the question of whether it was better to be eaten by a shark or a velociraptor.

Sheila felt that a shark would probably bite your limbs off first, and you'd have to watch yourself get eaten, which would be by far the worst fate. "At least," said Kenny, "you'd have time to kiss your butt good-bye. A dinosaur would just go for your guts—like you'd feel something really sharp in your middle and then you'd have to die looking into its cold carnivorous eye."

"Carnivorous!" hooted Sheila. "How could you know a word like that?"

"Ha, ha, and ha! I know *triskaidekaphobia* too."

Skip's sides hurt from laughing. She would have given up her job in Homicide for Jimmy Dee to have been there.

When the kids had gone back to their homework, and she was loading the dishwasher, Cindy Lou said, "So what are Kit's girls into? Witchcraft or something?"

Skip whirled. "How the hell did you guess that?"

"Is that it, really? Lucky, I guess. Anyway, half the world is. Why not them?"

"Half the world is? How come I never heard of it? I thought pentagrams meant Satanism."

"Get hip, Granny. The goddess is coming back to save her only begotten Earth from the patriarchal demons."

"When you put it that way, it sounds like a pretty damn fine idea."

"I can't pick any holes in it. Bring her on, why don't you?"

"Cindy Lou, you're not kidding? You know about this stuff?"

"Neopaganism? Sure I know. Black people never did stop doing magic. Voodoo's paganism. You know, I wasn't kidding about the demons. That's what every religion does with the last one—demonizes it. Like Astarte and Baal—a pair of perfectly fine deities until the Hebrews got into that golden calf stuff. All of a sudden, they were the devil. And Pan, I guess, became the modern-day model for him—horns and cloven hooves, you know."

"How come you know this stuff?"

"I've got a lot of Jungian friends. They're heavy into archetypes. Made me read books and take courses. They said every educated person should know about it. You know what? They're right."

But Skip's mind was elsewhere. "You think I could put a spell on O'Rourke?"

"You don't put spells on people. That's unethical."

"Oh. Maybe I could just kill him."

"Say, why don't we start a coven?"

Skip was bending over, loading in a couple of glasses. She straightened up. "Who?"

"You and me."

"You and me? A pair of rational, professional women?"

"Who better? We could teach Sheila the goddess made woman in her image. Healthier for a kid."

"A girl kid? I guess it is. It's the weirdest thing. I never thought about it."

23

• •

The software the TOWN used made it so cumbersome to edit that almost no one bothered. Lenore hated that, especially when she was writing to someone like Pearce, someone who might not realize her typos were really typos, might think she just couldn't spell or punctuate.

But he had just sent her a message, not E-mail, but the real-time notes the TOWNspeople called "sends." It said, "Sorry I haven't called. I miss you. Busy. Damn."

Very sweet, she thought. She kept her answer short and simple: "I miss you too." Good. No typos.

Next came, "I hope you're okay. I've been thining about you a lot."

So he didn't correct his typos either. That gave her courage. "I've been kind of down," she wrote. "Geoff's funeral really got tome. That's 'to me,' not 'tomb.' Though . . . one wonders."

"Sorry. So sorry," he sent back. "Can I help?"

Yes, he could help. He could damn well help. He could come over and hold her. He was a human being—that must mean he could provide a little human warmth. Did she dare ask for it?

Without even considering, she did, too desperate to do otherwise: "Love to se you F2F—migt cheer me up."

"On my way," appeared on the screen. No asking when, just on his way.

Lenore smiled to herself. She liked a man who took action. And things were under control, for once. Kit had insisted on keeping Caitlin overnight. She'd said Lenore needed to rest, but in the back of her mind, Lenore was worried. What if Kit thought she'd spend another night doing drugs? Didn't trust her with her own daughter? That was probably why she was so lonely tonight, because Caitlin was gone.

She had slept most of the afternoon, unable to get up after two nights of staying up and doing drugs and trying to do magic. She knew the two didn't go together, but she just felt so bad she needed whatever she could find, she couldn't get through without a little chemical help. It was as if her healthy and unhealthy sides had gone to war—or perhaps "constructive" and "destructive" was the way to put it. "Destructive" had won out.

She hadn't told Kit it was two nights on drugs. As it was, she was deeply, deeply embarrassed at what she'd done, and embarrassed didn't start it. Caitlin could have been hurt—could truly have been badly hurt if she really had forgotten and left her at home.

Yet she hadn't. Her destructive side might have won out in her own life, but the good mother still operated—managed somehow to go on automatic pilot and get Caitlin to day care.

When she woke up that afternoon, she'd promised Kit no more drugs. And wonder of wonders, she felt pretty much okay right now, except for not being sleepy. It was getting late, and she had to go to work tomorrow—that is, she had to show up. If she was fired, she'd find out when she got there.

She'd have a drink with Pearce, relax a little . . . and she'd sleep like a baby.

The living room was strewn with Caitlin's toys. She put them away, washed the supper dishes, and just had time to put on lipstick before he got there.

"Hello, beautiful."

She felt better already. Uplifted by his good cheer.

"I brought us some wine," he said, and held up a bottle.

She hadn't even remembered she didn't have any. How had she planned to entertain him?

"You're so thoughtful."

"You're nice to make time for an old man."

She was in the kitchen, looking for a corkscrew, but his words affected her so deeply, she marched out again. "You are not an old man, Pearce. You are a very kind, decent soul. And extremely attractive."

Having delivered her speech, she turned on her heel and marched out again. As she fiddled with the corkscrew, he came up behind her, slipped his arms around her waist, and nuzzled her neck. She wriggled away.

"I thought you said I was attractive."

She handed him a glass of wine. "You are. That wasn't the signal to jump my bones."

"Oh. Would you let me know what is?"

"Oh, come on." Following him back to the living room, she took her own glass and the bottle. When he sat on the couch, she sat beside him, to show friendliness. (Though not necessarily availability—she hadn't yet made up her mind about Pearce as a lover, knew only that he was a good friend and she enjoyed his company.)

He touched her under the chin, a gesture she wasn't quite sure she liked. She drew back a little.

He said, "Tell me what's wrong, little one."

"Nothing. I just . . ."

"I thought you said you were depressed."

He held out an arm and she snuggled into it. "Oh, I am. Mrs. Julian was my music teacher. Did you see her at the funeral? Nothing happening under her hat. I mean nothing—all lights out." She shrugged, which wasn't easy with his arm around her. "And then she died."

He poured them both some more wine. "Maybe that's a good thing."

"That she died?"

"She wasn't really living, anyway."

"It's just so—"

"Final."

"Exactly. How did you know I was going to say that?"

"Because I know you, my dear. You don't really know how well, do you?"

Nervously, she drained off half her wine. "What do you mean by that?"

"Oh, just that I've been watching you. I've watched you, and I understand you. I know you." He pulled her tight against him. His warmth was lovely, and his body too, so much bigger than hers yet still not fat; a good body for a man his age, a very good body. It was nice to be held by a man.

She simply lay against him, pressing her body to his, not wanting anything except what she already had, enjoying him completely.

He kissed her cheek and moved near her mouth.

"No," she said. "I don't think so."

He moved away.

"Why not?" He gave her a little more wine, poured the rest of the bottle into his own glass.

"I don't know. I guess I just don't feel sexy tonight."

"Uh-huh, that's what I thought." How did he keep reading her mind? "Come here."

He lay down on the couch and positioned her against him, tight against him, so she could feel every inch of him. She fit neatly into the curve he made for her, found it comforting and cavelike.

He put an arm around her and stroked her hair.

They stayed like that for a long time, until her mind started to wander, until she found herself thinking about him fuzzily. Thinking she wanted him.

But only if they could do it very, very slowly, building up, maybe touching an inch of each other's bodies at a time, maybe for an hour before going on to the next inch.

She realized that was what they had been doing.

She was gently massaging a small patch of his thigh, folded protectively over her.

269

She thought he had probably been rubbing her butt a long time.

She turned toward him, thinking the back of his neck was the next place she wanted to touch.

She was wearing a short dress, with black tights. It was easy for him to insinuate a hand between her legs. She was surprised that her tights were wet.

As she felt his hand against her, something exploded inside her body, something was set loose that traveled up her body and had to come out her mouth.

She already controlled the back of his neck. She touched it in such a way that his lips came to her, received her loneliness and the flow of love and lust and deep, despairing longing that she had for him.

When it was over, they were still wearing their clothes, or most of them. Her tights were on the floor, but her dress felt as if it would cut off her circulation at the neck.

Pearce's pants were around his ankles.

He groped for them. "What did you say to me a minute ago?"

She was embarrassed. "I said something? 'Yes, yes' or 'Don't stop?' Something like that?"

"It sounded like something else."

He was unnerved. So unnerved she had a good idea what it was she'd said. It was something she had thought, but hadn't meant to say.

" 'Oh, God, baby, that feels great'?"

"I don't know. Maybe." He was shaking his head as if he'd just been through something awful.

What she had said was "Thou art god." It was her religious goal never to make love with anyone she didn't feel that way about. Witches in books said it, and their mates said "Thou art goddess," which was as it should be, Lenore thought. To her, it meant she celebrated his masculinity. But since she didn't know any male witches she had to figure anyone she said it to would take her for a maniac. Would probably figure she'd stalk him.

How the hell to get out of this one? She hoped she hadn't said it more than once.

She touched his face and gave him a kiss. "How old did you say you were? Twenty-four?"

He gave her a grin.

"Want another drink?" That was good for forgetting.

"Sure."

She headed toward the bathroom, and when she came back found him going through her kitchen cabinets. "Uh-oh, we finished the wine. Hey, Caitlin's not here! I just realized I can go out. You want to go somewhere and have a drink?"

She saw him hesitate. He wanted to go home. She wanted him with her a while longer. "My treat," she said, and took his hand. "Oh, Pearce, you don't know how much I need it. There's a place on Magazine Street. Why don't we walk?"

He gave her a nice-daddy smile. She could use a nice daddy right now.

"Come on," she said, practically pulling him out the door.

She stopped on the way to pick up her purse, but she hadn't put her tights back on, just slipped on her shoes, and her dress was thin. When they were outside, she realized she'd made a big mistake. But if she went back in, she might lose him.

She was pretty sure she had an old sweater in the trunk of her car. Too bad about her legs, but it would be something.

"Aren't you going to be cold?" he said, and it surprised her. She wanted him with her so much right now, she somehow had the idea he'd be opposed to anything she wanted. She hadn't imagined he'd be this thoughtful.

"I've got a sweater in the trunk." She skipped forward to open it, and what she saw made her draw in her breath. "Oh, my God!"

"What is it?"

"Geoff's backpack. I remember now—we went to a restaurant the night before he died, and he didn't want to leave it in the car. He must have forgotten it." She fingered it, thinking of Geoff; gentle, strange Geoff, to whom she had never said, and never thought of saying, "Thou art god."

"What's in it?"

"I don't know. It's Geoff's. Was Geoff's," she forced herself to say.

271

Pearce grabbed for it. "Let's open it."

"No. It's not mine."

"Lenore, are you crazy? Maybe there's a clue to the murder in there."

Something in her resisted. "Not yet. Somehow I can't do it yet."

"Look. Let's don't go out. Let's go over to the Winn-Dixie on Tchoupitoulas and get some beer or something. And we won't open the backpack till we get back—we can be thinking about what's in it."

Why? Why don't we just forget it for now?

But she didn't say it because she didn't want to lose his attention again. Maybe he'd forget about what she'd said when they made love, maybe convince himself it hadn't happened. "Okay," she said. "Beer for you and wine for me."

"No, wine's okay. Your car?"

"Sure." She felt a little woozy from the first bottle of wine, but it seemed stupid to say so, considering that morning's escapade.

When they returned, wine and backpack in hand, Pearce made a big show of opening the wine, pouring it, "letting the suspense build."

What could be in there anyhow? Probably a couple of videos he forgot to return.

Finally, the moment arrived. "Here." He handed over the backpack. "You do the honors."

She opened it and saw that she'd guessed right. *The Little Mermaid* was lying right on top. Tears sprang to her eyes and spilled out. Suddenly all the grief she felt for Geoff came welling up, tearing at her heart, making her chest hurt, her throat close.

The thought of him in his little boy's room in his parents' house, lying alone on his bed and watching *The Little Mermaid*, was somehow the saddest, sweetest thing she knew about him.

Pearce put an arm around her, but she shrugged it off. This was a grief that had to be felt alone.

"What is it?" he said.

"The movie. *The Little Mermaid*."

He picked it up and stared at it. "The movie?"

Done with solitude, she threw her arms around his neck. "Ohhh, Pearce." He drew back, possibly in bewilderment, and then gingerly held her till she wound down.

When she was able, she said, "I'm sorry. I'm so sorry."

"It's okay." He stroked her head as if she were a little girl. "It's okay, but what happened?"

"I don't know exactly. I just felt sad all of a sudden."

"Shall we see what else is in there?"

She nodded and handed him the backpack.

He pulled out a book of some sort. It was covered with what looked like Chinese silk, woven into a gorgeous blue design and bound in burgundy leather. A ribbon bookmark protruded from its bottom.

"It looks like a journal," said Pearce. He opened it, and Lenore saw that Geoff's spidery handwriting covered the two pages thus revealed. Covered them completely, not even a margin left over. The first was dated June 4.

Quickly, Pearce turned the pages, looking at the dates. The last one was November 4, two days before Geoff died. Avidly, he started to read, but Lenore was suddenly angry. She took a gulp of wine.

"There's something cold about this," she said.

Pearce turned to her, reading glasses pushed down on his nose, looking rather old and utterly befuddled. "What?" he said. It might as well have been "Say whuuut?" for all he seemed to know about what was going on.

"You're like some old . . . raptor."

"Huh?"

"Rapacious . . . predatory." She knew she was out of control, but she couldn't help it; she was just saying whatever came to mind.

Miraculously, he got it. He laughed, but it came out a lot like "Hee-haw." "You mean like some salacious old journalist? Honey, they don't call us news hawks for nothing. I'll bet I've got a curved bill and little beady eyes by now."

She laughed too. "Your nose actually grew while you were doing that, did you know that?"

"You mean, when I was poking it where it didn't belong?"

"Did you see anything—uh—you know . . ." She was starting to feel slightly queasy.

He shook his head. "Not yet."

"I don't know if I'm up to this right now—would you mind?"

"What's wrong?"

"I don't exactly . . . feel right."

"You mean about reading Geoff's stuff."

"I don't know. I just feel slightly sick."

He took her wineglass away from her. "You know what I'm going to do? I'm going to tuck you in and sing you a lullabye."

Suddenly she was almost inconceivably sleepy. "You are?"

"Let's go." He took her hand. For some reason, she picked up the diary with the other.

She just barely had the strength to set the clock. She clutched Geoff's diary against her chest like a teddy bear, while Pearce held her other hand and sang her a pretty song about lying down in a big brass bed. He said it was an old Bob Dylan tune.

24

• •

Skip arrived at work looking forward to a morning with Wizard's printouts and disks, but there was something even more interesting on her desk. The lab had dropped off the report on Mrs. Julian. It said traces of blood and saliva had been found on the rocking chair pillow—Mrs. Julian's blood and saliva.

She phoned Teddy Troxler, the technician whose name was on the report: "What does it mean?"

"It means she probably had a seizure as she was dying, and bit her tongue. It's quite common—all the muscles clench down when that happens. If she had a pillow over her mouth at the time, she'd probably drool on it, and there'd be blood in the drool."

"Why wouldn't the murderer see it?"

"Are you kidding? I couldn't even see it—it was just a trace. Now, it would have been a little wet, but he probably just put the pillow back without looking at it. I'd think he was probably in a hurry, wouldn't you?"

"How about the glasses? Any fingerprints?"

"Uh-uh. All I've got's drool."

Jimmy Dee called next. "How would you like a pile of paper a foot thick?"

"You got Layne's program to work."

"Pretty neat once I figured it out. You wanted Geoff's stuff, right? Layne wasn't kidding, I can get you anybody's."

"Geoff's is good for openers."

"I'll bring it over."

It looked like a long dull morning—she had Wizard's material, and now this. She settled down comfortably with a cup of coffee, more or less under the evil eye of Frank O'Rourke, which she ignored.

The deleted stuff was about the flashbacks. But why had Geoff erased it? Maybe he'd thought twice about being so public about something so private. Or maybe someone had lectured him. Since she'd been logging on, she'd wondered whether certain posters were exhibitionists or were simply deluded. She imagined Geoff sitting at his desk, Mosey on his lap, a cup of tea close at hand, enjoying the illusion of privacy; of coziness—imagining he was among friends.

There were two provocative bits.

In a musing on the subject, Geoff said he thought he could remember a fight. There was no mention of who fought or where. The other interesting observation was this: "Sometimes I wonder if hypnotism would work."

She checked Jimmy Dee's printouts to see where and when the posts had been made. They were in the same session, but different conferences, about a week before his death. The first had been made in Confession about fifteen minutes before the other. The second, the remark about hypnotism, had been made in a conference called Irrelevant.

If the murderer had been online at the time, he or she could have tracked what Geoff was doing; if he had software like Layne's, he could have gotten a printout like Skip's that would have shown the direction Geoff's mind was taking.

If he thought Geoff might remember through hypnosis, the need to get him out of the way would have been urgent.

She remembered the books on hypnotism in his room. Perhaps he had learned to hypnotize himself. Or maybe he'd seen a hypnotist or hypnotherapist. Frantically, she looked through the printouts—both Wizard's and Dee-Dee's—for any follow-up to the remark. But to no avail—she'd have to ask Layne and Lenore if he'd ever mentioned such a thing.

And there was someone she could ask about the fight Geoff remembered. Marguerite had had a chance to get over the shock and it was time to see her again—to ask her some slightly harder questions this time.

But to Skip's disappointment, Cole, her shadow and protector, answered the door.

"Hi. I'm here to see Marguerite."

"I don't think that's a good idea. She's fragile today."

Good, Skip thought. *Maybe the truth's working its way to the surface.*

She said, "I'm afraid I really have to insist."

"Okay." He sounded dubious. "Come in."

Toots stood just inside the door, wagging her tail, not even bothering to bark.

I'm practically a member of the family.

The minute she thought it, something dark and heavy hovered over her.

She wished she could name it—could penetrate it and tame it. It was the unhappiness they were all sunk in—even Neetsie, who didn't live here anymore. It was the accumulation of all the years—starting with Christina Julian and Windy, the world's most boring man—of disappointment and failure and eventually violence.

Marguerite and Geoff and later Neetsie had been born into it, but Cole had been drawn to it, had volunteered for it. On the one hand, it seemed to Skip, he was bent on saving Marguerite, saving them all, and on the other he was as deeply mired in the muck as they were, and part of it was his own muck—his lifelong failure, his inability to achieve his dream.

She felt the darkness and heaviness as distinctly as if it were a curtain.

Marguerite entered with her customary drawn look, the one she always seemed to wear at home, and in her customary sweats. She seemed to do a lot of sleeping in the daytime.

Cole's arm was around her waist, guiding her. She moved with difficulty, as if she suffered a chronic illness, which was odd, Skip thought, since she hadn't seemed ill at the funeral. He settled her on the sofa and sat next to her. "You okay, angel?"

She gave him a long, honeyed look. "Fine."

He smiled back at her.

Even with the damn black cloud, they seem happy together. It's enough to give you hope or something.

Skip said, "Do you think we could talk alone?"

Marguerite looked alarmed. "Cole said—"

"That I'd stay with her. Sorry, but today it's got to be that way."

Well, what the hell. This is just Round One. Maybe I'll ask her the same questions eight or ten times. I'll come back every day till she cracks. "We haven't really talked about the night Leighton was killed."

"Omigod!" Skip could practically see the imprint of her hand on Marguerite's face, so vivid was the impression that she'd been struck.

"I'm sorry, but we really have to."

"What is there to say?" Her voice went up with each word, ending in a high whine on "say," so that it came out "sayyyyyy."

"Just tell me what happened, that's all."

"It was twenty-seven years ago!"

"Some things you don't forget."

Marguerite squeezed her husband's hand and gave an audible gulp. She spoke slowly and mechanically. "We were at my mother's house. . . ."

"Who?"

"Geoff and I."

"Anyone else?"

"No."

"Go on."

"We were there and we came home. Leighton was dead. That's all."

"Was anyone else in the house?"

"No!"

"Geoff remembered a fight."

Before Marguerite could answer, Cole did: "What do you know about Geoff? How could you possibly know that?"

It was time to get tough with these people. "Mr. Terry, I'm a police officer. It's my job to know things."

"Why should we believe you?"

"Frankly, I don't care if you believe me or not. Geoff remembered a fight." She pronounced each word separately and deliberately. "Geoff was killed because whoever killed Leighton thought Geoff knew his identity. That means he—or she—was in the house at the time—"

Cole said, "Wait a minute, wait a minute. I resent what you just said. Are you accusing my wife of killing her own son?"

"I didn't say that. Since we don't know who Geoff's killer was, I'm not assuming anything." She paused a moment, but Cole said nothing more. "He or she was in the house at the time. And Geoff almost certainly wouldn't have been there without you, Mrs. Terry. That's really pretty obvious, isn't it? Am I going to ask you down to the police station to answer the really hard questions?"

"You can't talk to me like this."

"Don't you think it's about time you got real? Your son's dead, Mrs. Terry, and so's your mother. Did I mention we're pretty sure she was smothered?"

Marguerite gasped. "My mother . . . ?"

"Your mother was almost certainly murdered too."

"But . . . no one told me . . ."

"I'm telling you. Three people have been murdered. Don't you think that's enough?"

"I didn't kill him, goddammit! I didn't kill him!" She was getting hysterical.

"I'm not accusing you of anything." Yet. "But tell me something. How well did you know Mike Kavanagh before your husband died?"

"Oh, I see what you're getting at. Oh, yes, I see. Well, you're barking up the wrong tree, Ms. Police Officer. I didn't know Mike Kavanagh at all until he started showing an interest in Geoff. Long after Leighton died. *Long* after."

"It couldn't have been that long. You married him eight months after."

Cole said, "I really think that's irrelevant."

But Marguerite had somehow entered a private world of her own, seemed scarcely aware that either of the others was in the room. "I would have loved to kill Leighton. Do you have any idea how abusive he was? Can you imagine what it's like to have your hair pulled when you come in—to be pulled around a room by your hair and thrown across a bed? Leighton did things like that because he didn't want to leave marks. He had a thing about that—leaving marks.

"It was always, 'Who've you been in bed with, bitch?' Not hello or good evening. Just that. Or 'Who'd you fuck tonight?' And a lot of hair-pulling. Sometimes slaps. But you know what he really loved? He'd hold my arm behind my back and push it up till I screamed. He'd bend my fingers back. Oh so lovingly. He just loved to do that."

"I guess you did want to kill him." *Maybe you even planned it.* "Did you tell Mike any of this?"

"Are you kidding? Mike thought he was a saint. Why would I tell Mike?"

"Maybe Mike was in love with you and you wanted him to kill Leighton for you."

"You're crazy, you know that? You're just a crazy bitch." She stood and, though she seemed unsteady on her feet, managed to look threatening. "You're crazy *nuts!*" Her arms flailed in the air.

Cole stood and caught Marguerite's waist with both arms. "I think I'd better get her back to bed."

"I need to ask her one more thing."

"You can see she's in no condition—"

Marguerite twisted out of her husband's grasp. "Quit talking about me in the third person."

"Remember the ring that was stolen that night?"

"You asked me about that before."

"And you said you never saw it again."

"That's right." It was strange—on this subject, she was eerily calm.

"Geoff said different."

"He was a child. He imagined things."

"And Neetsie says different."

"Neetsie?"

"The ring was stolen from her, Mrs. Terry."

"What? I have no idea what you're talking about."

"Yes, you do. You gave it to Neetsie and her house was burglarized."

Cole's face was turning purple. "Neetsie was burglarized?"

"Didn't she tell you?"

"No."

"Okay. Add that to the list. Your son's dead, your mother's dead, and your daughter's been burglarized. Let me know when you're ready to talk."

She left without a backward glance.

• •

When the cop had left, not even stopping to call Neetsie, Marguerite took two sleeping pills before Cole could stop her. It was just as well—better, because two of them at once, their fears naked and distorted the way they got, would be too much for him to handle. The other day Neetsie had had a lump in her breast; today she would probably have a stomach ulcer, and no telling what Marguerite would invent. This was the way with his women—he was used to it. They coped by hypochondria.

It was one way, he thought, as he headed his car toward All Systems Go. Cole needed a way right now. He almost envied them. It was beginning to dawn on him that his deal had fallen apart, that it was genuinely not going to happen. He wasn't sure what to do next. First he had to disentangle himself from Butsy; he had to deal with the IRS; he had to get Marguerite and Neetsie through the next few weeks.

But then what? There were only two companies he could think of who really needed his software that he hadn't yet approached. He'd have to send his suit to the cleaners, shine his shoes, and go through the whole sad business of business again.

Meanwhile, of course, he'd start on a new project, and if all else failed, there was always moving to California and getting a job as a programmer.

But that was wildly impractical. Marguerite was too fragile for a move right now. And the house, in its current condition, would be worth practically nothing if they tried to sell it.

Then there was leaving Neetsie. He just didn't think he was up to that. He'd been the strong one for so long, but there were certain things even he couldn't do.

They had royalties coming in from a couple of old programs he'd licensed, and they had the house. They could muddle along for a while. They'd been living more or less this way for a long time, except for a couple of helpful infusions from Burke Hamerton's company. A few more infusions wouldn't be amiss, but he'd come up with something. He always did.

Hell, the program was still valuable. The fact that his cretinous partner had fucked him meant nothing in terms of what he had to market—he knew it was important not to lose sight of that.

He found a parking place right in front of the computer store.

See. Luck is with me.

Takes a lot to keep a good man down.

He slammed out of the car and, without another thought, went in and asked for Neetsie.

"I'm sorry, sir, she's with a customer," said the oh-so-preppie young man who greeted him.

He saw his daughter across the room, her nose momentarily unornamented. She was wearing a black miniskirt, black tights and a burgundy sweater—Neetsie's version of corporate. He had to laugh.

"I'm her dad."

The young man looked suddenly alarmed. "I'll get her."

Cole watched him take over the customer and dispatch Neetsie to Cole's side of the room.

If the young man had looked alarmed, she looked terrified. "Dad, what is it?" Her face was contorted, as if warding off more bad news.

"I heard you were burglarized."

"That's what you came down here for?"

"Honey, I don't even know when it was. The cop just came by and happened to tell us. I couldn't believe you didn't call us."

Didn't call me, he meant. Marguerite, tending toward her own hysterics, wouldn't have been much help.

She mustered a smile. "I'm okay, Dad. It happened Saturday." She shrugged. "I'm fine."

"But—" He couldn't finish his sentence. He was at a loss. She'd had a near breakdown just the other day.

She glanced nervously at her customer, now in the care of the preppie. "But what?" she said.

She looked perfectly composed.

"Who did Dr. John for you?"

She laughed, a shrill, tickled laugh, almost delighted. "I didn't need Dr. John. I got through it okay."

"But you . . . I just thought . . ." *You're so fragile, just like Marguerite. You couldn't have gotten through it by yourself.* "It must have been awful," he said. "I hate to think of my poor daughter going through something like that alone."

"I didn't go through it alone. I just couldn't call you and Mom. Not after everything else you've been through."

"Honey, we're there for you. That's our job—we'll always be there for you."

"Well, listen, I appreciate your concern, but I really need to get to work." Her voice had a bite to it. For some reason, she was impatient with him.

"Neetsie!" Even to him, his voice sounded accusing. "Have you got a new boyfriend?"

Once again, she looked at her customer—longingly, Cole thought. "No. As a matter of fact, some women helped me through this." She paused a moment, thinking about it. "I would have thought you'd be proud of me. I stood on my own two feet, I called on my inner resources, and I didn't even need my daddy. I was *strong*." She emphasized the word, and he realized it wasn't a word he'd ever have applied to her.

She said "Aren't you proud of me?" in a voice that was anything but strong, a little girl's voice begging for approval.

283

"What women?" he said. But he knew. "Kathryne! You've got some kind of weird relationship with Kathryne."

"Daddy, I think we'd better talk about this later."

He realized his voice must have been louder than normal. "What do you know about her anyway?"

"Daddy, please. I'm at work."

"Do you realize she's my ex-wife?"

"I'm sorry, Daddy. Actually, I didn't know, when we first got to be friends, but eventually she took me aside and told me. I couldn't have guessed, you see—because you always referred to her as 'Kathryne with an *e* on the end,' and of course she was Kit, not that, and Brazil, not Terry."

"She got to know you because of me. She's up to something weird with you—some kind of strange revenge."

"Dad!" She said it like a little kid, making it two syllables: "Da-aad!"

"She didn't look for me, I sought her out." She raised her palms to heaven, as if the whole thing were too much for her. "Look, it's a long story, and I have work to do. Good-bye, okay?"

She turned and left him standing alone. His own daughter.

25

• •

*T*uesday night and I haven't heard from him. If he liked me, he'd have called by now.

Skip, will you stop it? You're a grown-up.

Is anybody? Even Cindy Lou, with all her posturing. Do grown-ups have anything at all to do with male-female relationships?

Probably not. We're all boys and girls when it comes to that area.

So Skip comforted herself. She found it shocking that she could be reduced to insecurity approaching sweaty palms by a man with whom she'd only had lunch. But she'd heard other people's tales of romance gone awry and as far as she could tell, this was simply one area in which maturity never set in.

Jimmy Dee, who was fifty, had recently said to her: "You've never seen me in love. It's not a pretty sight."

Well, am I a woman or a mouse? If he's not calling me I could call him.

No way. If they like you, they call.

Ah, but he has a second job. That bartender thing. How can he call me when he's working?

That explained it all. It was amazing how much better she felt. As soon as he could, he would call her.

But why wait? Why don't I just go have a drink with him? Come to think of it, I could see Tricia.

Tricia hadn't crossed her mind since Darryl mentioned her. She truly couldn't believe she'd forgotten a thing like that.

And suddenly she was seized with an almost uncontrollable desire to see her old school pal.

Let's see now, what was the name of the bar?

She closed her eyes and sat still. It was almost meditating, an act she was quite sure she couldn't be still enough to perform.

It came to her: The Monkey Bar.

She reached for the phone book and dialed the number. "Could I speak to Darryl Boucree?" From the background din, it had to be the noisiest joint in New Orleans.

"Is this the lovely Margaret Langdon?"

"How on earth did you know my real name?"

"You forget who I work with."

"Tricia. Well, actually, I remembered. Is she on tonight?"

"Uh-huh. Why?"

"I thought I'd come down and see both of you."

"Get your butt over here." He hung up without waiting for an answer. It wasn't elegant, but it was unquestionably welcoming.

She slipped into some leggings and a sweater, grateful that mode of dressing had been invented—so like sweats, but so flattering.

The Monkey Bar wasn't a place she would have expected to see either Tricia or Darryl. It had ceiling fans, a noisy tile floor, and lots of light—in many ways like a lot of other bars in New Orleans. But this one had a newish quality, a whiff of trying to be ultra-nineties while employing old-fashioned trappings, a look of the lowest bidding contractor.

The noise was almost intolerable, the crowd somewhere in its thirties, single and somehow yuppified. Yuppies were a concept one read about more than experienced in the Crescent City, Skip's brother Conrad being the only one she knew personally. Conrad was a young man on the make in an economically depressed, slow-moving town, a town in which legal secretaries were often temps so law firms wouldn't have to pay them benefits, a town that young men on the make would do well to leave.

Yet here was a room full of men who reminded her of Tom Cruise in *The Firm* and women who'd probably make good secretaries if anyone would give them a job. It was a Friday's kind of place, a place that would probably have been more at home in Atlanta.

Darryl waved at her: "Skiperoo!"

Normally she hated it when anyone nicknamed her, but when Darryl did, it made her feel warm and cheerful. She bellied up, and he slapped down a napkin. "What'll it be?"

"Are you kidding? White wine. What choice is there in a place like this?"

"Naw, you've got it wrong. It's an ugly-looking joint, but it's just a New Orleans crowd—Abita drinkers, most of them."

"I'll have the white wine—it'll be better for my nerves. How do you stand this place?"

"How do you think?"

"Mmm. Good tips, huh?"

"That and Tricia. I told her you were coming, but she's real busy. She'll be along, though."

"Hey, bartender! What's going on?" somebody hollered. Darryl left.

Skip sipped her wine in lonely splendor, thinking that people-watching wasn't even fun in a place like this. She shouldn't have been quite so impulsive.

Somebody poked her in the ribs. "Skippy Langdon."

Tricia hadn't undergone a transformation, a New York slicking-up, or even the onset of the first wrinkles. She was the same Tricia she'd always been—her face was slightly too long, her freckles still showed, her light brown hair was in a ponytail, and she wore the characteristic look Skip had almost forgotten—a scrutinizing look, as if she were staring down into your brain. If she underwent plastic surgery, it would give her away.

Skip had had no idea she'd be so glad to see her old friend. Tricia had a tray of used glasses, which meant she couldn't hug. But she put an arm around Skip's neck and still managed to balance it.

Skip said, "You came back and didn't call me."

"Well, frankly, you wouldn't have been glad to see me. I came back with a little drug problem."

"You?" Tricia hadn't been very adventurous in high school.

She shrugged. "Disappointment. Poverty. Despair. It'll get you if you aren't careful. That and the wrong kind of boyfriend."

Skip was too amazed to say a word.

"I'll be back. I have to get to work."

When she was gone, Darryl appeared and refilled Skip's glass without being asked. "Glad to see Tricia?"

"A lot of water under the bridge."

He nodded. "She's been through a lot." His face was as solemn as she'd ever seen it, except when Sheila was missing.

Is he in love with her?

I don't think so, but on the other hand, why not? Why is he content to be just her friend?

He said, "We've been through a lot together."

Drugs? Recovery?

"A lot of what?"

He waved a hand, indicating his kingdom. "Oh, three nights a week at this place. Life where there is no life. Adventures among the soulless."

"You love your job, I see."

A blonde who'd just arrived reached over Skip's shoulder. "Hey, Darryl." She pushed past Skip to kiss him.

"Hey, Gigi."

"Could I have an Abita?"

"You sure can." He looked slightly uncomfortable.

"Hey, did I ever tell you how my interview came out?"

"No. I bet you did great."

The woman was literally elbowing Skip out of the way.

It's his job, she thought. *He's probably a pal to these people.*

Yeah, and who knows what else?

She wasn't jealous so much as uncomfortable. Why didn't Darryl introduce her and include her?

She thought she knew the answer—he wanted the blonde to go

away, didn't want to prolong the encounter—but still, it didn't feel good.

Tricia came by again. "Sorry. It's a madhouse in here. In about an hour it'll let up, probably."

"I think I better go. Can I have your phone number?"

"Sure. Would you mind getting it from Darryl? I don't even have time to find a pen." She was off before Skip had time to answer. Skip felt oddly snubbed.

"Darryl, I think I better go."

He turned away from the blonde. "Awww. You just got here."

"Yeah, but it's not my kind of place."

"Hey, I'll walk you to your car." He signaled the other bartender. "Roy! Mind if I take five?"

Roy slammed down two beers, nodding as he did so, not even looking Darryl's way. Darryl turned to Gigi: "Back in a flash."

Skip said, "You don't have to. I'm fine."

"Of course you're fine. I know you're packing heat in that." He touched her purse. Gigi's blue eyes got big.

He leaned over and whispered. "I just want to see you a minute." His breath was hot on Skip's neck.

As soon as they were outside, he took her hand. "I just want you to know how much I appreciate your coming down here."

"You do? Really?"

"You don't know what purgatory that place is."

"Then why do you do it?"

"I told you—the money."

"You really need it that bad?"

"Skip, I've got a kid."

"You said you didn't!"

"Uh-uh. I hedged. I don't usually tell people until I get to know them a little."

"Well, I see the point of that." She paused, taking it in. "You were married?"

"Nothing resembling it. I was in high school." He gave her a look at his dental wonderland. "The Boucrees nearly shat. I think it's the real reason they sent me off to New Haven. For years and years, I didn't even think about it. Then out of the clear blue, Kimmie looked me up, brought over the kid.

"She'd just gotten divorced. She was trying to get through beauty school, and there I was with an Ivy League education I wasn't even using. Talk about feeling shitty." He let her hand go and spread his palms. "So I had to do something. She gets all the Monkey Bar money."

The man's a saint.

No, wait—only the devil could be so handsome. Therefore he's lying.

But she couldn't convince herself. She said the first thing that popped into her head: "Darryl Boucree, you are one nice dude."

They'd gotten to her car.

He kissed her, pushing her up against it. It wasn't a long kiss, or a particularly serious kiss, but it enabled her to feel his chest and take in his scent. "Good night," he said, and though she had a hand on the back of his neck, he pulled away and went back.

She thought it strange that he hadn't waited till she was in the car, but if the kiss had affected him as it had her, it was just as well. She realized she was shaking a little.

Oh, shit, she thought as she released her emergency brake, *I am really attracted to this man.*

He's got a kid, has he?

Is there no end to his little stories of helping out the human race? He's got to be lying. Cindy Lou's right—he's way too good to be true.

But once again she couldn't convince herself. She floated into her house and flung herself on the bed, engrossed in fantasies that had run amok.

She was imagining the child she was going to have with him, a little girl, half black, half white, with long, long legs and a probable career as a movie star, when Steve called.

"Skip. I'm so glad I got you."

"Oh. Steve."

"Is this a bad time?"

Why should it be? she thought. She was in a great mood. "It's fine."

"Are you still mad at me?"

"A phrase I've always hated, Steve Steinman—as if it's my fault.

Oh, sure, just give her a little time, she'll be all right. You just don't get it, do you?"

"A phrase I've always hated. It kind of leaves you without an answer."

I could try to explain to him what's wrong, but what would be the point? He really doesn't get it. He's not coming here and so there's no point arguing.

"Look, you're not coming and that's the end of it. Let's not prolong this; it didn't work out. Good-bye."

"Good-bye?" He sounded utterly bewildered. "What about all our plans? I thought we were committed to each other."

An icy calm had come over her. Now that she was actually talking to him, telling him how she felt, she could feel nothing, was all detached observer. "You keep stealing my lines," she said.

"What?"

"Yes, I thought we were committed to each other. What *about* all our plans?"

"I told you. They're just being delayed a little while."

"On the other hand, they were *our* plans. That's *your* decision. If you want the truth, that takes my breath away."

"What, I was supposed to consult you on this? Skip, we're not married."

"Look, what's done is done. I'm going to get on with my life now. I'd appreciate it if you didn't call me anymore."

"What? You're breaking up with me?"

How can you be so thick? Who wouldn't break up with you? She said, "I'm seeing someone else."

Silence. A long silence. And then he repeated it. "You're seeing someone else?"

"Yes." She felt her teeth clench.

"You're really breaking up with me?"

"Frankly, I don't look at it that way. I think you broke up with me."

A noise like a sob came over the phone. But it couldn't be. *Men don't cry.*

They especially don't cry over me.

"Skip, I'm so sorry." He was definitely sobbing. She didn't

know what to say. She sat there, teeth still clenched, more or less in shock, trying to think what to do next.

Finally, he said, "What can I do to change your mind?"

"I think you know."

"You mean give this up? You can't ask me to do that."

"We're at an impasse, aren't we?" It would have been a good time to end the conversation, but she found herself reluctant to do that, wanted to hold on to it.

"I guess so," he said.

"Good-bye."

He gasped, apparently stifling another sob. "Good-bye."

He hung up, leaving her with the odd sensation of being garroted, of her windpipe being squeezed by an unseen hand.

● ●

Pearce hadn't called.

Caitlin was home today and Lenore still had her job. Far from firing her, her boss at the bead shop had been solicitous. Lenore had mentioned Mrs. Julian when she called in. Her death on top of Geoff's would be hard for anybody to take, her boss had said, and wanted to know if Lenore needed even more time.

She probably doesn't think she could ever get anyone else to work so cheap.

Nonetheless, it was a relief to know her life was still intact after two days in the Twilight Zone.

Except that it wasn't. Pearce had bitten a big chunk out of it.

Why in hell did I sleep with him?

Was I nuts?

Yes. And needy. Maybe that's worse.

She hated being needy—and face it, she was needy again tonight. She had a big hole in her after all the things that had happened, and a night with Pearce couldn't fill it up. Instead, it had opened a new abyss of longing and loneliness.

For a long time Geoff had taken care of her, had met a lot of her needs. But he hadn't been a romantic partner or even, finally, a sex partner. Just a good friend.

Pearce awed her. She couldn't understand why she hadn't had a crush on him all the time she'd known him; probably she had, deep down, but it had simply never occurred to her that someone like him could be interested in someone like her.

Now Pandora's box had been opened.

All the troubles of the world, all the creepy-crawly insecurities, all the jagged-edged terrors, all the foul forms self-loathing could take, were beginning to ooze in Lenore's psyche, and to overflow.

She was panicked.

How the hell am I going to make it?

Call Kit.

No. I can't call Kit—I can't let her see me like this, I can't let anyone see me. They'd never let me keep Caitlin.

I could call Pearce. . . .

No, if he wanted to see me, he'd call.

Get Caitlin to bed—at least do that.

The child was slightly fussy, but glad to be home, Lenore thought. Once she had had her bath, she dropped off quickly.

Leaving Lenore with a terrible sense of aloneness and dread.

Should she have a drink?

What could it hurt?

She had dropped by Winn-Dixie on the way home from work and stocked up. Pearce liked bourbon, she thought, or maybe Scotch, so she'd gotten both. She'd have to drink something with him, so she'd bought some wine for herself. And she'd gotten some beer in case he was in a beer mood.

She needed a jolt. She crushed some ice, poured some bourbon over it, and tossed it down as soon as it was cold. The taste was so medicinal she poured herself a glass of wine before she sat down at the computer.

Pearce wasn't on the TOWN.

She was amazed to realize she hadn't logged on herself for days and days—when Geoff was around, she'd spent part of every day on the TOWN.

She went to a few conferences and realized she was just killing time. Finally, she called Pearce.

He wasn't home.

She was starting to get a headache, yet she was far too anxious to go to bed. She poured herself another shot of bourbon, then another glass of wine. She went back to the TOWN.

She E-mailed Pearce—"Love to see you if you don't get home too late."

To her amazement, he got back to her in less than an hour: "Still up for a visitor?"

"couldn;t be more felighted," she answered, not even worrying about her typos. He was there in fifteen minutes.

In the meantime, she had managed to change into a floor-length sea-green robe that she had made for a Beltane ritual last spring. It was some kind of chiffon stuff that was more or less transparent, and really pretty intriguing, she thought. Especially with what she wore under it—a black garter belt and whorey mesh stockings. She had pulled her hair up into a kind of Grecian ponytail—what she thought of as a Helen of Troy look.

When the bell rang, she didn't even bother to look out the peephole—simply tore open the door and flung out her arms.

26

• •

There was an earthquake somewhere.

Here. In Skip's apartment.

Her bed was shaking. In a minute, the ceiling would crack and fall on her.

She sat up, trying to orient herself, and realized it was only a pounding, a great crashing somewhere outside.

The pounding was followed by the shrillness of her doorbell—apparently she had a visitor who was alternately trying both wake-up methods.

Maybe the building's on fire.

What else could be so urgent? she wondered as she sniffed for smoke.

The air was not only pristine, she thought she could see her breath.

A little fire could only be a good thing.

She struggled over to her intercom. "This better be good."

"Skip. It's Pearce Randolph."

"What the hell are you doing here in the middle of the night? How do you even know where I live, for Christ's sake?"

The aftereffects of her evening were coming out in her mood.

"Lenore's dead."

"What?"

"Lenore Marquer has been murdered."

"How do you know?"

"I saw her. I was just at her house. She's floating in her swimming pool."

Skip was already pulling on clothes.

"Did you call the police?"

"What the hell do you think I'm doing now?"

"Where's Caitlin?"

"Caitlin?"

"Her baby, goddammit. Where is she?"

"How the hell would I know that?"

"Stay there, Pearce. I'll be down as soon as I call it in." She heard the fury in her voice. Didn't this man have a brain in his head?

She called for backup, saying there was probably a young child in the house and asking for at least two officers.

The gate with the intercom, a high wooden one, was on the side of the house. She couldn't see through it and for all she knew Pearce was standing on the other side with an AK-47.

"Pearce, are you armed?"

"Of course not."

"Would you mind putting your hands up?"

"Why?"

"Let's not waste time, all right?"

Seeing empty hands, she went through the gate.

"Mind if I pat you down?"

"No." He was grinning now, apparently beginning to enjoy himself.

Cold bastard.

"Come on. Let's go in my car."

She didn't speak after that, her silence letting him know how angry she was.

"Did I do something wrong?"

A lot. For openers: "You don't come banging on a police officer's door at two A.M. It makes us paranoid."

"Well, look—did you ever think about me? I find a body and I'm terrified. What am I supposed to do?"

"Go to the nearest pay phone and call 911. You know that. Everybody knows that. Why didn't you do it?"

"I thought you were my friend."

She sighed. "I have a feeling thereon hangs a tale."

"You don't know the half of it."

"How'd you know my address?"

He grinned again, making her want to kick him. "I'm an investigative reporter."

She had her red light on and she was going far too fast for city driving. But the district car beat her.

A uniformed officer, slightly wet, was just rounding the house. She identified herself.

He said, "There was a body in the pool all right, but it's real ugly. She wasn't exactly floating—she's got a concrete block tied to her foot."

Skip winced.

She ran up the steps and rang the doorbell. As expected, there was no answer. She tried the back door and found it open. Lenore's phone was ringing. "Check the house—make sure the baby's okay," she said to the uniform and stared hypnotized at the phone. She knew she shouldn't touch it, in fact could wait for the machine to pick up the call, but something told her it was important. She felt in her jacket pocket, retrieved a wadded-up tissue, and used it to grab the receiver. "Hello?"

"Lenore. Thank God." It was a familiar voice, but she couldn't place it.

"Who's this?"

"Skip? What are you doing there? This is Layne."

"Hang on a minute, will you?"

Though she knew the uniform was perfectly competent, she went to check on the baby, who was sleeping peacefully through the noise—she'd probably had a lot of experience at it.

Returning to the living room, she picked up the phone. "What's up, Layne? It's two A.M." She never said "What's up"; thought it the rudest phrase in the English language. But "rude" would have been

297

a gross understatement in describing her mood—and she hadn't even seen the body yet.

"Oh, shit—is everything all right?"

"Goddammit, Layne, this is no time to play games. Why the hell are you calling Lenore at this hour?"

"She left a suicide note on the TOWN. Is she all right?"

"What conference?"

"Is she all right, Skip?"

"Just tell me where the goddam post is!"

"There's no need to shout at me. If you feel like being polite you can call me back." He hung up, leaving Skip staring at the phone as if it had mooed.

Well, he's right. There was no need.

But there's no time to call him back now.

She hated herself when she fell into bullying; this was what gave cops a bad name. But the pressure sometimes got to her. The combination of Pearce's inconceivably stupid performance and her distress at Lenore's death (if it was she who was dead) had proved too much.

Oh, well, I'll apologize later.

She went out to look at the body, thinking that Jimmy Dee must have seen something in Layne that she hadn't—anybody who could stand up to an angry cop could probably stand up to Dee-Dee, and that was going some.

There was a sea-green garment of some kind floating in the pool. The body had been hauled up on the side in a futile rescue attempt and it was indeed Lenore—Lenore wearing only a black garter belt, black mesh stockings, and a rope around her ankle, the other end of which was tied through a cement block.

The officer who had pulled her out—the first one's partner—was sitting in one of the white chairs, drenched, she saw now, probably freezing, and trying to collect himself.

"She was just standing in the water," he said. "See, the light's on"—he pointed to the backyard light—"so you could see real good. Just the top of her head, her forehead, almost down to her eyes, sticking out. Then when you got close you saw the garter belt and everything—spookiest thing I ever saw in my life."

Skip saw that the rope on Lenore's ankle was a couple of feet long, so that if she happened to float up instead of sideways, indeed she would have been standing in the water.

"I've got a blanket in my car," she said, and gave him the key, upset at leaving the baby. She didn't know the other officer. What if Caitlin woke up? Would he know how to take care of her? "When you've got it," she said, "get on your radio and call the dispatcher. Say we need the coroner and the crime lab, and another car to take a baby to Juvenile."

Caitlin was still sleeping. Skip spoke to the first patrolman: "If she wakes up, can you take care of her?"

He gave her an Irish grin. "Are you kidding? I've got three kids."

She took a quick look around the house, saw that a bottle of bourbon and a wine bottle stood on the kitchen counter. Someone had dipped into the bourbon—about a cup was missing—and had all but demolished the wine. There were three glasses here—a wineglass and two tumblers, suitable for serving bourbon—as if Lenore had had two guests.

Her computer was set up in a small room in the back, still on— the screen indicated she'd been disconnected from the TOWN. Taped to her hard drive was a bit of yellowed, scruffy-looking paper with a gibberish word written on it in ink: "EtiDorhPa."

Skip was dying to get started with that computer, but she couldn't disturb a crime scene. The best use of her time right now was probably to get Pearce's story.

"I'm going to go talk to the witness," she told the patrolman.

Pearce was still in the car. Skip, considerably calmer than she had been half an hour ago, no longer wanted to kick his grinning teeth in. "I'm sorry I snapped at you."

"Snapped! You were a Class A bitch."

She got up in his face. "Pearce, let's get one thing straight. I'm a police officer; you either treat me with respect or you get more of the same treatment. Understand?"

"Just because you're a cop you can't——"

"I haven't got time for this crap. Look. You're a possible suspect. I'm going to read you your rights."

"What?"

"Before I ask you any questions, you must understand your rights. You have the right to remain silent. . . ." She watched the play of emotions on his face, saw his cockiness change to respect, noted, not for the first time, the sobering effect of the Miranda warning.

"I'll answer your questions," he said. "I have nothing to hide."

"First, let's hear you apologize." This wasn't necessary to the interview, but Skip liked things clean. The suspect had been disrespectful and she was giving him a chance to wipe the slate; she'd feel better about him, be less likely to lose her temper with him.

"Sorry." He lowered his head like a kid when he said it, practically whispered. It was all she could do not to grin. Like Geoff, this was a man who wasn't truly a grown-up—except this one was well into his fifties.

"That's better. Let's go up on the porch." The light was on there; she could see his face. "Okay, you said you came and got me out of bed because you thought I was your friend. What did you mean by that?" She had started here to let him know just how precarious his position was—if she was the easiest cop to deal with, he'd better not blow it.

"I'm kind of embarrassed about what happened."

"How's that?"

"It might sound crazy."

She nodded sympathetically. "I listen to crazy stories all day."

"Well, I've been kind of taking care of Lenore since Geoff died—trying to be her friend—and so when she E-mailed me to come over tonight, I felt I had to. I knew she was going through some rough times, and probably needed to talk to somebody."

"What time was this?"

"It must have been about nine or nine-thirty. I'd just gotten home from dinner with friends."

"Nine? Or nine-thirty?"

He thought about it. "Closer to nine, I guess."

"And you came right over."

"Yes. I got here near ten, I guess, and stayed about an hour and a half, maybe two; then I left. She was in a real bad way—I really felt lousy about it, so I ended up in a bar, having a couple of drinks, and then I remembered I left something and I went back for it. She didn't answer the door, so I went around the back."

"You went around the back. Did you think she'd be in the backyard?"

Despite the chill—it was a nippy night—he wiped perspiration from his face. "I thought the back door might be open."

"Oh. Why did you think that?"

"Well, while I was here, we went out the back door for a few minutes—to look at the moon. Lenore had a thing about the moon."

"You thought she left the door open?"

He shrugged. "She was pretty loaded."

"Well, if she didn't answer the door, she was obviously either not home or asleep—did you plan to just walk in?"

He mopped his face again. "We'd been making love."

She crossed her arms. "Fine. If you've made love with someone, that gives you the right to break into their house."

"Look, it was a stupid thing to do, okay? I just wanted to get the thing I'd left and go home. I didn't—" He searched for words, didn't seem to find any. "I didn't want to run into her."

Skip hoped she looked as skeptical and disapproving as she felt.

The coroner and Paul Gottschalk from the crime lab turned up. She filled them in quickly, and went back to Pearce.

As if there'd been no interruption, she said, "Why didn't you want to run into her? It was her house. You were her lover."

"I didn't feel too good about what was happening between us. When she invited me over, I thought she just needed someone to talk to, but she met me in this crazy getup with a garter belt and everything—look, I didn't even want to make love to her. But she grabbed me. . . ."

"She overpowered you. Great big Lenore and little tiny Pearce. Why didn't you just report her for rape?" Part of her nastiness was meant for effect, but Skip was also aware that an even bigger part was perfectly sincere—that this was the same reaction Pearce had provoked in her before.

The guy's a monumental dickhead.

"Look, I did it, okay? That doesn't mean I'm proud of it. She was loaded—I should have just left when I saw how loaded she was."

"But you didn't want to disappoint her."

He straightened his shoulders. "I didn't. Okay? I thought she might hurt herself."

"What do you mean hurt herself?"

"I mean commit suicide."

"Why did you think that?"

"She was self-destructive. You could see it from twenty paces. This was a woman with 'tragedy' written all over her."

"So you fucked her like the good friend you are."

He flared. "Why are you crawling all over me?"

She spoke calmly and slowly. "Because it's what you deserve. Because I'm a police officer. Because, as you yourself said, I'm the only friend you have in this department. If it was some other cop, have you got any idea what you'd be going through?"

"Oh, jeez. I wish I were dead."

"What was the thing you forgot?"

"My coat."

"I don't think so, Pearce. If it was your coat, you'd have said, 'my coat,' not 'something I left.' Also, you'd have noticed as soon as you got outside. It wasn't your coat, Pearce. It was something of Lenore's, wasn't it? You waited till you thought she was asleep and in fact went to the back because you knew it was open—you deliberately left it open yourself—and you thought you'd just sneak in and burglarize Lenore."

"No!"

"Well, then, did you kill her?"

He covered his face with his hands. Two more officers had arrived. One, a blond who looked like a football player, got out of a car and came over to Pearce and Skip. "There's a baby here?"

Skip introduced herself. "In the house. Her mother drowned."

"What about her father?"

"I don't know. The mother didn't live with him. But she has a grandfather—something Marquer. A woman named Kathryne Brazil would probably know—she was the mother's best friend."

The blond nodded. "We'll take care of it."

Skip turned back to Pearce. "Okay, I'm giving you a whole new lease on life. This is your big opportunity, Pearce—to tell the truth for once in your life. What was it you went back to get?"

He looked at her appraisingly, seemed to weigh his options. Finally, he lowered his head, just as he had when he apologized, and said in a low voice: "Geoff's journal."

It was all she could do not to repeat the phrase at top volume, followed by a chain of mental exclamation points. For that matter, it was all she could do not to jump on his chest and beat him senseless. Instead, she spoke gently, not wanting to risk losing the thread. "You want to tell me about that?"

"We found it in her car a couple of days ago—in his backpack. She didn't know it was there; I guess she'd forgotten. She opened up the backpack and there was his journal."

"Did you read it?"

"She wouldn't let me."

"Right. She wanted to make love."

He shrugged.

In fact, Skip had spoken only half in sarcasm. The notion of Lenore—loaded, needy Lenore—snatching it away from him and clawing at his clothes, was all too believable.

"She went to sleep holding it."

"Or you'd have stolen it then."

"I'd have read it then. Don't you think someone should have read it? This is a murder case, right?"

"That does bring up the interesting question of why both of you withheld evidence."

She was just needling, but to her surprise, he addressed it: "Lenore wasn't up to it, don't you understand that? She'd fallen into some kind of a funk that turned her inward. The first few days she was all over the map, getting coroner's reports, posting in ninety-three conferences, calling people up . . . but she was losing it. Somebody else died—her old music teacher—and she just couldn't handle it."

"That leaves you, Pearce."

"Goddammit, Skip, I'm a reporter."

"Okay, I'm leaving that one alone. So you got back to Lenore as quickly as you could. . . ." *In fact, you came back for the sole purpose of getting your hands on the journal. . . .*

"Yeah. I did. But she came out with the garter belt the minute I stepped in the door."

"What did the journal look like?"

"Book-size, I guess. Covered with Chinese silk—a blue pattern. And it had some leather on the side; cheap leather, nothing fancy."

"Okay, stay here a minute." If he tried to run, she had plenty of policemen to chase him. She went in and told Gottschalk about the book.

When she came back, she said, "Did you drink anything when you were in there?"

"Some bourbon. Why?"

"Did she drink anything?"

"I think she had some wine."

"Was anyone else there?"

"What? Skip, we made love, remember?"

"Did you see another person at Lenore's tonight?"

"No. Could we sit down? I'm tired of standing up."

"I'll send you to headquarters. You can wait there for me."

"Oh, hell. This is okay."

"Did you see her suicide note?"

"You guys found a suicide note?"

"Did you see it, Pearce?"

"No."

"So what did she look like?"

"What?"

"Let's go back to when you got there the second time—you went around back and then what?"

"The light was on, which it hadn't been before. This sort of see-through thing she'd been wearing was floating in the pool. And then I saw her arm and the back of her head, floating."

If he was telling the truth, the body must have floated sideways as well as up and down; who knew how many positions it had assumed before being removed—a silent sentry in the universe, subject to the whims of wind and water, performing a static, pathetic ballet.

"What did you do?"

"I got out of there. Fast."

"You got out of there. Did you try to pull her out?"

"Hell, no. I just split. Period."

"Maybe she was alive."

"No way. She was a former human being."

"I guess that's better than never being one."

"What?"

"Are you telling me you didn't even check to see if she was dead? That you made love to this woman and you couldn't even get your clothes wet finding out if she was alive or dead? You couldn't even call 911?" She was furious.

"I told you. There was no question. She was dead."

"Did you see her face?"

"No. She was floating facedown."

"Then how could you possibly know she was dead?"

"I just did, that's all." He was shouting. She'd finally made him mad.

"On the way over, you told me she'd been murdered. What made you think that?"

"I didn't know that. I just said it to get your attention."

Time to let him think that one over. "Okay, look, I've got a crime scene to take care of. You want to go back to headquarters and wait for me?"

"How would I get there?"

"An officer will take you."

"Do I have to?"

She waited a long time before answering, and narrowed her eyes when she did. "It would show good faith."

"Okay. Sure." He even tried his cocky grin again.

She went and got the first two officers to take Pearce to Homicide. Then she canvassed the neighbors—which turned up the usual nothing—nobody heard anything, nobody saw anything.

Finally, she went out for coffee—for herself and Gottschalk. She sat on the front porch, sipping, while waiting for him to finish. When he left, he still hadn't found the journal, so she turned the house upside down.

It wasn't there.

Next came the computer problem. The machine was off now, the keyboard filthy with fingerprint powder. She turned it back on, wishing she had a pair of rubber gloves. She logged on as Steve Steinman, suffering a slight twinge, thinking it wasn't quite ethical to use your boyfriend's TOWN account when you'd just dumped him.

Where had Lenore posted her suicide note?

Since Layne was the caller, it couldn't have been in the women's conference. It might be Confession, in one of the topics on Geoff, she thought, and went to the first, which had now split into two. She tried the second one, the more recent.

There was a post by Lenore at eight-fifteen, but not the one Layne had mentioned. To Skip's mind, it was almost more intriguing.

"Opened car trunk and guess what>?" it said. "Who knew? it was like a ghose come back from the dead. his backpack was thereQ@! Talk about freaked out! there it was, Heoff's backpack, right in my car. And guess what weas in it? Hiw journal. It was like Geoff could talk to me now, could talk to me over that biggest bridge of all. I lost someone else besides Geoff, all in a week. thsi means a lot to me, habving a little bit of geoff. I know a lot more about what hwappened than i did before, but don't want to talk about it yet. somebody fucked him over. We have to have a TOWN meeting to figure out wehat to do."

Other people had posted afterwards—innocuous notes of good cheer like, "Hang in there, Lenore"; "What a spooky thing!" But there was also a "More, more!" contingent, people who had read the post as if Lenore knew who the murderer was, who'd interpreted her request for a TOWN meeting (whatever that was) as a call for a public hanging. There was the scent of virtual blood in the air.

Lenore had been back online about three hours later—at twelve-eleven, with the note Layne must have meant: "don't think I can go on anymore. Life's just too much. Can;t think of a single thing that makes me happy any more. too much death; too mush sickness, toomuch incompetence (mine), i read that you ahve to love yourself to be happy just howthehell are you supposed to do that? id fomeboy knows would they kuuist kgivbe me lessons, please? don;t know if i was cut out for motherhood - - blowing it copletely. Caitlin deserves better, and anything would be better. Iwant to die.Q@! I could, too. I have a sweilling pool. I woulc just get in and hit bottom and never come up. Frankly, i think bottoem is where i am now."

Skip scrolled down to the present time. It was Lenore's last post in that conference. Since E-mail wasn't saved in the sender's file, Pearce could have safely lied about Lenore's having summoned him. Instead, what might have happened was, Pearce saw the first post, came over to her house, got the journal, left, read it, and found it incriminated him. Then Lenore, realizing she'd been used for something a lot more humiliating than a sex toy, had drunk everything in sight, taken every pill she could find, and begun rambling incoherently on the TOWN. And Pearce, fearing that Lenore had also read it, and seeing a fine opportunity, had dashed back, done the deed, and pretended to find the body.

That might explain his bizarre behavior in failing to call 911—the more attention he could draw to himself the better, since a murderer would never do such a thing, but would simply sneak off into the night. It was a distinctly inelegant plan, poorly suited to a person of Pearce's low cunning, but once again, that might have been its appeal for him.

I'm too exhausted for this kind of stuff.

But I'd better go see him.

She was about to turn off the computer when the tattered bit of paper taped to the hard drive suddenly gave her an idea. The word didn't seem to be English; indeed had all the earmarks of a made-up word. And it had capital letters where there usually weren't any.

A made-up word with internal caps—it followed the rules for a password exactly. She logged in as Lenore and then typed "EtiDorhPa."

• •

On her way to the police station, she stopped for more coffee and breezed in, speeding on caffeine, in a mood that came close to good. "Brought you some coffee." She slid a cup over to Pearce. His expression didn't change.

"So. How was that diary?"

"I told you. She wouldn't let me see it."

"Did she tell you what was in it? Taunt you or anything?"

"Taunt me?" He was doing his best to feign puzzlement.

"Oh, well, there was that post, of course."

"What post?"

"You know. The one in which she stopped just short of revealing the contents."

"What the hell are you talking about?"

"You didn't see it?"

"All right, I saw it. You think Lenore found something in that journal that incriminates me, don't you? And tried to blackmail me. But Lenore would never do that. I don't even have any money, Skip. That ought to be obvious to you. No one in their right mind would try to blackmail me."

"It could have been for drugs. But my guess is, it wasn't that. More likely it was love. What do you think of that?"

"I don't begin to understand this."

"See, I think it went kind of like this: 'You're my man now and it's our secret.' Boom. Fait accompli."

He shrugged. "She never mentioned the damn diary to me. I was the one always bringing it up, which just made her mad."

"Did you see it tonight?"

"No."

"Do you happen to know Lenore's password?"

"Now, how would I know that?"

"It's taped to her computer. But maybe she told you what it was—"

"Hey, she did. I do know her password. Or I could if I worked out where the caps are. She told me it's Aphrodite spelled backwards."

"Right. So you know her password. You could have just made that post yourself—about the journal. And then you went back to drinking with her, even made love with her. Then when she was thoroughly incapacitated, you drowned her and posted her 'suicide' note. Not a bad plan at all, except—"

"Bullshit! Why would I come to you in that case? If I was that cagey, why didn't I just go home?"

"The tipster's usually the guilty one. Didn't you know that?"

"Of course. You're dealing with a journalist here—do you really think I wouldn't know that? So I would only have done it if I was innocent—and a good citizen, I might add."

"You'd have only done it if you had to—which you did. Because you screwed up, Pearce. Quite literally, I'd say."

"What are you talking about?"

"You realized later you'd made the mistake of having sex with her. It suddenly occurred to you you could be nailed by a semen test. So you'd better damn well have a good excuse for being over that evening, even if it meant making up a cock-and-bull story no child would believe."

"Did anyone ever tell you you're a bully, Ms. Langdon?"

"Mind calling me 'Officer,' Pearce?" She was in such a good mood, she smiled at him.

"Look, if you don't believe me, go search my house. You're not going to find any journal."

Her coffee high vanished.

27

• •

She conducted the search as a formality only—he'd signed the consent forms for both his home and car far too willingly for a man who had something to hide. She knew she wouldn't find anything and she didn't.

Further making her day was an invitation to meet with her lieutenant, Joe Tarantino, and Cappello. Joe was a hands-on kind of lieutenant who liked working closely with his detectives. But he hadn't especially involved himself with this case; the fact that he wanted to meet with her now meant he was getting impatient. So what was normally a pleasure—trading ideas with Joe and Cappello—would have a whiff of shame attached.

Joe was holding the lab report on the grandmother. "I don't believe it, Skip. This started out as a simple little—"

"Accident," said Cappello. "Skip figured out it was a murder."

Joe arranged his hands in the "please-back-off" position. "I'm not blaming Skip." He turned to her. "You know that, don't you? It's just that—" He threw the report down in a gesture of pure disgust. "How did three people get dead, dammit? Three! There's a one-man crime wave out there."

"Or one-woman."

"I'm going to tell you something right now. Woman is right. The key to this is a woman, and that woman is Marguerite Terry. Either she did it or she knows who did. *Cherchez la femme,* Officers. I mean it—get her in here and lean on her like she was a fence post."

Skip knew he was right. She'd gotten sidetracked from Marguerite, failed to get her whole story, because she'd served the warrant and found the ring at Mike's. And now she had another suspect who looked almost as good.

But if Pearce were the killer, why had he bothered to frame Mike and then tried to get him off the hook? Last-minute nerves?

She hardly thought so. Not for a man who'd killed three people, one of them a helpless old woman. Why would a guy like that suddenly develop a conscience?

Mike was still her favorite.

But Joe was right—Marguerite had to know more. Skip was dying to bring her in and lean on her—why hadn't she done it before?

Cocksureness.

And pity. I was sure the killer was Mike and I felt sorry for poor, frail Marguerite.

Why was that, I wonder?

She just doesn't seem all there.

Skip was surprised at the realization.

What is it exactly? Doesn't she have her faculties?

But she does. She doesn't seem slow or anything.

What is it then?

By the time she arrived at Octavia Street, she still hadn't put her finger on it. Marguerite was her usual woozy kind of half-there self, and Cole hovered in the background.

Drugs! she realized. *She seems out of it because she is.*

"Mrs. Terry, I'm going to have to ask you to come to the police station with me."

"Am I under arrest?"

"No, ma'am. Not at this time." *God. I sound like an automaton. What's wrong with me?*

But she knew. She'd unconsciously adopted a robot voice to get some distance. She felt sorry for Marguerite, and she could keep her at bay by modeling a 'droid. Nobody would bother having a breakdown in front of a 'droid—it has no feelings and therefore wouldn't be affected.

Ah. There's information in that. I guess I think she's manipulative.

Marguerite wanted to change clothes, but Skip was insistent—this was urgent; they were going now.

Marguerite looked at Cole with big brimming eyes. He put an arm around her. "Of course I'll go with you."

Skip said, "That won't be necessary."

And Marguerite—fragile, pathetic Marguerite—replied, "I beg your pardon. It's not up to you to tell us what will or won't be necessary."

"I beg yours, Mrs. Terry. You are not the queen and I am not your footman. I am a police officer and you are my invited guest. If I were you, I'd certainly want to keep it that way."

"Is that a threat?"

"Of course not. Mr. Terry, you could follow in your car if you like—Mrs. Terry might like a ride home afterwards." She held her breath. Marguerite could refuse if she chose.

Cole held both his wife's shoulders. "Listen to me, darling. It's going to be all right. You're going to be fine. Do you believe that?"

Skip thought he sounded like something in a 1940s movie, but Marguerite seemed to be eating it up. She nodded and curled her body into his. In a peculiar way that had nothing to do with the gesture, it was moving. It had to do with the obvious bond between these two people—one of them was about half-gone on drugs and the other was the classic ne'er-do-well, yet they were obviously unaffected by each other's faults. Skip wouldn't want either of them in her life, but she respected their mutual admiration society.

She kept quiet on the ride back, trying to let tension build, make it clear this wasn't a tea party.

When she had Marguerite in an interview room, she looked so small and frail Skip felt her nerve going.

Get tough, Skip. She's a manipulator.

But she couldn't help it, she felt sorry for her. She needed reinforcements.

She went to get Cappello. "Would you mind sitting in on the interview?"

"Uh-oh. Is she belligerent?"

"*Au contraire.* She's a pussycat. A bedraggled little scrawny one."

Hearing her across the squad room, O'Rourke hollered, "What's the matter, Langdon? You developing a heart?"

"Ask your cousin."

Cappello squinted, annoyed at them both. "Let's go."

On the way back, Skip said, "You don't have to do anything. I just want you there, okay?"

"I get it. Like a teacher grading a test. If I'm there, you have to make an A. If I'm not, you're afraid you won't."

"God, I must be crazy. Listen, you don't have to do this. I just went nuts for a minute."

"Shut up, Langdon. You don't have to be the lone wolf all the time. Cops work in pairs all the time, you know? It's an okay concept; maybe you ought to do it more often."

Actually, she'd quite enjoyed working with Cappello on this case. The sergeant had seemed less stiff and formal than usual, not so much Little Miss Do-It-by-the-Book, and twice she had looked out for Skip as determinedly as the men protected each other. Something was happening between the two of them—or perhaps it was simply that they were both settling in, Cappello to her sergeant's role, Skip to Homicide. It was altogether a good feeling. Six months, a year ago, she'd never have asked Cappello or anyone else to help her with an interview—she was too afraid of being thought incompetent, young, inexperienced. Her theory was that if she screwed up, she'd rather do it with no one watching. Curiously, she didn't feel that way now.

And she was amazed by that.

Marguerite without her protector seemed smaller and more frail than ever. For once, she wasn't wearing sweats. She had on khakis and a J. Crew sweater. Her hair, probably cut to be blow-dried, hadn't been. It hung in lank sections, but at least it was clean, and she had put on a little lipstick. She looked a little better than the first time Skip had seen her, more as if she could function if she really had to; yet there was still something tight and drawn about her. Something that was too thin; stringy in the neck. For the first time, it occurred to Skip to wonder if she were ill.

She introduced Cappello, who smiled sweetly; the nice cop. But Cappello gave Skip a look as well, one of dismay, Skip thought.

Skip and Cappello sat down. Cappello read her her rights. Having previously called her "Mrs. Terry," Skip changed the tone by using her first name: "Marguerite, up till now, I've been worried about you, I really have. You had a lot to deal with, losing your son and your mother. But now you've had a few days to recover, and it's time we got some answers here."

Marguerite was already crying, tears streaming, sobbing, gulping, falling apart before their eyes. She said, "Oh, God, I wish I were dead."

Cappello handed her a tissue but kept her face stony.

"A lot of people are," Skip said. "Your family's looking like an endangered species."

Marguerite sobbed harder.

"I think you're protecting a murderer, Marguerite."

Marguerite gasped and shrank back as if shocked by the notion. Skip was beginning to feel less sorry for her. "Look, it was common knowledge you and Leighton didn't get along; you've told me that yourself. You went out every chance you could. You were a young, beautiful woman and you were having an affair."

Marguerite gasped again, turning fawnlike eyes on Cappello.

No help there; the sergeant only nodded agreement.

Marguerite put her arms on the table and sunk her face into the hollow they formed, like a kid in a schoolroom. Her shoulders convulsed with eruptive sobs. Sucking, asthmatic noise tore her chest.

Cappello caught Skip's eye. Loud enough for Marguerite to hear, she said, "Let's just wait it out."

Skip nodded: *My thought exactly.*

They sat there a while, Cappello smiling a little, to all appearances perfectly content. Skip wished she were so easily entertained.

After about twenty minutes, she gave up, decided on a different strategy. "I think maybe some coffee."

"Great idea."

"You, Marguerite?"

Slowly, Marguerite lifted her head. Her face looked like an open sore.

Marguerite nodded once, and Skip left, watching her out of the corner of her eye. Very slowly, Marguerite was starting to straighten her body.

Heartened, Skip got some doughnuts as well. When she returned, Cappello was offering more tissues and cooing. It was a side of the sergeant she hadn't seen.

In another minute she's going to put her arms around her. I should work with her more often. She's got a whole bag of tricks I don't even know about.

Marguerite grimaced at the sight of the doughnuts, but fell happily upon the coffee. Cappello helped herself to both. She broke her doughnut into halves, took a small bite, and chewed, setting a friendly, homey mood: just us gals around the breakfast table. She actually reached over and patted Marguerite's arm. "Feel better now?"

Marguerite nodded.

Skip could only marvel. She said, "Sorry you're feeling under the weather."

"It's not your fault."

Skip and Cappello exchanged glances. Excellent. She was apologizing to them.

"Look, I know it's hard. But if you think you can protect yourself by not telling what you know, you're wrong. This person is ruthless—he would as soon kill you as look at you. You know that, Marguerite. In your heart, you know that."

"You're being ridiculous." She spoke pettishly.

She's really a very childlike person. She's like Geoff—she just never grew up.

"Who was it?" said Cappello in a voice like velvet. Brown velvet, Skip thought. Chocolate.

Marguerite turned her face downward. She balanced her wrist on the table, but her Styrofoam cup shook violently. "Butsy," she said. "It was Butsy."

She spoke so quietly Skip could barely hear her.

"Butsy," she boomed back, repeating it loud and clear.

Now this was a development.

Testing the waters, Skip said, "I don't think so, Marguerite."

Marguerite frowned, the picture of a child who doesn't understand what the hell's going on.

"I don't think he'd kill his daughter."

"I don't understand what you're talking about."

"Somebody killed Lenore Marquer last night."

Marguerite gasped again, again made the shrinking motion, putting distance between herself and the officers. "Somebody else? Somebody else is dead?"

Odd, thought Skip. *She didn't say, "Oh, golly, not Lenore," didn't seem to care at all.* She said nothing.

Finally, Marguerite said, "He hated her."

"Oh?"

"When I knew him he was just a crazy guy. But he got born again and hated Lenore for having a baby."

"That isn't a motive to kill."

Marguerite sipped her coffee. "I don't think Butsy is a well man." Skip let the silence grow. Marguerite sipped some more, gathering her composure. "My husband and Butsy are partners. Butsy is . . . unstable."

Unlike you. It amazed Skip how quick people were to throw around accusations of mental problems.

She said, "Did you love him?"

Marguerite considered. "The energy that he now puts into hatred and fanaticism, he used to put into . . ." Skip waited.

She'll say "loving." She'll try to convince me what a great guy he was.

Marguerite looked her full in the face. "Sex," she said, coolly.

"And Leighton?"

"I beg your pardon?"

"I guess if you were so interested in sex, you weren't getting it from Leighton."

Marguerite stared at the wall, but her eyes seemed to look through it, as if she were seeing something on the horizon. "He used to handcuff me. He tied me up. He turned me over and sodomized me. He held my wrists above my head and made me stand against a wall. Leighton's problem wasn't lack of energy."

"Real violent sort of guy."

Marguerite nodded. "A regular sweetheart."

"It sounds as if he considered women personal property."

"Yes."

"Probably the sort who'd follow you—maybe have you followed—if he thought you were having an affair."

"He might."

She thought it time to up the ante. "Look, things happen. Sometimes there's a good reason for things. Maybe he found out and he started knocking you around. This time it got to be too much, so you got his gun and killed him."

Cappello shook her head in sympathy. "Battered wife syndrome. Ummm-ummm."

"A lot of women just get pushed a little too far. We know a lot more about it now than we did then."

Cappello said, "Good for you, Marguerite. Goddammit, you had to protect yourself."

"I didn't kill Leighton," she said simply. "I told you. I'd have liked to. I didn't."

"Are you saying Butsy did?"

"Butsy was a very different person then. A very loving person." Her eyes brimmed.

"You *were* in love with him."

"Yes. He was everything Leighton wasn't. Full of good cheer. Full of love. Nothing like he is today."

"Still, if he's a nut case now, he must have had hostility in him all along. Or maybe he just loved you so much he lost it with Leighton."

"I really don't think so."

"Why not?"

She was starting to cry again. "He never would confront things. Or people. He was a conflict avoider. The last thing he'd have done is cause trouble."

"I'm not saying he did. Leighton caused trouble. Butsy had to defend himself."

"No." She wasn't sobbing this time, but tears were dripping onto her sweater, falling fast. She sniffed.

"You must have loved him very much."

"I did, God help me."

"Then why'd you marry Mike?"

She stood up. "Goddammit. Goddammit. Goddammit. How dare you?"

Skip gave Cappello a glance. Cappello nodded briefly, moved one hand a tiny bit: *It's okay. I'm alert.*

She continued sitting, but Skip stood, not sure what Marguerite would do. "Why didn't you marry the man you loved?"

"Oh, goddammit, how can you be so cruel? I just don't understand some people. Why do you think I didn't marry him? Because he wouldn't marry me, goddammit. Because he already had a wife." She was screaming so loud, Skip heard hurried footsteps, officers coming to help.

Marguerite turned to the wall, put up her arms, fingers to elbows, as braces, and rammed her body hard into it. She pulled back, bowed her head, and began beating it against the hard surface.

When Skip and Cappello had subdued her, had turned her gladly over to Cole, they went back to the squadroom, Skip for one horribly discouraged. They were no closer than ever to knowing if Marguerite was the killer, and now had a new suspect, as if there hadn't been enough to begin with.

Outside the locked door to Homicide, the little reception room, was a man in a chair. Skip, in deep conversation with Cappello, noticed only that, that there was a man there, somewhere off in her peripheral vision.

"Skip," he said, and she felt, rather than saw, him stand.

She turned. "Oh, shit."

It was Steve Steinman. His face was a triangle of misery, pinched and drawn, not that different from Marguerite's.

"Steve," she said, before he could comment on her comment. "I'm . . . This is a bad time."

Wind whooshed past her as the door closed behind Cappello.

"I'll wait," he said. "I don't have anything else to do."

She looked at her watch. Nearly lunchtime, and she was starving. Losing sleep made her hungry. "Maybe we could have lunch."

"I don't think I could eat anything."

"Wait for me."

She went to get her purse, thinking she probably wouldn't be able to eat either. But she had to, to keep going. How dare he put her in this position?

She was furious.

Yet by the time she'd returned, she was a little shaken as well, moved by his coming here, but she wasn't sure how. She knew she felt something—but what was it?

I don't want to know. I haven't got time for this shit.

They went to a utilitarian restaurant not too far away, yet one you had to drive to—she had little time to waste walking back and forth.

And I don't want to spend that much time with him, either.

When they were seated and she had ordered a sandwich, he a Coke, he said, "I can't just let you kiss me off like this."

She didn't know how to answer. Finally, she said, "You're the one who did the kissing off."

That made him angry. "Can't you be patient? What's a year or two out of our lives?"

"Steve, I told you it wasn't a good time and it isn't. I'm in the middle of a case and I've been up all night. Every time I turn around, the whole thing blows up in my face. I can't think straight because I'm tired, and I certainly can't think about this."

"I shouldn't have come."

"I could have told you that."

"Good-bye, Skip," he said, and walked out.

That's it? That's what he came two thousand miles for?

She couldn't believe he was gone, couldn't fathom the disintegration of their relationship, could never in a thousand years have imagined they'd speak that way to each other.

Her throat closed, and she couldn't stop the tears. She pulled any old bill out of her purse—a ten, she was pretty sure—and left it, just wanting to get out. Once outside, a cold wind whipping, the sky gray and unforgiving, she felt at last the sadness at Steve's loss.

She'd used Darryl and the case to keep it at bay, and she couldn't do it anymore. Sobbing, hardly able to see, hoping she didn't trip, she hurried to her car.

Lines from a poem came to her and wouldn't go away:

> There is a singer everyone has heard,
> Loud, a midsummer and mid-wood bird . . .
> The question that he frames in all but words
> Is what to make of a diminished thing.

28

• •

She sat in the car a long time, pulling herself together, trying to breathe deeply, to calm down. Her body wanted none of it, wanted to cry until there was no salt left in her.

If only he hadn't come in the middle of all this.

But that was no good and she knew it. True, she was too tired and too tightly focused on her case to deal with it; true, she was interested in Darryl. But Steve had spent a lot of money and come a long way. How could you interpret that as something other than interest in keeping the relationship together?

I know how—he screwed up and he's backpedaling.

Yes, but he still cares—he wouldn't have come if he didn't care.

He made a unilateral decision.

On the other hand, he's right—we aren't married.

For the first time, it occurred to Skip to turn the tables: *What if I were the one with the great career opportunity?*

The answer came in a nanosecond: *I'd take it. And without asking Steve.*

So how could I ask him to do something I wouldn't?

She had that stomach-turning feeling you get when you've made a truly terrible mistake. But at the same time, she felt calmer; her breathing came less raggedly. The conflict inside her was resolving.

My life might be ruined, but at least I have peace of mind.

Someone tapped on her car window: *Are you all right?*

She tried to smile. The passerby went on.

To hell with this, I have to talk to Butsy.

She had his phone number back at the office, had noticed it in Lenore's address book. She went back, picked up the book, and saw that he lived quite near Cole and Marguerite.

All the easier to commit a murder, she thought, her heart giving an extra little thud. Geoff she could see, and the old lady—but his own daughter? Did people really kill their own kids?

Psychopaths do. All the time.

Butsy met her at the door with Caitlin in hand. That made sense; he was her grandfather and nearest relative. Of course she'd been turned over to him.

"Hey, Caitlin," she said, absently touching the baby's cheek.

She introduced herself and said she was sorry about Lenore.

"You knew her? You know Caitlin?"

"I haven't known them long."

"Lord help this poor child."

"May I come in?"

He looked surprised, as if he'd forgotten her presence. "Oh. Of course."

His old raised cottage looked as if he didn't know how to keep house and couldn't afford a housekeeper. Old-fashioned Venetian blinds—not even mini-blinds—were closed against what little sun there was. No lights had been turned on, which made for a depressing room, but might have been a good thing—even in the semidark, Skip could see dust.

The furniture was Naugahyde, an old sofa and an old recliner. An ancient carpet covered the floor.

He let Caitlin down: "I think she's wet."

Suddenly Skip realized that what had happened to Jimmy Dee had just happened to Butsy in spades. At least Jimmy Dee was prepared (though of course Butsy should have been if he'd knocked off Lenore). And at least his kids were out of diapers.

"Do you have Pampers?" Skip said.

"Pampers?"

"Disposable diapers."

"I don't have anything," he said miserably. "Lenore had a friend, didn't she? Someone older?"

"Kit Brazil?"

"Kit. That's it. I met her at the funeral. Maybe I could call her." He picked up a phone book from the coffee table. Simultaneously and for no apparent reason, Caitlin began to cry. "Oh, God, you wouldn't know how to change a baby, would you?"

Skip smiled. "I'm afraid not. Not if you don't have any diapers."

He looked so sad and helpless, she said, "You should be with relatives today. Can I call someone for you?"

He shrugged. "There isn't anyone. Just me and the baby now. Us and the good Lord." In the dim light, she thought she saw a glint that might have been a tear. He took out a handkerchief.

"Were you close to your daughter?"

"Not since she had the baby. Seemed to forget about me then. Say, you don't know where I could get a nanny, do you?"

"Sorry, I don't."

He'd picked Caitlin up, but she only wailed more. Skip didn't look forward to interviewing him over the din, but didn't see much choice. If she held Caitlin herself, she'd lose her focus.

"Mr. Marquer, it doesn't seem to me as if you know how to take care of a baby." It wasn't what she'd come about, but first things first.

He blustered. "I can do okay. I've got the key to Lenore's. I can go over and get some stuff—Caitlin's bed and everything. Mothers have babies and they don't know anything. It's no different. Lenore was only a kid—what did she know that I don't? I raised her, you know."

"From this age?"

"Her mother died when she was nine. But I was always around—I was a regular dad."

His blustery determination wiped away the sadness. He set Caitlin down.

"Okay," she said. "I'm sure you need to get to Lenore's. I'll tell you what I came about."

Skip longed to pick up the baby; she had a strange need to try to comfort this tiny being who'd lost her child-mother, a mother who was probably doing a lousy job, but who at least loved her child. Skip thought it possible that no one loved Caitlin now; Butsy didn't even seem to know her.

"I want to talk about Marguerite Terry."

"Marguerite? I barely know her."

"Maybe now, Butsy"—she was through with "Mr. Marquer"— "but you used to know her pretty well, didn't you?"

"No." He sounded puzzled, but it was probably an act.

"Come on. Go back in time about twenty-seven years. To when you had the affair with her."

"I beg your pardon?"

Caitlin pulled at Skip's hand, put out her arms to be picked up, as if she knew, somehow had intuited, what had happened, and she wanted to be held. Skip's attention, which should have been on Butsy, slipped over to her.

Perhaps because she was upset with herself, she spoke more sharply than she had to: "Can it, Butsy. The kid needs a home. You want to stay out of jail, you better talk."

"Jail? For what? Look, I'm a churchgoing man—"

She just loved that one. As if going to church meant a person never broke the law or his marriage vows. She spoke harshly. "You figure it out."

He was silent for a moment, either trying to catch on or pretending. "Wait a minute. If I had an affair, I must have shot Leighton? Which means I killed Geoff? Is that what this is all about? What about Lenore? You want to give me one good reason why I'd kill my own daughter?"

Caitlin set up a howl, a pathetic white heap on the dirty brown rug. Skip's nerves were starting to fray, badly.

"Don't fuck with me, Butsy. Start talking—loud enough for me to hear over that."

"I didn't even know her in those days. I mean, I saw her around. She sang in clubs and she was kind of a local figure about town. But I never met her to say hello to until Cole and I went into partnership. I didn't even meet him until six or eight years ago."

"Well, why would she say you were lovers then?"

"Marguerite said that?"

Caitlin yelled louder. Skip didn't speak.

"She's protecting Pearce." He said it in the tones of a person making a big discovery. "Pearce Randolph got it on with her. I remember it—that was the phrase he used. He 'got it on with her.' He bragged about it."

"When was this?"

"I don't know—you know what they say about the sixties—if you can remember, you weren't there."

"You better start remembering fast."

So I can get out of here.

Neither she nor Butsy was making a move to help Caitlin. Skip was fed up with Butsy for not taking care of her, upset that she could do nothing herself.

"Well, it was about that time. I remember because we were listening to her sing."

"Where?"

"Had to be the Dream Palace. I can see it so well in my mind's eye—that bar that ran the whole length of the room, the pinball machines. I was with Pearce and he was drunk. He started bragging about being with her. Then he turned up later as Geoff's friend— from that computer network."

"The TOWN. Are you on it?"

"Hell, no, I haven't got time for something like that. I know Cole and Geoff loved it." His voice dropped: "And Lenore, of course."

"How did you know Pearce in 1967?"

"Hanging out. We sat on many a bar stool together. That was it—our whole relationship. We never called each other up, arranged to meet, anything like that. We just both used to hang."

"I don't know, Butsy, you don't impress me as much of a hanger-out."

Finally, at long last, he picked up the kid, not that it helped—she screamed louder than ever.

"That was before I found Jesus."

This, Skip thought, *would probably be a good time to leave.*

On the way to her car, it came to her how very much she didn't want to talk to Pearce right then. She was about as out of sorts as it was possible to be, now that Caitlin's plight had become the whipped cream on an already nightmarish night and day. She tried to shake the depression brought on by the little girl's wails in that darkened house, her own decision to close herself off, and the hurt in her throat that decision had caused her. For Skip, that was a signal her mind was out of tune with her heart. It was the second time in an hour she'd felt it, a nail through the larynx.

Here in Geoff's old neighborhood, she found herself once again sitting in her car, staring out the window. If Pearce was the lover—and not Butsy—why had Marguerite lied about it? Could she still be in love with Pearce, still be seeing him?

It was possible.

Since Butsy only knew him casually, Marguerite probably didn't know the two were acquainted, therefore had thought it safe to give Skip Butsy's name. She had to know he'd deny it, but so what? He'd appear to be lying to save his ass (which might be more than simply appearance), and also, she might have some reason to frame him. Maybe his business deal with Cole hadn't worked out.

Pearce had never produced an alibi for the time of Geoff's death—indeed, had implied he'd been with a lady. Since Cole had been in Baton Rouge at the time, Marguerite could alibi Pearce if need be.

But why didn't she marry him?

Because he was already married. The reason she gave for not marrying Butsy.

What about the ring, though? Skip couldn't figure out how it fit in. Why would the murderer send it to Marguerite, and why would she lie about having received it?

She realized she'd never asked Neetsie about it.

Now that was someone she wouldn't mind talking to—someone young and vulnerable who'd probably, if she had one kernel of information, let it slip.

Where did she work? Some computer place. In the end, Skip couldn't remember, but she knew who'd know—and went to see Neetsie's neighbor, Miss Bertie La Grange.

In minutes, she was walking into All Systems Go.

She almost bumped into Neetsie, on her way out and looking the worse for wear. "Hi. I just heard about Lenore. Were you the one who found her?" She was crying.

"No, but I—" What to say here? "I was there. I'm sorry, Neetsie. You're having a really hard time."

Neetsie nodded so vigorously her myriad earrings banged into each other. She kept her head down and a tissue at her mouth.

"I have a quick question for you. How'd your mom happen to give you that ring—the one that was stolen?"

"Huh?"

"Listen, I promise it's relevant. I know you're hurting, but I have a reason for asking this."

She nodded again. "I asked her for it. I'd always liked it, so I just asked her. She said, 'Sure.' Why? What's the big deal?"

"Do you know where your mom got it?"

She shrugged. "No, it was just always there. I guess I thought she got it in the Dark Ages or something. She never wore it, that was why I thought she'd give it to me. Hey—" She stopped, apparently having just had a thought.

"I wore it one day and Geoff asked me where I got it. He said he thought he'd seen it, but he couldn't remember where. I said, 'Mom's jewelry box, silly.' And he said he never went in there. I guess that's something girls do, you know? Look at their mothers' jewelry. But it's weird about that ring—Kit did it too."

"Kit?"

"Yeah. Boy, was that strange, now that I think of it. It was way a long time ago. She asked me where I got it, made me take it off, tried it on herself—every kind of weird thing. I mean, she really gave me the third degree. It was like she thought I'd stolen it. I mean, like it was hers; like she thought I took it from her."

"Kit?" said Skip again.

29

• •

Kit wasn't in her office, perhaps had gone to Butsy's in response to a call about Caitlin. Fighting off nervous co-workers, Skip elbowed her way in and used Kit's phone to call him.

No answer.

She looked at her watch. It had been about an hour since she left him. If he'd gone to Lenore's as planned, he wouldn't have called Kit first. First he'd have picked up the baby's gear, at least gotten some diapers after Skip's admonition.

Anyway, he wasn't there—which meant she wasn't there. The young woman Skip had seen before, the one with the many braids, poked her nose in, looking for Kit.

Skip identified herself. "She's not here. If she left, where would she go?"

"She'd tell Lirette—someone has to be in charge if Kit isn't here."

"Can you take me to Lirette?"

The young woman nodded, suddenly quiet, picking up something from Skip that Skip couldn't yet herself identify. All she knew was her pulse was racing.

They went to another office. "Lirette?"

Lirette was a good deal older than Kit, or maybe she just had no use for hair coloring and fitness plans. She looked as if she could make a lot of roux-based dishes and the flakiest of piecrusts. Her gray-blue flyaway hair had the slightly crimped look of baby-fine locks that didn't take a perm too well but looked worse without one.

"This is Detective Langdon," said the young nurse. "She's looking for Kit."

Lirette looked alarmed. She didn't seem to know what to say.

Skip said, "She's not in any trouble, if you're worried about that."

"It's not that—I'm worried, that's all. She doesn't seem to be anywhere she's supposed to be."

"Thanks." Skip stepped out of her office and back into the corridor. She waved away the helpful young nurse, who seemed reluctant to be dismissed, probably imagining Skip was about to pass out and need assistance.

Things were happening too fast . . . first Lenore right after Mrs. Julian, then Marguerite's "confession," such as it was—bogus or not, Skip couldn't be sure.

And now this.

It might be perfectly ordinary for Kit to disappear for a few minutes—perhaps she'd stolen off to have a good cry over Lenore, but every instinct in Skip's body said that wasn't it, Kit was in danger, maybe already dead.

Kit knew something. Either the killer, like Skip, had just realized it, or he was systematically getting rid of anyone who knew anything about what had happened twenty-seven years ago.

Who says you can't rewrite history?

Skip called Security and identified herself. "I need help finding a nurse."

"Well, can I ask what for?"

"She may be in danger."

"What kind of danger?"

"Look, there isn't time for this. I need someone to help me search the hospital."

"Well, we don't really have nobody right now. Gerard's on his break and Tootie went home sick about an hour ago."

"How about you?"

"Well, I can't leave my post . . . there's nothin' I can really do."

Skip hung up. *Great. Just what I need right now. Bureaucracy.*

She felt time running out.

Barely thinking, driven by anxiety and adrenaline, she started walking, striding down the hospital corridors as if she were a nurse en route to a code.

I know what he'd do; he'd stage another accident—that's his specialty.

She headed to the roof, taking the stairs two at a time.

But no one was there.

The clouds had lifted, though, and she had a clear view. Somehow the metaphor of clarity rooted itself in her belly. She closed her eyes and let the blackness give way to whatever came, be it pictures or words.

She saw white—white walls, white cloths, bright lights, Kit all in nurse's white, swallowing, terrified.

This is a hospital, dammit! An ideal place for a drug overdose.

It's perfect—her best friend just died. She's too distraught to go on. She has a history of depression.

Dammit! Goddammit!

She was too late and she knew it—the murderer would be gone and Kit would be lying unconscious, maybe dead. But maybe not dead. That part, Skip's instincts told her, was very much open to debate.

She opened every door she came to, including broom closets and bathrooms, once surprising an old man sitting on a toilet. She hoped he wasn't a heart patient.

Running, she covered the fifth floor (closest to the roof), and descended to the fourth, not even pausing when anyone yelled at her, which was often.

She remembered something Suby had said—something about a room where Kit went to smoke, where the witches had had a secret ritual.

Would the killer have said he needed to speak to her? Something like: "Is there any place we could talk privately?"

Where was the room?

On the third floor, there was a wing that looked closed off. Could it be there? It wasn't locked. She went in, opening doors, not closing them behind her.

Was that a murmur she heard?

Voices?

Yes. At the end of the corridor.

Hand in her purse, holding her gun, she opened the last door on the hall. She could shoot through the purse or take her hand out, whatever she needed to do.

The room looked like a waiting room. It was small, with a wall of windows looking out on the back of another building. Worn couches and chairs had been placed awkwardly around the walls of the room, the upholstery hanging and discolored. Religious paintings in old wooden frames hung on the walls, probably from the days when the hospital had been a Catholic one. There was a porcelain water fountain in one corner, probably issuing barely a trickle. Kit was bent over it.

Standing behind her, holding her free arm bent, pulling up on it, his other arm around Kit's neck, was Cole Terry. As the fountain was low, he was forced to bend his knees awkwardly.

"Let her go or I'll shoot."

Instead, Cole pulled her upright and turned her around to face Skip. "No, you won't." The hand around her neck held a knife.

"Feeding her pills, is that it?" said Skip. "Another suicide so soon after Lenore? Do you really think that's going to fly, Cole? Especially now, with me here." She brought the hand with the gun out of the bag, slowly, yet as threateningly as possible. "As soon as she eats the last pill, you've lost your hostage—what's to stop me from blowing your head off?"

Skip heard herself speak and marveled at it. Her voice sounded as calm as if she were talking to Cindy Lou about what to order for lunch. Yet her blood pounded in her head, her crevasses were clammy, her underarms, the little V's between her fingers, her palms.

Cole smiled at her. In the act of holding a knife to a woman's neck, he simply turned his head and smiled as if meeting a neighbor picking up his morning paper. "You wouldn't do that. I'm a father."

His iciness unnerved her. She felt her teeth clench, but she opened her mouth wide to speak, trying to stay as loose as possible. "You killed your stepson."

"Don't be silly. He fell off a ladder."

"What about the grandma? What about Lenore? Think about it. The least I've got is attempted murder against Kit. That means it's over, Cole."

His eyes darted, calculating his chances, assessing what she'd said. "Put down the gun and I'll hand her over."

"Let her go, Cole."

Almost before she'd finished speaking, he did, flinging her against Skip. Both women were caught off guard. Kit landed heavily against Skip's chest, and Skip, who didn't have time to brace against the blow, stumbled backward.

Cole leapt forward, chopped her wrist. She felt her fingers open, the gun fall out. She didn't know which was louder, her own gasp or the clatter of the .38 on the tile floor.

Calmly, Cole picked up the gun and leaned against the wall. He was smiling again. Kit and Skip untangled themselves.

Where the hell is Security? Skip wondered. *Surely some of those people I upset must have called them.*

Yeah, but they would have known it was a police officer stomping around. Because I told them myself.

And how would they find me anyhow?

"It was this way," said Cole, "on that long-ago day." He spoke lazily, a man with all the time in the world. "When Kit found out I was having an affair with Marguerite, her idea of revenge was to tell Marguerite's husband. But she didn't know what a crazy bastard Leighton was, and he couldn't have begun to know how nuts Kit was. He drew his gun and ordered her out of his house, but she tried to grab it. There was a struggle and she killed him."

"Dammit, Cole, I didn't even know Marguerite."

"My dear, of course you didn't. Why would I introduce the two of you? But you were a jealous and determined woman, and Marguerite and I weren't the most careful of adulterers. It was easy

for you to find out what was going on—all you had to do was follow me."

He shifted his eyes to Skip. "I saw Marguerite across a crowded
room, and she wasn't even singing. She was sitting with a group of
people. I can see her blowing smoke and throwing back her head
to laugh. Remember smoke? Why doesn't it seem romantic anymore?"

There was something about the way he was telling the story
that Skip found even more unnerving than the fact that he was
holding a gun on her. As if he were the center of the universe. As
if none of his actions had any consequence because they were all in
the service of Cole Terry, king of the world. There was something
bloodless about the man.

They said that psychopaths were this way, but psychopaths,
theoretically, did not connect with other human beings, and Cole
obviously did. She had seen him with Marguerite. There was real
love there, love that had lasted twenty-seven years and survived
four murders.

"I saw her and my life was changed. We should have music at
this point, shouldn't we? It's too cornball for words.

"Have you any idea how many men wanted Marguerite then?
She'd sing and the love letters would pour in; marriage proposals,
every kind of thing. But I swear to God something happened the
night we met, and it happened to both of us.

"After a performance, I'd wait for her. Sometimes I'd sit at the
bar, but she'd never join me afterwards. In fact, the way we worked
it, she'd join somebody else and I'd sit there smoking, waiting for
her to leave, and then a few minutes later I'd follow her out. We'd
just about have each other's clothes off before we got to the corner."

Skip asked, "Where was Kit all this time?"

"Working nights." He gave Kit a discreet glance. "Don't worry,
dear. We didn't go back to our apartment. We always got a hotel
room—usually the same one, in an old hotel near Camp Street. It's
now been redone, I think. In those days it was quite romantic, with
its thin linens and bare light bulb—very Tennessee Williams.

"Of course, sometimes I wouldn't even go to hear her. I'd just go to our room and wait. We were good, if I do say so. I don't think we were ever seen together except the night we met, and then only for five minutes. I caught her hand at the bar and made a date with her. We met in Jackson Square and talked for two hours. We walked everywhere and saw nothing. We were in love within the first three minutes."

"What was it?" said Kit. "Why did you fall in love with her?" Her voice held nothing but curiosity, not fear, not anger or loathing, nor even regret. Skip wondered if she was dealing with two lunatics.

Cole spread his hands, casual as could be, even holding the gun. He turned it sideways while he did it. Skip nearly leapt, but in the end didn't have enough time. "We were soulmates," he said.

"You wouldn't have a child with me."

"It wasn't right. I knew it wasn't right. Neetsie was the child I was meant to have. She came when she was ready." His tone changed, from indulgent parent to professor, lecturing. "You see, Skip, Kit was a great deal more in love with me than I was with her. I thought she might even kill me—or worse, Marguerite. And that was far worse. So after she killed Leighton, I didn't dare leave her. Finally, I got up the nerve, even moving to another state. I had to, to protect Marguerite. But Kit was so obsessed she followed. She kept track of me through any means she could, the most recent being the TOWN. Then she actually moved back here.

"When Geoff started having flashbacks she knew she was in trouble. You see, she didn't know he was in the house until after the shooting. All she saw as she was leaving was a scared little boy at the door of his room.

"He got a good look at her—it was from a distance, but he saw her as well as she saw him. So she had to stop him from remembering.

"But she was too late. By the time she killed him, he already knew too much. He hadn't told anybody, but he'd written it in his diary; she had to kill Lenore to get the diary. Right, Kit?"

"You crazy bastard."

"But I figured it out, and so did our detective friend. The only problem is, I got here too late. You'd already killed her."

Again, he turned his attention to Skip. "There you were, lying dead on the floor. Kit was just putting the finishing touches on her suicide note—" He held up a piece of paper.

Kit said, "He made me write it before I started taking the pills."

"She was going to kill herself with your gun. I tried to stop her but it was the old story. We struggled; the gun went off. . . ."

"It's full of holes. Fire that gun and this place'll be overrun. This is a hospital—you don't think anyone'll notice the noise? You won't have time to fake a struggle—Kit'll still be alive, and you'll have the gun. In fact, you'll have just killed a cop in front of a witness. It won't even matter how many other people you've killed. You're dead, Cole. Your only chance is to give me that gun right now. If you don't kill a cop, you can probably plead insanity, be out in a few years. . . ."

But not if I have anything to do with it.

He looked flustered, staring first at Skip, then Kit. "Oh, bullshit. Say good-bye to your asses, ladies." He held the gun with both hands, raised it, arms outstretched. Skip heard the swishing of the door opening behind them.

She let out her breath. Security. Finally.

"Enough, Cole," said Marguerite.

His face darkened. "What the hell are you doing here?"

"No more killing, Cole. Give me the gun."

"Goddammit, you crazy bitch. Goddam you! All these fucking years I've protected you—"

"You killed Leighton. I didn't."

"What? After I've kept you out of fucking prison for twenty-seven years, you've got the nerve to say a fucking crazy thing like that—"

"Cole, you're getting upset."

"Marguerite, you better go lie down."

"Enough of this. Give me the gun. It's over."

"You've got a fucking nerve deciding what's over and what's not. Where have you been through this whole thing? I'll tell you where—asleep, that's where. And now you think you can come in here and . . ."

"You kept giving me those pills."

335

"What? Me? Now I'm a pusher or something? You couldn't wait to get your damn pills. I had to hide them from you."

"Cole, you've killed four people. Don't you think that's enough?"

"Four! How can you say that! You up and kill your damn husband and I spend the next thirty years protecting you, trying to cover your tracks, and this is what you do to me. I'm going to kill you, Marguerite. You're the next one—I'm just going to kill you." He trained the gun on her.

"You won't kill me." It was a high, strained voice. Neetsie's. The door swished again. "I came with Mom. I was listening. I heard everything. I can't believe you could talk to my mother like that." She was crying.

Crying and irrational. Her dad killed her brother, her grandmother, and her good friend, and all she can do is complain about the way he's talking.

The situation was getting more explosive by the moment.

"Neetsie, I didn't mean it. I was upset."

"I can't believe you did what you did. I really can't believe it. I thought you loved me."

"I do love you, baby." His face was a mask of misery—this one definitely had emotions.

"You broke into my apartment and scared me to death. You did that . . . thing . . . with the toilet. I just can't believe my own dad—"

"Oh, grow up, honey. You can get over that. Where would you be if your dad was in jail? How would you get over that? Look, it should have worked; I don't know why it didn't work. It was a damn clever way to get the cops off my back."

Neetsie looked as amazed as anyone Skip had ever seen. "You're not my dad. You're not the same person who does Dr. John. You're some *creature* who—"

"Shut up." He smacked her with the back of his gun hand.

Skip moved.

It would take two steps to get to him, but she had time for only one. She dived at his knees. She got a good grip, but he didn't go down—there was simply too much distance to make much impact.

He grabbed her by the hair and pulled. "Get up."

He put the gun to her temple. "Okay, we're going."

He marched her out of the room and through the corridor, out of the closed wing and into the hospital proper. It was brighter here; the place Skip had found so depressing on her previous visit seemed cheerful by contrast. A nurse was striding toward them; another was talking to a man in a suit, probably a patient's son or husband. All three saw the gun and began to run. Cole fired at the ceiling. "Let us through. Don't try to stop us."

He kept walking.

They turned a corner, nearly bumping into a nurse helping an old man on a walker. "Out of our way." Cole swept them away with his gun hand, the other still holding tightly to Skip. The old man fell, which made Skip furious.

She tried frantically to think what to do, but people were starting to litter the halls, some of them old, a great many of them sick. Instead of fleeing at the sound of the gunshot, the shouting, the clatter of the old man falling, they'd come out to rubberneck.

Anything she did would endanger them.

The good news was, she heard sirens. Cole heard too, and panicked. He shot once again at the ceiling. "Let us through."

People scattered, but it was no good. Others took their places.

Still, he kept walking. The stairs were open, not in a closed stairwell, so that they were able to descend without the risk of surprise at the bottom; first one floor, then another, the gun tight against Skip's scalp.

She was not even slightly frightened; seeing the old, the sick, the innocent so vulnerable in those halls, knowing what this man was capable of, she was nearly blind with fury.

They were almost at the door. Her tongue was tight against her teeth, every muscle tensed, in her own body's absurd effort to make sure no one got hurt.

Someone opened the door, and Skip got a glimpse of what was outside—police cars, a dozen at least. And it looked like more coming. Cole stopped dead. "I need a nurse. Now!"

There was scurrying behind them, and Lirette, the nurse from Kit's floor, approached warily.

"I want you to step outside" said Cole, "and tell them to send in an unarmed man."

The nurse disappeared. Skip stood in the middle of the corridor, the gun snug against her temple, every muscle tight against every other one. She ached to flay the son of a bitch alive. She was surprised at the hatred in her. She had never felt so much fury at a suspect.

An officer came in, but not the man Cole had asked for. "I'm Sergeant Sylvia Cappello."

Cappello's hands were up. Skip felt her throat tighten; she'd never seen Cappello helpless.

"Sergeant Cappello, you let us out of here or Officer Langdon's dead. You send those cops home, and those police cars home; but you stay. And you let us walk out of here quietly, peacefully, with no fuss."

"We can talk about that. Just let Officer Langdon go and we'll talk about whatever you want." Even at fifty paces, Skip could see the distress in Cappello's brown eyes; she'd never seen Skip helpless either.

"Don't be absurd."

"Nothing is impossible. You just need to let Officer Langdon go and we can talk."

Skip wondered if officers were pouring in other doors. She imagined they were, but maybe not. It didn't seem like such a hot idea in a hospital.

Cole, apparently deciding he'd get nowhere with Cappello, looked around, rotating his head quickly; nervously, Skip thought. His cool might be starting to crack.

"See that elevator over there? Let's go." He walked her over. "Push the Up button."

Skip wished she could catch Cappello's eye—this was her chance to break away, with another officer to help her. Almost as if Cole had caught her thought, he spun her around, pulled up on her arm so that she nearly gasped with the pain, and pushed her out to arm's length, so she couldn't get a kick in. He was staring Cappello straight in the eye. "Don't either of you move."

He was smarter than she'd thought, and that bothered her.

When the elevator came, it was empty.

" 'Bye, Sergeant." If he'd lost his cool, he'd now regained it.

Still holding Skip in a death grip, he took her to the fifth floor and they walked from there to the roof, not easy the way he was holding on to her arm.

He took her to the edge and stared over. The hospital was surrounded by police. Someone with a megaphone was preparing to shout up at him.

"Beautiful, isn't it?" he said. "Do you think a helicopter could land here?"

"What do you want, Cole? Do you really think you can get out of this one?"

"Well now, that depends, doesn't it? On how much your fellow officers want to save your neck."

"Oh, I don't think so."

"Don't you?"

She smiled to herself. It wasn't about to come to that. She was either going to be long dead before, or he was. It was the first time in her life she'd ever really wanted to kill someone.

This was no place to start a fight—right on the edge of a roof, but he wouldn't move away, not with an audience down there. She had to do it now. Her foot came up sharp to his groin just as her free elbow whammed him in the kidneys.

She heard the breath go out of him, but he tightened his grip on her. She relaxed for a moment, knowing he couldn't hold her. The pain would be too much. She whacked him again and twisted away, grabbing his gun hand. He went down on his knees.

She had both hands on his forearm, trying to get him to drop the gun. With his free hand, he grabbed her hair and pulled.

"Pull it out, you bastard!" She slammed his arm against the low railing of the roof, but still he held the gun.

He let go of her hair and punched her face. Furious, she tried to throw him off the roof. It was easy; she simply twisted more, and his weight shifted toward the railing. His back bent over it, but his arms pushed against her.

"Die, you bastard. Go off the roof. I don't care if I kill you."

His fingers opened. The gun fell.

And her anger started to dissipate. She kicked him. "Get up."

He came up swinging, but she swung back, both arms together, and landed a blow to his left cheek that sent him reeling. He was three steps from her now; she couldn't reach him, and she had no weapon.

It occurred to her that he might hurl himself from the roof, and that was unacceptable. She was aware that she'd just tried to throw him off it, but it was only a dim cognizance, like a childhood memory of a person she used to be. Her whole being focused now on stopping him.

She dived for him, and though the distance was greater this time, she'd judged it better. She brought him down just as a phalanx of cops burst through the door from the fifth floor.

She heard his head hit the concrete and bounce, exactly as Geoff's must have done.

30

• •

It was ending now, and it was all right. He'd done what he had to do. Looking at things in reverse order, Cole honestly couldn't think of a thing he'd have done differently, given what his motivations were, and the events that came before.

He'd had to kill Lenore after she made that stupid post about the diary. (Of course in the end, the book hadn't had a single incriminating word in it, but how was he to know that? It was her fault for saying it did.)

He'd done it rather elegantly, if he did say so. Writing the fake suicide note was brilliant, though perhaps the concrete block wasn't. It did get the job done, and he thought it had a nice Virginia Woolf–ish quality, but he could see now that it might not be the sort of thing one might have done to oneself. It might have made the cops suspicious.

Nonetheless, he had had to kill her. That wasn't in dispute, although Mrs. Julian might have been a bit superfluous—the chances of her remembering anything were probably nil. On the other hand, he had done her a favor. Her mind was gone; what was the point of living? He didn't have the slightest regret about that one.

He was being thorough and he'd been able to do a good deed in the meantime.

Geoff was another matter. He'd loved Geoff.

Well, actually, he hadn't. He loved Marguerite and Neetsie. He knew exactly what love was.

He had affection for Geoff, but not all that much. Besides, he'd always known something might happen, that somehow Geoff would remember something, say something, and he couldn't be allowed to do that, because Marguerite had to be protected.

Marguerite.

It was worth it. She was worth it.

He hadn't really been able to tell the cop about it, maybe because Kit was there, but it was like a fire, that first time he saw her. He touched her arm and his fingers got singed.

What he felt for her was so different from what he felt for Kit, with whom he'd really made a marriage of convenience, it seemed in retrospect. He hadn't thought that, he'd thought he was in love with her, but she wasn't willing to let him be who he was. Always nagging to have a baby, get a job, do this or that or the other thing.

He was deeply, deeply in love with Marguerite and yet it never once occurred to him he could be with her. He didn't know what he thought, he guessed simply that he was married and that was that.

After Leighton died, it didn't occur to him that he could leave Kit now. That she had served her purpose and Marguerite was free. But then they'd moved away and eventually she had left him. He couldn't believe it—she had left him.

For the first time he realized he could marry Marguerite.

But she was already remarried.

And then years later, it turned out he had an opportunity to move back to New Orleans, and she wasn't married. That was when he'd sent her the ring.

He'd taken it away as part of the plan to make Leighton's death seem a murder committed by a burglar. He'd never thrown it away—he knew a good place for it, in a sort of mouse hole in his old apartment, and he'd taken it when he and Kit moved.

Sending it to Marguerite was meant as a grand gesture, something no one but she would understand—a declaration of his intentions.

She'd responded (as he knew she would), and they picked up the courtship again. They'd been blissfully happy until Kit stuck her nose in.

The whole damn state of affairs had been caused by Kit. He'd just learned that last night. When he got Geoff's diary.

What it said was that Kit, who knew hypnosis, had offered to help Geoff with his memories. The blackmail notes would have started soon, Cole was pretty sure of that. He hadn't asked her how successful they'd been with the hypnosis, but he knew the slightest little snippet would be enough for Kit. She probably suspected all along anyway; probably made the offer hoping to find out after all these years.

You had to be careful with her, and he and Marguerite had been. He hadn't lied when he said they'd never been back to the Terry apartment.

But once they had made love at Marguerite and Leighton's. Just once, because Marguerite really wanted to. She liked the danger, but that wasn't what she said when she phoned.

"Cole, come over, I'm desperate to see you."

"I'm on my way." He wasn't of course. It was a game they played when they couldn't see each other.

"No, I mean it, I'm serious. There's no reason why not. Geoff's asleep and Leighton won't be home for hours and hours."

"I can already feel you against me, your hair tickling my chest . . ." He was playing their game.

Her voice exploded in his ear. "Don't, I can't stand it!"

"Ouch."

"Come."

"I can't come into your house. You're crazy."

"Come and I'll do things you never even heard of; I'll lick every part of your body and then I'll do it again."

He didn't answer.

"I need you, Cole. My skin heats up when I think of you, and I've been thinking of you for hours. I'm burning alive. I have to have you. I'm going to light all the candles in the house and think about you till I feel you next to me. I'll leave the key under the mat."

When he slipped into bed with her, on Leighton's side, at first he thought her skin felt rough. But she was wearing lace, black lace, and black mesh stockings, with three-inch heels, in bed. She'd actually worn her shoes to bed.

She had done what she said; she had lit all the candles and she had taken them into the bedroom.

She was on top of him, the candlelight playing on her face, her hair cascading down her back, her body lithe and white under the black lace, when they heard the unmistakable sound of a door opening.

The rest was a blur, the last real memory he had being Marguerite jumping off him. He remembered so well because it hurt so much. She had twisted her body, forgetting he was inside her, and had swung a leg over his chest, sitting on him rather than straddling, a lot of weight at once.

She had screamed and thrown her hands up, he didn't know why. And then he saw Leighton with the gun, looming over the bed, practically on them. But not quite.

Marguerite ran at him, threw her body at him, and they fought. Cole got out of bed, ran at them, but it was too late; the gun went off, he wasn't sure how, and Leighton was dead by the time he got there.

He and Marguerite figured out what to do: make it look like a burglary and leave. It was only about ten o'clock; Marguerite could come home and find the body by eleven-thirty or so.

They left Leighton where he was.

All they had to do, really, was make up the bed as if nothing had happened. And remove the candles, of course.

Then ransack the room a little.

Marguerite had kept a surprisingly stiff upper lip throughout the whole thing, had been almost chipper.

A good woman in a crisis, he had thought at the time.

As they were leaving, she gave him the ring and the gun to dispose of.

They'd kept the door closed, in case Geoff woke up, and when they opened it, he was in the hall. Marguerite knelt and gathered him to her, saying, "Oh, my poor baby," or something of the sort, and for the first time gave way to tears.

He patted her shoulder: "It's all right, Mommy."

"Sweetheart, how long have you been here?"

He looked at the floor. "I don't know. What was that big noise?"

"You must have been dreaming, honey. I didn't hear anything."

Cole made up Geoff's bed and put away his pajamas while Marguerite got him dressed to go to his grandmother's.

When he thought about it now, he was glad Geoff was dead, that he never had to find out his mother had killed his father.

• •

"Mom, are you all right?"

It was the last thing Neetsie had said before they stuffed Marguerite into the back of a police car as if she were the one who was guilty. Now she was hunched down, making herself as small as she could. She wasn't sure why she was sitting that way, but it was the way her life was.

Smaller.

She didn't know how to answer Neetsie. What did you say when your life disappeared chunk by chunk over the course of a week? When you realized the husband you loved had turned you into a drug addict? Worse still, that you had willingly collaborated.

Because I didn't want to know. I didn't want to think about it.

I knew he killed Geoff. I must have known, as soon as I heard about the TOWN, and the flashbacks. But I was so out of it, no one talked to me about it. I could keep quiet and I could sleep most of the time so I never had to think about it.

Now she couldn't stop thinking about it.

It's my fault. It's all because I insisted on his coming over that night. Why did I do that? Was I crazy?

But she knew she wasn't, really. She was just young and in love and rebellious. And the times were right for illicit love and daring trysts.

Yet how stupid. What a waste.

Not of Leighton's life. He was a small-minded sadist whose very unacceptability had attracted her—that and his cruelty, perhaps. There were things she wanted to explore then, things she had long since left behind.

It was a waste of her life, and Mike's. She had married Mike out of desperation and fury at Cole and out of guilt on Geoff's account.

But it should never have happened. It was a mistake for all three of them.

She had tried often to imagine what would have happened if she hadn't insisted that time, Miss Sexual Revolution spinning out of control.

Or was that what she was? Maybe she was Mrs. Leighton Kavanagh hoping to get caught.

If that was it, it didn't have to happen that way. She could have been indiscreet in some other way, some less dangerous way, and Leighton would have divorced her, and in the ensuing scandal Kit would have divorced Cole and that would have been it. No fuss, no muss. They would simply have changed partners.

Yet even now, even as guilt and contrition pounded within her like a headache, she could remember the pure excitement of that night, the thrill of waiting in bed for Cole, decked out in a black lace camisole and silk stockings. She had even worn high heels to bed, but that was too silly. She had taken them off before he got there and she and Cole had laughed about it later.

She wasn't laughing at the time. She was in another world, so clouded with her own desire that if Geoff had gotten up she couldn't have dealt with it. The sensation was so strong it was almost painful. Actually it did have an element of pain, a constriction in her pelvis that begged to be eased.

And later, the sculptured outline of Cole's arms and shoulders in the candlelight—then Leighton. She hadn't heard anything, not the key in the lock, not his footsteps, not anything except his voice: "What the hell is going on here?"

She knew what he would do if he caught an intruder in his home, had heard him say it a thousand times: "Shoot him on sight." Cole was the worst kind of intruder, the kind that needed shooting most.

She had to get to Leighton, had to get his gun. She had had her eyes closed, and had opened them when she heard his voice, and then all she saw was the way the room had become darker, as his body blocked the candlelight. But she knew he had his gun.

She got off Cole so fast he groaned; somehow or other she must have hurt him. She hit the floor, stumbled on one of the high heels, and went down on one knee. A vise grabbed her elbow—Leighton's left hand.

"Who the fuck is this?" he said, and drew his gun with his other hand.

Her head was almost at his hip level. She watched the gun leave its holster, saw him point it at Cole, all in one smooth motion; and she bit his thigh. Not hard, she thought now (or the autopsy would have shown tooth marks), but as hard as she could through his uniform pants.

He screamed—a man's scream, something like "Aaaaaaa"—and kicked at her, squeezed harder on her elbow.

Cole rose up from the bed, using his locked hands as a bludgeon, catching Leighton square on the nose. She didn't see that, but he told her later, as they were straightening the room.

What she knew was that Leighton lost his balance and stumbled, letting go of her elbow. She pitched her body into his, and was almost instantly sandwiched between Leighton and Cole, who had grabbed Leighton's right hand.

She bit her lip in a savage effort not to scream, so as not to wake Geoff. Terrified, she slithered down between the two men and, once more on the floor, saw her opportunity. She stuck her shoulders between Leighton's legs, which were now braced, feet somewhat apart, put one hand on each leg, and pushed. She didn't feel him start to fall, even to shake or seemingly to notice, until she heard the shot and he fell backward, away from her.

She never knew whether that bit of distraction had made the difference, whether he'd lost mental equilibrium if not physical. Her entire face was sore with the effort not to scream.

She had gone right away to check on Geoff, as soon as she could get something on, leaving Cole to cope with what had happened. The boy was awake, but only barely. She told him the

347

noise was upstairs, one of the neighbors had dropped something heavy.

He was a boy who watched a lot of television; even at four, he knew what a gunshot sounded like. He probably didn't believe her.

She knew why Cole killed him, killed her only son twenty-seven years later and it hurt almost more than the fact that he did it. It was the real reason she never balked at taking the pills, why she wanted to sleep all the time.

Leighton's killing was done in self-defense. She was the only witness and she knew that. Cole wasn't going to jail even if Geoff remembered seeing him there, remembered how he and Marguerite covered up what had happened.

But he might have been dragged down to the police station, might even have been arrested and had to stand trial, would almost certainly have been subjected to public scrutiny.

He killed Geoff because of his damn business deal!

What's wrong with me? How could I have been so passive? How could I have let it happen?

But she knew why. She could only face it now because that morning there weren't any pills. Last night there had been some, she was almost sure. . . .

Oh, Jesus. He gave them to Lenore!

She had found the diary. Feeling more energetic than usual, she had picked up in the kitchen a little, and discovered it under some newspapers. It meant nothing to her, she'd noted only that Geoff was trying hypnotherapy with Kit and thought how odd that was, considering Cole had once been married to Kit, and wondered if Geoff knew that.

All day she'd felt odd; she was probably in withdrawal, now that she thought of it. But that wasn't all; she'd felt uneasy and angry. Then when the cop had come and dragged her off, she'd directed her anger at her, at the cop.

Cole took her home and left. Left her after what she'd been through! And he didn't even say where he was going.

Then Neetsie came over to ask about the ring. And she mentioned Kit's strange reaction to it. Marguerite knew Cole had had it all those years before he sent it to her, but until then it never occurred to her that Kit might have seen it. She remembered the entry in the diary—after that, she couldn't remember much at all.

Had she told Neetsie what happened that night in 1967? She didn't know.

She did know that somehow, somewhere, in that conversation, her veil against the world had finally dropped, that she had admitted to herself that Cole killed her son and her mother.

And Neetsie knew too.

She'd been clinging to that Baton Rouge thing, telling herself that it couldn't have been Cole because he was away.

That seemed ludicrous once she said it out loud.

It was only an hour there and an hour back—Cole could have been back in bed at his hotel by seven-thirty, even allowing half an hour for Geoff to wake up and try to rescue the cat.

It was Neetsie who figured out that Kit was in danger, Neetsie who'd taken her to the hospital, had known about Kit's private place, the solarium in the old leper ward.

But Marguerite was firm—she'd insisted the girl stay out of the room with Cole. Her father.

Marguerite realized something strange on the way to the hospital—that Neetsie knew Kit well, and she loved her. In some odd way, Cole's ex-wife, a woman she hated—in principle, anyway—was a mother of sorts to her daughter.

She was hunkered down now, wishing she didn't know that or any of it, wishing for the pills. How to answer when her daughter, who was all she had left, asked her if she was all right?

She had touched Neetsie's shoulder to make sure she was really there and not in the past like Geoff and her mother and Cole. Neetsie must have taken it as a good sign. She had hugged her mother, something she hadn't done in years, not even the day Geoff died.

She knew what Neetsie knew. She had been a mother one last time, when she had forbidden her daughter to enter the solarium, but in the end she had failed and Neetsie had had to face down her own father. Marguerite had exhausted her strength. Neetsie was her mother now.

31

• •

Once again Cappello had come to Skip's aid. She had gotten her out of there and into a car with no one except the two of them, and had asked her if she was okay, if she needed some coffee before they went back to headquarters.

"No, I'm fine. Let's go right over." In fact, her adrenaline was pumping, and she was dying to get there, go into action again.

"I don't think you realize what just happened to you. I want you to take five."

"No, really."

"Humor me. Just walk around the block with me." She parked in the garage and led Skip outside.

The wind in Skip's face was a caress.

Cappello shivered. "I'm freezing."

"I feel great."

"I'll bet you do. You were in that tunnel with all your dead relatives beckoning."

Skip was surprised. "I guess I was. I was too mad to notice. That asshole could have hurt somebody, you know that?"

Cappello hooted, but Skip was impatient, in no mood to join in.

They didn't walk around the block, just to the corner and back, and they made it to the office before the others had found parking places. Joe met Skip at the door with his arms open wide. "Baby, don't you *ever* scare me like that again."

Joe was Mr. Professional. He never called her pet names and never hugged the detectives. She guessed she must be suffering from shock—everyone seemed a good deal more upset than she was. She was more or less flying.

She had put together most of the remaining pieces on the ride back, but what she didn't know, she thought she could get from Kit, who'd arrived to give her statement before she and Cappello had. She called Kit into a room.

"Are you doing okay?"

"I feel like I've been up about seventy-two hours."

"Yeah, me too."

"I thought you might still be at the hospital."

Kit grinned. "Fortunately, the asshole gave me capsules. They dissolve slowly enough that all I had to do was throw up. Since I was in a hospital, they knew just what to do."

"I'm glad you're okay."

"You want to know about the hypnosis, don't you?"

"That and the ring."

"Oh, the ring. Well, I saw it years ago. I went in one of Cole's drawers for something and there it was. I didn't even know the stone was citrine—frankly, I thought it was topaz. It was just some-thing I'd never seen before. I thought he'd probably bought it for my birthday. He didn't give it to me, but by that time I'd forgotten all about it. I never thought of it again until I saw it on Neetsie's finger. Which was before Geoff began to post about the flashbacks and before Lenore told me about his mother's 'stolen' ring. Are you following?" She was talking fast, as if she had coffee nerves.

"Come on, Kit. That practically convicts him. How come you didn't tell me?"

"I was afraid it sounded silly, I guess. It's funny—it sounds very damning now, but you can't imagine how thin it seemed at the time. Also, I wasn't at all sure it was the same ring. Remember, I only saw it once and really didn't give it much of a look."

"Was that why you asked Geoff if he wanted to try hypnosis? You thought you could get to the bottom of it?"

"That was one reason. But not the main one. I really thought I could help him. A lot of good work is being done with hypnosis these days."

"For heaven's sake! Okay, you didn't mention the ring because you weren't sure. Why in hell didn't you mention the hypnosis?"

"Because I'm not licensed—or certified. Whatever you have to be."

"You don't even know?"

"It's got to be something. I didn't want to end up in some kind of legal trouble."

Skip sighed. Similar fears probably caused more witnesses to clam up than lawyers did.

"And because ethics prevented my talking about a client."

"Your client was dead."

"And because I didn't learn anything that could possibly help."

"No?"

"No. Not even in retrospect. We worked on the ring, but it didn't come up in his memories, except as something he'd seen his mother wear. Apparently, he didn't see it the night his father died."

Skip considered. "Okay, thanks." She stood up.

"I can go?"

"Sure." Skip smiled at her, aware that it was the first time she'd smiled in hours, days maybe. "I'm sorry if I was hard on you. I'm feeling a little . . . wired, I guess."

"Oh, forget it. You've been through a lot." She looked down at her folded hands. "We all have."

"Yeah."

"Look, I wish I'd said something about the ring . . . I truly, truly do. It's all so crummy. Something good has to come out of this. It just has to."

She started to cry.

• •

It was only after she got home that Skip could really think about what had happened, and the thing that chilled her, the thing that absolutely paralyzed her, was not how close she had come to death but how close she'd come to killing Cole.

Jesus. I would have dumped him off that roof if I could have.

No, I wouldn't have. I'm not that kind of person.

Don't do that. You would have. You went crazy up there.

I'd better talk to Cindy Lou.

Steve was who she really wanted to talk to. Thinking of Steve made her think of Darryl—could she talk to him about it? She didn't know, didn't know him well enough. If Cindy Lou was right, she couldn't—a butterfly man wouldn't stand still for it.

And anyway, he hadn't called.

Let's get real, Skip—you've had lunch with him once and then when he didn't call, you called him. He hasn't called since then. Is that a man you can rely on?

He hasn't had time.

He isn't interested.

It didn't matter; she knew perfectly well it didn't matter.

She wanted Steve.

Where was he?

He must be staying with Cookie Lamoureaux, the friend they had in common. She called Cookie and Steve answered. "It's Skip."

"Yes."

"I need to talk to you."

"My flight leaves in two hours."

"I'll come get you. I'll take you to the airport."

"Cookie's taking me."

"Stay there. I'm on my way."

He was waiting in the living room, his coat already on, and he didn't smile when he saw her.

He had always been so quick to smile, so accommodating, so easygoing. This was a new Steve, this sullen, quiet one.

One that I made.

When they were in the car, she said, "Listen, I think I made a big mistake."

"No. I'm the one who did."

"Look, I'm really sorry I couldn't talk to you at lunch. You surprised me, that's all. It's been an awful day and—"

"All we ever talked about is your work. Do you realize that?"

"Steve, that's not fair!" It certainly wasn't. She knew him—no subject on earth was more fascinating to him.

"Oh, great. That's not fair either. Nothing I do is fair. I can't do anything right. I get the message, okay?"

"You came all this way and you won't even talk to me?"

"It looks to me like you're the one who won't talk."

"Steve, I reversed things. I thought about what would happen if I got a great business opportunity in another town."

"I know what would happen. You'd take it if you wanted it. Just like that. I'd be the last person you'd consult about it."

"Well, I realized that."

"So did I, and I just don't think I want to be with a person like that."

"Wait a minute! This is theoretical—you're the one who *did* it."

"I tried to talk to you about it. You weren't interested."

"I couldn't talk about it. I thought you were breaking up with me."

They'd reached the airport. She moved as close as she could get to the curb. He turned to her. "Look. We just weren't a good match, that's all."

His eyes were dark, fierce with anger. Hers were swimming. "I'm sorry. I'm so sorry. I didn't mean to let it go—I was trying to protect myself. But I realize now I couldn't, because it's too late. . . ."

"You did okay. You got another man."

"What?" For a moment she had no idea what he meant. "No, I didn't. That was a smoke screen."

A car behind them honked. She glanced around. They were blocking a long line of traffic. Steve said, "I've got to go."

And he left.

32

• •

About a week later, Kit called. "You know how I said something good had to come out of all this?"

"Did you?" Skip had barely slept since the last time they saw each other. Dee-Dee had made something special for her every night and she had pushed it around her plate to please him. Kenny had given her a model he'd made, and Sheila, who listened only to rap, had bought her a tape by the Boucrees. She remained inconsolable.

Why, she wasn't sure.

Because of Steve, partly.

Because of Darryl, a little, though she had seen him—one night he had come for dinner at the Big House.

Because she had lost it so badly up on that roof—had come face-to-face with evil and its name was Skip.

Because, Cindy Lou insisted, she had come close to death.

That was a lot of things to make you miserable. And there was one more—anger at herself for losing Steve. It was her fault, she had accepted that. Cindy Lou had called it.

The fact that she had let it happen was killing her.

Then there was the case. It had had a very successful conclusion. No one doubted Cole would be convicted and everyone
thought Skip a hero. Television hadn't gotten there in time, but an
amateur photographer on another roof had taken a series of pictures of Skip and Cole. Two had run in the *Times-Picayune*—one of
Skip with the gun to her head, another of her bending Cole over
the railing.

On the other hand, a peculiar thing had come out of it—her father, who hadn't spoken to her in a year or more, had called to
congratulate her.

But still. The bottom line was that three people had been killed,
and one was someone Skip had gotten to know.

Rationally, she knew she couldn't have prevented Lenore's
death, but the horror of it, the senselessness, wouldn't leave her.

Kit said, "You don't sound so good."

"I guess I'm tired."

"Maybe I should call back later."

"No, talk to me. If you have good news, I want to hear it."

"Well, it's good news for me. Butsy feels he can't take care of
Caitlin, and he's agreed to let me adopt her."

"Kit, that's wonderful. I think you'll be a terrific mom."

"I do too, to tell you the truth. I'll tell you why I'm calling.
We're having a ritual to say good-bye to Lenore and to celebrate
my getting Caitlin—I know it sounds weird, but to us they're part
of the same thing. We'd like you to join us."

"I don't think—"

"Neetsie will be there. She'd especially like to see you."

"I'll probably have to testify at the trial, and Neetsie might be
a witness as well—"

"If you both turned up at Trinity on the same Sunday, would
there be something wrong with that?"

"No, but this isn't Trinity."

"If the First Amendment means anything, it's no different." Her
voice softened. "We'd love to have you, Skip. We all went through
this together—you were sort of our guide through it all—"

"Me!" She felt like nobody's guide.

"We all appreciated the way you helped us through it."

She said she'd think about it and hung up.

In the end, what she thought was that Kit was right. It was her job to guide the course of the investigation and out of that course had come consequences—inevitable ones, some bad, some horrible. But it truly was part of a process and she was pleased that these women saw it this way. She had nearly killed Neetsie's father. She had torn apart Suby's father's house. They had plenty to be mad about if they wanted to be.

She found she wanted to see them. This often happened to her on a case. She liked the people she met; she missed them later.

And she certainly needed to say good-bye to Lenore.

They had set the ritual for the new moon, to symbolize new beginnings.

I could use a few of those, she thought as she drove to Suby's. They were meeting there instead of Kit's because Caitlin, though it was partly her ritual, wasn't invited. The witches thought the part about her mother might be too sad for her.

They had asked Skip to dress in black and white, but they were in their black robes. This time the altar had on it, not a skull, but some baby gifts and pictures of Lenore and Caitlin.

They cast the circle and called the directions, as they had done before. Once again, Skip was struck by the beauty and simplicity of the ceremony.

Neetsie took the role of high priestess. She called Hecate, goddess of the crossroads, who presumably would preside over both Lenore's and Caitlin's journeys.

"Sisters, we've come to say good-bye to one of us. Lenore was someone we loved. She died so suddenly we had no chance to say what we felt for her. Let's say it tonight." She picked up a talking stick. "Lenore, thank you for being a good friend to my brother." She passed the stick to Kit.

Kit thanked her for having Caitlin and taking care of her, and for letting Kit be part of the family. Each person said something similar.

Skip thought she wouldn't say anything, she'd hardly known Lenore, but when the stick came to her, she couldn't stop herself. She wondered later how magic worked, if the stick had some sort of spell on it, but the witches said not. "Forgive me," she blurted. "Forgive me for not being there, for not knowing. For not being able to stop it."

To her everlasting horror, she started to cry in front of a roomful of potential witnesses.

Oh, God, I shouldn't have come. I must be crazy.

Kit came and held her until she stopped, and they went on as if nothing had happened.

When Lenore had been thoroughly bidden good-bye, the witches took off their robes. Their white ones were underneath.

Neetsie said, "We've celebrated Lenore's life and now we'll celebrate Caitlin's."

Skip hadn't thought of death as quite so festive, but suddenly she realized that what they were doing was like the end of a jazz funeral, when exuberant music is played to celebrate the release of the soul.

For Caitlin's part of the ritual, Suby brought out a huge basket tied with ribbons. Inside were more ribbons, which she explained would represent symbolic gifts to go in the basket. Each person was to tie a ribbon and give Caitlin something for her new life—wish her something, Skip thought, because it was easier to grasp that way.

But when it was her turn, she didn't say it like that. She had been thinking what she wanted for Caitlin, and it surprised her what it was. By the time she said it, she wished it with such conviction that she believed she could marshal her energy and somehow give it to her, and so she said it as if it were more than a wish: "I give you the freedom to be Caitlin Marquer, always, no matter what your mother says or your teacher says or anybody says."

It was a simple thing, but she wanted Caitlin to have it.

After they had all given their gifts, they did the spooky chant to raise what Neetsie called a cone of power, which they sent across the city for Caitlin. That was what made the magic, the ladies said; you could project energy that way.

Someone had made chocolate chip cookies—Lenore's favorite— which they washed down with milk out of deference to Caitlin's kid status. This was the part of the ritual Kit was pleased to call "sacred bullshit." As the witches chattered lightly about restaurants and movies, Skip, who after all barely knew them, dropped out of the conversation and went into a reverie of her own.

The next day was Saturday, she was thinking. She could shop for some plants and a rug, see about getting that watercolor she wanted.

Or maybe I'll skip the rug for now. I could go to California instead.

When she woke up the next morning, she found something had stuck in her head. It was what the witches had said when they wished Hecate good-night: "Lady, enjoy us. Lady, destroy us."

JULIE SMITH's *New Orleans Mourning* won the 1991 Edgar Award given by the Mystery Writers of America for Best Novel, making Smith the first American woman to win the award in that category since 1956. Detective Skip Langdon, introduced in *New Orleans Mourning*, returned in *The Axeman's Jazz* and *Jazz Funeral*.

A former reporter for *The New Orleans Times-Picayune* and the *San Francisco Chronicle*, Julie Smith is also the creator of two San Francisco sleuths: lawyer-detective Rebecca Schwartz, who appears in *Death Turns a Trick*, *The Sourdough Wars*, *Tourist Trap*, *Dead in the Water*, and *Other People's Skeletons*, and ex-reporter-turned-mystery-writer Paul MacDonald, who appears in *True-Life Adventure* and *Huckleberry Fiend*.

Julie Smith lives in the San Francisco Bay Area.